Praise for Jeremy Robinson's

ISLAND 731

"Robinson puts his distinctive mark on Michael Crichton territory with this terrifying present-day riff on *The Island of Dr. Moreau*. Action and scientific explanation are appropriately proportioned, making this one of the best *Jurassic Park* successors."

—*Publishers Weekly* (starred review)

"This is the stuff that comic books, video games, and successful genre franchises are made of."

—*Kirkus Reviews*

SECONDWORLD

"Jeremy Robinson's latest thriller is massive in scope and brilliantly apocalyptic. *SecondWorld* is far from second best."   —James Rollins

"Plan to hunker down for an all-nighter with this one. I did."
—Steve Berry, *New York Times* bestselling author

"Robinson blends myth, science, and terminal velocity action like no one else."
—Scott Sigler, *New York Times* bestselling author

ALSO BY
JEREMY ROBINSON

The Jack Sigler Thrillers

Pulse
Instinct
Threshold
Ragnarok

The Chess Team Novellas

Callsign: Queen—Book 1
Callsign: Rook—Book 1
Callsign: Bishop—Book 1
Callsign: Knight—Book 1
Callsign: Deep Blue—Book 1
Callsign: King—Book 1
Callsign: King—Book 2—Underworld
Callsign: King—Book 3—Blackout

The Antarktos Saga

The Last Hunter: Descent
The Last Hunter: Pursuit
The Last Hunter: Ascent
The Last Hunter: Lament
The Last Hunter: Onslaught

Stand-Alone Novels

Kronos
Antarktos Rising
Beneath
Raising the Past
The Didymus Contingency
SecondWorld
Project Nemesis

Island 731

Jeremy Robinson

St. Martin's Paperbacks

This is a work of fiction. All of the characters, organizations, and events portrayed in this novel are either products of the author's imagination or are used fictitiously.

ISLAND 731

Copyright © 2013 by Jeremy Robinson.
Excerpt from *XOM-B* copyright © 2014 by Jeremy Robinson.
Excerpt from *Project Maigo* copyright © 2014 by Jeremy Robinson.

All rights reserved.

For information address St. Martin's Press, 175 Fifth Avenue, New York, NY 10010.

Library of Congress Catalog Card Number: 2012042087

ISBN: 978-0-312-55247-3

Printed in the United States of America

St. Martin's Press hardcover edition / March 2013
St. Martin's Paperbacks edition / March 2014

St. Martin's Paperbacks are published by St. Martin's Press, 175 Fifth Avenue, New York, NY 10010.

10   9   8   7   6   5   4   3   2

*For Dad, again, because you're
still joking about red flakes and I appreciate it.*

ACKNOWLEDGMENTS

I release something like five or six novels every year. It's kind of a ridiculous amount, but made possible thanks to the hard work and dedication of the people who support me professionally and personally. So it is with great appreciation that I point out the contributions of the supremely helpful folks who took part in the creation of *Island 731*.

Thanks to:

- Scott Miller, my agent at Trident Media Group, for his tireless efforts and shrewd mind.
- Peter Wolverton, my editor at Thomas Dunne Books, for forcing me to improve with every book and for supporting my solo-publishing efforts.
- Anne Brewer, my associate editor at Thomas Dunne Books, for being speedy and delightful to work with.
- Rafal Gibek and the production team at Thomas Dunne Books, for copy-edits that always make me look like a better writer than I am.
- Ervin Serrano, art director at Thomas Dunne Books, for designing covers that stun and for including this author in the design process.
- Kane Gilmour, my solo project editor, friend, and supporter, for advance reading and comments on *Island 731*.

- Hilaree, Aquila, Solomon, and Norah Robinson, my four muses whom I adore, thank you for your excitement, creativity, and love.

PROLOGUE
Pacific Ocean, 1942

Master Chief Petty Officer James Coffman awoke to find his leg being eaten. The pain felt dull. Distant. The connection between his mind and limb had somehow been numbed. But he could clearly see the gull tugging at the sinews of his exposed calf muscle. The wound, fresh and bloody, should have sent shock waves of pain through his body, but he felt nothing. *It's a mercy*, he decided as he sat up. He'd seen men with similar wounds—inflicted by Japanese bullets—howl in agony.

The seagull opened its wings wide and squawked indignantly as though Coffman were a competing predator. Even as he reached out for it, the bird took two more pecks at the meat of his leg. When the gull flew away, a string of muscle hung from its yellow beak.

Coffman reached down, grabbed a handful of beach sand, and flung it after the bird. He tried to shout at it, but only managed a raw, rattling sound.

Like many young men in the United States, Coffman had enlisted in the navy shortly after the bombing of Pearl Harbor. He began his naval career as a petty officer third class serving on the USS *Yorktown*, an aircraft carrier in the Pacific fleet. Through grit, determination, and several battles, Coffman had worked his way up to master chief petty officer. But he took no greater pride than when the *Yorktown*, with his assistance, drew Japanese blood.

He'd grown accustomed to the sounds and smells of war

over the years, so when he drew a long breath through his nose, he found the fresh scent of earth and lack of machine sounds disconcerting. He'd been deposited on a peaceful, white sand beach.

Coffman craned his head around, growing dizzy as he moved. With a hand buried in the sand for balance, he took in his surroundings. That he was sitting on a beach was clear. The sand was smooth, almost soft, and stretched around a crescent-shaped cove. The water lapped at the sand just below his feet, and it appeared so calm that he nearly mistook it for a freshwater lagoon, but he could smell the salt in the air. Following the water out, he saw forty-foot, palm-covered ridges. He couldn't see the ocean, but could see where it entered through an opening in the natural wall, sheltered from the force of the ocean.

I'm inside a volcanic cone, he thought. Coffman knew most of the Pacific islands were created by volcanoes that sprung up along the "ring of fire." He didn't have any real interest in geology, or island life, but since millions of soldiers were fighting and dying over islands just like this one all across the Pacific, he'd picked up on a few facts.

Coffman looked behind him and found a jungle, thick, lush, and tropical. He'd been to Hawaii on shore leave once. This looked similar. Could he be on Hawaii? It didn't seem possible. It was too far—an entire time zone away from Midway.

Midway . . .

The last few days were a confusing blur. He thought back, trying to remember how he arrived on the shore of this island. The USS *Yorktown* had sustained significant damage at the Battle of the Coral Sea, but had come out victorious. The ship needed three months' work to be fully functional, but aggressive Japanese tactics wouldn't allow the respite. Undaunted, the *Yorktown* returned to Hawaii and yard workers completed the three months' work in just three days. Days later, the Battle of Midway began and the *Yorktown* once again sustained heavy damage at the hands of Japanese dive bombers.

Covered with heavy debris and ruined planes, the giant ship began to list. The crew feared the carrier would capsize, so the ship was abandoned, the men taking refuge on the USS *Hammann*, a Sims-class destroyer. But the stubborn *Yorktown* did not sink that night. Coffman returned with a salvage and repair crew the next morning. They worked through the day, breathing air laden with smoke from the burning boiler room. Despite the conditions, the skeleton crew pushed planes and heavy equipment overboard, reducing the vessel's topside weight. The effort began to work. The list lessened and it seemed the carrier would once again limp back to Hawaii for repairs.

But the Japanese returned, using darkness and the debris-filled ocean to cloak the submarine's approach. Coffman, who stood on deck wearing coveralls coated with black soot and oil, saw the four approaching torpedoes first. He shouted a warning, but there was nothing the crew of the *Yorktown* could do. The ship was dead in the water.

But they were not alone. The USS *Hammann* opened fire with her 20mm guns in an attempt to destroy the torpedoes. For her effort, the *Hammann* was struck amidships. The explosion tore the destroyer in half and the *Yorktown*'s would-be rescuer jackknifed and sank, taking the rescued crew with her.

Two of the torpedoes struck the *Yorktown,* punching holes in the hull and flinging Coffman from the deck. He remembered the cool air as he fell from the smoky deck to the open ocean. After that, there was a lull. He woke hours later. The sun dipping below the horizon cast silhouettes of the now distant fleet. He immediately thrashed and called out. But no one would hear him. No one, but the three men adrift alongside him. They'd managed to slip him into a life jacket and had saved his life, but over the next few days he'd wondered if he would have been better off dead.

As days passed, his throat and tongue swelled from dehydration. The skin on his forehead burned with boils from sun exposure. His body ached. And as hard as he tried, he couldn't move his legs. The last morning he remembered, he woke to find one of the men missing. They didn't know if he'd simply died and slipped beneath the waves, if a shark took him, or if he'd swum away in delirium. But the end, for all of them, was near, so they didn't worry about it too much. Resigning himself to death was the last memory he could recall.

Then he woke up here, on this beach.

The boils still stung his forehead.

His throat felt scoured.

And his legs. . . . He tried to move them again, but couldn't. He'd assumed they were broken, but having felt no pain from the gull's attack, he knew better. His back had been broken. Either when he'd been flung from the *Yorktown*, or when his body had struck the water.

But if he had made it here, perhaps the others had, too? He looked around for some sign of life.

Palm leaves shifted a scratchy tune powered by an ocean breeze. Cumulus clouds drifted past high above, their passage reflected by the calm lagoon water. But he couldn't see any bodies nor could he hear any voices. But there was an aberration in the sand next to him.

Four gouges, like the beach had been tilled by miniature oxen, traced a path back to the jungle. The lines were so straight and evenly spaced that Coffman had little doubt they were manmade. He leaned over to inspect the nearest tracks. The motion sent a stabbing pain up his back.

He growled in agony as he realized that his time in the ocean had kept pressure off his back. Perhaps it had even healed him some. But now, on land, every motion could have dire consequences. As the pain subsided, he opened his clenched eyes and saw that the lines in the beach were framed by footprints.

Booted footprints.

The other men had been dragged away, their heels plowing twin paths through the sand. But who took them?

As pain flared anew, Coffman straightened out and looked out over the lagoon. He imagined the shape of this inlet from above and recalled nothing resembling it on any of the maps

he'd studied. Had they somehow landed on an uncharted island? Had the men been dragged away by local islanders? If
so, there might still be hope of survival.

A crunch of dry palms caught his attention. The sound
came from directly behind him, so he couldn't turn to see it.

Crunch. Closer this time. The steps were slow. Furtive.
Careful. As though Coffman might present some kind of a
threat. That meant whoever was there saw him as a threat.
Which meant . . .

Coffman lay back down, craning his head backward.
Through an upside-down view of the jungle, he saw black
boots and tan pants step into the open. He turned his gaze
skyward, but the figure charged and all Coffman saw was the
butt of a rifle. Then nothing.

He woke to an all-consuming pain. His scream was dulled
by a gag tied tightly 'round his mouth. He fought to move,
but had been restrained.

"Calm yourself," came a voice. The accent was distinctly
Japanese.

No . . .

He'd be tortured for information, kept alive for months
until they were sure he'd told them everything he knew, and
then he'd be shot.

The gag went slack and was pulled away.

"Just kill me now," Coffman said. His voice sounded better. In fact, despite the pain enveloping his body, he felt hy-
drated. *They'll heal me first*, he thought, *and then torture
me.* It seemed likely, but the pain he felt told him they'd gotten a head start on the torture.

"You are far too valuable alive," said the voice.

"Show yourself."

The man didn't reply.

Coffman stared at a bare cement wall in front of him. He
couldn't see the lamp mounted to the ceiling above him, but
felt the heat from it on his skin. He tried to turn his head,
but found it restrained.

"I'm going to free your right arm," came the voice. "When I do, try to move it. Slowly. You were injured."

Coffman had a list of questions, but when the restraint on his right arm loosened, he felt them melt away. His hand tingled as blood flowed more freely into the limb.

"Go ahead," the man said. "Move your arm."

The limb felt heavy. Stubborn. Like it didn't want to move, but Coffman needed to see something more than this barren cement wall. To know he still existed and this wasn't hell. Pain pulsed from his shoulder as he moved the limb. He didn't remember injuring the arm, but he didn't remember much. His memories of the *Yorktown* felt distant. Years old.

"Good," the man said. "Very good."

When his hand came into view, it glowed in the bright light cast from above. His hand looked different. Thicker. Swollen, perhaps. But that wasn't all. The shape was wrong. The thickness, too. And the pattern of his arm hair, once thin and faint, now appeared thick, and dark. He turned his arm over and found a tattoo of a naked woman sitting upon the guns of a battleship.

"That's not my arm," he said. "That's not my arm!"

The man behind him *tsk*ed a few times and then reached out and pulled the arm down, restraining it once more. "You've suffered a great deal," the man said. "You're confused."

Coffman tried to understand. Tried to remember. Images came in flashes. He saw the ocean. A seagull. A beach. Then darkness. And lights. Always lights, blinding him to the shapes around him. Men. Their voices, speaking Japanese, returned like a song heard too many times. But he didn't know what had been said.

"Now then," the man said, the tone of his voice as pleasant and soothing as Coffman's own grandmother's. "Try to move your other arm."

There was no tingling this time. In fact, he barely felt the limb, but it was there. He sensed the movement. He needed to see it, to know if he was going mad. Gritting his teeth, he willed the limb up. His eyes clenched with pain and he didn't see his arm rise, but he felt it.

When the man said, "Wonderful," Coffman opened his eyes.

And screamed.

This arm wasn't his, either.

It wasn't even human.

ONE
Pacific Ocean, Now

"Man overboard!"

Mark Hawkins reacted to the words without thought. He hadn't even seen who'd fallen and couldn't identify who had shouted the words. But he heard the confirming splash and saw several crewmembers on the main deck look over the port rail.

At a run, Hawkins leapt up onto the port rail and launched himself over the side. But he wasn't on the main deck, which was just eight feet above the waterline. He was on the second deck, twenty-five feet up and six feet in from the main deck's rail. As he dove out and looked down he saw an undulating, solid mass of plastic, rope, and wood. He had no idea how thick the layer of garbage was, or how dense, but when he didn't see a body languishing atop it, he knew the crew member who'd fallen overboard was trapped beneath it. He also knew that his landing would hurt.

He heard a gasp as he fell past the main deck, just missing the rail. His feet struck the layer of trash a moment later, punching through like a blunt spear. The rest of his body followed, slipping through the chunky film, but not before becoming tangled in rope. Stunned by the impact and chilled by the Pacific waters, Hawkins nearly panicked, but the memory of someone in need of help kept him focused.

His eyes stung when he opened them. Visibility was poor thanks to a swirling cloud of small plastic chips churned up by his explosive arrival, and worsened by the noonday sun being filtered through layers of colored plastic, casting the depths in dull, kaleidoscopic shades.

He tried to swim, but something tugged at his ankle, rooting him in place. He leaned forward and pulled his leg in close. His ankle was wrapped in a loop of rope bound to a lump of congealed refuse that floated like a giant buoy. Had he landed on the mass, his rescue effort would have been cut abruptly short. Not that it was going well at the moment.

But Hawkins was not completely unprepared. He unclipped the sheath on his belt and freed his seven-and-a-half-inch San Mai Recon Scout hunting knife. The razor-sharp blade cut through the rope like it wasn't there. After sheathing the blade, Hawkins pushed off the heavy chunk of garbage and swam deeper. Six feet from the surface, he came free from the lowest traces of floating debris and immediately saw the kicking feet of the fallen crewmember just twenty feet away.

As he swam closer, he saw that the small feet were attached to a pair of smooth, lithe legs. The man overboard was a woman.

Dr. Avril Joliet.

Despite being a genius, or damn near close to one, Joliet didn't always make the best choices. How she'd earned two Ph.D.s in biology and oceanography without getting lost at sea, eaten by a predator, or hit by a bus was beyond Hawkins. It wasn't that she was absentminded, just impulsive. Quick. But it was those same qualities that allowed her to learn fast, blow the doors off conventional theories, and make discoveries while her peers spent time wondering if they should bother. But this time, Joliet's speed might have finally caught up with her.

Her quick, jerky movements confirmed his fears. She was stuck. Hawkins swam up behind her and put a gentle hand on her shoulder. Her white blouse billowed as she spun around, eyes wide with fear. There were a number of predators—large sharks, mostly—that prowled beneath the Garbage Patch, waiting for prey animals to become stuck.

When she saw him, she relaxed, but as she turned, a large,

beaked face came into view, startling Hawkins. A burst of bubbles shot from his mouth as he shouted in surprise. When the bubbles cleared, Joliet stared at him with a single eyebrow raised. A second glance over her shoulder revealed the face of a sea turtle, its black eyes staring lifelessly into the abyss.

Confused, Hawkins moved around the oceanographer for a better look. She wasn't tangled at all!

The turtle, on the other hand, looked like a sacrifice bound to a pillar for some ancient god. Loops of rope around the fins held it tight, the struggle for freedom long since abandoned. The loggerhead sea turtle looked like all the others Hawkins had seen, with one startling exception—the body and shell were pinched at the middle, narrowed to a diameter no thicker than Hawkins's forearm.

What the hell?

Desperate for air, and confused by Joliet's actions, he hitched him thumb toward the surface and kicked through the layer of trash. Pushing through the refuse, Hawkins took a breath and craned around, looking for the *Magellan*. The ship cut through the ocean two hundred feet away, coming around in a wide arc.

Joliet surfaced next to him, sucking in three deep breaths and then saying, "You have to help me!"

"The turtle is dead," he replied.

"Hawkins. Mark. This is an important find. It's tangible evidence. Provoking. Something like this will be hard to ignore. Who doesn't love a sea turtle?"

Hawkins didn't disagree. The loggerhead turtle was an endangered species and images of the deformed creature would make a compelling photographic addition to the article he was writing, but that didn't mean she had to dive in after it. "It's not going anywhere. Drake would have come back for it."

"There isn't time!" Her eyes were wide. Frightened.

Hawkins had only known Joliet for a month, but in that time he'd seen her step between two fighting crewmen, go toe-to-toe with Captain Drake, and haul in a thirty-pound bluefish, which became a meal for the crew. She wasn't a timid person. But something had her spooked. In the middle of the Pacific Ocean that usually meant one thing.

Shark.

"Please tell me it's not a great white," Hawkins said with a frown.

Joliet's eyes somehow widened a little bit more.

He had no doubt she was rethinking the wisdom of her actions. She'd seen the turtle, and then the shark—probably just the dorsal fin—and leapt in without thinking. Like he did when he gave chase.

Just like he did the first time he found himself in a similar situation. And while he had no desire to relive that particular event, they were already in the water, and she was right about the turtle. He drew his knife and held it above the water for her to see. "I'll cut it free, you hold it."

A nod.

Hawkins looked over his shoulder. The *Magellan* finished its turn and headed back toward them. The crane, which normally lowered submersibles and Zodiacs into the water, rotated out over the water, a line dangling down. If they held on to the wire, the winch would have no trouble plucking them from the ocean. He waved his knife in the air, hoping the glint of sunlight off its blade would alert them to their position. A shark was bad news, but being run over by a two-hundred-seventy-four-foot, three-thousand-ton research vessel could really ruin a guy's day. "It's going to be dead weight once it's free, so we're going to have to time this right."

With the *Magellan* closing in, Hawkins said, "Ready?"

"After you," she replied.

Hawkins didn't really understand how he'd become the ringleader of this unauthorized salvage, but he was determined to see it through. He pushed the air from his lungs and descended through the debris.

The turtle, still bound to the lump of plastic detritus, was easy to find, despite the poor conditions. Hawkins kicked over to the loggerhead and began cutting away its bonds. As the first flipper came free, Joliet slipped up next to him and took hold of the turtle. He had no idea if the turtle would be buoyant at all—it might sink like a stone—but he hoped there was enough gas trapped in its deformed body to keep it afloat. If it sank, there was no way he and Joliet could keep it aloft.

He moved to the second of the four bound flippers and began hacking away at the ropes. The lines fell away like overcooked spaghetti. Free from its bonds, the turtle fell forward, but its descent stopped when it leveled out. Hawkins allowed himself a grin. Gas trapped beneath the shell would make the job much easier.

Gripping the cut lines, Hawkins pushed himself down and started on the line binding one of the back flippers to the mass. But the knife had no impact.

Steel cable, Hawkins thought. *Damn.*

A distorted shout and hard tap on his shoulder brought his eyes around. Joliet clung to the turtle with one hand, but the other stabbed out toward the open ocean.

A shadow slid through the debris like a wraith through fog. Circling. Closing in. Sharks weren't above scavenging the dead, but the electric impulses of their racing hearts and kicking feet drew the predator toward the promise of a fresh meal. Man-eating sharks, bears, and big cats were often treated as aberrations needing to be hunted and killed, but Hawkins knew his place in the food chain.

With renewed urgency, Hawkins moved the knife up and hacked off the turtle's rear flipper. The large reptile came loose, but it didn't sink. Joliet kept it aloft. Hawkins looked for the shark again, but it was lost in the field of debris. That he couldn't see the hunter didn't put him at ease. The shark's ampullae of Lorenzini—jelly-filled electroreceptors on the snout—would easily detect the electric field produced by their bodies. While they were blind, the shark would see them with the clarity of a falcon hovering overhead.

A loud rumble through the water announced the presence of the *Magellan,* reversing its screws and coming to a stop. Hawkins slid over the top of the turtle, took hold of its shell on either side, and kicked for the surface. He felt lumps of hard plastic bounce off his back as he rose. The debris grew bigger as he neared the surface.

Almost there, he thought. But a garbled scream and jarring impact told him he wouldn't be reaching the surface. He turned to the right and saw the maw of a great white shark open to envelop him.

TWO

Hawkins clung to the reddish-brown loggerhead shell, hoping the armored carapace would shield him from the snapping jaws. The shark's snout hit the turtle's underside, scraping deep grooves in the softer underbelly as it manically snapped its jaws open and closed, searching for a bit of flesh to bite into. The impact drove the deformed shell into Hawkins's torso, knocking out what little air remained in his lungs.

The turtle rolled around the shark's nose and spun past its gills, bumping Hawkins into the large predator's body. The unexpected collision caused the shark to twitch. It craned its head, and open jaws moved toward Hawkins and bit down hard, finding a limb.

With a vicious shake of its head, the shark's serrated teeth went to work, carving through flesh and bone as easily as Hawkins's knife. The limb came free, clutched in the giant's jaws. With surprising speed, the great white gave a twitch of its tail and sped away to devour its prize.

Still reeling from the attack, Hawkins watched the shark swim away, keenly aware of how close the shark had come to eating *his* arm. Luckily, the loggerhead wouldn't miss its fin. Not that the two-foot-long appendage would satiate the shark's hunger for long. It would soon return, and the turtle had only one large fin left to sacrifice.

A hard tap on Hawkins's shoulder made him flinch and spin around so fast that he let go of the loggerhead. After catching a glimpse of Joliet above him, he swam after the turtle without a second thought, not because he'd already risked his life recovering it, but because it was his only protection against the great white. Without looking for signs of the shark, he took hold of the turtle's shell once more and hoisted it back toward the surface.

His lungs burned with a longing for air, and he'd soon instinctively open his mouth to draw a breath, but he couldn't let the turtle go, not after nearly dying for it. Joliet greeted him just beneath the thickest layer of plastic refuse. She held a thick metal carabiner at the end of a metal wire in her hands. He knew the wire had been lowered by the crane in order to pluck them from the water, but it would easily handle the turtle, too.

As Hawkins took the line and moved it around the turtle's torso, he realized the creature was perfectly designed for what he had in mind. The cable wrapped around the shell and slipped into the foot-deep groove where the turtle's body had been abnormally constricted. He secured the carabiner and shoved himself up to the surface.

The layer of trash fought to keep him submerged, but Hawkins pulled himself up the cable until he cleared the surface and took a long, deep breath. He tried to speak, but couldn't. His body craved oxygen and each breath sounded more like a gasp.

The pale, blue hull of the *Magellan* rose up out of the water some twenty feet away, though the end of the crane hovered directly overhead—nearly three stories overhead. Most of the small crew stood at the rail, shouting to them and watching the scene play out. None of them knew that a hungry shark circled below.

With a frantic spin of his hand, Hawkins motioned for the crane operator to pull them up. But no one seemed to be in a rush. Thankfully, Joliet, who'd been up for a breath once already, found her voice before he did.

"Shark!" she shouted. "Pull us up! There's a shark!"

Her plea was instantly repeated by everyone on deck and the crane operator quickly received the message. The cable went taut as it was drawn up through the crane's arm and rolled tightly around a winch attached to the *Magellan*'s aft deck.

As his torso slid free of the water, Hawkins began to feel relief, but he couldn't shake the feeling of impending doom. "Higher," he said to Joliet, who clung to the cable just above him. "Climb higher!"

She managed to pull herself up one arm's length, but then slipped and nearly fell. The metal cable hadn't been designed for climbing. "I can't go any higher!" she shouted.

But the effort was enough. He hoisted himself up and pulled his legs out of the water. The turtle followed next, dripping water and clumps of plastic as it tore a hole in the layer of trash. The giant loggerhead on the end of the line drew a sting of gasps from the deck crew. Joliet had apparently failed to tell a single person about what she saw before leaping to the dead creature's "rescue."

And people think I'm *impulsive,* he thought.

A high-pitched shriek from above drew his eyes up just in time to see Joliet's backside falling toward him. He leaned back and let go of the cable to avoid being knocked off the line. Joliet landed in his lap and together they slipped down the line, only stopping when they reached the turtle's shell, just two feet above the surface of the water.

"Sorry!" Joliet said. "I slipped."

"It's okay," Hawkins said, glancing down at the water.

But it was decidedly *not* okay, because just beneath the water, he saw a pair of black eyes roll white and the gleam of the noonday sun on countless rows of razor-sharp teeth. The hole punched in the surface layer by the turtle had provided the great white with a clear path toward its dangling meal.

The behemoth rose from the surface and was greeted by the shocked shouts of the crew on deck. With its nictitating membrane—a white, third eyelid—protecting its eyes, the shark could no longer see its prey, but it didn't have to. The open jaws would find something to close down upon.

A string of curses rose in Hawkins's throat, but he never let them loose. Instead, he swallowed his fear and tried something stupid. An act of desperation. He wrapped his arms around Joliet and clutched the wire. "Hold on tight!" Then, he leaned back, tilting the turtle sideways and offered the shark one last sacrifice. As soon as the loggerhead's remaining flipper struck the shark's lower jaw, the trap sprang shut. The shark descended into the abyss with the still-attached appendage. It gave a single vicious shake of its head and tore the limb free.

Hawkins, Joliet, and the one-finned turtle were propelled like a kid clinging to a lakeside rope swing. They careened around in a wide arc. Their momentum came to an abrupt and painful stop against the metal hull of the *Magellan*. The impact nearly knocked them free. If not for his steadfast grip and the turtle attached beneath them like a tire swing, Hawkins had no doubt they would have been knocked free.

As the line swung back out over the open sea, Hawkins found his voice and directed it at Peter Blok, the first mate and crane operator. "Get us out of here or I swear to God, I will climb up this cable and throw you in!"

The winch whined as it sped up, pulling the still-swinging trio up out of the shark's reach. The crane soon deposited them gently upon the presently empty aft deck. Hawkins loosened his grip on the cable and leaned his head around Joliet's wet hair. "Are you okay?" he whispered.

"I owe you a beer," she said.

"You owe me a lot more than that," he replied.

She glanced at him with a cut-the-bullshit expression, and he grinned. "I'd say that was at least worth a twelve-pack. Microbrew. Not the cheap stuff."

"I can do that," she said.

"And if you share it with me, I won't tell anyone about how you screamed like a girl."

Joliet smiled and visibly relaxed. She stood, turned, and slugged him in the shoulder. "I *am* a girl."

Hawkins stood, rubbing his shoulder, and said, "Don't hit like a girl."

"That was damn near the craziest thing I've ever seen at sea," came the rough voice of Harold Jones, the ship's engineer.

The man's wide eyes looked bright white next to his dark skin. He rubbed a hand over his close-cut gray hair. "And I've seen some things."

Jones had two junior engineers on his team, Phil Bennett, who was something of a whiz kid with engines, and Jackie DeWinter, his daughter from a woman he'd never married, who'd been apprenticing with him for nearly three years. Despite being a self-proclaimed grease monkey, DeWinter always looked put together with long, styled hair and longer legs. In short, she was Joliet's opposite in style, though both women had striking faces.

DeWinter stepped around her father wearing an expression that cycled between happy, terrified, and relief. "Oh my God, are you two okay? What were you thinking? That was awesome!"

"Fine," Joliet said. "Better than fine. Look what we found." She stepped aside, allowing the father-daughter team to see the dead, nearly limbless turtle.

DeWinter winced, then saw the pinched shell and gasped. "What is it?"

Hawkins was about to tease her, but the single fin and a severely deformed shell made it look like something alien. "Once upon a time, it was a loggerhead turtle."

Jones leaned over the specimen, looking at it from all angles. "What happened to it?"

"Aside from becoming a meal for Jaws," Hawkins said, "that's what we need to find out."

"Looks like it got into something," Jones said, pointing to a band of red where the turtle's constricted midsection came together.

"Nasty," DeWinter said. "But this is actually a good thing, right? We're here to find things like this."

He felt horrible for it, but Hawkins agreed. Finding this deformed turtle was a very good thing, but as he looked down at the ruined creature, it certainly didn't *feel* good. "Yeah, this is why we're here. But I wish we weren't."

That wasn't entirely true. He looked at Joliet. She met his eyes. They both smiled.

Silence lingered for a moment longer than Jones could bear. He cleared his throat. "I'll go get a stretcher so we can move her."

Hawkins turned toward him and saw DeWinter smiling like she knew something he didn't. *Does she?* Joliet did spend a good amount of off-time with DeWinter. They were the only two women on board. Before Hawkins could dwell on the idea, a sea of frantic voices that sounded something like a gobble of frightened turkeys drowned out his thoughts. The rest of the crew had arrived, all asking questions and retelling their version of the story at once.

Hawkins heard Phil Bennett, the youngest crewmember on board, ask, "Should we try to kill that shark?"

It was a stupid question. The *Magellan* had been sent to research the Garbage Patch to help preserve the environment for creatures like the shark. That someone on board, even if he was a mechanic and not a conservationist, would ask that question revealed what an uphill battle cleaning up the Garbage Patch would be. The idea of killing a shark simply because it tried to eat someone made little sense to Hawkins, but he knew it made perfect sense to many people. The problem was, people were still terrified of the unknown, which included most everything in the ocean, and reacted to dangerous animals with violence. Humanity liked to think they were at the top of the food chain, but without modern weapons, people weren't top dog, and being eaten was, and always had been, part of the gig. Animals ate people. People ate animals. A shark eating a human being was as natural as a twenty-piece serving of chicken nuggets, perhaps more so.

That was his take on the situation. He'd like to believe there was some kind of natural law that said sharks wouldn't try to eat people, but he knew better. Even *people* ate other people when tradition, or desperation, required it. And those people weren't hunted down and shot like crazed beasts. Sometimes they got movie deals.

Hawkins decided to ignore the question. Bennett was young and allowed to be stupid. The man who spoke next would have to cut the conversation short, either way.

"What in the name of St. Peter were you two thinking?" shouted a voice that parted the crew. Captain Jonathan Drake, a sixty-year-old man with the body of a forty-year-old professional wrestler stepped up to Hawkins. The crew encircling them stepped back when Drake crossed his arms over his chest, as though the man's muscles produced some kind of invisible force field.

Hawkins and Joliet knew better than to reply right away. Engaging the captain when his hackles were raised never worked out well for his verbal sparring partner. Best to wait it out and offer an explanation when Drake's face lost a few shades of red.

What Hawkins did do was take a single step to the side, revealing the deformed loggerhead turtle on the deck. Drake saw it immediately, but made no comment. He rubbed his square chin, scratching at the neatly trimmed white hair that framed his face and head. Drake wasn't just the captain of the *Magellan,* he also believed in its mandate—to study the harmful effects humanity has on the planet's oceans and try to affect change. The ramifications of the turtle's state wouldn't be lost on the man.

Joliet opened her mouth to speak, but Hawkins knew it was too soon. He placed his hand against hers. Her voice caught in her throat, but when he glanced at her she appeared more confused than angry, which is what he expected. They'd become friends over the past month at sea, but Joliet couldn't stand to be told what to do. Only Drake got away with it, and sometimes not without a fight.

Drake turned to the bystanders and pointed to the four standing nearest the turtle. "You four. Take Stumpy here to the biolab."

The four grumbled, but immediately began working out how to transport the creature. The biolab was on the main deck, so they wouldn't need to go up or down any stairs, but the several-hundred-pound dead weight still wouldn't be easy to move.

Drake turned his attention back to Hawkins and Joliet. He looked each of them in the eyes and said, "You two, wash up and come see me on the bridge in thirty. We need to talk."

With that, Drake spun on his heels and stormed away. The man had let them off the hook without a public verbal beatdown, but Hawkins couldn't help but feel he might have been better off staying in the water with the shark.

THREE

Hawkins washed himself clean in just over a minute. Showers were supposed to be brief while at sea, so he used the rest of his allocated five minutes to languish under the hot streams of water. The close encounter with the great white had bunched up the muscles on his back and the heat helped relieve the tension. As steam billowed around him in the small shower stall, he took a moment to reflect.

Today marked the third time in his life that he'd looked down the throat of an animal intent on sinking its teeth into him. The first had been as a child when he was attacked by a rabid raccoon. He'd been standing in his driveway, trying desperately to sink a basketball shot, but his seven-year-old arms weren't up to the task. He first noticed the scrawny raccoon as it walked past him, in broad daylight, carrying a bagel pilfered from a neighbor's trashcan. If not for a missed shot, the raccoon may have continued on its way, oblivious to Hawkins's presence, but the ball landed just a few feet from the animal's side.

The sharp *thunk* of the ball hitting the pavement had the same effect a hand grenade might have. The raccoon launched itself into the air, arms splayed, bagel twirling away. At some point during its twisting flight, the raccoon must have seen Hawkins because upon landing, it shrieked and launched toward him. If not for his father's nearby minivan and Hawkins's monkeylike climbing skills, the coon might have enjoyed a much fresher snack. But thanks to his father, armed with a broom and trashcan cover, Hawkins escaped unscathed. In some ways it was a good memory, since it was one of the few nice things his father did before deciding not to be his father anymore.

He wasn't so lucky during his second confrontation with a hungry mammal. Hawkins ran his fingers over his bare chest. The four long scars had healed long ago, but still stung under his touch. Not from any physical pain. It had been five years since that dark day in the woods of Colorado, but the memory of that confrontation still felt fresh.

A loud banging snapped him out of his reverie. "Five minutes!" The voice belonged to Bob Bray, his roommate aboard the *Magellan*. The Massachusetts native was a high school science teacher, and spoke like a man used to fighting to be heard—very loudly. Despite his cacophonous disposition, he was regarded as one of the leading teachers in the country and had written three books, two of them on what he called "incarceration-style learning" and "experience over textbooks." He promoted experience-based learning at the high school level and had taken a sabbatical of sorts to join the *Magellan*'s crew. His goal was to see how much more he could learn about the ocean and its denizens than he could if he just read the typical high school or even college textbook.

Bray's third and most popular book, *Sinister Science,* was a graphic, nonfiction account of science gone awry throughout the course of human history, including sections on church-altered science, torture—both ancient and modern—chemical and biological warfare, and experimentation of all sorts. He'd brought a copy on board for anyone who was interested, but the photos and illustrations turned most people away. The study was intensely dark, which was appropriate given the subject matter, but it caught most people off guard because Bray was generally a pretty happy guy.

"What're you doing in there?" Bray banged on the thin shower stall wall again. "Wait. No. I don't want to know."

"I'm coming, I'm coming," Hawkins said. "You do the same thing to kids in the locker room?"

"I teach biology," Bray said. "I've never set foot in the locker room."

Hawkins took his towel from the shower door and quickly dried his upper torso. He threw on a T-shirt and wrapped the towel around his waist before stepping out into the small bathroom known to seafarers as "the head." Bray stood in the doorway, holding on to the doorframe above his head. In addition to being loud, the man had issues with personal space, but Hawkins had become accustomed to it. "How come you can say 'room' just fine, but not 'locker'? *Lockah.* Lockah room."

"You're wicked funny," Bray said with a grin. "So that shark was crazy."

"Shahk."

"I'm being serious," Bray said. "You could have died."

"I didn't," Hawkins said.

Bray grinned fiendishly. "You did it for her, didn't you?"

Hawkins applied a liberal amount of deodorant. It would be a week before his next shower. "You've already determined the turtle was a female?"

"Joliet, asshole. She's a little too flat for me, but—"

Hawkins raised an eyebrow. "Flat?"

"Kind of boyish. I prefer something to hold on to."

"I can't believe the next generation is going to be taught by you," Hawkins said.

"Men have a natural proclivity toward women with wide hips and large breasts. Child-bearing hips. This is like Biology 101 here. The real weirdos are guys like you, who prefer boyish waifs like Joliet. Makes me wonder if you're not, you know—" Bray raised his eyebrows a few times and gave him a wink.

"Hey, I'm not the one keeping a half-naked man from leaving the bathroom, am I?"

Bray quickly lowered his arms and backed out of the doorway. He was a big man, standing six-five, and while not completely out of shape, he sported a belly he called a "keg-pack." His short-cut black hair and round cheeks gave him the look of an oversize dwarf, a fact that had earned him the nickname

"Eight," as in Snow White's eighth dwarf. "You're not half naked. You're wearing a T-shirt. Why do you do that, anyway? I've never seen you without a shirt on."

Hawkins slipped past Bray and entered their small room. "Gotta give you *something* to fantasize about. Keep the mystery alive."

Bray grunted and turned away when Hawkins dropped his towel, but he didn't leave. "So are you in the shitter with Drake, or what?"

"Not sure," Hawkins said, pulling up his boxers.

"He looked pissed."

"You're not helping."

"If you know your enemies and know yourself, you can win a hundred battles without a single loss."

Hawkins quickly put on a pair of cargo shorts. "You're a man of wisdom if ever there was one."

"That's Nichee or something."

"Nietzsche, and it wasn't." Hawkins slipped into a pair of boat shoes. He'd gone barefoot a lot lately, but felt he should dress up for the meeting with Drake. "I thought you were a history buff?"

"*Scientific* history," Bray corrected. "I wouldn't call myself a connoisseur of philosophy."

Hawkins smiled. "By the way, that wasn't philosophy. You were quoting Sun Tzu's *Art of War.*"

"Really? Awesome."

"Just awesome? Not 'wicked awesome'?" Hawkins quickly rubbed the towel over his short brown hair and hung it over the end of his top bunk.

"Funny. Hey, I'll be in the biolab when you're done getting verbally spanked. Your boy toy—Joliet, sorry—asked me to prep the loggerhead for dissection. You coming, Ranger?"

Hawkins smiled at the nickname. It had been five years since he was a ranger at Yellowstone Park, but once the crew found out, it stuck. "I'll be there, Eight."

Bray opened the room's door to leave and stumbled back. Joliet stood there, her face serious.

"Shit, ahh, you couldn't hear us, right?" Bray wrapped on

the door with his knuckles. It bonged loudly. "We were having a private talk. Guy stuff."

Joliet, who was nearly two feet shorter than Bray, leaned her head around his chest. "Coming?"

"You heard, didn't you?" Bray said, backing slowly out the door. "I'm going to go now." He hustled away, glancing over his shoulder twice like Joliet might pounce on him, then disappeared around the staircase.

"You didn't hear a thing," Hawkins said, "did you?"

"Not a word. Should I be upset?"

"Only if you take him seriously." Hawkins stepped around Joliet and entered the hallway. "C'mon, let's get this over with."

Hawkins stepped into the *Magellan*'s pilot house three minutes later. Captain Drake stood at the room's core, looking out the windows, which offered a full three-hundred-sixty-five-degree panorama. The view, which should have been blue ocean and bluer sky all the way to the horizon, was marred by an endless stretch of bottles, jugs, lighters, clothing, ropes, fishnets, and countless other buoyant, manmade items collectively known as the Great Pacific Garbage Patch. The several-thousand-mile-wide trash heap, while quite spread out in parts, came together in several areas to form more condensed layers of refuse known as plastic islands. The *Magellan* was smack dab in the middle of the largest such island, a nearly thirty-square-mile slick of garbage brought together by the circular currents of the Pacific Ocean.

The pilot house was a technological marvel. High-tech displays revealed computer-controlled navigation, communications, and environmental systems, not to mention sonar, radar, and weather stations. Even with the lights out, in the dark of night, the bevy of screens and lights illuminated the room like the sun.

"Lovely view," Hawkins said, trying to start the conversation off with a light tone.

"Isn't it, though?" Drake said, turning his piercing blue eyes toward Hawkins.

Before Hawkins could speak again, a head popped up from behind one of the computer screens at the back of the room. Kamato Shimura, a young Japanese intern, pushed his glasses higher on his nose and acknowledged their presence with a smile and a wave. The kid wore his typical uniform— dark blue khaki pants and a tucked-in, red polo shirt—the formality of which was balanced by the Red Sox cap on his head.

"Hi, Kam," Joliet said, sounding happy to see the kid.

Drake craned his head toward Kam. "How long have you been here?"

"Since before you came in," Kam replied. His voice held just a trace of a Japanese accent, and his English was better than Bray's. "I'm updating the video chat software. Mr. Bray said his last classroom conference call was glitchy. I won't be long. Just pretend I'm not here."

"You going to be up for another round of fishing when we clear the Garbage Patch?" Hawkins asked. He strolled up to Kam and held up his hand like he wanted to arm wrestle. Kam took his hand and they performed a complicated handshake that ended in failure and a laugh from both of them. Hawkins wasn't a fan of practiced handshakes. In his opinion, only people who thought they were cool, or really wanted to be cool, practiced the adult male version of patty-cake. But Kam got such a kick out of it, in a very noncool way, that Hawkins overcame his dislike and had fun with it. Every time they perfected the shake, they added a new element. In a way, it had become a mind game between the two, to see who would forget the new step first. Kam enjoyed it because he never forgot. Kid had a brain like quantum computer.

Right now, the handshake was a delaying tactic, but the invitation to fish was an honest question. Long before the handshake challenge, Hawkins had been slow to get to know Kam, but their mutual love of fishing had eventually bridged the gap. Before entering the thickest part of the Garbage Patch a few days previous, he, Kam, Bray, and Joliet had gone fishing off the aft deck. The long day melted into evening and by the time the sun hit the horizon, Kam was one of the gang, despite being fifteen years younger.

"So," Hawkins said when Kam was done laughing. "Fishing?"

Kam's eyes all but disappeared when he smiled. "Definitely."

"Maybe you'll let the rest of us catch a few next time," Joliet said with a smile.

Kam waved her away. "If that shark comes back, it's all yours. Otherwise, not a chance."

Drake cleared his throat. "Speaking of the shark . . ."

Kam's smile fell. "Right. Sorry. I'm not here." He slipped a pair of earbuds into his ears and lowered his head back down behind the screen.

Drake shook his head. "Kid's ancestors must have been ninjas. Been here for ten minutes. Didn't hear a sound."

"Sir, about the shark, and the turtle," Hawkins said. "The whole thing. I take full responsibility for it."

Joliet's head snapped toward Hawkins. "You do?"

"And here I thought chivalry was dead," Drake said. "Truth is, both of you acted impulsively. I saw this one"—he motioned to Joliet—"swan dive into a milk jug. Then not ten seconds later, the Ranger here takes a twenty-five-foot plunge to rescue the damsel in distress."

"I didn't know who was in the water," Hawkins corrected.

"You didn't?" Joliet asked.

"Doesn't matter," Drake said. "What matters is that two of the smartest people currently serving aboard my ship threw themselves in the Pacific Ocean, which at our current location is mired with trash so thick you're lucky you didn't become trapped beneath it."

Hawkins remembered the rope around his leg. If he didn't have his knife, escape wouldn't have been so easy. The Garbage Patch frequently trapped seals, dolphins, sharks, and turtles.

Drake continued. "Not to mention that these waters teem with sharks, a fact you two are now intimately familiar with. And for what? To save a turtle. A *dead* turtle."

Joliet stepped forward. "Captain, with all due—"

"Stow it, Joliet." Drake turned back toward the view. "I actually think you two did a fine job."

Hawkins and Joliet glanced at each other. The words coming out of Drake's mouth were as strange as the deformed loggerhead waiting for them in the biolab.

Drake crossed his arms. "There could have been a bit more communication and a lot more coordination, but you got the job done. That turtle of yours is going to get a lot of news coverage and raise a lot of eyebrows. We're here to collect evidence that this swath of shit is harming the environment, but all the data in the world isn't going to change a thing. But you can't ignore that turtle. A few more finds like that and maybe we'll get someone to come out here and clean this mess up. And maybe I'll get to enjoy this view again."

Drake turned toward the stunned pair. "But I didn't ask you here to pat your backs, either." He paused, rubbing his bearded chin.

"What is it?" Joliet asked.

"I want you to know," Drake began, but paused again. "The point is, you two are capable. You can do what we came here to do. But . . . you're going to have to keep doing it on your own."

"What are you talking about?" Joliet asked, her voice getting tense.

"The *Darwin* isn't going to make it."

The *Darwin* was the second of three ships in the privately funded science fleet. The ship, coming from Hawaii with supplies and ten more scientists, was scheduled to rendezvous with them in two days. The *Magellan* currently operated with a fourteen-person skeleton crew and Joliet was the only real scientist on board. Hawkins knew more than an average amount about wildlife and the natural world, and Bray, despite being a wiseass high school teacher and author, was a decent biologist, but neither of them were published in scientific journals, and neither had Ph.D.s—Bray didn't even believe in them. Hawkins could write all the articles in the world, and Bray could Skype with high schools across the country, but without the collective minds of professional oceanographers, biologists, microbiologists, climatologists, and a slew of other experts, their discoveries might not be taken seriously.

"Before either of you can complain, you should know the reason the *Darwin* isn't going to make it. There's a storm, a big one, coming up from the South. High winds. Twenty-foot swells. Real rough seas. The *Darwin* sustained significant damage and—"

"God, is everyone okay?" Joliet's brewing agitation disappeared. A lot of the scientists on board were her colleagues, if not friends.

"A lot of injuries," Drake said. "No souls lost. But they were forced to return to port. Going to be at least another month before they can get underway again and three weeks after that before they reach us."

"We're scheduled to head back before then," Hawkins observed.

Drake nodded. "Which is why I want you two to find as much compelling evidence as you can. Photograph it. Document it. Everything by the books. Maybe we can still make a difference."

Joliet was nodding when Drake finished talking. "We can do this. Public opinion shapes policy, right? We'll focus on the big picture. On what's most shocking."

"Glad to see you rolling with the punches, Joliet," Drake said. "Now, you two best get to that turtle. Do what you need to do and secure the body in the freezer by twenty-two hundred."

Hawkins took a step toward the door. While the *Darwin*'s return to port was a blow to their mandate, he appreciated the bold approach it required they take. It was more his style. But then he paused and asked, "Why so fast?"

Drake frowned. "That storm I mentioned? It'll be here tonight."

FOUR

The loggerhead's plastron—the underbelly—came free with a slurp. Joliet had drawn a scalpel around the turtle's soft flesh that divided its top and bottom shells. The cut on a healthy turtle would have been shaped like a stingray, but this specimen, pinched at the midsection, had a figure eight-shaped body.

"Slowly," Joliet said, pulling on the top half of the plastron.

Hawkins held the lower half, lifting up so the entire shell could come free at once. Bray stood behind a video camera, documenting the dissection. All three wore blue surgical aprons over their shorts and T-shirts, but only Hawkins and Joliet wore bright blue, elbow-length rubber gloves.

The turtle lay on a table at the center of the biolab, a four hundred-square-foot space on the port side of the *Magellan*'s main deck. Foam blocks had been wedged under the sides of the turtle's shell, keeping it from wobbling, or from slipping off the table. Bright fluorescent lights hanging from the ceiling illuminated the body. The only other source of light came from a single porthole, through which the sun—now heading for the horizon—shone brightly.

As the plastron lifted away from the body, the tangy scent of turtle insides wafted into the sterile-smelling "clean" lab, which normally smelled like bleach. Hawkins nearly gagged. He wasn't sure which smell was worse—guts or bleach—but combined, they sent a wave of revulsion through his body and made him wince.

Bray lowered the camera and said, "Good God, that reeks."

Joliet paused and looked at Bray. "Keep the camera up."

Bray lifted his shirt collar over his nose and continued recording the scene.

"The plastron came free after cutting along the seam between the marginal and inframarginal scutes, and then along the posterior margin," Joliet said, describing the work she'd completed. She tilted her end up so that it was facing the camera. "As you can see, the subject's body is quite deformed."

"What was the cause of this deformity?" Bray asked.

Joliet appeared annoyed for a moment, but then nodded. They hadn't recorded that portion of the dissection. Hawkins and Joliet placed the underbelly on an adjacent workbench.

"The deformity of this specimen was caused by a thick band of red plastic, which we cut away." Joliet picked up the hard plastic ring and held it up for the camera to see. "I'm not sure what its original purpose was, but there is some faint Japanese script, here on the side."

She turned the band around so that all the text could be captured by the lens. "It seems likely that the turtle, still very young, swam through the plastic band, which then became stuck around its midsection. As the specimen grew, the ring restricted its growth, resulting in this severe abnormality. That it survived into adulthood is something of a miracle."

Joliet moved back to the table and Hawkins followed, hoping he wouldn't puke on camera. He'd been hunting several times in his life, but quickly cleaning out a freshly killed deer wasn't quite the same as slowly poking around the insides of a decomposing sea turtle.

The inside of the turtle was bright red and pink mixed with bits of dull gray. Hawkins swallowed and turned his eyes toward Joliet, hoping her words would distract him. They didn't.

"The ventral surface of the specimen is covered by three muscle groups." She pointed to the exposed neck. "The longitudinal." She pointed to the upper body, where a pair of feather-shaped muscles had been exposed. "The large pinnate, which power the turtle's front flippers." She moved to the lower extremity. "And the pelvic muscles, which we already separated from the plastron. Despite the upper and lower portions of the body being separated by the deformation, the muscles appear whole and healthy. There is no disease present." She looked at Hawkins. "Hand me the knife."

A metal tray next to Hawkins held three large metal bowls, sliding calipers, metal snips, scissors, hemostatic forceps, toothless forceps, tweezers, three scalpels of various sizes, a turkey baster, a pair of pliers, a hacksaw, and a razor-sharp knife that looked rather like a fishing blade. He picked up the knife, pinching the flat side of the blade between his fingers, and handed it to Joliet, handle first.

Knife in hand, Joliet made quick work of the large muscles, cutting them free from the shell, ligaments, and bone where they were attached. "Bowl," she said.

Hawkins held out the largest bowl and Joliet placed all six slabs of turtle meat inside. When she was done, the bowl weighed quite a lot and Hawkins grunted as he carried it to the corner of the room and placed it in the large metal sink.

"This is where it gets interesting," Bray said, raising his eyebrows at Hawkins.

Joliet spoke quickly, keeping them on task. "The peritoneal cavity is now exposed. It should be noted that I would normally now separate the flippers and shoulder girdles, but they were . . . removed prior to recovery by a large Carcharodon carcharias—"

"A great white shark to the layman," Bray added.

"—that has learned to feed on creatures that become entangled in the Garbage Patch."

Joliet motioned for Bray to move closer. He moved to the end of the table, where he had a clear view of the loggerhead's exposed organs.

Hawkins took a deep breath and instantly regretted it. The smell had worsened significantly. The sight of the organs didn't help, nor did the guacamole-like green mush oozing around the cavity's perimeter. *Man up*, he told himself. *This is important.*

"The heart is here, in the center, and is hugged by the large tan liver on either side. The intestines, however, are severely out of place, running down the core of the turtle's body, to the posterior." She moved to the lower half of the disfigured subject and pointed out the jumble of pink intestines. "The intestines, normally bunched up just beneath the liver, have been elongated through the pinched midsection. It's likely that this resulted in poor digestion and nutritional health."

Hawkins frowned. This wasn't the slam-dunk revelation they were hoping for—most of America suffered from poor digestion—but it was a start.

"Let's take a look at the heart, before moving to the stomach," Joliet said and then reached a hand out to Hawkins. "Baster."

Hawkins handed her the turkey baster. "What's this for?"

Joliet moved over the heart, scalpel in one hand, baster in the other. "The pericardial cavity often contains liquid." She slowly made an incision and put the tip of the baster inside. After pushing it as far as it would go, she gave the baster a couple of squeezes, each one sucking up pink fluid. "Bowl."

Hawkins held out a fresh bowl, but leaned his head away from it. The baster burped as Joliet squirted the liquid in the bowl, and then repeated the process two more times until the cavity was empty. Hawkins quickly brought the bowl to the sink. He placed it down a little quickly and some of the fluid splashed out. He glanced down and saw small globs of green, some white stringy fibers, and a swirl of nearly clear and deep red fluids.

He moved away from the sink and took a deep breath, once again regretting it.

"You okay, Ranger?" Bray asked.

When he looked up, Hawkins found the camera turned toward him. He put on a brave face and gave Bray a thumbs-up. "Never better."

"If you're not feeling well, Mr. Hawkins, I can help."

The three of them turned toward the voice. Kam stood in the doorway, staring at the turtle. He looked simultaneously interested and disgusted, sentiments Hawkins shared.

Hawkins was glad for the respite, but wasn't sure if Kam could do the job. He spent most of his time in front of computers, not dissecting animals. Still, it beat puking on camera, so he swept his arm toward the turtle. "Be my guest."

Kam stepped up next to Joliet and nodded at her. "Umm, okay. I'm ready."

Bray gave Hawkins a look that asked, Is he for real?

Hawkins just shrugged.

"You're sure?" Joliet asked. "It's pretty bad."

Kam gave a semiconfident nod. "I've seen my mother gut fish. I should be okay."

"All right. If you say so," Joliet said. "Hey, while you're here, can you read this for us?" She handed him the red plastic band that had been removed from the turtle's midsection.

Kam turned the ring around in his hand, squinting at the text. "Uh, broccoli. It says 'broccoli.' Must have been used to hold stocks together."

"Don't they usually use rubber bands for that?" Bray asked.

Kam shrugged. "I'm not a farmer."

"Either way," Hawkins said, "we know it's trash and had no business being in the Pacific Ocean. Can we finish? There's still a storm coming."

Hawkins wasn't worried about the storm. It was still a few hours away. But it made for a handy excuse to press forward and get this business finished.

"Right," Joliet said. She pulled open the pericardium and looked inside. "The heart, aorta, and pulmonary arteries all appear healthy. There are no signs of heart disease. But it is a little small for a specimen this size."

Kam's hand went to his mouth, his face barely containing revulsion. When all three turned toward him, he took a deep breath, held it, and then removed his hand. "Please. Continue."

Joliet made quick work of the rest of the major organs, describing the health and state of the lungs, liver, spleen, cloaca, and mesenteries as she removed them from the body and placed them in a bowl held by the unflinching Kam. When the stomach was revealed, her eyes went wide. "The, ahh, stomach appears to be distended. It's at least twice the size as expected." She poked the stomach with her index finger. "It's quite firm." She looked at Hawkins. "Come feel this."

"I'll pass," Hawkins said, gloved hands raised.

She turned to Kam. "How about you?"

Kam quickly shook his head. The kid looked like he was a hiccup away from puking.

The door to the lab swung open. Phil Bennett stepped inside. "Hey," he said, looking apologetic for intruding.

The lanky kid had tussled brown hair and pale skin, but enough freckles to almost make his face look tan. He looked too young to be an engineer, even a junior engineer, but then again, Kam looked even younger and he was in charge of the ship's computers. Hawkins thought neither could be over twenty, but also knew that the older he got, the more twenty-somethings looked like teenagers to him.

"Captain Drake asked me to let you guys know the storm will be here soon. Says to wrap it up ASAP." A flash of confusion crossed Bennett's face when he saw Kam. "What are you doing here?"

"Just helping," Kam said.

"He's manning up, that's what," Bray said with a grin. "You want to give it a try?"

Bennett looked unsure, but walked closer. Kam stepped aside as Bennett got closer, revealing the opened turtle and its mottled organs. Bennett stopped at the sight. He winced. "That's . . . gross."

"Sure you don't want to lend a hand?" Bray asked.

"I think I prefer engines, but it's really not that different, I guess," Bennett said.

"How do you figure?" Bray asked.

Bennett stepped closer, eyeing the carved, open body. "Well, for starters, the *Magellan* has an inner steel framework and hull—the bones and skin. The bridge is like the head." He wandered around the table and tapped the turtle's head with his finger. Then suddenly, as though realizing what he'd just done, he winced and wiped the finger on his oil-stained pants. "The bridge contains the high-tech computer system, which is really like a brain. It can perceive the outside world through radar, satellite data, and an array of on-board sensors that measure temperature, wind speed, and even the visual spectrum. The computers are also connected to every area of the ship. The engine, the doors, the hull, air-conditioning, the boiler, everything. It's really a fairly complex nervous system. The ship can't technically feel pain, but when something goes wrong, and those alarms go off, it sure sounds like a scream."

Bennett wandered around the turtle, looking at the insides with less disgust.

Is he really looking at it like it's just a machine now? Hawkins wondered.

"This turtle and the *Magellan* both need chemical fuel to operate. The fuel gets processed and turned into kinetic energy. Both need a continuous supply of oxygen. When the engines are used, they get hot and are cooled with liquid."

He looked down at the array of organs on display. "It's really nothing more than an open car hood." He pointed to one organ at a time, naming them. "Gas tank. Carburetor. Air pump. Exhaust." He pointed to the heart. "Just one piston, though."

The look on his face had changed from repulsion to full-on interest.

"That's kind of messed-up thinking," Bray said, snapping Bennett's attention back up. "Historically speaking, it's when people start seeing each other as nonhuman, or machinelike that the worst atrocities are committed."

"It's a turtle," Bennett said. "Not a person."

Bray rolled his eyes. "Flesh and blood is flesh and blood. The same logic applies."

"Actually," Joliet said, "everything he said is correct and fairly insightful."

"For a mechanic?" Bennett said, sounding a little defensive now.

"For anyone," she said.

Bennett shrugged like it was nothing. "I'm interested in engines of all kinds."

"All kinds," Bray said. "*All* kinds."

Hawkins knew that Bray was just messing with Bennett, but he wasn't sure the kid knew that. Actually, he was sure of it when Bennett grew suddenly serious.

"My father died of a heart attack when he was forty," Bennett said. "My mother and I had to move in with her parents. Heart disease is genetic. Figured I better know how my engine works so I can service it right and not join him in fifteen years." He dipped his head toward Bray's stomach. "You should probably start thinking about that, too."

"I'm a high school teacher," Bray said. "You'll have to do better than that if you're trying to insult me."

The pair stared at each other for a moment. Bennett looked like he was ready to say something and Hawkins knew Bray would already have thirty different one-liners lined up. He was about to say they didn't have time to argue, but Bennett beat him to the punch.

"Just forget it, okay?" Bennett took a step back toward the door, looking wounded. Before anyone could apologize, he paused. "Have you found anything interesting? I mean, for why we're out here. The Garbage Patch."

"We're getting there," Joliet said.

Bennett backed toward the door. "Right. Okay. So yeah. Drake says to make it snappy." He stopped at the door. "Hey, Kam—good luck with the turtle, buddy." And with that, he stepped out of the room and closed the door.

"I knew he wouldn't stay," Bray said.

"Not sure pissing off the guy who controls the air-conditioning in our room is a good idea," Hawkins said. "Could make our lives hell."

Bray grunted, but didn't argue the point.

"Didn't know you two were friends," Joliet said to Kam.

Kam shrugged, still looking queasy. "Neither did I."

"Right." With a reassuring smile, Joliet turned back to the turtle's stomach and placed a scalpel against the organ. "I'm going to open the stomach now. Ready?"

Kam took a breath, swallowed, and nodded.

She made the cut as she spoke. "If the turtle ate anything—oh my God."

Hawkins stepped closer, interest overriding revulsion. "What is it?"

"Get this," she said to Bray, waving him closer. She finished the cut and spread the organ open. A rainbow of colors greeted them. She reached in and scooped out a handful of the undigested meal. "Plastic. It's all plastic."

She dug out two more handfuls. Most of the plastic chips were unidentifiable globs, stuck together by gelatinous goo and undigested fish parts, but Hawkins saw a bottle cap, a scissor handle, and what looked like a full spool's worth of dental floss. The items seemed random, unconnected, but all had one thing in common: They were trash, either thrown into the ocean intentionally or lost by some sunken cargo ship.

"Likely cause of death is starvation," Joliet said, reaching into the open cavity once more. "The stomach filled with debris over time and eventually became so packed with indigestible particles that food could no longer fit. The disfigured body was bad enough, but this is . . ." Joliet's forehead scrunched up. "Hold on. Something's stuck in here." She tugged at something, but couldn't pull it free. "Can I have the pliers?"

Hawkins picked up the tool and handed it to Joliet. He leaned in closer, sour stomach all but forgotten. This is what they'd been looking for. No one could deny the damage being done to the ocean once they saw this video. That the specimen was a relatively cute creature helped, too. If this were a shark, some people might actually cheer.

"Got it," Joliet said. She pursed her lips and pulled. "It's really stu—"

Whatever it was came free and Joliet spilled backward. Hawkins caught her with an arm under her back. But neither of them commented on the fall, or quick save. Both sets of eyes were on the object clutched in the pliers' grip.

"What the hell is that?" Hawkins asked, standing Joliet back up.

The object looked like a plastic cube. On its base were four stainless-steel prongs, each tipped with a bit of torn stomach lining. A thin, five-inch-long, black wire emerged from one side. And what looked like a small LED light sat on top of the device.

"I think it's a transmitter," Bray said. "Radio tracker. Gives off a pulsing signal."

"Inside a turtle?" Kam said. "Is that unusual?"

Joliet raised a single eyebrow at Kam. "Are you serious?"

The kid just shrugged.

"It looks like it was designed to be ingested," Hawkins observed. "Those hooks kept it planted to the stomach wall. But the light's not on. Must not be working."

"I can open it up," Kam said. "See how it works. Maybe find some clue about who made it on a circuit board or something?"

"That's actually a really good idea," Bray said.

They were right. Kam was the perfect man for the job.

"Just take off the—" Kam wiggled a finger at the bits of stomach lining clinging to the barbs.

"I think Kam is asking the right thing. Who would have done this to an endangered species? Or really any species?" Joliet asked. "And why?"

"I think I know," Hawkins said. With all eyes, and the camera, on him, he picked up the red plastic band. "Whoever put the tracker in the turtle wanted to be able find it again. For some reason, the tracker failed and the loggerhead grew to adulthood. But look at the size of the band around its waist. It's small. And the turtle would have been small when it first got stuck in the band. The tracker wouldn't have fit in its stomach at the time, let alone down its throat. I think the turtle was kept in captivity until it was large enough for someone to shove that tracker down its throat and attach it to the stomach lining. The turtle might have been killed by the plastic it ate, but the deformation was done on purpose." He looked Joliet in the eyes. "This turtle was an experiment."

FIVE

The storm arrived sooner than expected. After hastily bagging and tagging the loggerhead's internal organs and putting the disassembled creature on ice, Hawkins returned to his quarters with Bray. Not because he wanted to, but because Drake had ordered all nonessential crew to "weather out the weather"—his words—in their berths with close access to the head. In other words, he didn't want any of them puking on his ship. Of course, confining the crew to their quarters, which were located at the bow of the ship, almost guaranteed seasickness.

The room canted at a sharp angle.

"Oh, good God," Bray said, clutching the mattress of his lower bunk.

Hawkins typically slept on the upper bunk, but he didn't feel like being catapulted if a wave struck the ship's side. He stood across the small room, holding on to the wall-mounted desk for support. As the ship angled up a wave, Hawkins bent his right knee and leaned into it, keeping himself more or less upright. "You'd feel it less if you stood up. Let your inner ear adjust to the tilt."

"You going to do that all night?" Bray asked.

Hawkins grinned. He'd spent a lot of time on the ocean as a boy. Even these strong waves wouldn't make him seasick. Bray, on the other hand, had been on a few whale watches in his lifetime and not all of them had turned out well. His first few days aboard the *Magellan* had been . . . messy, but he'd gotten his sea legs. Until now. "You think you're going to sleep?"

Bray clutched his eyes shut. "I just need to get used to the motion, that's all."

"C'mon, it's not that bad," Hawkins said as the bow began to lower. He shifted his weight in toward the ship's aft. The *Magellan* crested the wave and dropped so fast that even Hawkins felt his stomach twist.

Bray groaned.

"I was thinking about going to get some raw clams," Hawkins said. "Want some?"

"I hate you," Bray said, but he couldn't hide his grin.

As the ship entered the trough between waves, Hawkins's mind returned to the loggerhead dissection. That the stomach showed evidence of environmental damage was horrible, but fantastic for their cause. But the plastic band constricting the turtle's midsection being part of some kind of experiment took the wind out of their sails. It would have made a powerful image. And sure, they could still use it, but it wasn't quite ethical. But if it helped save the environment, and through its protection, human lives, perhaps omitting the existence of the tracking device was defendable, if not noble. Then again, someone had performed a horrible experiment on an endangered species. The park ranger in him couldn't let that slide. Someone had to be brought to justice.

"You're not even here, are you?" Bray asked.

Hawkins realized they'd gone over another wave. "Just thinking. About the loggerhead. About the radio tracker. Have you ever heard of anything like that?"

"Outside of the low-IQ kids throwing frogs at chain-link fences, no. And they have stupidity as an excuse."

Hawkins gave a nod. "The plastic band and tracker had to have been done by the same person. It was intentional. The question is, why?"

"People have done a lot of screwy things in the pursuit of knowledge," Bray said. "And I'm not just talking animals. I'll just focus on my neck of the woods. Did you know that the Atomic Energy Commission and Quaker Frickin' Oats gave the residents of Fernald, Mass—my hometown— breakfast cereal with radioactive tracers?"

Hawkins didn't. It sounded unbelievable.

"My grandfather died of throat and stomach cancers before I was born. Big shocker there, right? The U.S. Navy had a Harvard biochemist inject sixty-four prisoners with cow blood. And, get this, Oak Ridge Labs injected eleven patients—*patients*—at the Massachusetts General Hospital in Boston with *uranium*. The United States has a long history of injecting foreign elements into peoples' bodies to find out what will happen. Sure, sometimes they find a cure to something, but it's usually accidental."

Hawkins had no reason to doubt the man. If Bray was an expert on any two things, it was biology—including the history of the science—and his home state. "But what could be learned by binding the turtle's shell with a plastic band?"

"Adaptability," came Joliet's voice. She stood in the open doorway, clutching the frame as the ship rose up on another wave. "To see how the growing turtle's body would adapt to the constriction. We know the intestines elongated, and the muscle groups separated, but there is still more to uncover, like how the turtle's neurology and nervous system were affected." She looked at Bray lying in the bed. "You know, it's easier if you stand."

"I know, I know!" Bray threw his legs over the side of his cot and sat up. He looked about to say something when he groaned and held on to the top bunk. "I hate both of you."

"It's possible the turtle would have lived far longer if not for all the plastic it consumed." Joliet frowned. "While I would never condone the experiment, there is a lot to be learned from it."

"Might as well benefit from someone else torturing the animal, right?" Bray asked. "I thought you Canucks were all touchy-feely, leave-your-doors-unlocked types."

Joliet's face scrunched up with anger. "Hey, this is different!"

"Not to PETA," Bray said, his grin revealing that the dig was in jest. "That was for making me sit up."

Joliet was still fuming when she looked at Hawkins and saw his smile. He tried to erase it, but failed. He sensed her frustration with Bray extend to him.

"Have either of you seen Kam?" she asked.

Bray answered quickly. "I didn't think he was your ty—"

"*Bray*," Hawkins warned. Continuing the roast of Joliet might help the man keep his supper down, but it wouldn't end well—for either man, it seemed. "Not since we left the lab. He looked a little green. Probably in his quarters trying to forget what the inside of a loggerhead looks like."

"Well, he's not."

Kam, like the three of them, was nonessential to the ship. As a technology intern, his official duties included software updates and hardware fixes, but since the systems on the *Magellan* were fairly new and up-to-date, Kam most often found himself cleaning, or fetching coffee. Hawkins wondered if the young man's performance in the biolab was an attempt to elevate his status, and perhaps be invited to take part in endeavors more rewarding than brewing the perfect cup of Folgers Classic Roast.

"Why are you so worried about him, anyway?" Bray asked. "He's a big boy."

"Asks the man hiding in his room with his big, strong Hawkins to take care of him." She said the last part with a pouty face that made both men grin. "Try to deny it, but you like Kam as much as the rest of us."

Bray just stared.

"You show him your god-awful magic tricks," she said. "He's sat through each and every one of your boring Webcasts. And I know he helped you with the Saran Wrap prank. I caught him in the hallway, keeping watch while you covered the toilet."

"That little shit," Hawkins said. He'd been on the receiving end of that prank. He'd gotten Bray back, but now he had to get Kam, and it seemed, Joliet, who'd kept her mouth shut.

"Fine," Bray said, and then groaned as the ship tilted forward. "I like the twerp, but I'm not his mother. I'm not going to Hulk smash my way through the ship just to find him. Maybe he's in the head?" Bray asked with a groan. "I might be headed there myself."

"Checked there, too," Joliet said.

"There are nearly forty bathrooms on board," Hawkins noted. "Maybe he wanted privacy?"

Before anyone could answer, the ship listed sharply to the side. Hawkins fell forward, landing on Bray in the lower bunk. Joliet spilled to the floor, sliding until she slammed to a stop against the wall.

As the ship righted itself, Hawkins pulled himself off of Bray. "That's not good."

"What the hell happened?" Bray asked.

Joliet pushed herself up, leaning against the wall. "Wave hit the starboard side. The ship must have turned."

"Aren't you supposed to steer *into* the waves?" Bray asked. "Why would Drake let the ocean T-bone us?"

The ship rolled hard again, pushing Hawkins back onto the bed. When it passed, he said, "He wouldn't."

Joliet made for the door. "Something's wrong."

Hawkins stumbled out of the room behind her.

"Where are you going?" Bray asked.

"The bridge," Hawkins answered as he moved down the hall.

"Oh, hell," Bray muttered and gave chase.

Hawkins paused with Joliet at the bottom of the staircase leading up. They hung on to the railings as the floor shook and a loud rumbling echoed through the ship.

Bray stumbled up and took hold of Hawkins's offered arm. "The hell is that?"

"Waves are breaking against the hull," Hawkins guessed.

"Doesn't sound like water," Bray said.

Joliet started up the stairs. "That's because it's not just water. The ocean is full of a million floating projectiles."

Hawkins realized that they were in a very precarious situation. At two hundred seventy-four feet in length, the

Magellan wasn't a small ship, but the right storm could sink even the largest vessel. Worse, they seemed to be out of control and the ocean was full of debris, some of it rock solid. Rescue in the middle of the Pacific was fairly unlikely on a good day, but surrounded by endless miles of garbage, they'd never be found.

He kept his thoughts to himself as he motioned for Bray to follow Joliet up the stairs. Halfway to the top, the ship shook from a massive impact. A loud bang from the top of the stairwell was followed by a swirling torrent of sea water.

SIX

The roiling water carried a slick of worn plastic chips past Hawkins's feet with enough force to sweep them out from under him. If not for the railings he clutched by both hands, he would have toppled down the stairs. He felt thankful that Joliet and Bray had been holding the railings, as well, or they would have all fallen together.

As the ship canted in the other direction, the flow of water stopped. *We're not sinking*, Hawkins told himself, *a wave just found a way inside.*

"Mark!" Joliet shouted from above. She'd reached the top of the stairs on the main deck and fought to stay upright on the sharply tilting, very wet floor. "A door is open!"

Hawkins reached the top of the stairs right behind Bray. Nearly horizontal rain whipped into the hallway, stinging his face. Had Joliet lost her balance and fallen, she'd have been tossed out the open door, over the rail of the main deck, and into the torrid ocean. As the ship tilted, pushing them away from the open door, a flash of lightning lit the scene outside the door.

A cresting twenty-five-foot wave laden with garbage reached out for them like a giant. They were about to be pulverized. Hawkins struggled to climb the steepening floor, hoping to reach the door before the wave.

"Take my arm!" Bray shouted. He held onto the stairway

railing with one hand and stretched out the other to Hawkins. "We'll both pull."

Understanding what the man had in mind, Hawkins reached forward and took Bray's hand. They pulled in unison, accelerating Hawkins up the incline. He'd covered half the distance when his speed dropped quickly. The ship was still listing. Desperation fueled his leap and he caught hold of the open metal door with the tips of his fingers.

Thunder boomed through the opening door, so close that it made his ears ring. But it didn't slow him because he knew the next boom would be the wave striking the ship. He pulled himself up the door, found his footing, and pushed against the heavy metal. His progress felt impossibly slow, but he managed to get the watertight door closed. The first drops of the descending wave hissed against the hull as Hawkins took hold of the locking wheel and gave it a spin.

The door's locking pins snapped into place, securing the hatch and keeping the water at bay, but it did little to spare the ship, or Hawkins, against the force of the wave. The impact pushed the ship to a forty-five-degree angle and tossed Hawkins away from the door as though it had exploded.

Hawkins shouted as he fell toward the other side of the ship. But his topple was cut short as something snagged his shirt. He swung to the side and struck the wall hard, but not nearly as hard as he would have struck the far wall. When Bray shouted a strained "Yearg!" Hawkins knew that it was the big man who had caught him. And likely saved his life.

When the ship righted itself, Bray let go of Hawkins's now stretched-out T-shirt and rubbed his shoulder.

"You okay?" Hawkins asked.

Bray rolled his shoulder around. "You owe me one."

"I'll give you one of the beers Joliet already owes me," Hawkins said with a grin and gave Bray a pat on the shoulder, causing the man to wince.

"Let's go!" Joliet shouted as she started up the next staircase. They were still three flights below the bridge.

With no more open hatches along the way, the ascent went

more smoothly, though they were still tossed back and forth. Beaten and bruised, they staggered up the last flight of stairs only to find the door leading to the wheelhouse locked.

Joliet wasted no time hammering the door with her fist.

Peter Blok, the ship's first mate, unlatched the door quickly, shouting, "Cahill, where the hell have you—?" Blok looked like he'd been slapped in the face when he realized who was at the door. His eyes were wide behind his wire-rim glasses, but his eyebrows were furrowed in frustration. "What are you three—you're supposed to be confined to quarters!"

"What's going on up here?" Hawkins asked, though it sounded more like a demand. "We're being pummeled down there."

"We don't have time for this right now," Blok said. The man spent most of his free time reading novels, and he was generally soft-spoken. His raised voice instantly alerted Hawkins to the seriousness of their situation.

"The computer's fried," Blok said. "We're sailing blind."

"We're not sailing at all," came the angry voice of Captain Drake. He arrived a moment later. "If they want to see the end coming, I won't deny them that." He looked Hawkins in the eyes. "Just stay out of the way. Clear?"

Hawkins nodded and stepped past the seamen with Bray and Joliet in tow. The ship rolled, forcing everyone to cling to whatever nearby bolted-down object they could find. "Is no one steering the ship?" Hawkins asked.

"Can't," Drake said. "Controls aren't responding."

Bray's eyes widened. "We're dead in the water?"

"Not exactly," Blok said. "The ship's systems are functioning. We're just not in control of them."

"How is that possible?" Joliet asked.

"The *Magellan* is run by computers. Every system—navigation, communications, environmental—everything, is managed by the computers," Drake said. "And those computers have a mind of their own at the moment."

Hawkins looked out over the wheelhouse. Every computer screen flickered, offering brief glimpses of the aberrant system. Even the radar screen was a jumbled mess of green lines and random blobs of color. The three other crewmen in the wheelhouse just clung to their stations with white knuckles. There was nothing else to be done.

Hawkins nearly asked if they'd tried switching the ship to manual control, but decided the question would insult Drake. Of course he'd tried. An old sailor like Drake would probably prefer to spend the night behind the wheel, battling the storm on his own rather than let the computer take control. But there was another possibility. "Could it be a computer virus?"

Drake shrugged. "Not my area of expertise."

"What about Kam?" Joliet asked.

"We sent Cahill to find him fifteen minutes ago," Blok said as the ship rolled hard in the other direction. He stumbled, but Hawkins caught him by the arm and kept him upright.

Ryan Cahill was both the second mate and the ship's medic. When the storm abated Hawkins thought the man would have his hands full. "We just came from the science quarters," Hawkins said. "Cahill's not down there."

"Neither is Kam," Joliet added. "We didn't see either—oh, no . . ."

"What is it?" Drake asked.

Hawkins knew what Joliet was thinking and answered for her. "The stairwell hatch on the main deck was open. Took at least one wave, maybe two before we closed it. It's possible one, or both of them, went outside."

The ship tilted back as it rose up over a wave, spilling Daniel Sanchez, a deck hand, to the floor where he slid until he hit the back wall. His head struck the metal wall hard. He slumped to the floor. Bray made his way to the man and knelt down. "He's unconscious."

"Dammit," Drake grumbled, then shouted to the other men. "I thought I told you three to strap in!" He turned to his new arrivals and repeated the message. "That goes for all of you, if you want to stay. Pick a seat and strap yourself in."

"What about Kam and Cahill?" Joliet asked.

Drake gave her a look that said, Do not argue. "If they're

outside, they're dead, and there is not a thing you can do about it. Now sit yourself down and—"

"Sir!" Jeff Allen, a young deckhand, shouted. This was his first long-term voyage aboard the *Magellan* and the storm had managed to bleach his normally tan complexion.

As the ship tipped forward over the crest of the wave, Drake made his way to the front of the wheelhouse. Ignoring the captain's orders, Hawkins, Joliet, Bray, and Blok followed him to the front windows, where a battery of windshield wipers were losing the battle against the endless sheets of rain.

They peered out the fore windows and saw a curved, trash-filled ocean in the bright glow of the *Magellan*'s floodlights. The ship entered the trough between waves, leveling out, but the view didn't change.

"Oh my God," Bray said, backing away from the window.

Hawkins followed the vertical wall of garbage up. It disappeared into the darkness above the ship. A flash of lightning illuminated what Bray must have already realized—a fifty-foot wall of garbage-laden ocean was about to crash down on them. This wave couldn't be climbed. The *Magellan* would have to go through it.

"Hold on to something!" Drake shouted as he dove to the floor and held on to the base of a bolted-down chair.

The last thing Hawkins saw was a frothy wall of white dropping on them like a mammoth curtain call. Then there was a sound like thunder, but louder, and a jarring impact that sent him sailing. He blinked once, caught a glimpse of a refrigerator, felt a momentary pain in his head, and then, nothing.

SEVEN

Water lapped against sand. Sea birds called. The gentle undulation of a ship in water. Hawkins sensed all of this as he
awoke, and for a moment, they combined to put his mind at
ease. Memories of a two-week vacation in Bermuda, and the
woman he'd met there nine years ago—what was her name?—
drifted through his waking thoughts. Lazy days aboard a
catamaran. Fishing. Snorkeling. Eating. Drinking. And the
nights . . . . Where the days passed calmly, the nights burned
with passion. Belowdecks. On deck with only the stars watching. Even in the water.

Water . . .

Memory of the crashing wave woke him fully.

Hawkins gasped and sat up straight. Pain bloomed immediately, pounding at the back of his head. He moved his
hand back and found a lump matted with blood. He'd struck
something when the giant wave had slammed into the ship,
but had no memory of what it was.

He found himself against the back wall, his view of the
wheelhouse impeded by a workstation and, to his right, a
refrigerator. The fridge looked new. In fact, it was still wrapped
in plastic. That's how it had stayed afloat, he realized. The
plastic had kept the water out, and the air trapped inside
kept the fridge buoyant. It might have been floating in the
Garbage Patch for years before being turned into a projectile. The top of the fridge was crumpled now, and smeared

with rich, red blood that seemed to glow on the white surface. The blood made his stomach twist, not so much because it disgusted him, but because he knew it had come from one of the other crewmembers.

A seagull squawked so loudly that Hawkins surmised it was actually in the wheelhouse. He pushed himself up slowly, pausing to let his spinning vision focus. The first thing he saw was a blurry mix of bright green and blue. His eyes refused to focus on the distance, but Hawkins could tell they'd made it out of the storm and found themselves . . . where? At an island? The nearest island should have been nearly two hundred miles away. They couldn't have covered that much distance overnight.

Turning his attention to the interior of the wheelhouse brought his eyes into focus. Bray lay on the other side of the fridge. He looked dead, but his rising chest revealed he was merely unconscious. Hawkins stepped over the fridge, into the center aisle of the bridge, and found Joliet on the floor.

The seagull stood beside her, violently tugging at her hair. *What the hell?* Hawkins had never heard of a seagull entering a ship, never mind trying to scavenge a meal from a living human being's body. Was it rabid? He couldn't be sure, but it was the biggest damn seagull he'd ever seen, a fact that didn't slow him down as he charged the bird, waving his hands and shouting.

At first, the bird didn't back down. It opened its wings wide and squawked at him.

"I don't care how tough you think you are," Hawkins said, unclipping his knife from his waist and drawing it out, "I'm not going to let you eat her."

The seagull seemed to recognize the threat and, with one last angry squawk, spun around and flew out of the wheelhouse through a large hole in one of the big windshield windows. Given the size of the hole, the fact that it was bent inward, and the positioning of the fridge, Hawkins guessed that appliance had punched the hole.

Joliet stirred with a groan. "What happened?"

Hawkins helped her into a sitting position. "Not really sure. Just came to myself. But we're safe now."

He helped her into a chair where she sat, holding her head. "I'm going to check on the others," he said. "Don't move."

"You don't have to worry about that," she said, rubbing her temples.

Hawkins went back to Sanchez, who'd been knocked unconscious just before the big wave struck. After checking for a pulse and finding one, he shook the man's arm. "Sanchez." He tried to wake the man as gently as possible, but Sanchez didn't move. Hawkins pinched the man's arm hard. Sanchez didn't flinch. He was out for the count.

Hawkins moved to Bray next and smacked his cheek a few times. "Bray. Wake up."

The big man grumbled.

"Wake up, Eight."

Bray's eyes popped open. He shouted in surprise and tried to scramble away.

"Bray!" Hawkins said, holding his friend's shirt. "It's over. We made it through the storm."

"Everyone okay over there?" came Drake's voice.

As Bray calmed down, Hawkins looked up over the console blocking his view. Drake stood on the far end of the wheelhouse. A streak of blood ran down his forehead and face. "We're alive," he replied. "How 'bout you?"

"Not so much," Drake said, his voice turning solemn.

Hawkins quickly double-checked Bray, who waved him away, saying, "Go. Go." Then he stood and made his way toward Drake, who was helping Blok to his feet. Drake motioned with his head to the floor at the front of the wheelhouse. Hawkins steeled himself as he walked around the front row of consoles. He'd seen death before, up close and personal, but he didn't think repeated exposure to something like that would ever make it easier.

When he rounded the corner and saw the caved-in head of Jeff Allen, he knew he was right. A pool of watered-down blood covered the floor around the body. Hawkins covered his mouth with the back of his hand and stepped back so only the man's legs could be seen.

"Near as I can tell, that fridge caught him on the way in," Drake said. "Would have been quick."

Hawkins nodded. The young man wouldn't have had time to even register the injury before he ceased to exist, which was preferable to a long, drawn-out, painful death. No one deserved that.

Joliet gasped when she staggered up to Hawkins's side and looked around the corner. "Oh, no . . ."

"Where are we?" Bray asked. He stood on the starboard side, looking out the windows.

Happy to turn his attention away from the body, Hawkins joined Bray at the windows. Toward the bow he saw a crescent-shaped, light gray sand beach. Behind it was a thick, tropical jungle that eventually rose up over a string of steep hills. The beach and jungle wrapped around the starboard side, eventually dwindling down as steep, rocky cliffs rose up, blocking the view of anything beyond.

Hawkins turned aft and saw that the cliff ended nearly a football field's distance away. The break in the wall was perhaps seventy feet wide—just big enough to allow the *Magellan* passage—and picked up again on the other side, where it merged with more tropical jungle. The water below them was dark blue, but toward the shore, it glowed light blue from the gray sands beneath. Had they discovered some kind of lost paradise?

"It's beautiful," Joliet said.

"Any idea where we are, Drake?" Hawkins asked.

Drake stood on the port side of the ship, looking out over the palm-filled jungle. "Some kind of lagoon. Beyond that, your guess is as good as mine."

"There aren't any islands on the charts for this part of the ocean," Blok said, his voice more subdued than usual. He rubbed a hand over his bald head and repositioned his glasses. "It's not supposed to be here."

A loud knocking came from the locked hatch at the back of the wheelhouse. "Open up!" someone shouted.

"That's Jones," Drake said to Hawkins, who was nearest the door.

Hawkins understood the unsaid order and quickly unlocked the door. A disheveled Harold Jones, the ship's chief engineer, stood on the other side. Blood covered the dark skin of his forehead and his thinning gray hair. "Where's the captain?"

"Here," Drake said, stepping into the center aisle and heading for the door. "How are the engines?"

"Functional, but not controllable. Whatever happened during the storm hasn't stopped. Computer still has control."

"And your crew?" Drake asked.

"A little roughed up, but we managed. I checked on the Tweedles on my way up—" "The Tweedles" was the crew's nickname for their two chefs, brothers who were two years apart, but looked like twins. Chubby, bald twins, hence the name. Jones smiled. "Looked like they'd eaten before the storm, so they've got a mess on their hands. But they're—"

Jones's smiled faded. His eyes had stopped on the pair of feet poking out from behind a console at the front of the wheelhouse. "Who's that?"

"Jeff Allen," Drake said.

"He's . . . ?"

Drake nodded.

"Dad!" DeWinter took the stairs two at a time, arriving by her father's side with a look of horror in her eyes. Her skin, normally a few shades lighter than Jones's, was covered in grime. When she saw Drake, she addressed him instead of her father. "Captain . . ." She paused, out of breath. "We found Cahill . . ."

"Good," Drake replied. "Is Kam with him? We need to get—"

"You don't understand," DeWinter said. "Cahill. He's dead."

Drake's face reddened. "How?"

DeWinter collected herself and answered. "He's bound up in some netting tangled off the port crane. Looks like he fell overboard. Drowned."

"The hell was he doing outside?" Drake grumbled.

"Have you found Kam?" Joliet asked.

DeWinter shook her head. "Should have been in the science quarters with you."

Drake rolled his neck, the vertebrae popping audibly. He pointed to Jones and DeWinter. "You two, fish Cahill out of the water. We'll use the wet lab as a morgue. Put the dead on ice and return them to their families. Blok and I will get Sanchez to medical and Allen to the wet lab. The rest of you, find Kam. I want control of my ship and I want it yesterday."

As the group split up, Hawkins was thankful he wasn't in Drake's shoes. There was nothing that could have been done to save Allen or Cahill, but Drake took his responsibilities as captain seriously. The deaths of his second mate and a deckhand had to be eating him up.

Hawkins followed Jones and DeWinter down the stairs to the main deck, where the outer hatch was once again opened. The door must have been left open by Cahill, but why had the man gone outside? It was a suicidal move. The only reason he could think of was that someone less experienced—namely Kam—had ventured outside first. The theory didn't bode well for their search.

Jones and DeWinter stepped through the open hatch and headed for the back of the ship, where the body of Cahill waited for them.

"I'll start looking belowdecks," Bray said. "Don't feel ready to see another corpse."

"That makes two of us," Hawkins said. "I hope you're the one that finds Kam."

"I will," Bray said. "I'm sure of it." Then he descended the stairs toward the lower decks.

Hawkins followed the father and daughter team outside, but stopped at the port rail. Joliet joined him and together they looked out at the hilly jungle. A squawk brought his eyes up to the clear blue sky. Five large seagulls circled overhead, like vultures.

Joliet put a hand over her eyes and looked at the birds. "What are they waiting for?"

A scream replied, but it didn't come from the birds. It came from the stern.

"That was Jackie," Joliet said and, without a moment's pause, ran toward the stern deck with Hawkins hot on her heels.

EIGHT

Hawkins stumbled over a loose buoy as he sprinted toward the starboard side of the *Magellan*'s bow. The first deck at the front of the ship was normally clear of everything except for the occasional sunbathing crewmember. But now it was covered in a layer of refuse that came up to Hakwins's knees in places. He caught himself on the rail, pushed off, and continued after Joliet, who had hopped through the debris with surprising agility.

After stepping past empty jugs, an army of rubber duckies, and endless loops of rope that made the whole mess look like some kind of giant plate of spaghetti, Hawkins arrived to find Jones holding DeWinter against his chest. His normally composed and confident daughter shook with fright.

"What happened?" Hawkins asked.

"I didn't see it," Jones said. "But something took the body. Cahill is gone."

"Come look," Joliet said.

Hawkins joined her at the rail and peered over the edge. A large swath of thin netting hung over the rail and descended into the water some sixteen feet below. It was the kind of net used to catch large fish, like tuna, but worked just as well on sharks, dolphins, whales, and apparently human beings. But there was no body in this net. Not anymore.

Joliet pointed at the water beyond the net. "Look. There's a footprint."

Hawkins had recently learned that a footprint, in the ocean, was an area of flattened water caused by a disturbance by something beneath, most often a surfacing whale. But this wasn't a footprint in the traditional sense. The water here was calm. There were no waves to flatten. Instead, the footprint left behind were widening ripples spreading out from the net, presumably where Cahill's body had been caught in it.

The mystery of what happened to the body wasn't hard to solve. "Shark," Hawkins whispered. "Had to be."

Joliet nodded. "A big one. These nets are strong enough to entangle whales. Shark's teeth would cut some of the lines, but not all of them."

Hawkins stared into the deep blue water surrounding the ship, looking for a shifting shadow, but found nothing. If there was a shark down there, it had either retreated to the depths with its meal or headed back out to sea. He hoped for the latter, but had a feeling the shark would stick around to see if anything else fell into the water—like a dog at a dinner table. "Think it's our friend come back for the rest of the turtle?"

"Wasn't a shark," DeWinter said. She pulled away from her father's grasp and wiped her wet eyes.

"Had to be," Hawkins said. "What else in these waters could do it? Squid?"

Joliet shook her head no. "A squid big enough to pull a man free from this netting would have to be huge, and they live in deep waters."

"This looks pretty deep," Hawkins said, looking down into the water.

"Not nearly deep enough. Maybe—"

"It *wasn't* a shark!" DeWinter shouted. "I *saw* it. It didn't stop to bite, or to shake its head. I know how sharks bite. They shake their heads so the serrated teeth can cut. Whatever took him, took him as it swam past. It never slowed down. He was there, and then he wasn't. A shark couldn't do that."

Joliet crossed her arms and frowned. "She right. A shark would have made a mess of things."

"Then what did it look like?" Hawkins asked.

"Maybe we should give her some time?" Jones said, placing his hands on DeWinter's shoulders. "She might remember the details better if—"

DeWinter shrugged out from her father's arms. "I remember the details just fine, not that there is much to remember. It was black, fast, and at least eight feet long, maybe bigger. It came from beneath the hull, took the body, and went deep. That's it. Was too fast to see anything more."

Hawkins thought about the possibilities. A shark still felt right to him. They were the biggest deep-sea predators that could also hunt in shallow waters. But DeWinter was sharp and her testimony hard to ignore.

He shook his head. This wasn't like an attack at a national park. He'd investigated several attacks at Yellowstone during his stint there. The culprit could always be identified. Even if no one witnessed the attack, there were always tracks. Or scat. Or easily recognizable bite marks. Sometimes claw marks. Hawkins rubbed a hand over his chest. And the potential offenders were few: bears, cougars, and sometimes herd animals like elk or bison provoked into action by a heckling tourist.

But out here in the ocean, there were an array of predators that could arrive and escape unseen. Not only that, while Yellowstone is 3,468 square miles of wilderness, the ocean and its depths are essentially limitless. New species of predator, including sharks and behemoths like the giant squid, were still being discovered. Since most ships avoided this stretch of water because of the thick Garbage Patch, it was possible that a new species of predator hunted here. That the island wasn't on any charts supported his theory, but with no facts to support it, Hawkins decided to keep his speculation to himself.

A loud splash spun the group around toward the port side of the ship, beyond which the lush, green tropical jungle swayed back and forth, as though beckoning.

"What was that?" DeWinter blurted, fear filling her voice.

"Could be Kam," Joliet said quickly, and before anyone could offer another possibility, she was off and running across the cluttered deck.

"Joliet!" Hawkins shouted as he gave chase. "Slow down!" But he could see she had no intention of slowing down. She'd jumped into shark-infested waters to save an already dead turtle. He had no doubt she'd jump in now to save Kam. But they didn't even know if it was Kam. It could be the shark tearing apart Cahill's body. It could be any number of things that wouldn't be wise to dive-bomb.

Halfway across the debris-strewn deck, Hawkins could see that Joliet wasn't going to slow down. Ignoring the mess, he risked not watching his step and sprinted forward. *Look before you leap*, Hawkins thought. The old catch-phrase had become cliché over time, but no less effective at saving lives.

But Joliet seemed unfamiliar with the phrase. She leapt up, planting her right foot on the rail, and bent her legs, ready to spring out into the air. As her leg extended, Hawkins reached an arm around her waist. When she pushed, he pulled.

For a moment, Hawkins thought she might take them both overboard, but Joliet's one hundred twenty pounds were no match for Hawkins's two hundred. Still, the effort it took to pull her back sent them both sprawling to the deck, where she began kicking to get free.

"What the hell!" she shouted. "Hawkins, let me go!"

"Calm down," Hawkins said, and then grunted as he caught an elbow in the gut. He understood the emotions driving her—it *could* be Kam, and to Joliet, not jumping in meant she was abandoning their friend. Hawkins felt similarly, but the splash could have been made by whatever had taken Cahill, and one close encounter with a predator in any given month was more than enough. If it had been Joliet who was missing, Hawkins might have jumped in himself. As he fought with her, he recognized the strong emotions fueling his fight to keep her on board, and safe. He was hooked like a tuna and she was reeling him steadily in. Of course, she might not talk to him after this. "You need to start thinking things through."

As they struggled, Jones stepped past them and looked over the rail.

"Mark, I swear to God, if you don't let me go—"

"Nothing down there," Jones said.

The struggle stopped.

"Would have jumped in for nothing," the engineer added. "You should listen to your man."

Hawkins let go of Joliet. She stood up, gave Hawkins a kick in the leg, and turned on Jones. "He's *not* my man." She stepped up to the rail and looked over the side.

Jones helped Hawkins to his feet, and gave him a nod. "You did good, son. She'll thank you later."

Hawkins looked at Joliet. "We'll see about that."

When he stepped up to the rail, Joliet was back to business, scouring the water. Hawkins saw nothing, but a few random chunks of flotsam. "There's nothing down there."

He was about to follow up his observation by pointing out that she would have jumped in for nothing, but she pointed toward shore and said, "But something was."

Rings of water rippled across the lagoon. But they weren't just moving away from the *Magellan*, they were also moving toward it. "Whatever it was that made that splash, it didn't fall from the ship. It was closer to shore."

"It wasn't Kam," she said.

Hawkins scoured the scene with his eyes, looking for some sign of what had been in the water. But like most everything in the ocean, whatever made the splash had left no other trace, save for a few ripples on the surface. That's when he turned his eyes to the sandy shore and saw something he recognized without any trouble.

"Footprints," he said. "On shore."

"Where?" Joliet asked. "I don't see anything."

Hawkins pointed toward the prints, but knew she wouldn't see them. They were indistinct and masked by the glare of the white sand in the bright sun. But he knew footprints when he saw them.

"Here," Jones said, tapping Hawkins on the shoulder.

Hawkins turned to find a small pair of binoculars in Jones's hands.

"Like to watch for whales in my free time," Jones explained.

The binoculars weren't very powerful, but they worked well enough to reveal the details on the beach. The footprints were more like toeprints. Whoever had made them was both barefoot, and running. They emerged from water, turned a hard run, cutting a line parallel to the water, and then into the jungle. "Someone was in the water," he said. "Whoever it was exited the lagoon in a hurry, then moved along the beach."

"I knew it was Kam," Joliet said and then snatched the binoculars from Hawkins's hands. She searched the beach for herself and lowered the binoculars. "You should have let me go."

Hawkins's patience began to wear thin. "Whoever was in the water—"

"Kam," she said.

"*Whoever.* He was gone before you got to the rail. If—*if*—you managed to cross the lagoon without being eaten by whatever took Cahill's body, you wouldn't be able to track them in this jungle. It's too thick."

"And *you* could?"

Hawkins could see Joliet was responding out of frustration. She liked Kam a lot and was clearly concerned. He was, too. But her knee-jerk reaction would put herself in danger and, if she went tromping through the jungle in hot pursuit, was likely to wipe out any trail left behind. "Yes, Avril. It's what I do."

That sunk in slowly. Joliet's tense shoulders relaxed. "Sorry."

Hawkins thought about his time as a park ranger. He'd loved the job. The outdoors. The scenery. The pay was shit; but the life, it was good. Most of the time. But sometimes people got lost. Or attacked. And when that happened it was Hawkins's job to find them. He had an almost unnatural ability to find missing people, though he knew it was simply a result of having the best teacher.

Hawkins grew up in Durango, Colorado, right on the border of the Southern Ute Indian Reservation: 1,058 square miles of protected land, if you ignored the Sky Ute Casino and Resort. Hawkins's love of nature brought him to the reservation to hike and explore and, after meeting them on a trail, he became friends with Jimmy GoodTracks and his father, Howie, who took the boys hunting whenever possible. Hawkins's mother had died in childbirth and his father, who never forgave him for it, was a drunk. So Hawkins spent as much time with the GoodTracks as he could.

Tragedy struck a year into their friendship when Jimmy was hit and killed by a truck, whose driver had fallen asleep at the wheel. Not long after Jimmy's death, Hawkins's father up and left. For good. Sharing a mutual grief, Hawkins and Howie GoodTracks adopted each other. While the adoption wasn't legal, he had no living grandparent or relatives who cared, so no one came calling. They became the father and son both had lost.

The GoodTracks name came about on account of Howie's ancestors being expert trackers. Tribe legend said that they could find a man lost in the mountains blindfolded, tracking by scent and sound alone. Howie spent the next six years teaching Hawkins everything he knew. By the time Hawkins went to college, he could follow a trail that was invisible for most people.

"Your name is fitting," GoodTracks had said after Hawkins followed a three-week-old trail that had been windswept and rained on to find a feather hidden beneath a stone—a final test. "You see like a hawk."

Hawkins had never been more proud. When he finished college with a degree in conservation and a minor in English, he decided to carry on the GoodTracks legacy by becoming a park ranger specializing in rescue and recovery. And no one was better.

But the beautiful landscape of Yellowstone was sometimes a very dangerous place to be. The scars on Hawkins's chest were a stark reminder of what could happen when people lower their guard. He'd become so good at his job—a legend in the business of finding people—that it went to his head. Blinded by overconfidence, he'd stood his ground, hunting knife in hand, against a grizzly bear intent on ransacking a campsite. The campers had fled, but rather than join them, Hawkins had stayed. The result was etched on his chest . . . and dead at his feet. He would have likely died himself if one of the campers hadn't returned and dragged him out of the woods.

Howie had visited him in the hospital. "You've lost respect for the power of nature," he had said. "Step back and find *your* path again."

Trusting Howie above all else, Hawkins had taken his mentor's advice and pursued his second passion: writing. But his thoughts and dreams remained in the forest, which he still visited but hadn't worked in for the past five years. And he wasn't sure he ever would again. But now, someone—likely Kam—had fled into the jungle and was likely lost.

Joliet turned to him and said, "Don't you mean, 'did'? Past tense. You're a writer now. You don't find people lost in the woods anymore."

Hawkins looked out at the distant shoreline and the barefoot tracks lining the beach. "Today, I do."

NINE

Mark Hawkins's father had been a strict man. Not the modern "time out" kind of strict. Closer to the "boy, don't make me take off my belt and give you a whuppin" kind. His father's belt's sheen had been worn off, mostly on Hawkins's backside. But he'd grown accustomed to the anger, and the violence, and even the angriest man, woman, or animal couldn't make him flinch.

So when a furious Captain Drake went on a verbal rampage upon hearing the news that Cahill's body had been snatched away, that Kam was missing and likely lost on the island, and that his ship was still dead in the water for no reason anyone could fathom, he vented his uncommon rage with a string of curses punctuated by throwing a mug across the wheelhouse.

The sharp crash of shattering porcelain against the hard metal wall snapped the man from his flare-up. He put his hands behind his head and turned away from the crew, taking a deep breath as he looked out at the island.

Hawkins waited for the man to speak. Joliet, Bray, Jones, and Jim Clifton, the younger of the two Tweedles, stood silent, waiting for the captain to regain his composure.

Despite being the second-largest man on the ship, outsized only by his brother, Clifton looked ready to bolt. His face glowed red. His bald forehead and jowls were slick was sweat. The big man did not like confrontation. Hawkins felt bad for the man. His job was to cook, a task he and his brother were quite good at, so he wasn't accustomed to being on the receiving end of the captain's anger. Hawkins was about to tell the man he could leave when Drake turned to face them again.

"Let me make sure I understood everything," the captain said. "A shark took Cahill's body."

"My daughter didn't think it was a shark," Jones said.

Drake nodded. "Noted. But I think we can all agree a shark is the only thing that makes sense."

Hawkins, Joliet, and Bray all nodded. Jones didn't look so sure, but eventually consented. The younger Clifton just stared, looking petrified. Drake noticed and softened his tone. "Jim, how are things in the galley?"

"Everything works. Power is on so all the food is good. We can cook. Just need to finish cleaning up the, ahh, the mess."

Drake offered the man a smile and gave him a pat on the shoulder. "First good news I heard all day. Why don't you head back down and help Ray finish cleaning. Then see about lunch."

"I'll need mine to go," Hawkins said.

"Mine, too," Joliet added.

Bray raised his hand. "Make that three."

"Okay," Jim said before hurrying belowdecks.

When the nervous chef was gone, Drake's scowl returned and he turned to Hawkins. "May I remind you that I'm the captain of this ship and no one—" He glanced at Joliet. "I mean no one, makes a decision about what happens aboard the *Magellan* without my say-so." His eyes turned to Bray. "That goes for you, too, funny man. Am I clear?"

"Yes, sir," Hawkins said, knowing that a show of respect would help calm the man.

"Fine," Joliet said.

"You think I'm funny?" Bray asked.

Hawkins gave his head a slight shake. Drake was an old

navy man and as captain of the *Magellan*, his orders were as though from God himself. Hawkins made a mental note to explain this to Joliet and Bray.

The captain, to his credit, let their comments slide. "Think you can find him?" Drake asked, looking at Hawkins. The captain knew Hawkins's past and had no doubt realized that Hawkins intended to look for Kam.

"There are too many unknowns to give you a definite answer," Hawkins said. "We don't know how big the island is, or what kinds of natural dangers there might be."

"Natural dangers?" Bray asked.

Hawkins stepped up to the shattered wheelhouse windshield and looked out at the island. He could smell a hint of something sweet mixed in with the sea air. "Cliffs, sinkholes, sharks. Those kinds of things. If he kept running, it's possible he injured himself after escaping the water. It seems likely that he was running away from the . . . shark that took Cahill's body. If that's true, we might be lucky and find him not too far from shore."

"And if we're not lucky?" Drake asked.

"If this island is as big as it looks, and the jungle as thick, it could take some time to find him. Days even. But it *is* an island. He can only run so far. Our best bet is to take everyone on shore and walk a spaced-out grid until we find him."

"Afraid we can't do that," Drake said.

"Sir," Jones said. "If it would help, my crew can—"

Drake raised his hand, silencing the engineer. "Kind of you to offer, Jones, but I need you and your crew working on a way to get the ship under manual control. Physically separate the computer system if you can. I want my ship back."

"Yes, sir," Jones said.

"Are you sure that's wise?" Joliet asked. "Kam might be able to fix the computers. If something is broken—"

Drake turned to Joliet. "Unless you can guarantee me that you'll get Kam back in one piece, and soon, this is the way it's going to be."

"We—*I* can't," Hawkins said. "There are no guarantees with search and rescue."

"Jones," Drake said. "Be gentle."

The elder engineer headed for the stairs. "I will. We'll get started now."

Drake stepped up next to Hawkins and they looked at the island together. "I appreciate you leading the search."

"Not a problem."

Drake gave a confident nod. "You'll bring him back."

Hawkins smiled. It was as close to a pep talk as the gruff captain would offer. "I will," he said, but then added, "dead or alive."

During his years as a ranger, Hawkins had taken part in more than seventy-five search and rescue operations in Yellowstone, most of which he coordinated. Ten of those searches had ended with fatalities. Before every search someone would invariably ask, "Will you find them?" To which he would answer, "yes," but would then think, "dead or alive." He'd never expressed that extra bit of information before. For some reason, he felt Drake would appreciate the candor.

Drake locked eyes with Hawkins. "Can't ask for anything more. Sometimes people die and there's nothing we can do about it. Just let me know what you need," Drake said.

Hawkins held up a slip of paper upon which he'd written a list of supplies. Nothing extravagant: food, water, bedrolls, first-aid kit, and a radio to communicate with the ship.

Drake read through the list, but paused halfway through. "Bedrolls?"

Bray repeated the question. "Wait, bedrolls? You want to sleep out there?"

"Once we're out there, we're not coming back until we find him."

Drake crossed his arms. "Sorry, Hawkins, but I want you back on board by the time the sun hugs the horizon."

"We'll lose time and ground," Hawkins said, losing his patience. "We can only walk so far before turning around. It limits how far we can search."

"It's summer," the captain said. "The days are long. And as you pointed out, this is an island. If he keeps moving, he'll make it back eventually."

"And if he doesn't?" Joliet asked.

"Then you better hope Jones figures out how to get my ship back. I don't need to remind you that we have no propulsion, and no way to contact the outside world. Our food and water will only last so long. You may end up becoming intimately familiar with every nook and cranny of this island." Drake looked at the list again. "Look, how about this? If you have a solid trail, spend the night. If you're just running search grids, I want you back." He offered his hand to Hawkins.

Hawkins took the captain's hand and shook it. "Agreed."

Drake handed back the list. "Blok is clearing the aft decks. He'll get you everything you need."

"Thank you, Captain," Hawkins said.

Drake grunted.

Joliet rushed toward the outside door. Hawkins followed. Then Bray.

As they exited the wheelhouse onto the exterior staircase, Bray looked at the jungle and asked, "Are you really planning to stay out there overnight."

Hawkins descended the stairs. "Yup."

"And if there isn't a trail? Will we really come back?"

"There'll be a trail," Hawkins said.

"But what if—"

Hawkins stopped and turned around. Bray wasn't understanding. "There *will* be a trail." He left out the words "even if we don't find it," but Bray seemed to understand.

"Shit."

TEN

The front end of the ten-foot-long inflatable Zodiac boat rose high out of the water as Bray twisted the throttle. Hawkins dove forward, putting his weight on the bow of the Zodiac, but wind and acceleration were working against him.

"Slow down!" Hawkins shouted, but Bray either couldn't hear him over the whine of the engine or was ignoring him. Hawkins lifted up his head and peeked over the front end. The distance between the Zodiac and the white sand beach shrank quickly. "You're going to ground us!"

Joliet didn't weigh much, but when she added her weight to Hawkins's, the front end lowered and revealed the beach, now just twenty feet way. As they entered the shallows, Bray opened up the throttle all the way, for just a moment, and then shut the engine off and tilted it forward, lifting the propeller out of the water.

Momentum carried them through the two-foot-deep shallows. Fish scattered as they passed by. Hawkins imagined how easy fishing would be here and thought they would have no trouble staying alive if they were, in fact, stranded. A loud sifting sound coupled with a jolt announced their arrival at the beach. The boat slid halfway ashore before stopping and Bray wasted no time leaping onto the sand.

Hawkins took a backpack of supplies and tossed it hard to Bray, who caught it, but not well. "What the hell was that?"

"What?" Bray said.

"You nearly flipped the boat," Hawkins pointed out.

"You want to be eaten by a shark?" Bray answered.

"Sharks don't eat ten-foot Zodiacs," Hawkins said.

"*If* it's a shark," Bray said, "and it's strong enough and big enough to make short work of that fishing net, I don't think it would have any trouble with an *inflatable* Zodiac."

"He's right," Joliet said, catching Hawkins off guard. "Sharks routinely attack small boats. Even if it's just out of curiosity, one bite would sink a Zodiac."

Hawkins wasn't above admitting he was wrong. "Okay. I'm sorry. How about a little warning next time?"

"Done," Bray said.

The three of them dragged the boat up onto the beach and Hawkins tied it off to the base of a palm tree. After securing the boat to ensure high tide didn't sweep it away, he looked up at the palms shifting in the breeze above. "No coconuts."

"Who cares?" Bray said. "You planning on having a piña colada?"

"Nevermind."

"You think we're stuck here," Joliet said. "Don't you?"

Hawkins stepped past the pair and started down the beach. "Let's just find the footprints."

"Well, that's a yes if I ever didn't hear one," Bray said as he gave chase.

Hawkins quickly found the line of footprints and knelt to inspect them, hoping they would distract Bray from his line of questioning. While he didn't know for sure that they were stranded, he wanted to be prepared for the possibility. He'd keep track of every food and water source they came across. There were eleven crew members to feed—not including Kam—and while their supplies would last a while, especially if rationed, eleven people wouldn't be easy to feed. And while there were plenty of fish in the water, there were also sharks, which apparently could eat people *and* boats.

"He was running before he hit the beach," Hawkins said, looking at the footprints, which were actually closer to toe-prints.

"Unless he was tip-toeing," Bray said, and when Joliet and Hawkins both gave him disapproving glances, he added, "What?"

"No blood," Hawkins noted. "I don't think he was injured."

They followed the tracks, which led along the shore for thirty feet before veering to the left and disappearing into the jungle. They stopped at the line of trees and brush that fringed the beach.

"Does this not make sense to anyone else, or is it just me?" Bray asked.

"What doesn't make sense?" Joliet asked.

"First of all, Kam goes outside during the middle of a storm—a storm that killed Cahill, an experienced sailor. We have to then assume that Kam fell overboard, or was swept overboard by a wave. Yet he somehow stayed with the *Magellan*."

Joliet answered, "He could have been caught in a net, like Cahill, but higher. Above the waterline."

"Okay," Bray said, "so he's caught in a net, on the *outside* of the ship, where he spends the night being pummeled and nearly drowned by waves. He survives until morning, and instead of calling for help, or climbing the net, he drops into the water, has the energy to swim to shore, with a killer shark at his heels. Then he runs—*runs*—onto the shore, along the length of the beach and finally into the jungle. No open wounds. No broken legs. And full of energy. I don't know if you noticed, but we were in the wheelhouse and knocked down for the count. So how did a little guy like Kam pull that off? And if he was so afraid of the shark, why didn't he run straight into the jungle?"

Hawkins replayed Bray's words in his mind. He couldn't find a single flaw in the man's reasoning. "Right, right. It doesn't make sense."

"Unless he was panicked," Joliet said. "He would have been delirious when he ran along the beach. Not thinking. And then he saw something that both of you have missed." She pointed to the edge of the jungle where the footprints led.

Hawkins eyed the brush. It was subtle, but he could see what Joliet had already seen—a break in the overgrowth.

"I don't see a thing," Bray said.

Hawkins stepped up to the jungle and placed his hand on a large-leafed tropical plant. "There's a path," he said, and then pushed the big leaves aside.

The revealed path was subtle, but present. Like a long, thick snake, the dirt path wound its way around trees, brush, and rocks, leading into the dimly lit jungle. A wash of humidity and earthy scents rolled over them. The place had its own scent, fertile and organic. Living. Hawkins noticed goose bumps rising on the skin of Joliet's bare arms.

She noted his attention and said, "You feel it, too."

"Feel what?" Bray asked.

"Nothing," Hawkins said, stepping back onto the beach. He turned back to the *Magellan* and removed a small two-way radio from his pocket. He depressed the Talk button. "Captain Drake, this is Hawkins, do you read? Over."

After a burst of static, Drake's voice came from the small speaker. "I read you, Hawkins, and I've got my eyes on you, as well. Found a trail? Over."

"Yeah, we're going to head in after him. Over."

"Copy that," Drake replied. "Go find our boy and bring him home. Over and out."

Hawkins put the radio back in his cargo shorts pocket. He found the captain's choice of language amusing. Kam was certainly not their "boy," though it's possible that Drake did think of the *Magellan* as home. He'd been captain of the vessel for ten years and spent more time aboard the ship than he did on land.

"You know," Bray said. "You guys sometimes have this psychic communication thing where you think the same thing—usually something bad—and don't tell me what it is. It's kind of annoying."

As Hawkins turned to Bray, he felt something hard beneath his foot. He glanced down and saw a strangely shaped stone poking out from beneath the sand. He nearly didn't give it a second thought, but a portion of the sand covering the object slid away. *Not away*, Hawkins thought. *Inside*. The shape of the opening left behind was instantly recognizable. He'd seen it before, when he recovered the body of a woman who'd been lost in the woods for three months. She'd been scavenged by wolves, birds, and bugs. She was just bones when they found her, just five hundred feet from a marked trail.

The skull confirmed Hawkins's suspicions. He bent down, put his finger in the eye socket, and pulled. The skull came free, sand pouring through its various openings, concealing its shape.

"What is that?" Joliet asked.

"Confirmation." Hawkins turned the skull over so that its blank stare faced at the other two.

Bray jumped back. "Holy shit!"

Joliet gasped, but then quickly took the skull from Hawkins, inspecting every inch.

"This is what we were thinking," Hawkins said. "We're not the first people to find this island."

"It looks like he was bludgeoned," Joliet said, pointing out the caved-in hole in the top of the skull.

"Yes," Hawkins said. "*She* was."

Somehow the idea that the skull belonged to a woman revolted Joliet. She handed the skull back to Hawkins and wiped her hands on her shorts.

"How can you tell it's a woman?" Bray asked after taking a few steps back.

"The narrow jaw, chin, and cheekbones. The skull size and lack of a brow line are good indicators, too." Hawkins turned the skull over in his hands. "The skull is discolored, so she's been dead for a long time, but there's no way to say how long. Could be ten years. Could be a hundred. She's been buried beneath the hot, dry sand, above the waterline, so she's been well preserved."

"What's holding you up? Over," Drake's voice said from the two-way radio in Hawkins's pocket.

Everyone, including Hawkins, jumped at the sound, and he nearly dropped the skull. After fishing out the radio, he pushed the Talk button and replied, "Drake, we found a skull. Over."

"A skull?"

"She's old, sir. Nothing to worry about. But we're not the first people to find this island. Over."

"Copy that," Drake said. "Would have been surprised if we had been. Any idea what happened to her? Over."

"Honestly," Hawkins said, holding down the button. "Best guess is that she was murdered. Over."

"Murdered?" Drake said, his voice full of surprise.

Hawkins inspected the caved-in skull. "Yes, sir. Without a doubt. But I think it's safe to say that this is a mystery to be solved another time. She's long since dead. Over."

After a moment, Drake replied. "Agreed. Over."

"Actually," Bray said. "I think I'm going to stay behind. See if I can't uncover more of the body."

"What?" Joliet said. "Why?"

"Doesn't seem right just leaving her here," Bray said, stepping closer and taking the skull for the first time.

"I don't mean to be micromanaging you all from the ship," Drake said. "But what's the holdup? The sun isn't going to stay in the sky all day. Over."

Hawkins sighed. "Sir, Bray is requesting to stay behind and exhume the rest of the body. Over."

After a moment, Drake replied. "Let him stay. The pudgy bastard's just going to slow you two down. Over."

Hawkins and Joliet laughed.

Bray bristled and said, "Hey!"

With a shrug, Hawkins said, "He's right."

"Assholes," Bray said, but he couldn't disguise the thin smile on his face.

Hawkins pushed the Talk button on the radio. "Joliet and I are heading out now. Bray is staying behind. Keep an eye on him. If we're not back by nightfall, help him get back to the ship without crashing the Zodiac into the side. Over."

"Copy that, Ranger, good hunting. Out."

After shaking hands with Bray, Hawkins led the way into the humid jungle. The air was thick with the scent of rot. He knew there was little to fear on the island. Beyond a few bird species, the island would be unpopulated. Even though he'd never admit it, the skull had him spooked. He didn't believe in ghosts, but had no doubt something awful had happened here. The very air seemed tainted by it. He pushed his irrational fears aside and focused on the mission at hand: Find Kam and get the hell off this island.

ELEVEN

Ten feet into the jungle, Kam's footprints included deep, round heel marks. This was good news because they would catch up to him more quickly if he was walking, but also added one more layer of confusion to the young intern's disappearance. If he'd entered the jungle in a panicked state, why had he stopped running as soon as he'd no longer been visible? Since then, the footprints revealed a calm, measured gate, which stayed on the muddy path.

This is going to be easy, Hawkins thought. Howie Good-Tracks had taught him to notice the minutest aberrations in the natural world. Every scuff, scratch, indentation, or patch of grass bent in the wrong direction told a story. The depth of a footprint in mud could reveal the target's size, weight, and sex. When tracking people, the gait, or distance between steps, and what part of the foot sank deepest revealed a person's mind-set—calmly strolling, running flat out, or ambling randomly, like most lost people do. The angle of a bent branch could even hint at the target's speed and, based on the freshness of the break, when they'd passed through. Skills like these weren't taught in many schools, and certainly not by people like GoodTracks, who didn't just know these things, but lived them. With Kam not hiding his path, most of these skills wouldn't be necessary, but if Kam wandered off the trail, Hawkins would be able to follow him just as easily.

Twenty minutes into their rapid-paced hike, the trail rose

up a steep grade. They slowed as they followed the path up, occasionally needing to scale short rock walls. At the top of one such stony rise, Hawkins leaned over the edge and reached his hand down to Joliet.

She took his hand and quickly scaled the eight-foot wall. At the top, she sat with her legs hanging over the edge and caught her breath. Hawkins sat next to her and opened his pack. After taking a swig of water, he offered her the bottle and she helped herself. The air in the jungle felt thick enough to drink and their bodies were saturated. But they still sweated in the late-afternoon heat and needed to drink often.

Hawkins took the bottle from Joliet when she offered it back to him, took one more swig, and capped. Neither had said a word as they followed the path to this point, but the silence wasn't uncomfortable. They'd often spent quiet days on the deck of the *Magellan*, reading books, writing, or just catching some rays. It was one of the things he liked most about her, but the silence was beginning to feel uncomfortable.

Joliet spoke first. "What are you thinking?"

"You don't want to know," Hawkins answered. And he believed it. During the last twenty minutes, he'd allowed his imagination to run wild, filling in the blanks of Kam's disappearance and working out several different scenarios. Some were farfetched and easily dismissed. Others fit, but seemed unlikely, which was unfortunate because they had happy endings. But there was one scenario that nagged at him. The sequence of events lined up and the evidence seemed to support it. Unfortunately, that scenario wouldn't have a happy ending.

"Can't be as bad as what I'm thinking," she replied.

Hawkins knew she wouldn't give up. Her dogged persistence in all things was one of her attributes that he respected, but with which he often felt annoyed. Still, he'd learned that giving in right away kept things pleasant. "Okay, here's my theory. Kam and Cahill had some kind of falling out. Best guess is that Kam somehow screwed up the computers by accident. When Cahill confronted him, he ran and ended up on deck. When Cahill followed into the storm, he was knocked overboard. Kam made it back inside and hid until the storm ended. Fearing discipline or even legal action because of Cahill's death, Kam fled to the island. He wasn't running from a shark, which is why he ran along the shoreline, rather than straight across it. He ran because he didn't want to be seen. Concealed in the jungle, he slowed to a walk. Kam feels responsible for Cahill's death, and possibly for screwing up the ship. That's my best theory."

Joliet sagged. "I came up with the same thing. Do you really think Kam would run? If it was an accident—"

"There is the possibility that it wasn't an accident," Hawkins said. "That their confrontation on deck ended in violence."

Joliet's eyes widened. "You think he *murdered* Cahill?"

"Not premeditated. But if they fought, and that's what caused Cahill to fall overboard, it's still manslaughter."

Joliet shook her head. "I just can't picture Kam doing something like that. He's such a sweet kid, not to mention half the size of Cahill."

"People do stupid things," Hawkins replied, thinking of the drunk man who'd been gored by a bison after walking up to the sleeping giant and slapping its snout. "Was Cahill a drinker?" It was an awful thing to hope for, but he wanted Kam to be innocent, too.

"I've never seen him drink," Joliet said. "Not even before we left."

Captain Drake had taken the crew out to a restaurant the night before they'd left. Hawkins tried to remember that night now, but his own drinking fogged the memory. He did remember flirting with Joliet, and being shot down, but had no memory of Cahill imbibing.

"You didn't drink that night, either, did you?" he asked.

"Nope, and I remember every word, story, and grope."

Hawkins froze. He slowly turned to her. "I didn't . . . ?"

Joliet's serious expression softened with a smile. "Don't worry, Ranger. Wasn't you." She stood up, brushed off her shorts, and straightened her tight, blue T-shirt.

As she started up the trail again, he stood and gave chase. "Wait, who was it then? If it was Bray, I'm going to—"

Joliet stopped and raised an open palm in his direction. He fell silent and stood next to her. She pointed up the steep, jungle-covered hillside.

"I don't see anything," he whispered.

"Between the trees near the top," she said. "There's something gray."

It took him a moment, but when he saw it, the flat gray surface stood out. "The hell?"

His hand went to his waist, feeling the handle of his hunting knife. Its presence put him at ease. "Let's check it out."

Following the path, they wound their way up the hillside. As they neared the top, the incline grew steeper and the path became a series of switchbacks. Hawkins didn't like that they had to pass in front of the aberration several times. Something about it made him wary, and every pass left him feeling more exposed. Vulnerable.

But nothing happened. They followed the last path to the top where it wrapped around a stand of trees. Hawkins's hand went to his knife again as they rounded the palms, but when he got his first look at what waited for them, he knew the weapon wasn't needed.

Vines covered much of the gray concrete, but given its location at the top of the hill, Hawkins could see the structure for what it was. "It's a pillbox."

"A what?"

"Pillbox. From World War Two. The Japanese must have occupied this island." Hawkins stepped through the open back-side of the concrete octagon. A long, thin opening stretched across the side facing the hill. He looked out and could see patches of the path below. "Anyone advancing up the hillside would have had a hell of a time reaching the top without being cut to pieces by machine gun fire. They probably had a lot of the brush and trees cleared away back then."

"If this island was occupied during the war," Joliet said, "why isn't it on any maps?"

"If the island was never discovered by the U.S., the Japanese stationed here probably just deserted and went home when the war ended." Hawkins searched the small space for

WWII relics, but found nothing. "Looks like they cleaned up shop when they left, too. They didn't leave a thing behind."

"Aside from a giant concrete octagon, you mean?"

"Right." Hawkins turned to a pile of dirt and leaf litter on the side of the room. A splotch of red color next to the debris caught his attention. He knelt down and picked it up. The thick cloth was easily identifiable as a piece of baseball cap. The remnant of a *B* confirmed Hawkins's suspicion that it was Kam's Red Sox cap. That it was ruined was cause for concern—the kid rarely parted from it—but it being here was also the first real evidence that Kam had made it to the island and not drowned in the storm.

"That's Kam's hat!" Joliet said, taking the fabric from him.

"Yeah, but why is it—"

A loud squeak made him jump back and Joliet shouted in surprise as a black shape shot across the floor and out the door.

"What . . . was that?" she asked, catching her breath.

"A rat," he said. "I think."

Joliet inched toward the open door, looking for the rodent. "Looks like the Japanese left something else behind, too. Where people go, rats follow."

"Mmm," Hawkins said, but he'd only heard half of what she said. He walked back to the window and looked down the hill, scratching his chin.

"What is it?" Joliet asked.

"The rat," he said.

"You don't like rats?"

"Rat," he said. "Singular. Rats tend to live in colonies. Sometimes several hundred in a single colony. And each female in the colony can have sixty young, per year, half of which might be females. Eleven weeks after birth, those females start cranking out young of their own. On an island like this, left to breed for the past seventy years, their population should have expanded until the place was overrun."

"But it's not," Joliet said. "This is the first we've seen."

Hawkins placed his hands on the windowsill, watching the jungle floor below for movement. "And there are plenty of food sources out there. Rats aren't picky. It's possible that their population exploded and suffered a massive die-off because of starvation, but that still doesn't explain the lack of a colony. Rats live just two years. For there to be one rat, there needs to be others, and we run into the colony explosion scenario again, unless . . ."

"Unless what?"

"Unless something is keeping them in check."

"What do you mean?"

"There's a reason Yellowstone is never overrun with rats. They're there—they're everywhere—but their population is controlled—" He looked her in the eyes. "By predators. Mountain lions, wolves, foxes, lynxes, bobcats, eagles, hawks, owls, and a variety of other predators keep the rodent and rabbit populations in check."

"So what? The seagulls here have a taste for rat?" Joliet said with a grin.

"No," he said, "to keep a rat population down to where they're not scurrying everywhere requires a healthy population of a number of different predators."

"How do you know there are different predators?"

"If there were only one species of predator, they would face the same overpopulation issue as the rat. They'd be everywhere. Predators are kept in check by competition. Other hunters."

Joliet's smile faded. "How come we're not seeing them then?"

"Because they're predators," Hawkins said, eyes still on the hillside below. "They don't want to be seen."

TWELVE

Hawkins let the moment drag out for a moment and then smiled. "Don't worry, any predators on the island would have come with the Japanese, too. Feral cats. *Maybe* wild dogs. And some bird species, like the seagulls, which seem aggressive enough to handle a rat."

Joliet's let out a breath. "Bastard."

Hawkins chuckled, but it was only partly sincere. The combination of a dead woman, a WWII fortification, and the presence of an active ecosystem that included predatory animals had him on edge. The island appeared to be as close as you could get to a tropical paradise, but the history of the place trumped the environment. And he had no doubt the lush jungle hid more secrets.

But he wasn't a historian. Nor was he here to speculate on wildlife. He came to the island to find Kam and take him back to the ship. He stepped out of the pillbox and scanned the clearing outside. He'd lost Kam's trail before they'd reached the switchbacks, but he couldn't think of a reason the kid would have gone trailblazing. If anything, Kam had cut straight up the hillside, ignoring the switchbacks altogether. He'd hoped to pick up a trail atop the hill, but saw nothing.

Nothing at all. No rocks. No trees. No overgrowth. The clearing around the pillbox entrance looked almost manicured. Grass covered the ground, but it was neatly trimmed.

Not good, he thought, but didn't voice his fears. Once they had Kam, they could theorize about the island all they wanted. Until then, Hawkins would stay on task.

He spun around, looking at the pillbox again, and noticed that the trees surrounding the building were just barely taller than its domed roof. If he stood atop it, he'd have a good view and might be able to gauge the size of the island.

Joliet stepped outside as he walked to the side of the pillbox and tested the strength of the vines with his hands. They'd make decent handholds, but he wasn't confident they'd hold his weight. "Give me a boost," he said.

Joliet looked at him like he was crazy. "You know I'm half your size, right?"

Hawkins found a thick vine high up on the wall and gave it a tug. It would do the trick. "I need to take a look at the island."

"Why don't you lift me up, then?"

"The operative word is 'I,'" Hawkins said. "No offense. But I need to see the island for myself."

Joliet strode over to him. She linked her fingers together and bent down to take Hawkins's foot. "You know, Tarzan wouldn't need Jane's help."

Hawkins placed his foot in her hands, held on tight to the vine, and said, "Jane was a helpless damsel in distress."

Joliet lifted and Hawkins pulled. He rose up the side wall and reached over the top with his free hand. Once he had a grip, he reached his other hand up and pulled. Joliet pushed until his foot rose out of her reach. After swinging a leg up and over the top, Hawkins made short work of the climb. He got to his feet, standing on the flat edge that surrounded the dome. He turned back to Joliet and said, "That was a compliment, you know. The Jane thing."

Joliet smiled up at him. "I know."

She stood there for a moment, staring up at him with a smile and squinted eyes. He was frozen in place. His stomach knotted uncomfortably, but his own smile widened. *Screw Bray and his curvy women*, Hawkins thought, *she's amazing*.

Hawkins thought she must have read his thoughts, or at

least seen a glimmer of them in his eyes, because she let out a laugh and asked, "What?"

You know what, he thought, but said, "Nothing."

Hawkins thought he saw her blush, but she turned away and said, "Just take a look, will you? We need to keep moving."

Over the past month, he and Joliet had formed a bond neither of them would admit to, and thus far it hadn't included a physical element. But he could sense them growing closer, and the way her sweat-soaked T-shirt clung to her body made him hope things moved forward sooner than later. Before Joliet could catch him staring, Hawkins turned toward the domed roof.

The structure looked sound enough, but it had been exposed to the elements for seventy years. He stood slowly and gave the dome a couple of hard kicks. When nothing gave, he leaned forward and put his weight on it. The dome, known to be a naturally strong shape, held his weight. Moving slowly, he crawled to the top on his hands and feet.

Then he stood.

And gasped.

He could see over the tops of the trees and had a view of the jungle below. The mottled sea of green fell away as the hill descended, stopping at the lagoon. He could see the crescent-shaped beach and a small, moving figure he assumed was Bray. The *Magellan* lay in the lagoon, silent and motionless. From this point of view, he could see that the entrance to the lagoon was actually a curved channel through the cliffs. From the outside, it would be hard to see.

How the hell did the ship get through there without crashing?

Beyond the cliffs, the endless blue Pacific Ocean stretched to the horizon. With his eyes on the outer fringe of the island, he made a slow turn, taking in every detail. His wonderment over the view quickly turned to dread. The island was large. The far end was perhaps three miles away, easy to cover in a day, but he figured there were at least nine square miles of land—nearly six thousand acres—to cover. And that wasn't including the many hills he could see. There was enough land to stay lost in for a long time.

Toward the far end of the island, between a pair of hills, he saw the sparkle of water, behind which lay more land. *A lake*, he thought. People were invariably drawn to fresh water. *If Kam keeps moving until he finds the lake, he might stay there. And if we're stuck here . . .* Hawkins pushed that thought aside. *Focus.* Between the distant hills and the lake sat a lighter patch of green. He couldn't see exactly what it was—there was too little to make out—but it looked like a large clearing.

Maybe an old airfield, he thought. "The island is volcanic," he said, noting the raised perimeter. Like most islands in the Pacific, this one had once been the top of a very large, active volcano.

"You don't see any steam, do you?" Joliet asked as she explored the fringe of the clearing.

"No, it's dormant. Probably been for a long time. There're a couple of tall hills, a lake—probably at the island's lowest point—and a large, flat clearing, but all of it is inside a very large crater."

"Probably multiple craters," Joliet said. "Volcanic cones tend to shift in the ocean."

Hawkins heard the sound of shifting vegetation.

"Hey, I found the path," Joliet said from below.

Hawkins looked down. Joliet stood on the far side of the small clearing, holding a large-leafed plant aside.

"I think I see footprints, too."

Something about the word "footprints" triggered a new question. "Why is Kam barefoot?"

Joliet just stared up at him.

"Did you ever see him go barefoot on the ship?"

She thought for a moment and then shook her head. "He wore sandals all the time."

"So why is he barefoot now?"

"Maybe they fell off in the water."

That made sense, but still felt wrong. They were missing something. "Maybe."

What the hell aren't we thinking of?

"Hey, look at this," Joliet said. She held the plant up in the air. The large leaves were bound together at the bottom. "The leaves were staked into the ground. He covered the path on purpose. Why would Kam do that?"

The mental floodgates opened.

Kam wouldn't.

"We need to go back to the ship," he said, sliding down the dome to the edge of the pillbox roof.

"Why? It will still be daylight for a few more hours. We can—"

"It's not Kam," he said, lowering himself over the front end of the pillbox. He held on to a vine for support.

Joliet rushed up and put her hands under Hawkins's foot, supporting some of his weight. "What do you mean, it's not Kam?"

"Why would Kam—"

The vine supporting most of Hawkins's weight tore free from the concrete above the pillbox entryway. Taking the vine with him, Hawkins fell. He and Joliet spilled onto the grass in a heap.

Hawkins pulled his legs off of Joliet and got to his feet. He helped her up and as they both brushed off their damp clothes, he continued. "Why would Kam swim to shore, run straight to a path in the jungle, come all the way up here, and then conceal his tracks?"

She had no answer.

"Exactly," he said. "Kam wouldn't. Someone was already here."

"But Kam is missing," she said.

"He might have been lost in the storm with Cahill."

"Or he was taken," she said.

Hawkins didn't think so. The footprints weren't deep enough to suggest someone was being carried, but he couldn't discount the theory, either. Kam wasn't very big.

"Either way, we need to get back to the ship. The island is too big to search on our own, and the presence of an unknown person . . . or people, changes things. We need help."

As Hawkins turned toward the path leading back down to the cover, he glanced at the pillbox and noticed something different. Something was painted above the doorway, where the vine had been.

He brushed away the moss and vine bits still clinging to the wall and looked at the writing.

七百三十一

"Is that Japanese?" Joliet asked.

"That'd be my guess, but I have no idea what it means." He looked at each character individually, trying to remember them, but stopped when he heard a faint scratching sound behind him.

"Got it," Joliet said, capping a pen and slipping a small notebook into her cargo shorts pocket. "Now, let's get the hell out of here."

As Joliet started down the switchback path, Hawkins took one last look around the small clearing. When thinking about dogs and cats being left behind on the island, he made the logical leap to the idea that they'd be feral after seventy years of breeding, hunting, and surviving on an island. But now he had to consider another possibility.

What would people be like if they'd been left here, cut off from the rest of the world, for seventy years?

THIRTEEN

Hawkins led the journey down the hill much faster than they'd ascended it, in part thanks to gravity, but mostly because he'd been spooked by their discoveries at the pillbox. His neck had grown sore from looking back over his shoulder as they hiked, but his paranoia had company. Nearly every time he looked back, Joliet was already doing likewise.

He'd once spoken to the survivor of a mountain lion attack; a young woman who'd been jogging a trail in Yellowstone in the early morning. She hadn't seen or heard anything. But she *felt* it. The danger. Had she not unclipped her bottle of pepper spray from her belt in advance of the attack, she'd have been easily killed. Instead, the cat got a face full of liquid pepper and would probably think twice before attacking another human being.

Is that what I'm feeling? he wondered. He'd encountered wild animals on several occasions, but had never felt that advance fear. He liked to think it was because he was on equal footing with the world's predators, and to an extent, had proven that to be true. That he was feeling spooked now only increased his building sense of doom.

Halfway between the hill and the beach, something snapped.

Hawkins froze.

Joliet stood beside him.

Neither spoke. They just watched. And listened.

After a full minute, Hawkins said, "Man, this place has me on edge."

Joliet gave a nervous laugh. "I know, right?"

But then the sound repeated. Closer. And overhead.

Both of their heads craned up. The tall palms, mixed with other exotic, leafy trees, swayed, creaking quietly. Sunlight filtered through and the bright green leaves shimmered on the jungle floor. But there was nothing else there.

"Do rats climb trees?" Joliet asked.

"Not usually," Hawkins replied. "Unless they're trying to make it easy for the birds that eat them."

"Right," Joliet said before glancing down and seeing the hunting knife in Hawkins hand. "You know something I don't?"

He didn't really remember drawing the blade. "I hope not."

Brush along the path, just twenty feet behind them, shook. He'd normally write the movement off to a squirrel. Or in this case, a rat. But he didn't think that was the case here. They were being stalked.

"Go," Hawkins whispered. "Run."

Joliet seemed surprised. Did she not see the brush moving, or was he really just being paranoid? Better paranoid than dead, he decided, and said, "All the way to the beach. Don't stop. Go. Now!"

As he raised his voice, movement swirled around and above them. He saw shifting shadows and flickering sunlight as something moved through the canopy. Nothing more. But he had learned something—the creature stalking them wasn't alone.

There was a pack.

Joliet needed no more convincing. She took off down the winding path, moving swiftly. Hawkins took one last look around and saw nothing. Sensing the predators moving in, he followed after Joliet, knife in hand.

The trail made running easy, but it also wound a meandering path through the jungle. *Fastest way between two points is a straight line*, he thought, and then went off-path, cutting straight through the jungle, tearing through brush, hopping fallen trees and making a racket.

Joliet heard him coming and whipped her head in his direction. Her face was twisted with fear, but quickly turned to relief when she saw it was him.

"Don't bother with the path!" he shouted. "Just cut through the trees!"

When the trail wound to the right, Joliet plowed straight ahead, leaping through the forest like a frightened deer. She moved so quickly that Hawkins had a hard time keeping up. Her small size let her pass by obstacles that he had to crash through, like a tank following a sports car through a slalom course.

The trees thinned and the bright glow of the beach beckoned to them. But they hadn't made it yet. The movement around them had grown frenzied. He glanced to the side a few times and got quick looks at something yellowish, stumbling with each look back. But he didn't have to see them to know they were moving in to strike. The creatures' frenzied approach grew louder, their movements combined with shrill chirps.

"Go, go, go!" he shouted.

A shadow drew his eyes up and what he saw held his attention. The creature was silhouetted against the bright green canopy. He couldn't see colors, or details, but its overall shape had been revealed. It had a rounded head, like an oversize, dull arrowhead. He saw four legs sporting clawed feet, splayed wide. The body was just a foot long, but its tail, which wagged frantically back and forth, extended another foot. But none of this held his gaze for long. It was the two translucent wings, for lack of a better word, extending out from the creature's midsection that had him transfixed—and caused him to run into a fallen tree.

The limb caught him across the waist and flipped him ass over tea kettle like a professional wrestler. The loud "oof!" that escaped his lungs and the thud of his body hitting the jungle floor spun Joliet around.

"Mark!"

He pushed himself up and shouted, "Keep going! Get help!"

As he caught his breath, Hawkins noticed he no longer held his knife. While keeping his eyes up and on the lookout for danger, he searched the area around him with his hands. *I'm lucky I didn't fall on the blade*, he thought. *What an idiotic way to die that would have been.*

A chirp that was one part whistle, one part growl spun him around. The creature stood upon the fallen tree, staring into his eyes. It was three feet long from snout to tail and covered in yellow- and black-striped scales. Its size wouldn't normally intimidate him, but the hooked inch-long claws it used to cling to the tree looked dangerous. And when it chirped again, he saw two rows of needlelike teeth accompanied by two snakelike fangs. The wings he'd seen were now gone, folded beneath the creature's pale belly.

Even though the lizard looked imposing, and its ability to fly was certainly surreal, Hawkins felt he could handle the creature, even without his knife.

But the chirps closing in reminded him that this creature was not alone, and nature is full of predators that worked together to take down much larger prey. Including people.

Hawkins's hand struck something hard. He reached his fingers out and felt the familiar shape of his knife's hilt. He clutched it tight, waiting for the right moment to strike.

He didn't have to wait long. The lizard sprang from the tree. Its wings snapped open from beneath its body and it covered the distance between them in a flash. Hawkins fell back and as the creature passed overhead, he slashed out with the knife. The blade slid through the wing's membrane so easily that Hawkins wasn't sure he'd struck a blow.

But then the lizard crashed to the jungle floor, shrieking in agony.

The sound seemed to agitate the other lizards. They bounded from tree to tree, flying and clinging, closing the distance. Everywhere he looked, serpentine eyes stared hungrily at him.

A rustling on the jungle floor alerted him to danger. He stood quickly and saw the wounded lizard charging him. Instincts born of a childhood on the soccer field took over. Hawkins kicked the thing and sent it flying, though much less gracefully than it was accustomed to.

"Hawkins, get down!"

He obeyed the voice, ducking quickly. He heard an impact above him. A large stone fell to the ground next to him, accompanied by one of the lizards. It was stunned, but far from dead.

Hawkins turned toward the voice and saw Joliet, armed with another stone. He ran to her. "I told you to leave."

"And I just saved your life," she said before turning and making a beeline for the beach.

Hawkins thought Joliet's claim was a little exaggerated, but kept it to himself. Now was not the time for arguing the details, and he couldn't deny he owed her a "thank you." Still, she should have listened. In a different situation, *she* could have been killed.

Spurred by the knowledge that the jungle's denizens really did want to maul them, the pair charged toward the beach, blazing a new path through the jungle. The chirping behind them grew louder. Frantic. And then, all at once, it stopped. The jungle fell silent.

The sudden silence was so powerful that Hawkins and Joliet actually stopped. Hawkins spun around, knife at the ready. "What the hell?"

"Where did they go?"

Where he expected to see dozens of flying lizards, or at least several clinging to trees, he saw nothing. Not a living thing. The jungle was just as empty as it had been the first time they'd entered it.

Still, he knew they were there.

He backed away, toward the beach, which was just a few feet behind them now. He could hear the faint lapping of waves, smell the salty air, and feel the hot sun on his back. *Did the creatures sense the beach?* he wondered. *Do they not like the light? Or is there something else about the beach that frightens them?*

When Joliet stepped out onto the beach and let out a shout of surprise, he feared his last guess was correct. He charged out after her, ready for action. The first thing he saw was Bray, shirtless, filthy, and covered with sweat. Then he saw what lay at Bray's feet and for the first time since they left the pillbox, he thought he might prefer the jungle to the beach.

FOURTEEN

Hawkins remembered what it felt like to look at a corpse. Fresh or long since decomposed, the sight of a human being with the life drained from it left a mark on his soul every time, even more so when the evidence of a violent death was plainly visible. He kept his resolve while on the job, but occasionally found himself washing the images from his mind with alcohol. He'd never abused the substance, but had no trouble using it to forget, at least for a few hours, the poignant reminder of his own frailty.

The scene on the beach reminded him how easily human life could be lost.

Fifteen times over.

Bray stood at the end of the line of uncovered bodies—skeletons, really—out of breath and soaked with sweat. His eyes were swollen and red. Had he been crying? The man had exhumed a mass grave on his own, after all. And from where Hawkins stood, it appeared each and every one of the dead had been murdered in the same fashion as the first they'd stumbled upon.

"Oh my God," Joliet said. "This is a mass grave?"

"This is just the top layer," Bray said. "There are more underneath."

Hawkins saw a body with what looked like a third arm and came to the same conclusion as Bray. Other bodies had been buried below. After quickly scanning the jungle behind him and finding no shifting shadows or striped reptilian skin, he knelt down at the head of the nearest body. The skull had been caved in by something blunt, and powerful. *Death would have been quick, at least,* he thought, assuming this was the one and only wound these people suffered.

Joliet walked down the line of bodies, stopping to look at each one. "Who are they?"

"Three of them were Americans," Bray said. "World War Two sailors. I'm not sure about the rest."

Joliet turned to Bray. "Americans?"

Bray held out his hands and let three sets of dog tags dangle from their chains. He separated one from the others and read the name. "Coffman." He pointed to the body at his feet. "He's this one here. Just finished clearing him off."

Hawkins moved down the line to Coffman's body, his eyes jumping back to the jungle every few moments, looking for motion.

Bray read the rest of the tag. "Coffman. J. P. 452386 C. That's his serial number. The 'C' means he was Catholic. 'Type A.' That's his blood type. They didn't do positive or negative back then. Next line is the date of his last tetanus shot. 4/1942, which is how I dated them. 'USN' for United States Navy. And I suspect that's all his interrogators got out of him, too, considering his wounds."

Hawkins had just noticed the multiple breaks in the man's ribs. It's possible he was punched repeatedly or just whacked a few times with whatever crushed his skull in. Straight nicks and scratches covering his arms, legs, and face; the kind caused by blades or, in the wild, claws and teeth. There was no denying the man had been tortured before he died.

"We need to cover them back up," Bray said.

"I thought you wanted to remove the body?" Joliet asked.

"When there was just one body," Bray said. "This isn't simply a murder anymore. It's a mass grave. Evidence of war crimes. Some of the guys who did this stuff during the war are still alive. Barely, but that doesn't mean whoever did this should escape justice in the history books. Someone is going to have to search this whole island for more,"

Bray straightened suddenly as though waking from a dream. "What happened with you two? You didn't find Kam?" He squinted at them. "And why were you running?"

Hawkins offered Bray a bullet list of everything they'd discovered: the rat, the pillbox that supported evidence of the island being populated during World War Two, the size of the island, and finally their flight from the flying lizards."

When Hawkins finished, Bray eyed the jungle nervously. "Flying lizards? Geez. Can you describe them?"

"I can draw one for you back at the *Magellan*," Hawkins said. While far from an artist, he sketched in his free time and, according to Bray, he was a "regular Picasso." But Picasso represented the extent of Bray's knowledge of the arts outside of the multiplex movie theater.

Hawkins stood and took the two-way radio from his pocket. He pushed the Talk button and said, "Captain Drake, this is Hawkins. You read?"

After a moment of static, the captain's voice came from the speaker. "I read you, Hawkins. Didn't think I'd hear from you so soon. Did you find Kam already? Over."

"No, sir. It's a long story and I'd prefer to give you the details in person. But the short version is that we think Kam either fell overboard . . . or he was taken. Whoever fled the ship and left those footprints in the sand knows this island well. Over."

"That doesn't sound good," Drake said.

Hawkins looked out at the pale blue hull of the *Magellan*. If he didn't look at his feet, or back at the foreboding jungle behind him, the scene appeared picturesque. Real postcard material. But the beauty of this place was cosmetic. Beneath the stunning views lurked a dark and bloody past. "It's not, sir. How are things on your end? Over."

"Making some progress actually, hold on."

The line went silent. During that time, Hawkins's eyes lowered to Coffman's body. He looked at the legs and saw that both had been fractured multiple times and allowed to heal incorrectly. He couldn't imagine the kind of pain this man endured. What could he have known that would make him endure this kind of torture? *Unless*, Hawkins thought, *this wasn't torture.*

Coffman had been tortured. Of that there was no doubt. But were they trying to extract information from him or simply entertaining themselves?

"This is odd," Joliet said, bending down to the skeleton with the illusion of a third arm.

Hawkins glanced at her, but as he did, he saw something strange, too. He turned back to Coffman's body. The left arm looked strange. He turned his head to the side, trying to get a good look at both arms at once. He knelt down and placed one hand at Coffman's shoulder and the other at his wrist—the hand was missing. Without shifting his hands, he picked them up and moved them to the right arm. *The hell?* While his system of measurement was crude, he felt positive that Coffman's left arm was at least three inches shorter than the right. The bones in the left arm were also thinner.

Was Coffman deformed? Hawkins wondered, but then discounted it. He doubted a man with a deformed arm would have seen active duty outside of an office setting or hospital. It might not have been much of a handicap, but in a war setting, a weaker arm would definitely be a liability. Then what? Malnutrition? That didn't make sense, either. It wouldn't affect a single arm.

Hawkins leaned in close. The left arm almost looked dainty. Feminine. His head snapped to the left, where the woman they'd first discovered lay, three bodies over. The woman's right arm lay to her side. The left arm was missing.

He faintly heard Bray asking him what he was doing, but ignored the man. He could barely hear him over the rushing of his own blood. He measured out the left arm again. Doing his best to keep his arms in place, he stood and walked to the skeleton missing an arm. He placed his hands over the right arm.

They matched.

He leaned up, eyes wide, but not seeing. "Fuck."

Hawkins snapped out of his daze. Joliet had muttered the same curse, at the same moment he had.

"What is it with you two?" Bray asked as he stomped toward them. "What are you doing?"

"Coffman's left arm," Hawkins said. "It's not his." He looked down at the woman missing a limb. He pointed to the empty shoulder joint. "It's hers."

Bray stumbled back a few steps. "What?" His eyes darted back and forth between Coffman's body and the woman's. "That can't be right."

"It's right," Joliet said and then pointed to the body she'd been inspecting. "You thought there was another row of bodies beneath these because of the extra limbs." She looked up at Bray. "There is no second row. The third arm—" Her eyes moved to Hawkins. "It's been surgically attached."

Hawkins and Bray both leaned over the woman. Joliet had cleared the sand away from the arm, revealing a shoulder ball joint with a pin in it. The pin ran straight through the bone where it attached to the sixth rib. It wasn't hard to picture this person in life, in agony, with a limp arm hanging from the ribs.

"These people weren't tortured," he said. "They were experimented on."

A deep roar filled the lagoon valley. All three of them jumped back, spinning around in search of the sound's source. Hawkins found it in a cloud of gray smoke issuing from the *Magellan*'s exhaust.

The engines were running.

"How you like that?" Drake said over the radio, sounding pleased. "It's about as piss-poor a rig as I've ever seen. We'll have to two-way radio every course change to the engine room so they can manually adjust the ship, but we'll be mobile."

Hawkins stood and looked down at the three-armed body. "You have no idea how happy I am to hear that, sir."

He knew they couldn't leave without discovering Kam's fate, but it was nice to know they could, if they had to. He didn't think getting through the sharply bending channel that led into the lagoon would be easy, but if they moved slowly enough, they could do it. They could escape the island grave-yard.

"Let's get back to the *Magellan*," Hawkins said. "Figure out what to do next."

Neither Bray nor Joliet disagreed. They quickly and qui-etly made for the Zodiac. Hawkins took one last look at the jungle and the bodies and hoped that if Kam were in the hands of the people who had committed these crimes, or their descendants, that he was being treated well, or already dead. The alternative was unthinkable.

FIFTEEN

The lavish spread on the mess hall's long dinner table felt inappropriate, given the fact that two men were dead, another missing, and they'd just uncovered the bodies of fifteen mutilated war crime victims, at least three of which were United States Navy. But it seemed surviving the storm and getting the engines back up was cause for celebration. At least it was to the Tweedle brothers.

In attendance were Captain Drake, Blok, Bray, Joliet, and Hawkins. Ray and Jim Clifton remained in the kitchen preparing meals for Jones and Bennett, who'd kept working in engineering, Sanchez, in case he woke up, and DeWinter, who manned the bridge. The crew normally ate in shifts, and the captain almost always ate alone, but this was as much a group debriefing as it was a meal.

The table held an assortment of foods. Grilled steaks sat in front of everyone except for Blok, a vegetarian who got pasta instead. Sides included mashed potatoes, green beans, and salads with dried cranberry, sugar-coated almonds, and avocado, served in frozen bowls. Not exactly high on the fancy scale, but filling, comforting, and served with red wine that helped ease Hawkins's tension.

He'd eaten quickly, devouring the food while listening to Jones explain how the young Phil Bennett had been the one to figure out the engine problems. He heard the details, but only retained what was important—the engines worked. After Jones finished speaking, conversation faded to little more than "pass the salt." It seemed that discussing what they'd found on the island, both living and dead, would wait until everyone had finished eating. During the silence, Hawkins sketched the strange lizard he'd seen. He drew a top view, a side view, and a nasty close-up of its strange, fanged teeth.

His mind drifted as he used a paper stump to smudge the dark charcoal he employed to draw the image. The shading brought the lizards face to life, its black and white eye staring at Hawkins as it had in the jungle—with grim intention.

Drake cleared his throat loudly, snapping Hawkins out of his memories. He flinched and dragged a smudge across the creature's extended wing.

After wiping his bearded face with a cloth napkin, Drake said, "I don't normally do things this way, but given the gravity of our situation, I want to hear from all of you before I make any decisions." He tossed the napkin on his cleared plate and continued. "We've got two men dead, one that might be in a coma, and another missing. We have the most basic control of the *Magellan,* but still no communications, no radar, no navigations. If we try to leave we'll be sailing by the stars with no weather service. We'd be on our own.

"Way I see it," the captain said, "we have three choices. First, we stay right here, find Kam, and then leave."

"Uh-uh," Bray said, nibbling on an almond. "If someone boarded the *Magellan* and took Kam, I don't think we should make ourselves a target by staying in the lagoon."

Joliet wielded her fork like a laser pointer, aiming it at Bray. "You think we should leave Kam behind?"

"No, no," he said. "I think we should get the ship out of this lagoon, anchor off shore—far enough to make swimming the distance tough—and come back in the small boats."

"Which is option number two," Drake said. "Park off shore and return to search in shifts. We'll set up a search grid, and—"

"Won't work," Hawkins said, not lifting his eyes from the page as he added stripes to the lizard's top view. "The island is too big to search a grid with so few people while returning to the ship every night. From what I could see, most of the island meets the sea with a cliff. The lagoon might be the only way to make land. We also have to assume that Kam—if he's alive—or the people holding him, might be mobile. You can't search an area and then assume he won't be there later. We'd be better off leaving, getting help, and returning with a small army."

"And that would be option three," Drake said.

"I can't believe you're suggesting that," Joliet said.

"Makes sense," Blok said, running his hands over his bald head. "It's possible Kam is already dead and we'd be risking our lives for nothing. Returning with more people, and weapons, is the only way to be sure and not lose any more lives."

"*You* can stay on the ship," Joliet said, growing angry. She turned to Hawkins. "Both of you can. Kam is our friend."

"I wasn't suggesting we leave," Hawkins said. "Only that a search grid wouldn't be much better than leaving."

"Then what *are* you proposing, Mr. Hawkins?" Drake asked.

"The sun set thirty minutes ago, so it's too dark to take the *Magellan* out of the lagoon tonight. I'll take the Zodiac back to the beach in the morning, while you take the *Magellan* off shore. I'll pick up the trail again and find Kam. On my own. Come back to the beach in a week. If I find Kam, we'll be there."

"And if *neither* of you are there in a week?" Bray asked.

"Then do like I said, come back with an army."

"You can't go alone," Joliet said. "You were almost killed. We're coming with you."

"When you say 'we're,' are you including me?" Bray asked. Joliet glared at him.

"Thought so."

Hawkins lowered his sketch pad. "I'm going alone."

Joliet locked eyes with him. "Bullshit."

"I won't risk your life," he said.

"It's mine to risk."

Hawkins sensed that arguing wouldn't help, but if he'd

known the island was populated, he'd have never agreed to let her join him the first time out. "You'll slow me down."

"We did just fine before *and* I saved your life." Joliet crossed her arms over her chest.

The captain tapped a fork against his glass like he was about to give a toast at a wedding. Everyone turned to him. "I understand that this is a tense situation, but please try to keep your heads."

"Not the best choice of words," Bray said.

The captain ignored Bray's comment. "I think we've ruled out leaving, and when it comes to finding Kam, I trust Hawkins's opinion." Drake raised his hand to Joliet, who was about to protest. He turned to Hawkins. "But I can't let you go alone. Blok, what do we have for weapons?"

"Ahh, there's the rifle. Two spearguns."

"There's a kitchen full of knives," Ray Clifton said from the door, which he nearly filled. He dried his hands on a towel and stepped into the room. He paused behind Hawkins's chair. "Overheard your conversation. We got cleavers, too. Keep 'em sharp." He motioned to Hawkins's drawing. "Make short work of those dracos there."

"Draco?" Hawkins said, looking up over his shoulder at the behemoth of a man.

"That flying lizard," Ray said. "It's called a draco. Saw it on Discovery. That's what you saw on the island, right?"

Bray stood up across the table and reached out for the sketch pad. "Let me see that." He took the pad and sat down with it.

"Here's how we're going to play it," Drake said. "In the morning, we'll take the *Magellan* through the strait. I'm going to need every set of eyes to help us maneuver through there, so no one is leaving the ship until we're out. Then Hawkins, Blok, Joliet, and if he chooses to, Bray, will return to track down Kam. Take whatever weapons you can find. I'll give you three days to find him."

Hawkins began to protest. "Three days is—"

"As much as you're going to get," Drake said. "When the sun heads for the horizon on day three, I'll bring the *Magellan* closer to the island so you can rendezvous with us, with or without Kam. Understood?"

Hawkins nodded, but didn't speak. The three-day deadline wouldn't give them enough time to cover a lot of ground, but whoever took Kam wouldn't just be wandering the island aimlessly. That path would end somewhere, and he felt confident they could find out where inside three days. But he had no way of knowing if Kam would still be there when they arrived, or even if he'd still be alive. He did, however, have an idea.

"What about you, Captain?" Hawkins said, looking at the old captain's bulging muscles. "Let them take the ship out and you help me find Kam."

A wide grin formed on the captain's face. "Much as I'd like that, I'm the captain of this ship, and this isn't *Star Trek*. My duty is here."

Hawkins figured as much, but had to ask. While Bray was overweight, Blok a skinny rail of a man, and Joliet not much bigger than a fourteen-year-old boy, the captain was strong and in good shape. They'd cover a lot more ground and he had no doubt that the old sea dog would be good in a fight. Not to mention the fact that he wouldn't worry about Drake as much as he would Joliet, or even Bray. His relationship with the captain had remained professional. He'd become attached to Bray and Joliet. Their welfare would be a distraction.

"Are these teeth right?" Bray asked, looking up from the drawing.

"Yeah," Hawkins said. "Why?"

"It had fangs?"

"Yes. Like a snake, but shorter."

"What about color?" Bray asked.

"Yellow with black stripes," Joliet answered.

"And you got the size right? It was this slender?"

Hawkins lost his patience with Bray's rapid-fire questions. "Yes. That's what it looked like. Do you know what it is?"

"I told you," Ray said. "That's a draco."

Bray stood and turned the pad around so they could all see it. "You're right," he said to Ray. "But you're also wrong. The wings are formed by a thin membrane stretched between ribs that the draco lizard can open. But they can't fly, like a bird. They glide. Usually to escape predators. The wings, limbs, and head are all draco, but the rest . . . that's something else."

"Something else?" Joliet asked.

"You of all people should see it," Bray said. He propped the sketch pad against his belly. Using both his hands, he covered the creature's open wings and limbs in the top view Hawkins had drawn. "Remember the coloration. Ignore the size of the head, but take the fangs into account."

Joliet looked for just a moment before she gasped. "Hydrophis melanocephalus."

"Hydro-what?" Ray asked.

"A sea snake," she said, her voice suddenly full of dread.

"That's bad?" Hawkins asked.

"Sea snakes have the most potent venom of any snake. Far more deadly than any land snake. In fact, it's the most deadly natural substance in the world." She looked at Hawkins. "If either of us had been bit . . ."

"How come we don't hear about people dying from sea snake bites?" Hawkins asked.

"Because they're docile," Joliet said. "You can swim right up and play with them. Millions of years of not being screwed with have made them nice. Probably why their fangs are shorter than the average venomous snake, too. They don't bite unless severely provoked."

"Like if you're trying to eat them," Bray said. "But just about everything in the ocean knows not to bother."

Ray looked dubious, "Doesn't look like a sea snake to me."

"Nor does it look like a draco," Bray said. "Because it's neither. And both."

"Just what the hell are you talking about, Bray?" Drake asked, raising his voice.

"It's a chimera," Joliet said.

The captain didn't look impressed. "Which is?"

"Two or more creatures merged to form something new," Bray answered.

"Something unnatural," Hawkins added. His stomach twisted. There was another word he believed could describe the creature. "Another experiment."

SIXTEEN

"I don't understand," Hawkins said. "How is any of this possible?"

He lay on his cot, staring up at the ceiling, hands clasped behind his head and feet crossed. Outwardly, he looked no tenser than a vacationer lying in a cot and sipping a mixed drink. But the tension gripping him made his body ache, never mind the fact that the jungle hike, and run, had worn him out. A month on board a ship with less exercise than he was accustomed to had taken a toll on his stamina.

"Which part?" Bray asked. He sat at the room's only desk, looking at Hawkins's sketch of the draco-snake, which Bray had dubbed "minidrakes," by combining "draco" and "snake," but also because drakes were a type of dragon.

Bray hadn't used the term in front of Captain Drake yet, but Hawkins had a feeling the man wouldn't appreciate being associated with the creatures, so he tried to refer to them as chimeras or draco-snakes. "Let's start with the chimeras."

After the revelation that the draco-snakes were two creatures merged into one, and likely another experiment, the dinner group had gone silent. Perhaps sensing that a conversation based on the few, but frightening, facts they'd uncovered would lead to wild speculation, Drake had quickly dismissed the group. He asked them to go to bed early so that they might be rested for the search, but Hawkins suspected the dismissal was more for the benefit of the nonscience crewmembers.

Their jobs required focus. Worrying about flying lizards and freakish experiments could slow their work, or result in sloppy work, which could endanger all of them in the long run. So they'd returned to their quarters, staying silent for nearly thirty minutes, each lost in thought. Joliet had left, saying she'd needed time to think and process, but she'd come see them soon. She had yet to return.

Bray stood, turned around, and sat back down in the backward-facing chair. "First of all, the idea of a chimera is nothing new. Homer describes a creature in the *Illiad* that is part lion, part goat, and part snake. The Bible mentions creatures called the Nephilim, which are half-human, half-demon, but then goes on to say that all flesh—including animals—became corrupted. Some people actually believe that the Greek myths, which are full of chimeras, might be based on actual creatures alluded to in the Torah—the first five books of the Bible—as well as the Book of Enoch, an ancient text supposedly written by Noah's great-grandfather, but not included in the Christian canon. The manticore—part human, part lion, and with three rows of shark teeth. The griffin—part lion, part eagle. The hydra—part serpent, part squid, which might explain its regenerative abilities."

"But that's all myth, not reality," Hawkins said. "Nephilim and hydras might make great fiction, but I can't take them seriously." He didn't care if the pope himself believed chimeras were real. As far as he could tell, myths stayed in the past and he was much more concerned about the present. As much as Bray's passion and knowledge about history impressed him, thinking about flying lions with shark teeth couldn't possibly help him understand the draco-snakes.

"Okay, let's talk science." Bray rubbed his chin for a moment, collecting his thoughts. "First, it's important to understand that chimeras can form naturally."

"C'mon," Hawkins said, fearing that Bray was about to make a case for the reality of mythological chimeras.

"Just listen," Bray said. "Chimeras are formed when two fertilized eggs, or embryos, fuse in the womb. I'm not talking cross-species chimeras here. A chimera can develop from a single species if two distinct embryos become one."

"Like conjoined twins?" Hawkins asked.

"In the loosest sense, sure, but what I'm talking about is a much deeper joining. Okay, here's a gross example. A farmer in India went to have a massive tumor removed. Was so big it made him look pregnant. When the surgeons opened him up, the tumor had hands. And limbs. A jaw. Hair. Even nads. Wicked gross, right?"

When Hawkins grimaced, Bray continued. "The body was seriously deformed, but lived inside the guy for thirty-six years. When he was an embryo, he wrapped around his twin brother and the two merged into one." Bray raised his index finger. "Oh! There was this lady in Britain who merged so completely with her twin, down to the cellular level, that she actually had two different blood types. She was literally two people at once. What's really crazy is that chimerism is becoming more common in people because of in vitro fertilization. So we're doing it in labs all the time, just not on purpose."

"So we're accidently merging twins," Hawkins said. "I'm still not seeing how it applies to flying sea snakes."

"Minidrakes," Bray said, "and it does apply. If you'd let me finish a thought, you might learn something."

"You have very long thoughts."

"Thank you," Bray said.

Bray had a habit of saying "thank you" whenever someone described something as being large, long, or delicious. He never said it, but everyone knew he was implying they'd been talking about his manhood. Hawkins had no doubt Bray had picked it up from one of his high school students. Had that vibe. It *was* funny at first, especially when he did it to Joliet, but the joke was getting old so Hawkins tried not to grin. It would only encourage the man. "Continue, Professor Bray. Educate me."

"Gladly," Bray said. "This is where things get freaky."

"I thought we crossed into 'freaky' five minutes ago."

"It's far freakier when it's intentional," Bray said.

Hawkins couldn't argue with that. The idea of someone merging a sea snake and draco lizard together just felt wrong. Never mind the fact that they'd also tried to transplant adult human limbs from one person to another.

"The main difference between natural chimerism and laboratory chimerism is that the process can be controlled in a lab. Instead of randomly merging—which, by the way, most often results in both fetuses dying before birth. That the farmer was born and then lived thirty-six years with a twin in his belly is miraculous. Anyway, instead of randomly merging embryos, scientists can select specific embryonic cells from one organism—say, a bird's wings and breast muscles strong enough to use them—and transplant them onto the embryo of something else. Like a lion."

"So griffins could be real?" Hawkins asked with a raised eyebrow.

"In theory, yes."

"But isn't that just a hybrid? What makes the draco-snakes chimeras?"

"Hybrids are a fusion of gametes."

"Lost me already," Hawkins said.

"Did you ever take biology in school?" Bray asked, shaking his head. "Gametes are cells that merge with others cells during fertilization. Eggs. Sperm. Those kinds of things."

"So humans are hybrids?" Hawkins asked.

Bray nodded. "Kind of, but not really, because we're talking about gametes from different species, not Mom and Dad. So these gametes come together and form a single zygote. That's a fertilized egg to the layman. This can pretty much only happen in a lab, or with very closely related species, like lions and tigers."

"Ligers," Hawkins said. He'd seen some of the giant cats on TV. They occasionally made the news when an illegal private zoo got shut down. Lions and tigers kept together could mate and have offspring that were equal parts of both species, but often twice the size.

"Exactly," Bray said. "The end result is a new species with a single, merged genetic code. A chimera is different because each individual part has distinct genetic codes."

"Like the lady with two blood types?"

"Right. The minidrakes aren't a new species. They're still two distinct species with separate genetic codes brought together as a single organism. Like the Trinity. God the Father. Jesus. Holy Spirit. Separate, but joined."

Hawkins just stared at him.

"Sorry," Bray said. "Raised Catholic. Forget it. Okay, here's a question for you. Ever heard of a geep?"

"No."

"'Course not," Bray said. "Geep are lab-created goat-sheep. They were created in the eighties. Lived full lives. Gets worse. In China, a human-rabbit chimera was created. They claim to have destroyed the embryos, which I doubt, but the point is, the cells were successfully merged."

"That's sick," Hawkins said.

"Seriously," Bray said. "A rabbit? Were they trying to make an Easter Bunny? Why not give someone tiger claws? You're probably thinking that shit went down because it was China. Well, guess what? The University of Nevada School of Medicine made a chimera that was eighty-five percent sheep and fifteen percent *human*. Now *that's* nuts."

A dull sound suddenly reverberated through the ship. The low, rumbling tone sounded like a fog horn. The lone blast of sound lasted three seconds and then faded.

"Someone must be testing the horn," Bray said.

A thud on the floor above them turned their heads up.

"Sounds like the horn caught someone by surprise," Bray said with a grin.

Hawkins just looked at the ceiling like he could see through it.

Bray gave a shrug. "On to the craziest thing you'll hear all day. Spider silk. Stuff is stronger than steel, but fibrous. Lots of potential applications. Bulletproof vests. Airbags. Hell, someone could probably make space suits out of the stuff. But they can't harvest it in large quantities. Spiders aren't only small, but when researchers set up a spider farm, the spiders went on a *Highlander*-like killing spree."

Bray saw the confusion on Hawkins's face. "*Highlander*, the movie. 'There can be only one.' No? Nothing? Forget it. When they couldn't get a lot of spiderwebs from the spiders, they made a chimera from spiders. And goats. Instead of producing milk, the goats now squirt out spider silk. How fu—"

A second thud, louder than the first, reverberated from the floor above.

"What's going on up there?" Bray asked.

Hawkins said nothing. He sat up in bed, listening. But the sound did not repeat. He slid his feet onto the floor. "I'm going to check it out."

Bray once again shrugged off the interruption, but had finished his lecture. He picked up the sketch pad from the desk and flipped through the images. Most were quick sketches of wildlife, sometimes landscapes or random images of whatever happened to be in front of Hawkins at the time.

Hawkins stood to leave, but Bray's next words froze him in place.

"Oh ho!" Bray said, stopping his rapid-fire page flipping. "Nice."

He turned the sketch pad around so Hawkins could see the drawing. It was a detailed sketch of Joliet. In a bikini. She'd been tanning on deck when he came across her. He had realized she was sleeping when he spoke to her, but got no reply. After finishing the sketch, he woke her with a cough so she wouldn't get sunburned. But he never mentioned the drawing. Not to Joliet. Or Bray. "Say a word about that and I'll make you afraid to close your eyes at night."

Bray laughed and turned the pages again. "Fine. Fine. Just say something to her soon. Your pining is killing me."

"I don't pine," Hawkins said.

"I work in a high school," Bray replied. "I know pining when I see it." He stopped flipping pages again. "What's this?"

Bray showed Hawkins the image. It was a sketch of the pillbox he'd done from memory before drawing the draco-snakes.

"That's the pillbox," Hawkins said.

Bray pointed to the text above the entrance. "Looks Japanese."

"Know what it says?" Hawkins asked.

"I think we've established that neither of us reads Japanese, or maybe you think I just struggle with the word 'broccoli'? Drake might know, though. He's been around the world a few times."

A third loud bang sounded from above. This time, the boom was followed by rapid-fire bumps moving across the ceiling.

"Someone's running," Bray commented.

Hawkins looked at him. "Where's Joliet?"

SEVENTEEN

Hawkins went for the door as the thumping sound overhead moved quickly away. *Someone's running,* he thought as he twisted the door handle. *But why?* He pulled the door open to an empty hallway. The stairwell on the right side of the hall was also empty.

But he could hear someone descending the stairs two at a time. The light step and quick puffs of air revealed the runner as Joliet. Running a treadmill in calm or rough seas never gave her any trouble and she breathed the same way when she exercised.

"Joliet, what are—"

"Back!" she shouted before reaching the bottom. "Get in your room!"

Joliet emerged from the stairs a moment later. Blood ran from her forehead over her cheek.

Hawkins stayed frozen in place, trying to comprehend why Joliet was running and how she'd been injured.

Joliet, on the other hand, barreled toward him like a Pamplona bull. "Get back!" She shoved Hawkins back inside the room.

Hawkins was about to ask her what the hell was going on when he heard a second set of footfalls coming from the stairwell. And those feet sounded much heavier. Joliet was being chased, by someone large. He clenched his fist and headed for the door. "Bray."

"I'm with you, Ranger," Bray said, coming up behind him.

But Joliet stopped them in their tracks by slamming the door closed. She pushed the button lock, but didn't look relieved at all. "We need to block the door!"

"Block the door?" Bray said. "Who the hell is out there."

"I don't know! Just block the door!"

Loud footsteps approached the door. Hawkins thought he could actually feel each footfall vibrating through the floor.

"Joliet," Hawkins said, taking her shoulders in his hands. "If it's anyone from the crew, we can handle them."

She shook her head, eyes darting back and forth. She shrugged away from Hawkins and darted across the small room. She picked up the metal desk chair and ran back to the door. She wedged the chair under the doorknob and stood back.

Bray smiled and shook his head. "Okay, so now that we have a locked metal door with a chair, would you mind telling us what—"

An explosive impact pounded the door from the other side. It shook, but remained intact. The very loud and sudden sound made Joliet, Bray, and Hawkins jump away from the door.

"Hey!" Bray shouted, his embarrassment about being frightened turning quickly to anger. "Who's out there! Cut the shit or I'm going to—"

The second impact bent the top of the door inward. The bend was slight, not quite an inch, but the strength it would require to bend the metal door wasn't lost on Hawkins.

Or Bray. "Goddamn, is he using a sledgehammer?"

Hawkins took Joliet's face and turned her eyes to his. "*Who* is it?"

"I—I don't know. I only saw a shadow. But he's big."

The door shook from another impact. The chair slipped free and fell to the floor.

"Really big," Bray said. He quickly put the chair back into place and leaned against it, holding it in place.

"I went to medical," Joliet said. "To check on Sanchez. I think . . . I think he's dead. The lights were out. Broken. But I could smell blood."

Bang! The door bent a little more.

Bray grunted as the impact shook the chair. "Hawkins, be ready if this guy gets through!"

"When I called for help, I saw him. Just a shadow. And when I ran, he chased. That's all I know."

Bang!

Hawkins went to his dresser, opened the top drawer, and took out his knife and sheath. He quickly buckled the sheath around his waist and drew the blade.

Bray did a double take when he saw the knife in Hawkins's hand. "Sure you want to use that? We don't know for sure that Sanchez is dead. If this is just Ray on a bender—"

"It's not Ray," Hawkins said. "It's a local."

Bray and Joliet both stared at Hawkins, digesting his deduction. Bray finally nodded. "After the next strike, he'll be winding up for another. I'll open the door, you—"

"Hold on," Hawkins said. "Listen."

The thump of heavy footsteps receded and then pounded up the staircase.

"He's leaving." Bray let go of the chair and stood up.

Hawkins pulled the chair away from the door.

"What are you doing?" Joliet asked.

"I have to warn the others." Hawkins grabbed the door handle and spoke to Bray. "Lock the door behind me."

Hawkins could see that Joliet and Bray were both about to argue. "This isn't a request." The words were spoken with enough force to startle the pair. Neither argued when he opened the door and slid into the hallway. He listened as the door closed, the push-button lock was engaged, and the chair wedged into place. Satisfied his friends were safe, Hawkins tightened his grip on the hunting knife and started up the stairs.

Halfway to the top, Hawkins paused. Thumps reverberated through the ship, but he couldn't tell if they were coming from above, or below. He was about to turn around and head to the lower levels when a gunshot rang out.

From above.

He charged up the stairs, knife in hand, ready for a fight. The outside door at the top of the stairwell lay open. Indistinct shouts filtered in through the warm nighttime air. He stepped onto the main deck of the *Magellan* and was greeted by a shouting voice.

"There he is! I see him!"

A rifle blast was immediately followed by a loud ping as a bullet ricocheted off the metal wall just above his head. Hawkins ducked down. "It's me! It's Hawkins!"

Footsteps pounded toward him. "Hawkins. God. Are you all right?" An out-of-breath Jim Clifton stopped next to him.

"Wouldn't be if you had better aim," Hawkins said, eyeing the hunting rifle that was kept on board in case they came across an animal that needed to be put down.

"Sorry 'bout that," Jim said. "Thought you were him."

"Him, who?" Hawkins asked.

"Somebody's on board. Knocked Blok on his ass."

"Port side! At the bow!" This voice belonged to Captain Drake and Hawkins responded immediately. He snatched the rifle from Jim's hands and sprinted toward the bow.

When he arrived on the starboard side of the bow, he scanned the area. The ship had been cleaned of debris, but the large net that Cahill had been entangled in lay at the center of the bow deck, folded into a large square.

A large shadow shifted on the other side of the deck. Hawkins raised the rifle, but didn't pull the trigger. He wouldn't shoot at a target he couldn't clearly see. It could be Ray, for all he knew, and he wasn't about to make the same mistake Jim had. Keeping the rifle raised, he stalked forward. "Stop where you are! Identify yourself!"

The shadow paused and Hawkins felt a pair of eyes looking at him.

"Who are you!" Hawkins shouted.

In a blur, the figure disappeared. At first, Hawkins wasn't sure what happened, but then he heard a splash. "He went over the rail!" Hawkins ran to where he'd last seen the figure standing.

Footsteps pounded up behind him.

"Where'd he go?" Jim asked.

"Someone get a good look at that son of a bitch?" Drake barked.

Hawkins aimed the weapon toward the water. The half-moon provided a little light, as did the *Magellan*'s remaining outside lights—it seemed several had been broken by the intruder—but Hawkins couldn't see anyone. Water sloshed near the shore and he saw a shape emerge.

How the hell did he swim so far so fast?

Didn't matter. He wasn't about to let him escape. He aimed low, hoping to hit the man's leg and incapacitate him. Ignoring several more sets of approaching footsteps, Hawkins wrapped his index finger around the trigger.

He exhaled. Held his breath. Applied pressure.

"Hold your fire!"

The voice was ragged and wet, but Hawkins recognized Jones's voice and didn't fire. The man sounded wounded, physically and emotionally. He turned toward the voice.

Jones stumbled into view. "It took her. It has Jackie!"

The old man fell to his knees where light illuminated his face and torso. He was soaked with blood. His eyes rolled back.

Drake ran to Jones and caught him as his body collapsed.

Hawkins quickly scanned the beach. The intruder had escaped. Again.

"We're going to find her," Drake said to Jones, whose body had gone limp. "We're going to get your girl back."

Hawkins knelt next to Drake, who for the first time seemed overcome with emotion. He checked Jones's neck for a pulse and was relieved to find one. As he pulled his hand away, Drake snatched his wrist in a tight grip. "You're going to get that son of a bitch. You hear me? This is an island. He can't run forever."

Hawkins knew only one reply would be accepted, so he nodded and pulled his arm away. But he wasn't so sure. First, they didn't know if the intruder was alone. There could be an entire population on the island, for all they knew. Second, Jones's warning about Jackie kept repeating in his mind.

It took her. It has Jackie.

It.

Not he. Not she.

It.

EIGHTEEN

Hawkins followed the barrel of the hunting rifle like a donkey behind a carrot. If anything in front of him so much as twitched, it would get a .44-caliber round before Hawkins bothered to introduce himself. The only other person wandering the ship was Bray, and he stood just behind Hawkins, brandishing a fire ax. Everyone else was locked inside the ship's lounge on the first deck.

After the attack, Drake and Blok had run around the *Magellan*'s upper decks, closing and locking outside doors. Since the wheelhouse window had been punched in by the refrigerator, they'd locked that interior doorway, too. With the crew sealed inside, they had gathered in the lounge. Hawkins and Joliet had tended to Jones's wounds—a bump on his forehead and a few scrapes—using the ship's lounge as a makeshift medical room. While Drake fumed, pacing back and forth, deep in thought, Hawkins had offered to search the ship, level by level, to be sure they were alone. Drake agreed, but sent Bray along for backup.

They searched the first deck first, making sure that the lounge level was clear. Then they headed down to the lowest deck so they could work their way up. It had taken them twenty minutes to inspect the third deck, which housed a large generator room, laundry facilities, and several storage rooms including large dry, cool, and frozen food stores. They'd moved up to the second deck, searching from stern to stem.

They'd found a few spots of blood—presumably Jones's—in the prop motor room where the attack had taken place. They still didn't know exactly what had happened. Jones had gone in and out of consciousness, but had never stayed awake long enough to give an account of what happened. And Bennett had been in the generator room. The winch room, upper generator room, and switchboard were all clear, as were the workshop, exercise room, and empty crew quarters. As they neared the front of the ship, Hawkins and Bray grew tenser. The science crew quarters were just ahead. This is where they'd had their own encounter with whoever, or whatever, had taken DeWinter.

As Hawkins nudged open one door at a time, sweeping the room with the rifle, he replayed the events in his mind. The invader had smashed their door, nearly knocking it in. After giving up, he ran straight to the rear of the ship, disabled Jones, and took DeWinter. He then ran up to the main deck, rounded the port side of the ship to the bow, and jumped into the water, crossing the distance to shore like an Olympic swimmer, all while holding an unconscious—or dead—woman over his shoulder. And he did all of that fairly quickly, sprinting to the back of the ship, up, and then back again.

But why? Why come after Joliet on one side of the ship and then run all the way to the back to take DeWinter? Something nagged at him. The answer was there, at the fringe of his thoughts. But other questions rose up, vying for attention. The horn that sounded before the attack. They had all heard it, but it didn't originate from the *Magellan*. Did it come from the island? Or perhaps a passing ship? There was no way to find out, or even attempt to communicate. The idea that rescue might have passed by the island infuriated him. Made him want to punch something.

Then he rounded the corner and saw the door to his room. "Oh my God."

"I told you," Bray said. "It's crazy."

Hawkins had a hard time taking his eyes off the bent metal door, but dutifully checked the two rooms and single head on the way to his room. With the way clear, he searched his own room and then turned his attention back to the door. The top right of the metal door was bent inward. When closed, a two-inch gap separated the door from its frame. But the bent metal was just part of the picture. Large dents pocked the white door's surface. At the center of each dent, the paint had chipped away to reveal the gray metal beneath.

"These dents are at least an inch deep," Hawkins said, rubbing his fingers over the surface of the largest of the dents.

"I'm telling you, the guy had a sledgehammer," Bray said. He raised the ax over his head and pretended to strike the door.

Hawkins shook his head. "The angle is wrong. The dents wouldn't be so straight."

"Maybe he used it like a battering ram?" Bray offered.

"The shape would be more rectangular." Hawkins traced a finger around one of the nearly circular indentations. "You'd lose a lot of force using a sledge like that."

"Then what do you think?" Bray asked.

Hawkins stood to the side and motioned Bray closer. "Feel this." He pointed to the largest dent.

Bray rubbed his hand over the surface of the dent.

"Feel the ridges?"

Bray nodded.

"Three of them, right?"

Bray felt the ridges with his fingertips. "Yeah. So?"

"Make a fist," Hawkins said.

Bray looked dubious, but complied. Hawkins directed Bray's fist, placing it in the hole.

"Your hand is a little smaller," Hawkins said. "But it fits."

"Geez, he was *punching* the door?" Bray said. "The guy must have been huge. And there's no blood? How could someone do this without breaking their hand to bits and not opening a wound?"

Hawkins shrugged. "A glove?"

"An *armored* glove," Bray added.

Hawkins could have spent a long time looking over the door and trying to theorize how it had been decimated, but they weren't here to play detective. They had a ship to search. After clearing the next room, the pair headed up to the main deck, which held most of the ship's labs—hydro, wet, computer, biology, and more—as well as a machine shop, the ROV bay, specimen freezers, which currently contained the dissected sea turtle, and the medical bay.

They searched stern to stem once again. Not because it was more efficient or had some kind of strategic value, but because of what they might find in medical. Sanchez. Joliet hadn't gotten a good look at his body, but she'd been positive the man was dead. Had there been any doubt, she would have been the first person back to check on him. So after checking the rest of the interior main deck and coming up empty, Hawkins and Bray slowly approached the door to medical.

The metal door lay open. Darkness concealed most of the room. The only light came from the open door, which created a cookie-cutter streak of light across the white tile floor. But it was enough. A pool of dark red lay at the end of the light's reach. The scent of blood hit Hawkins so hard, he could taste it like a mouthful of pennies.

Hawkins covered his mouth with his arm, stifling the odor and a groan. He paused at the door. The dark room would be the perfect place for an ambush. But he had no choice. He stepped into the room, cutting the beam of light with his shadow, and reached for the light switch. He flipped the switch and nothing happened. "Lights aren't working," he said. "Must have broke the bulbs."

"There's a portable lamp to the left, I think," Bray said. "The bright kind. For doing surgery or putting in stitches. That kind of thing."

Made sense, but with Cahill dead, if anyone needed stitches, they'd be the messy kind that leave ugly scars. Hawkins could do the work in a pinch—he'd helped sew up a few wounded animals—but animals never complained about scars.

"If you cover me," Bray said. "I'll switch the light on."

"I won't be able to see you."

"If something happens, I'll fall to the ground and scream. Just keep your aim up." Bray slipped past Hawkins. "Ready?"

Hawkins tried to think of another way to do this, but couldn't. "Fine."

Bray moved into the darkness slowly, hands extended to keep from walking into a wall. He disappeared from view a few feet from the doorway's light.

Hawkins kept the rifle against his shoulder, but pointed away from Bray. He'd been taught to keep the safety on until he'd picked a target. Helped prevent hunters from accidentally shooting each other. But he ignored that rule now. Whatever they were looking for was strong enough to bend a metal door and fast enough to abduct a crewmember without being seen. If he had to fire, he suspected he wouldn't have time to disengage the safety before pulling the trigger.

A loud crash of metal on tile floor spun him toward Bray. When the big man shouted, Hawkins's finger went to the trigger.

"Fuck!" Bray shouted. "Don't shoot! Don't shoot!"

Hawkins slowly took his finger off the trigger, which he'd begun to squeeze. That the weapon was far from sensitive had been a blessing twice now.

"Tripped over a chair," Bray said. "Found the light, though."

With a click, the floor around Bray lit up. He stood next to a lamp that looked like it could have been used on a film set. Bray loosened the joint, adjusted the lamp so that it faced the room, and retightened it.

"There," he said, but Hawkins didn't reply.

The bright lamp lit the horrible scene in stark detail. Sanchez lay in a cot across the room. The floor around the bed was covered in congealed blood and the once-white sheets were now dark red—brown where the blood had begun to dry.

Hawkins inched closer to the body, lowering the rifle as he stepped forward. Sanchez lay on the cot, but no longer in one piece. His body had been separated at the center, the two halves joined by drying entrails. His eyes were opened wide, turned to the ceiling, his face contorted in an expression of raw pain. He'd either regained consciousness before the attack, or the pain had woken him. Either way, he'd experienced the agony of being split in two.

Bray groaned and backed away, performing the sign of the cross and saying "Oh God," again and again.

Hawkins forced himself closer, looking for details about how this had happened. When he found it, he backed away, too. A portion of the man's right lower leg had been crushed, the flesh stretched and purple. The same mark had been left on his shoulder.

"He was *pulled* apart," Hawkins said, his voice almost a whisper.

"What kind of person could do this?" Bray asked.

Hawkins wasn't sure if Bray was referring to the brute strength it would take to rend a man in half at the waist or the mental state a person would have to be in to perform the task. He looked back at his friend, who did nothing to hide the fear and revulsion on his face. "Maybe 'what kind of *person*?' is the wrong question."

Hawkins forced himself back to the bedside. He took a blanket from a neighboring bed, opened it, and flung it over the body. He turned back to Bray. "Because I can't even begin to imagine a human being capable of something like this."

NINETEEN

Drake's face twitched as Hawkins gave his report, detailing the state in which they'd found Sanchez's remains. The good news, however, was that he and Bray had searched every nook and cranny of the *Magellan*'s interior and found nothing. Locked inside, they were safe. When Hawkins finished, the remaining crew—Blok, Bray, Joliet, Bennett, and Ray and Jim Clifton—sat silently, faces turned down to the blue rug beneath their feet.

Jones lay on the couch, conscious now, but silent, staring up at the ceiling. He'd regained consciousness just a few minutes after Hawkins and Bray had begun their search, but hadn't said anything. Hawkins had seen the look once before, seven years ago, on the face of a man whose son had fallen over a cliff. It was the look of a man mourning the loss of a loved one.

Jones looked like he'd given up hope, which Hawkins resented. DeWinter might still be alive. Giving up on her now would be a mistake and would certainly seal her fate. They didn't know why Kam or DeWinter had been taken. Both could be dead, or alive, but there was only one way to find out.

Bennett lowered his face into his hands and mumbled, "Why is this happening?"

Hawkins thought the question was rhetorical, but Joliet

knelt down in front of him and pulled his hands away. "Phil, we're safe now. You don't need to be afraid."

"But it took her," he replied. "Jackie is gone."

"Kam, too," Bray muttered. "Thought you two were pals?"

"Eight," Hawkins said, using Bray's nickname. "Give him a break."

Bray shrugged. "Just saying."

Bennett wiped his arm across his nose and pulled away from Joliet. "I'm fine."

Joliet stood and shot Bray a look.

He raised his hands in frustration. "What?"

Hawkins could feel the tension building in the room. If things weren't worked out, and soon, they'd all be at each other's throats. "Sir," he said, his voice stopping Drake mid-pace. The man's face burned red. His sharp blue eyes flicked to Hawkins. "I know it might make sense to cut our losses and leave, but—"

"The hell with that," Drake said. He pointed to Jones. "That man is my oldest friend. I'm Jackie's godfather, for shit's sake. We're *not* leaving."

Hawkins held up his hands. "I don't want to leave. I want to go look for her. And Kam. Bray, Joliet, and Blok will accompany me. We'll take weapons and enough supplies for a week."

"Not good enough," Drake said.

"I don't understand," Hawkins replied.

Drake picked up the fire ax Bray had used. The muscles in his forearms twitched as he twisted the wooden handle. "I'm coming with you."

The captain had at least fifty pounds on Hawkins and held that ax like he knew how to use it. He'd be good to have along, but given Drake's previous reservations about leaving the ship, Hawkins felt he should play devil's advocate, just in case the man wasn't thinking straight. "What happened to staying with the ship? If something were to happen to you, would we be stuck here, working engines or not?"

Drake mulled the question, patting the ax handle in the

palm of his hand. "Blok will stay on board. He'll have no trouble getting the *Magellan* back to the mainland."

Hawkins glanced at Blok. The man nodded, validating the captain's statement, though Hawkins wasn't sure if the man was simply afraid of leaving the safety of the sealed ship.

"This is no longer a search and rescue mission," Drake said. "Our people are not *lost*. They were *taken*. We're not going to find them sitting on a rock, munching coconuts. We're going to have to take them back. By force. You and I both know that you can handle that. But can he?" Drake pointed to Bray, who looked supremely uncomfortable at being singled out, and equally confused. Drake's finger shifted to Joliet. "Can she? I can tell you from experience that Blok here can't stand the sight of spiders. That the kind of man you want in a hostile environment? Or do you want someone like you? Someone who can do what needs to be done?"

While Hawkins didn't know Drake's detailed past, he suspected the man had been in the navy—maybe even as a SEAL. In his current state, he definitely seemed capable of defending himself. He looked at Blok. The skinny bookworm probably wouldn't be much use in a fight. With a nod, he said, "I never disagreed. Just wanted you to be sure."

"I'm sure," Drake said. "Jim, Ray."

The Clifton brothers both looked up. They wore twin masks of discomfort, probably wondering what Drake was going to ask of them. "See to Jones while we're gone. Anything he wants, you get it for him."

The brothers looked relieved. Ray even gave a salute. "We will. Of course. No problem."

"Bennett."

The skinny kid stood silently, looking at Drake. He kept his head up, but a quivering lowered lip revealed the boy was terrified. And rightfully so. Being brave while looking at a dissected turtle was one thing; facing the possibility of being kidnapped, killed, or maimed was something else entirely. Some people just couldn't do it, no matter how desperate the situation. The look in Bennett's eyes was easy to read—a little more pressure and he'd break.

To his credit, Drake adjusted his tone and body language. He placed a hand on the young man's shoulder. "Look, Phil, I know you're scared. But here's the situation. Jones isn't feeling like himself right now. DeWinter's missing. That makes you my chief engineer. You copy?"

Bennett nodded quickly. "Yes . . . yes, sir."

"While we're gone, I want you to keep working on the ship's controls. See if you can't have us in a better situation than we are right now. You're a smart kid. You can do it."

Bennett lowered his head. "But . . . down there is where—"

"The ship is clear," Hawkins said. "Seal the doors after we leave and don't open them until we get back. No one will bother you."

Bennett still looked unsure, but nodded. "Okay."

"One last thing," Hawkins said to Drake. "On the ship, you're in charge without question. But out there, in the jungle, you need to do what I say. If I say jump, you jump. If I say duck, you duck. Not listening to me could get you killed. Deal?"

Drake stared at Hawkins for just a moment before allowing a slight grin. He took Hawkins's hand and shook it. "Deal."

Hawkins turned to Bray and Joliet, who were standing by the door, looking ready to leave. He appreciated that neither had to be asked to join their little rescue mission. They were good people, and good friends. "Ready to go?"

"Lead the way," Bray said.

While Hawkins, Bray, and Joliet gathered by the door, Drake knelt down next to Jones. "We'll get her back."

Jones mumbled something.

"What was that?" Drake asked.

"I said," Jones said, speaking loudly, "she's already dead."

Drake looked stunned. He just stared at Jones.

"Bullshit," Hawkins said. "She was alive when it took her. That's why you stopped me from shooting."

"Would have been better if you'd shot her," Jones said.

"How can you say that?" Joliet said. "She's your daughter!"

"You didn't see it!" Jones shouted.

Drake took Jones's arm. "Dammit, Harry, what did you see?"

Jones's turned to the captain. "I'm not sure. Something. Large. Fast. Its eyes. They were . . . human. But the rest . . . I don't know. It was dark. But if you'd seen it, you'd know." Tears filled his eyes. "She's dead. My baby is dead." He waggled a finger at Hawkins. "Ask him. He saw it."

"I saw a shadow," Hawkins corrected.

"But you *know*. I can see it in your eyes."

"I've seen enough," Hawkins said. "*It* is big, and fast, and strong. *It* is a killer. And *it* is not a human being. It's an animal. Maybe something like draco-snakes. Another experiment. I don't know. But here's something I do know. The Earth is in the middle of its sixth mass extinction. But the cause isn't climate change, or an asteroid, or a biblical flood. It's mankind. Us. There isn't a creature on this planet we haven't figured out a way to kill. We're the top predator and we're pretty goddamn good at killing things. I don't care if it's a lion with eagle's wings waiting for us, we'll find a way to kill it. And we'll get your girl back."

Jones just shook his head.

Hawkins nearly lost his patience with the man. No matter what he'd seen, how could he give up on his daughter? Hawkins opened the door and stepped into the hallway. "Let's go."

Drake gave Jones's arm a squeeze and stood up. "We'll find her."

As Drake headed for the door, Jones shouted after him. "You're all going to die out there! Don't go, Jon. Don't—"

Hawkins slammed the door closed, cutting off Jones's voice.

"Don't hold it against him," Drake said. "He's speaking out of fear. Jackie's his world. He'll be lost without her."

Hawkins allowed his anger to melt away. He motioned to Bray and Joliet, but spoke to Drake. "Our packs are still ready to go from yesterday. If you want to get your pack ready, we'll find some weapons."

"Thanks for doing this," Drake said. "It's above and beyond. All three of you."

"Thank us when we make it back," Hawkins said. He wouldn't admit it, but Jones had gotten to him. Still, there was little in nature that could take a few .44-caliber rounds and keep coming. He just needed time to pull the trigger. He turned and headed toward the stairs that would take him to the dive room and two high-powered spearguns. "We leave at first light."

TWENTY

The warmth of the new day and scent of flowers in the air did little to calm Hawkins's nerves as he powered the Zodiac across the lagoon. He knew the picturesque setting concealed something much uglier, the evidence of which lay straight ahead, uncovered on the beach.

Hawkins angled the Zodiac away from the mass grave of deformed bodies. He beached the boat and the four passengers hauled it high up onto the sand. As Hawkins tied the Zodiac to a palm tree, Drake inspected the bodies.

"What kind of person would do this?" Drake said.

The captain spoke loud enough for all of them to hear, but Hawkins knew it was a rhetorical question, because none of them had an answer.

"We should cover them," Bray said. "We forgot to yesterday."

"We'll lose daylight," Drake said. "No time."

"He's right," Hawkins said as he unloaded their gear—four backpacks with food, water, medical supplies, and assorted survival gear. He quickly checked over their weapons. They had four "heavy-hitting weapons"—Bray's term—the fire ax, two pneumatic spearguns, and the rifle. They also brought several smaller weapons, including several knives and a can of pepper spray. The ax could be used again and again until the user grew tired, which is why Drake had requested it. The spearguns were high powered and out of the

water would have ridiculous penetration power, but reloading took time as the air pressure needed to be recharged by
a hand pump. Aiming the weapons would also be difficult,
so they were weapons of last resort, to be fired up close and,
most likely, just once. Bray and Joliet agreed to carry the
spearguns.

Hawkins slung the rifle over his shoulder. With plenty of
hunting experience under his belt thanks to Howie Good-
Tracks, Hawkins was the obvious choice. The Remington
lever-action rifle held ten rounds, which was nice, but was
considered a short-range weapon. The range didn't concern
Hawkins, though. The one-hundred-yard reach was far better than anything else in their arsenal and they weren't likely
to have a hundred-yard view once they entered the jungle. The
only real drawback was that he had only ten extra rounds.
Twenty shots total. Against one adversary, they'd be enough,
but he wasn't sure if they were dealing with a larger population. If they were, twenty rounds might not do the trick.

Hawkins looked at the crescent-shaped beach that wrapped
around the lagoon. There was enough gray sand to conceal
hundreds more bodies. The thought of it sent a chill up his
back. Shaking off the image, Hawkins tossed a backpack to
Bray. "The dead can wait. Time to go."

He headed for the jungle's edge while the others grabbed
their gear. He slid past some brush and stepped into the canopy's shade. The jungle seemed different. Not as quiet. He
could hear things moving. Distant calls. They'd spooked the
island's natives when they'd first arrived, but the creatures
had either grown accustomed to their presence or no longer
considered them a threat after they'd been chased away by the
draco-snakes.

Hawkins scanned the area, looking for the yellow- and
black-banded creatures. Part of him hoped they would attack now. He'd much rather fight them with his energy high,
weapon fully loaded, and the bright beach nearby if the fight
went south and retreat was required. But he saw nothing but
an endless sea of tree trunks, green leaves, and shifting light
as the morning sun filtered through the foliage.

A hand clasped him on the shoulder. He turned to find Joliet smiling at him. "Ready to go, Ranger."

He nodded. "Stay close. Only speak if you have to. We'll rest at the switchbacks and not a moment sooner." Hawkins took the lead as they entered the jungle. Drake brought up the rear. The group, all dressed in packed cargo shorts and T-shirts, would have looked like vacationers on a hike. The weapons they carried and looks of determination told a different story.

Hawkins kept their pace brisk and steady, but slowed every time he heard something move in the brush, or saw a shift of shadow from above. When they reached the switchbacks, he removed his backpack and helped himself to his canteen while the others caught up. Drake arrived moments later, a layer of sweat covering his forehead. But he seemed oblivious to the heat. His eyes remained wary and on the jungle.

"Have something to drink," Hawkins told the captain.

Without taking his eyes off the jungle, Drake unclipped his canteen, took three long drinks, and put it back. The man's vigilance never wavered.

Hawkins was glad to have him along. He really was a far better choice than Blok.

After a five-minute rest, Hawkins broke his bad news to the group. "We have a problem."

"What is it?" Joliet asked.

"There aren't any tracks," he said.

Joliet pointed to one of the clearly indented footprints left by Kam, or his captor. "What do you mean? Kam's trail is still here."

"Not for Kam," he said. "For whoever took DeWinter. There were no tracks on the beach, either, which means they were covered up. There weren't any broken or bent branches at the jungle's edge. Whoever took DeWinter left no trail. The point is, we might find Kam by following these tracks, but DeWinter could have been taken somewhere else on the island. We don't even know if they were taken by the same person."

"Then what do we do?" Bray asked.

"Only thing we can do," Drake replied. "Follow this trail to the end. If we find Kam, we take him with us. If we don't, we keep looking. It's an island. We'll find something eventually."

"Also," Hawkins said, "we're being followed."

Bray and Joliet both reacted with surprise, craning their heads around in search of their pursuers.

"I don't see anyone," Joliet said.

"Your little friends picked up on us about a half mile back," Drake said. "They're keeping to the trees. Staying mostly out of sight."

Bray and Joliet looked up.

"Why didn't you tell us?" Bray asked. He looked at Drake, but then turned his attention to Hawkins. "Why?"

"They're keeping to themselves," Hawkins said. "I didn't want to spook you. When the adrenaline rush wore off, you'd have grown tired quickly."

Bray looked dubious, but relented. "Okay. Fine. But why are you telling us now?"

"Just about to ask him the same thing myself," Drake said, taking his eyes off the jungle just long enough to give Hawkins a stern look.

"Because," Hawkins said, "when they attacked Joliet and me yesterday, it wasn't to eat us. We're far larger than their normal prey."

"Then why attack?" Bray asked.

"They're territorial," Hawkins said. "The beach is the edge of their territory."

"They were escorting us out!" Joliet said.

Hawkins nodded. "And letting us know we weren't welcome. Which is part of the problem. Returning has pissed them off even more."

"And the second part?" Drake asked.

"I'm pretty sure the switchbacks are the inland edge of their territory, at least in this part of the jungle."

"Why is that?" Drake asked.

"Dracos can't glide up," Bray said.

Hawkins gave a nod. "Exactly. This is where they started following us yesterday. I'm telling you because they might come at us again when we leave their territory."

Bray looked back up. "Okay, so what's the plan?"

A shadow shifted overhead. Bray aimed at it, but nothing was there.

The sound of claws on tree bark filled the air.

Leaves rustled overhead.

Low vegetation shook.

"The plan," Hawkins said, stepping to the first of several switchback rises, "is to run like hell. Go!"

He sprinted up the first rise with the group close behind. But they weren't alone. A chorus of angry shrieks rang out behind them.

Waves of draco-snakes descended like a squadron of kamikaze fighter jets.

TWENTY-ONE

Knowing it would be nearly impossible to shoot one of the fast-moving draco-snakes with the rifle while running, Hawkins turned it around and wielded it like a club. A shriek drew his eyes up. A large chimera specimen fell toward him, wings tucked under its belly, limbs pulled in tight, jaw unhinged and open. It fell like a missile with fangs, straight for Hawkins's face.

Hawkins swung up with the rifle, but what should have been a direct hit missed completely. The lizard extended its wings with an audible *fwap*. With a twist of its head, the creature spun away, sailing downhill until it clung to the side of a tall palm.

He couldn't decide if they were smart or just easily intimidated. Either way, swinging the rifle around seemed to keep the creatures at bay. "Stay aggressive and they'll keep back," he shouted to the group behind him.

Just as the words exited his mouth he felt an impact on his left shoulder. He turned to find a draco-snake clinging to him. A line of sharp pinpricks stung his flesh as the creature's needle-sharp claws slipped through the fabric of his olive green T-shirt just as easily as it did his skin. But the sting of his pierced arm was quickly forgotten as he saw a pair of short fangs dripping venom just inches from his face.

Something coughed behind him and suddenly the draco-snake was no longer there. Hawkins caught sight of it when the three-foot-long spear through its chest pinned it to a tree with a *thunk*.

Bray frantically tried to reload the second of his three spears, but the ungainly weapon wasn't cooperating.

"No time for that," Hawkins said, heading to the second switchback. "We need to get to higher ground!"

He swung out with the rifle, striking a draco-snake inbound for Bray's head. The butt of the rifle struck the creature's spine with a crack, breaking its back and knocking it to the ground. The creature twitched at Bray's feet.

Bray wound up with the speargun, mimicking Hawkins's rifle club technique. He brought the weapon down with a savage strike, finishing off the draco-snake—and the speargun, which bent at a sharp angle. It wouldn't be firing any more spears. Bray discarded the weapon and held his two spears, one in each hand. They whooshed loudly as he swung them at passing dracos.

"Move it!" Joliet shouted as she passed the pair.

Drake followed her, swinging the ax at everything that got close.

Hawkins and Bray charged up the switchback trail, swinging and shouting. Hawkins knew that anyone, or anything, nearby would hear them coming, but the element of surprise only worked if you were still alive.

With each switchback, they rose higher above sea level so that the draco-snakes at the bottom of the hill would have to scurry up after them. The creatures weren't nearly as fast, or agile, on land as they were in the air. By the time they reached the fifth switchback, the creatures had all but vanished. Only their angry shrieks from below remained.

Propelled by adrenaline, the group kept a swift pace to the top of the hill. Hawkins retook the lead as they approached the pillbox clearing. Moving more slowly, he shouldered the rifle and scanned the area. Seeing no danger, he lowered the weapon, stumbled into the clearing, and sat down in the neatly trimmed grass to catch his breath.

Bray sat himself down next to Hawkins, then lay down

on his back and stared at the blue sky above the clearing. "That . . . was awful."

Joliet sat between them, her canteen already at her lips. After taking a long drink, she pointed to Hawkins's arm. "We should patch that up."

Hawkins looked at his shoulder. There were eight overlapping quarter-size bloodstains on his shirt, four on one side, four on the other. He pulled the sleeve up, which stung as the coagulated blood peeled away with the fabric and started the bleeding anew.

"So this is the pillbox," Drake said. He looked it over and stepped inside.

Bray turned his head toward the small bunker. "You did a good job with the sketch. Looks like the vines have shifted, though. The numbers are covered."

Joliet took a small first-aid kit from her backpack and shuffled closer to Hawkins. She inspected the wounds, poking the skin around them. "Well, I don't think you'll need stitches, which is good because I don't know how to give them."

She let go of the shirt to clean the wound, but the fabric sprang down, making the job difficult. "Take off your shirt."

"You sure that's necessary?" Hawkins asked.

"Girl asks him to undress and he asks if it's necessary," Bray said.

"Shut up, Eight," Hawkins said.

"Just stating the obvious. She's clearly—"

"Shut up, Bob," Joliet said, a little more forcefully than Hawkins.

Hawkins started to remove his shirt.

Bray turned his head to the sky once more. "I'll just lie here and—"

"Oh my God."

Bray turned to the sound of Joliet's voice. Her eyes were locked on Hawkins's chest and the four long scars etched across it. Bray sat up fast. "Holy shit. What did that?"

"You've never seen him without a shirt on?" Joliet asked.

Bray shook his head no. "Never without a T-shirt. The hell did that to you, Ranger?"

"Later," Hawkins said.

Bray raised a single eyebrow. "Ask yourself this question: Will Bob ever stop asking me about my big-ass freaky scars?"

Hawkins sighed. Bray was persistent like no one else on the planet. He wouldn't have a moment's peace until he told the man the truth. "Grizzly bear."

"Geez," Bray said. "I know you were a ranger, but shit, you stood up to a grizzly?"

"Shouldn't have," Hawkins said. "We could have gone our separate ways, but I'd lost respect for nature. It's not something I'm proud of."

"Not something you're proud of—holy shit, did you *win*?"

"Bray . . ." Joliet said, her tone a warning. "Let it be."

Hawkins was lost in the memory as he spoke. "I killed it." He drew his hunting knife. "With this."

Bray smiled wide. "Your parents should have named you John Rambo."

"What I did was wrong," Hawkins said.

"What? Why?" Bray asked. "A bear attacked you. You defended yourself."

"Actually," Hawkins said, "it was the other way around."

"*What?*" Joliet said.

Even Drake looked surprised.

"I was taught how to fight predators by Howie Good-Tracks, an elder in the Ute tribe. After my father headed for the hills and Howie's son died, we kind of adopted each other. Howie taught me that when a predator attacks, the best way to defend yourself is to be the more aggressive predator. If you're a dangerous meal, most animals will back down. But that's not what happened. The bear didn't attack me. I attacked it. I killed it. And I shouldn't have."

A weight fell over the group. Bray didn't say another word. Joliet silently finished patching up Hawkins's shoulder. When the two long bandages were taped in place, she quietly said, "You can put your shirt back on."

Hawkins slipped into his shirt and pulled it over the old wound. "Thanks," he said to Joliet.

"Did you say something about Japanese characters?" Drake asked as he strolled out of the pillbox.

"Above the door," Bray said. "But we don't know Japanese, so we couldn't read them."

Hawkins stood up and rolled his shoulder. The wounds still stung, but the bandages felt secure. "Meant to show you earlier, but—well, you know what happened."

Drake moved the fallen vines to the side. The muscles in his face tensed. "Seven thirty-one."

Bray gasped and then choked. After a brief coughing fit, he said, "What? What did you just say?"

Drake looked grim as he spoke the words again. "Seven thirty-one."

Bray looked like he'd been sucker punched in the gut. "You're sure?"

"Wish I wasn't," Drake said.

Hawkins and Joliet just stared dumbly at the pair.

"Seriously?" Bray said. "This doesn't ring a bell for you two? *Unit* Seven thirty-one."

When they didn't reply, Bray stood, walked to the pillbox, and looked at the numbers again. He shook his head. "Chapter twelve. *Sinister Science*. Did *anyone* read my book?"

No one had. He sighed. "There have been several nations and individuals who have done horrible things in the name of biological scientific progress throughout history. But none hold a candle to Unit Seven thirty-one. They were Japan's covert R and D division during World War Two. They performed sadistic experiments on human beings."

"The Japanese tend to gloss over that bit of their past," Drake said. "They'd prefer it didn't exist. A lot of Japanese know nothing about it. Most schools even teach that the U.S. was the aggressor in the Second World War. Modern Japan has very little in common with the 1940s version. It was a dark time. They fought ruthlessly with little regard for the sanctity of human life, on the battlefield or in the laboratory.

Was kind of a mass corruption that sometimes happens to nations."

"Like Nazi Germany?" Hawkins asked.

"I don't recall the Nazis eating POWs, conquered peoples, or little girls," Drake said.

Joliet looked horrified. "You can't be serious."

"He's right," Bray said. "Once again, you'd know this if you read my book. Widespread Japanese cannibalism was proven during the War Crimes Trials after the war. Japanese soldiers could eat POWs and locals, but not Japanese dead. It was *policy*. Like what I was saying to Bennett before— they dehumanized human beings outside their race. Eating people became no different than eating a cow." Bray shook his head. "And that was just the regular military, never mind Unit Seven thirty-one. The Nazis did similar experiments, sure. Tested the effects of chemical and biological agents. They froze people's limbs and rapidly heated them. But they were also fond of performing live vivisections. Liked to see working organs. Beating hearts. Nasty shit. They'd remove the organs, or limbs, and the victims had to *watch*. Test subjects were usually Chinese since the unit was based in China, but they also experimented on POWs, including Americans, and women, and children. Even pregnant women. Nothing was off limits."

"The people on the beach," Joliet said.

"I don't know why I didn't think of it then, but Unit Seven thirty-one also experimented with repositioning limbs, and switching limbs, and organs between bodies, including animals. If it were just the numbers, I might be able to write it off, but when you take the bodies into consideration—"

"And the chimeras," Hawkins said.

"And the sea turtle," Joliet added.

"This island must have been a second Unit Seven thirty-one base that was never discovered. Given the sophistication of the Drakes—"

Drake cleared his throat.

"The dracos, I'd say they kept operating for some time after the war."

"Considering we've got two people missing," Drake said, "I'd say they never stopped operating."

Bray's face contorted with a look of extreme confusion.

"What now?" Drake asked.

Joliet stepped toward Bray. "Bob?"

"You feeling okay, Eight?" Hawkins asked.

Bray raised a hand and pointed past the three of them, toward the opposite side of the clearing.

Hawkins spun around fast. He raised his rifle, braced it against his shoulder, and took aim at the creature standing there. But he didn't pull the trigger.

"Umm," Bray said. "Was that goat here before?"

TWENTY-TWO

The goat returned the group's silent stare, slowly chewing on a long strand of dry grass like a hillbilly named Bubba sitting on a front porch. Hawkins half expected the thing to say, "Git off my land," but the goat just offered a feeble bleat and went back to chewing, pulling the grass into its mouth, inch by inch, with its tongue. As a child, Hawkins had always felt unnerved by goats' rectangular pupils. He'd overcome the fear as an adult, facing down far worse than goats, but when this goat craned its head slightly and locked eyes with his, Hawkins felt the childhood paranoia return.

The all-white goat with five-inch-long curled horns stood just three feet tall and sported an impressive potbelly and full-looking udder. Hawkins glanced at the udder and re-membered Bray's story about spider silk-producing goats. Knowing goats could jump great distances from an idle posi-tion and having witnessed the flying draco-snakes, he half expected the goat to leap up and swing around on spiderwebs shot from its swollen udder. But it just stood there, chewing.

The goat took a step forward, jangling a small bell at-tached to a red plastic band wrapped around its neck. Hawkins focused on the collar. It looked familiar. It looked . . . "Just like the one on the turtle."

"What?" Joliet asked.

"The collar," Hawkins said. It looks like the plastic band we found around the loggerhead's midsection."

Joliet shifted, but her movement brought the goat's attention to her and she couldn't get a better view.

Bray started calling to the goat the way someone might call a dog, with clicks and squeaks. He knelt down on a knee. "My uncle owned a farm in New Hampshire. Alpacas, llamas, and goats. Weird combination, but they did okay." He opened his pack and began rummaging through it. "Lots of goat's milk products. Soap. Cheese. Stuff like that. My parents sent me there for a few weeks. To teach me how to work hard. But all I really learned is that I hated farming"—he began unwrapping something—"and that goats have an affinity for oats, sugar, and anything sweet."

Bray held out the unwrapped chocolate-chip granola bar and started clicking at the goat once more. "Come on, girl."

"Don't think a goat living on an island in the middle of the Pacific will know what a granola bar is," Drake said.

"Doesn't need to," Bray said. "Goats have an excellent sense of smell. Eyesight, too. Those rectangular pupils give it crazy night vision."

The goat cocked its head to the side, flaring its nostrils. Then, with a sharp bleat, it trotted to Bray and began nibbling on the end of the crunchy snack. Bray pet the goat's back. "Good girl." He looked to Hawkins. "She won't move until the bar is gone."

Hawkins wasted no time inspecting the collar and quickly confirmed his suspicions. "Same red plastic. Japanese text, too, though the characters are different. Definitely doesn't say 'broccoli' again."

"Broccoli?" Drake asked.

Joliet knelt next to the goat and stroked its side. As her hand passed over the goat's fur, the skin beneath it rippled, as though twitching with excitement. "It's what Kam said was written on the plastic band we took off the turtle." She gave the goat a gentle scratch behind its ear and it paused eating to let out an ecstatic bleat. "I don't think this goat has ever been petted before."

"Let me have a look," Drake said, stepping up next to the goat.

Something about Drake put the goat on edge. It shifted away from him, but the granola bar kept it from fleeing. When Drake stood still, hands on knees looking at the collar, the goat relaxed and focused on its meal.

"Goat three hundred fourteen," Drake said.

Bray turned to the captain. "Huh?"

"That's what the collar says," Drake explained.

Bray looked doubtful. "How well do you speak Japanese?"

With a sigh, Drake explained. "Passable, but not fluent. I met my wife in Japan. Learned the language so I could speak to her parents. Ask her father's permission. Do things right."

"Didn't know you were married," Bray said.

As soon as the words escaped Bray's mouth, Hawkins saw the subtle change in Drake's expression and knew the truth before the man spoke. "I'm not. She died ten years ago. And before you ask, it was cancer. The fast, merciful kind. If there is such a thing, but it took her just the same."

Bray lowered his eyes to the ground. "Sorry."

"Ten years ago," Joliet said. "That's when you became captain of the *Magellan*."

Drake gave a nod. "Called in a favor." He looked at Hawkins. "Needed to escape." He stood and stepped away from the goat. "Now, if we're done with our trip down memory lane, what's the big deal about the collar, other than the fact that it confirms the island is populated by people with access to the outside world?"

Hawkins hadn't thought about the ramifications of the people here having plastic. Drake was right. Whoever lived here hadn't been isolated since World War II, but that didn't mean they weren't off-their-rockers crazy. "I'm not sure."

"I know what it means," Bray said, petting the goat. He waited for the others to look at him and then said, "It means Kam lied. The band around the turtle didn't say 'broccoli.'"

Joliet scoffed. "There's no way to know that."

The goat finished with the first of the two crunchy granola bars. Bray offered it the second, which it happily accepted. "Why would a plastic band that matches the one around this goat, which is accurately labeled 'goat,' identify a logger-head turtle as 'broccoli'?"

"There's probably a hundred different possibilities," Joliet said.

"Including that Kam lied," Bray said. "You agree that the turtle had been experimented on. The tracker in its gut was proof of that. Given what we found on the beach, the presence of the dracos, and now a matching collar makes a pretty air-tight case that whoever screwed with the turtle is, or was, on this island. If they took the time to accurately label a goat, why call a turtle broccoli?"

"Could have been to throw off anyone that found the turtle," Drake offered.

Bray nodded his agreement. "One of the hundred possibilities. But whoever experimented on the turtle didn't expect the tracker to fail. They might not have intended it to live more than a year or two before recapturing it. Even then, I doubt they expected it to survive into adulthood. Just doesn't make sense to me. It's . . . unscientific."

"Experimental science is full of code names," Joliet said. "Especially those born out of the Second World War."

"I'll give you that," Bray said as the goat finished the second bar. He stood up. "But I'm not sure 'Project Broccoli' has much of a ring to it, especially if we're talking about Unit Seven thirty-one, whose members subscribed to the bushido code just as much, if not more so, as the soldiers who eviscerated themselves after losing a battle."

Both sides of the argument made at least some kind of sense, but everything was based on pure speculation and Hawkins knew that did no one any good. "How about this? We'll ask Kam when we find him."

"Works for me," Drake said. "It's time we got moving and our guide is waiting for us."

The goat's bell jangled as it wandered to the hidden path at the edge of the clearing. It paused at the jungle's edge and bleated at them.

Bray zipped up his backpack. "Hold on, Pi."

"Pi?" Hawkins asked.

"Three fourteen," Bray said. "Three point one four. Pi. It's amazing you can tie your shoes, Ranger." He stood and headed for the goat, which turned and entered the jungle.

"We're being led by a goat," Joliet said. "Great."

"It's not leading us," Hawkins said. "Just happens to be headed in the same direction." He chased after Bray, reclaiming his position on point. He paused at the clearing's edge and peered into the canopy-dimmed jungle. Once his eyes adjusted, he saw the goat waiting for them twenty feet down a switchback trail. It stood next to a footprint.

Hawkins shook his head and thought, *We* are *being led by a goat.* And he was actually okay with that. The bell jangling around the goat's neck would make it a predator's first target, and would help disguise their approach to anything or anyone that recognized the sound. In fact, if they could get the bell off the goat, Hawkins thought it might be a good idea to take it. But for now, they'd follow the goat, as long as it didn't start swinging from spiderwebs or sprout sea snake fangs.

TWENTY-THREE

As the group neared the bottom the switchback trail on the opposite side of the hill, Hawkins kept expecting an attack. The longer the goat's bell rang, the more it sounded like a dinner bell. The high-pitched voice of his childhood neighbor calling her cat filled his thoughts. "Here, Draco! Come on! Time for din-din."

But they were never bothered.

"Has anyone seen a draco-snake?" Bray asked.

"Not a one," Hawkins replied. "Doesn't mean they're not there, though. I think they can hide pretty well when they want to."

"It's possible we're out of their territory," Joliet said.

Hawkins shook his head. He'd thought of that, too, but the theory had flaws. "Based on their size and the number of individuals we saw, I'd guess the whole island is technically their territory. Would have to be to support that many."

"Maybe they just lost our scent when we went over the hilltop," Bray said.

"I don't think so," Hawkins said.

Bray shook his open hands at Hawkins. "Then enlighten us, O wise wilderness sage."

Drake's voice startled them all when he spoke from the back of the group. "It's the bell."

"The bell?" Bray sounded incredulous.

Before Bray could launch into why he thought that was a

stupid idea, Hawkins spoke up. "Actually, I agree. The dracos are either afraid of the goat for some reason, and the bell warns them away, or they've been trained to avoid the bell."

"Huh. Like a Pavlovian response?" Bray said. "So instead of salivating when they hear the bell, they run for the hills, or the trees, in this case."

"Something like that," Hawkins said. "Either way, I think we should stick close to our goat friend."

"Or take the bell," Drake offered.

Hawkins nodded. "If we have to. But I couldn't use the rifle. It would give away our position." He motioned to the harpoon in Joliet's hands. "We'd have to use that."

Joliet looked mortified. "I'm *not* shooting the goat."

"Her name is Pi," Bray said. He sounded serious, but the grin on his face said otherwise.

"I'll take care of it," Drake said.

As Hawkins rounded a stand of palms at the corner of the last switchback, he froze. He thrust an open palm toward the others, stopping them in their tracks.

"What is it?" Joliet whispered.

Hawkins gestured with his hand like he was ringing a bell.

Eyes widened.

The bell had fallen silent.

With the rifle at his shoulder, Hawkins crept around the sharp turn in the trail. When he saw what lay ahead, he relaxed his grip on the rifle, but didn't lower it. Pi stood at the center of the trail, her white tail twitching. She turned her head slightly and lifted her nose.

Hawkins wasn't sure if the goat smelled something dangerous, or was tasting the air for a potential snack, but he suspected the first option. Pi hadn't stopped eating the whole way down the hill. If she took this route often, they probably had her to thank for keeping the path so pristine. At times he felt like the path was part of some kind of nature park. That there were switchbacks meant the trail had been created by men, but its current condition was thanks to Pi, and any other goats on the island.

With a bleat, Pi expressed either her disinterest in the scent or the all clear. She continued her casual pace into the jungle, where the path leveled out and meandered into the distance.

Hawkins followed, but kept the rifle at the ready and quickly scanned their new surroundings. The scenery here looked similar to the jungle on the other side of the hill, but there were fewer palms and larger, leafy trees with tangling roots, branches, and vines. The air felt more humid here, if such a thing were possible, and the air lacked any trace of the ocean's salty scent. If he didn't know better, he'd have thought they were deep in the Amazon jungle. Of course, the Amazon is alive with noise. Here, there wasn't much to hear beyond the clang of Pi's bell.

When Hawkins reached the spot where Pi had paused, he stopped and smelled the air for himself. There was a subtle change. A slight coolness on the breeze coupled with something fresh. Is this what the goat smelled? He looked down and saw a pair of bare human footprints. Whoever had left them, Kam or his kidnapper, had stopped here, too.

But why?

"I hear water," Joliet said, stepping up next to Hawkins.

Hawkins hadn't heard anything, but focused on his ears anyway. And then he heard it. A faint, monotone static. "Sounds like a river."

"On an island?" Bray asked.

"It's not common," Joliet said. "But I think some volcanic islands have fresh water springs. And Mark *did* see a body of water separated from the ocean. Could just be overflow from the storm."

Drake pushed past them. "It's going to take months to find anyone if you all keep stopping to discuss the island and its critters. Best way to find the answers is to keep moving." He continued down the path with his fire ax perched on his shoulder.

The man had a point. No one argued. Hawkins motioned for the others to follow them and he took up the rear. He was going to suggest the position change anyway. If the bell really was a deterrent, an attack would come from behind.

And if that happened, he wanted to respond quickly with the rifle.

They walked for ten minutes. The static hiss became a roar. The air grew cooler. And the darkness of the jungle gave way to sunlight pouring through the open canopy above the river.

After passing through a field of waist-high ferns, the moist earth path gave way to gray sand. The ten-foot-long beach was hemmed in by lush plants that grew along the banks of a narrow but fast-moving river. But the most dramatic feature of the river was a waterfall emptying into the river from a forty-foot cliff to their left. A rainbow arced through the mist that clung to their skin and saturated their clothes. A series of vertical ridges covered the dark gray cliff face. They looked unnatural, almost manmade—like incredibly tall, square organ pipes—but Hawkins had seen volcanic formations like this before. Plants clung to every ledge, lavishing in the combination of mist and bright sunlight.

Pi, however, was on edge. The goat stopped several feet short of the water. Her thighs rippled with tension as though ready to spring away. The goat seemed fearless on land, but it definitely didn't like the water.

Or whatever it thought might be in the water.

"Stay back from the river," Hawkins said quickly.

Bray and Joliet jumped back quickly. Drake responded less slowly, but stepped back and readied his ax.

Pi's large belly bounced as she sniffed the air. Her eyes remained locked on the water.

"What's that?" Joliet asked. She had a hand over her eyes, blocking out the sun as she looked up toward the top of the waterfall. "Is that a rock?"

Hawkins followed her eyes up. At first he couldn't see anything, but then he saw an aberration between the mist and the jungle at the top of the cliff. The gray coloration looked lighter than the stone of the cliff, and far smoother. They'd already seen something similar. "Another pillbox."

He was going to suggest they check it out, but Pi gave a

bleat and started through the water. He thought the goat would have to swim across, but it never sank more than knee deep. Hawkins edged up to the water's edge. To his left, the waterfall basin was dark, turbulent, and coated in mist. Anything could be down there and he'd never know it. To his right, the river flowed smooth and fast, five feet deep, but clear. But directly ahead, a smooth gray surface cut across the river. "Looks like a concrete bridge. The water must be high from the storm. It's covered by a few inches of water."

Hawkins took a step onto the concrete. It felt solid beneath his feet, but he could feel the tug of fast-moving water on his lower legs. He made his way across and then waved for the others to follow. Bray and Joliet quickly joined him on the other side. Drake took one last look around and started across.

When Drake reached the halfway mark, Pi, who had continued along the path into the jungle on the other side, began bleating. The rapid-fire, high-pitched staccato call from the goat sounded like nothing Hawkins had ever heard before, but apparently Bray had.

"It's a warning call!" Bray shouted. "The goats on the farm did that when a fox or coyote came near. Get out of the water!"

Drake heeded the warning and focused on crossing the remainder of the river. To his credit, he didn't panic or move too fast. A misstep would send him into the water.

Joliet stabbed a finger to the river beyond Drake. "Oh my God, what is that?"

Hawkins saw an impossibly large shape slipping through the water. It glided toward Drake with little effort. He took aim with his rifle, but didn't fire.

"Shoot it!" Bray shouted.

Drake turned to look and slowed as he did.

"Shoot!" Bray repeated.

"Bullets don't penetrate water," Hawkins said in a stern voice. "Have to wait for it to surface. Captain, move your ass!"

With a burst of speed, the shape closed in.

Drake discarded his previous caution and ran through the shin-deep water.

Tracking the creature's swift passage through the water, Hawkins could see it would reach Drake before he made it to the shore. Seeing just one option available to him, Hawkins lowered the rifle—

—and dropped it to the ground.

TWENTY-FOUR

As the rifle fell to the ground at Hawkins's feet, he twisted around and snatched the speargun from Joliet's hand. She had already begun to take aim, but he couldn't risk her missing the shot. Unlike the rifle, there would only be time to get off a single shot. They had replacement spears, but reloading was time consuming and cumbersome. And while he could squeeze off ten shots with the rifle in just as many seconds, water did a remarkable job stopping bullets. The speargun, on the other hand, was designed to slip through water with ease.

Looking down the length of the speargun, Hawkins took aim at the submerged creature surging toward Drake. Only a few feet separated the pair.

He fired.

With a puff of compressed air, the spear shot away. The three-foot-long metal rod passed beneath Drake's arm as he ran. It found the water a fraction of a second later and pierced the surface like no bullet could. There was a snapping sound as the sharp tip of the spear struck the creature's midsection—and ricocheted away toward the opposite bank.

Realizing that neither spear nor bullet would stop the creature in time, Hawkins discarded the weapon and lunged toward Drake. He reached out his hands, intending to yank Drake forward and hopefully out of reach.

He glanced down and saw the large shape in the water

had stopped moving forward. But then a reptilian snout broke the surface. Green-skin-rimmed nostrils snapped open as the creature took a breath. Hawkins felt Drake's fingers reach his and began wrapping his hands around the other man's wrists.

Water exploded as the creature rose up and revealed itself. A crocodile. He wasn't sure exactly what species of croc, but it was easily eighteen feet long and would have no trouble devouring a man. Hawkins saw the long mouth lined with thumb-size teeth snap open. But still, the apex predator didn't move in to strike.

Is it just trying to scare us out of its territory?

The question was just a flash in his mind, answered nearly at the same moment he thought it. The flesh at the back of the croc's throat, where its tongue should have been, expanded. Rolls of undulating muscle unfurled in a flash. At first, Hawkins thought the croc was regurgitating a meal, but then he saw it move. Two long, squid tentacles unfurled from the croc's mouth, slipping out of cavities at the back of its mouth. As they emerged, the limbs began twisting and shaking like wounded snakes. At the center of the throat, Hawkins saw that where the croc's esophagus should be there was a beak. Loud clicks came from the croc's mouth as the beak repeatedly opened and snapped closed.

Another chimera. This one a vile perversion of nature.

The twin tentacles shook with tension and then sprang from the reptile's mouth. Part of Hawkins's mind registered seeing the flesh stretch out toward Drake, but then he had his arms locked with Drake's and yanked.

A loud slap filled the air as Hawkins pulled Drake beyond the waterline. The two men began to fall back but stopped halfway to the ground. Hawkins looked into Drake's eyes and for the first time saw fear. Then he saw why. Drake's right leg was being lifted off the ground. There was a tug and Hawkins was pulled upright.

Hawkins looked over Drake's shoulder. The croc sat in the river, its yellow eyes locked on Drake. Two long, pale tentacles as thick as Hawkins's forearm stretched between the crocodile's mouth and Drake's leg. The two tentacle clubs were stuck to Drake's calf. And if they were anything like actual squid tentacles, they'd have buried rows of sharp hooks into the meat of Drake's leg.

And then, it pulled.

Hard.

"Bray!" Hawkins shouted as he felt himself lean forward.

The big man was there in an instant. Bray wrapped his arms around Hawkins's waist, locked his hands together, and fell back. The extra two hundred-plus pounds had an immediate effect. The three men once again began to fall back toward shore, but Bray's back never hit the ground. They were held at an angle, frozen in midair, as though by some kind of magnetic force.

With the tug-of-war at a momentary standstill, Hawkins searched for a solution.

Joliet was one step ahead of him.

The report from the rifle ripped through the jungle like thunder. The sudden sound was so loud that everyone, including the crocodile, flinched.

"I hit it, but I don't think it's hurt!" Joliet said, sounding out of breath. "Most of the body is under water." She pulled the rifle lever down, expelling the spent round and chambering another.

The second shot had little effect on the men. They were expecting it. But the crocodile lurched away from the sound. The sudden tug pulled Hawkins and Bray upright again.

The tug-of-war was about to become a no-contest event. The tentacles were strong enough to pull a lone man off his feet, but had trouble with two, and reached a stalemate with three. But flinching from the gunfire had revealed the predator's ace up its sleeve. With the limbs stretched to their maximum range, all the crocodile had to do was move backward. Three men couldn't compete with eighteen feet of prehistoric muscle.

Drake shouted in pain as the croc pulled and the men dug their feet in and leaned back.

Hawkins nearly cried out in pain, too. Drake's huge hands were crushing his wrists.

"Hawkins," Drake said through gritted teeth. "Let me go."

"Not a chance," Hawkins said.

"It will kill us all." Drake's grip loosened.

There was no way in hell Hawkins would let go of Drake. Even if it was the right thing to do, he couldn't. Howie's advice returned in a flash. "When you have no choice," Howie had said. "When flight is impossible. Turn and fight. *Attack*. Strike hard and you will survive. Hold back and you'll be lunch." Hawkins had incorrectly applied that advice in the past, but now seemed the perfect example of when to heed it.

The problem was that to be aggressive in this situation meant letting go of Drake. He had no doubt that if he let go, Drake would be pulled into the croc's jaws before he could do anything about it.

At the moment, they were in Joliet's hands.

"Aim for the tentacles!" Hawkins said.

The shot echoed off the cliff. Then a fourth. And a fifth.

"I can't hit it!" Joliet shouted. She stood just short of the water. The croc's tentacles were close enough that she could have nearly placed the barrel against one of them, but the crocodile had begun to thrash, yanking its limbs—and Drake's leg—back and forth. Shooting Drake along with the monster was a very real possibility.

An idea, as crazy as it was stupid, came to Hawkins. But he didn't see any other choice and his feet were now in a half foot of water to the side of the submerged concrete bridge. Drake was even deeper. In a moment, the crocodile would be able to reverse course and quickly catch them.

A tearing sound preceded a sharp scream from Drake. A portion of the large, tentacle clubs had come free, but left a series of open puncture wounds in their wake. Blood oozed from the line of holes.

Drake's grip loosened. "Let go."

Hawkins ignored him. "Bray, when I say, let go of both of us."

"But—"

"Just do it!"

Crack! Another shot. Another miss.

Hawkins let go of Drake with his right hand and reached down for his hunting knife, sheathed on his belt. The strain on his left arm quickly became unbearable, but at least Drake, who had seen him go for the knife, held on with both hands. With his shoulder feeling like it was about to be popped from its socket, Hawkins shouted, "Bray, now!"

Bray unlocked his arms and opened them. The result was something like the freeing of a catapult arm. Drake and Hawkins were suddenly airborne. But they were far from helpless. As the croc pulled them in, Drake and Hawkins pulled, as well. The combination of forces acted like the classic roller derby slingshot, propelling Hawkins *over* Drake.

As Hawkins overtook Drake, he looked down and saw the tentacles attached to Drake's leg. He also saw the large jaws and twitching beak awaiting them. In fact, he was now poised to enter the monster's jaws *before* Drake, and head-first.

Joliet's fear-filled voice shouted from shore. "Mark!"

Hawkins took careful aim and swung out with the knife. He felt a gentle tug on the blade, but the sharp metal had no trouble slicing through the soft squid flesh. A deep red, two-inch-deep wound opened up on one of the limbs and then began to tear.

Both tentacles instantly released and shot back into the croc's mouth as it thrashed and sped away. While apex predators like the crocodile—and squid—are essentially killing machines, they're also terribly fearful of injury.

Without the limbs pulling them, gravity became the dominant force. Hawkins and Drake plunged into the river. Hawkins surfaced a few feet beyond the concrete bridge. Drake came up next to him. Without asking if the man was all right, Hawkins shoved him toward the bridge, where Bray waited to pull them out. The current was strong, but they could move against it. Slowly.

Bray caught hold of Drake's hand and pulled him onto the bridge.

"Go!" Hawkins shouted, nearly at the bridge. He got his

hands on top of the bridge and began pulling himself up while the other two men ran to shore. He heaved on shaky arms, fighting the swifter current flowing over the bridge, and pulled himself halfway up.

Crack! The rifle shot startled him more than before and he nearly fell back in. But Joliet's next words spurred him forward. "It's coming back!"

With a quick glance back, Hawkins saw a large, triangular head closing the distance.

Crack! A geyser of water erupted next to the croc.

There was no time for Hawkins to climb atop the bridge and flee to shore. At best, he'd wind up in the same situation as Drake. At worst, he'd be plucked from the bridge and eaten. He'd injured one of the tentacles, so the crocodile might not use its long-range weapon, but the giant reptile wouldn't have much trouble snatching him from the bridge old-school croc style. If it worked on zebras, it would work on a man.

So instead of standing and making himself a larger target, he slipped over the top of the concrete bridge and pushed himself into the waterfall's basin. Partly concealed in mist, he turned around and shouted. Massive jaws snapped closed and stopped just short of his face. The crocodile had bitten the bridge. As the croc let go and moved back, Hawkins fled in the only direction left available to him.

Down.

TWENTY-FIVE

The water pounding down from the waterfall above the basin helped propel Hawkins deeper. He followed the bowl-shaped slope of the basin toward the bottom. He hoped that the crocodile, whose eyes were positioned atop its head for spotting prey on or near the surface, wouldn't spot him below.

A look up told him his plan was working. The silhouette of the croc circled the basin above him. Its massive body blocked out the already diffuse sunlight and cast swirling shadows on the basin walls. Hawkins paused his descent, willing the croc to give up the hunt. He couldn't hold his breath forever.

He quickly noticed that the crocodile's search pattern brought it deeper with each pass. It would soon be able to spot him.

And then, Hawkins thought, *I'll be lunch.*

He pushed deeper. Water pressure squeezed his ears and compressed his chest. He let out some air. The bubbles made for the surface and as they passed the croc, it snapped at them.

Hawkins didn't watch to see if the predator was smart enough to realize the bubbles had come from him. He just kicked for the bottom, which he could see just ten feet below. He'd have nowhere left to hide, but figured he could push off and maybe sneak past the croc long enough to reach the surface. He doubted it, though.

As he neared the bottom, he noticed it looked different from the walls. The water depth coupled with the turbulent surface conditions and the croc's shadow had filtered a lot of the sunlight, but the difference in color between the gray stone wall and bright white bottom was easy to see.

Is there sand at the bottom? he wondered, but decided against it. Any silt below the waterfall would most likely be gray, like the volcanic stone that made up the cliff and basin walls. In fact, with the swift current swirling around the basin, he doubted there would be any sand at the bottom at all. *So what is it?*

A shrieking face appeared out of the gloom. He reeled back and let out a bubbly shout. When his mind finally registered that he was looking at a human skull, he calmed, but then cursed himself for shouting. The croc had undoubtedly heard the sound. It had also cost him most of the air remaining in his lungs.

But his thoughts lingered on the skull, and the field of bones surrounding it. *There has to be at least fifty people here*, he thought. The bones covering the basin floor looked deformed. *Not deformed*, Hawkins realized, *worn down, like sea glass. These bones have been here for a long time.*

Hawkins dug an arm into the loose collection of bones and found that they shifted easily. He reached down to his shoulder and didn't find the bottom. His guess about the number of bodies lodged at the bottom of the basin had been grossly conservative. *There might be hundreds of bodies!*

A change in water current tickled Hawkins head as a large shadow shifted around him. Without looking back, Hawkins twisted himself down, piercing the layer of bones like a drill. When the shadow returned, he froze. He lay on his back, covered by bones, but with a view of the basin.

The croc swam just a few feet above the bone layer, its head cocked to the side so that it could look down.

It knows I'm down here. It just doesn't know where.

Hawkins jumped when the crocodile lunged out with its

open maw and snatched a skull. The loud snap of the jaws closing on the old bone felt like an electric jolt, but it wasn't nearly as frightening as when the skull imploded under the croc's crushing bite.

With a twitch of its tail, the agitated crocodile surged through the water. Hawkins couldn't tell if the beast was furious, injured, or just impatient, but there was no doubt it was growing more dangerous. It dredged a path through the bone yard, snapping at everything it passed, and sending chunks of white pluming into the basin.

It passed just a few feet to Hawkins's right, pushing a femur hard into his ribs, but the impact didn't hurt nearly as much as the ache in his lungs.

You're going to die down here, he told himself. In a few months his flesh would be picked clean by fish and crocs. In a few years, his bones would be just another polished, water-worn skeleton.

Be aggressive, he thought. *Stop hiding!*

Hawkins clenched his hands and realized that he still held his hunting knife. He looked for the croc. It circled near his head, angling to make a pass. He slowly twisted his hand around, pointing the blade up.

Aggressive. He repeated the thought like a mantra. *Be the more aggressive predator.*

The tip of the croc's jaw appeared over his eyes as it swam just a foot above him.

Aggressive.

The croc's head and neck passed, revealing its true size. The creature could easily fit a man down its gullet.

Attack!

Hawkins thrust the knife up. A momentary resistance of tough crocodilian skin quickly gave way and the seven-and-a-half-inch blade slid into the croc's lower jaw, all the way to the hilt.

The crocodile's reaction was immediate and violent. It thrashed forward, which only increased its pain as the blade cut down the length of its lower jaw. Before Hawkins could withdraw the knife, it struck bone, dug in, and stuck. Unwilling to release the weapon that had now saved his life from *three* top predators, he held on tight.

The croc accelerated through the water like a torpedo bound for the surface. Hawkins was yanked from the bottom, rising with the croc, attached to its belly like a remora on a shark. The pressure on his lungs lifted, but the ache to breathe increased.

The light of day grew brighter as they ascended, then struck him with its full force as he and the croc launched from the water. Hawkins gasped loudly, sucking in air as the panicked reptile continued swishing its mighty tail, propelling them both higher into the air. They crashed through the waterfall's spray, through the rainbow-colored mist, and toward the concrete bridge.

Seeing the bridge, Hawkins wrenched the knife free, pushed away, and twisted around. Had he not turned around, the impact with the concrete bridge might have broken his back. As it was, he took the collision in the gut. What little air had found its way into his lungs was driven out. Pinpoints of multicolored lights danced in his vision, but he managed to cling to the bridge for just a moment, which was long enough to realize the croc had also landed atop the bridge.

The giant continued thrashing as blood dripped from the wound Hawkins had inflicted. But it had no interest in him. It was trying to flee from the more aggressive predator, or the very lucky one—Hawkins couldn't decide. His mind was a fog and his vision fading. He tried to breathe, but his body hadn't recovered from the blow. He slipped back toward the basin, slowed more by the water rushing past him than his grip.

Then something took hold of his wrists. Through pinhole vision he saw Joliet above him, shouting at him. Her voice was indistinct, but he understood what she wanted: a little help. As she pulled him up, he managed to swing a leg up onto the bridge. With Joliet pulling and the water pushing, he soon found himself on his hands and knees on the bridge, gasping for air.

"It's okay," Joliet said. "Just breathe."

After sucking in a few desperate breaths, Hawkins asked, "The croc?"

"Gone," she replied. "Whatever you did to it worked. It took off downstream. What *did* you do to it?"

Hawkins lifted the knife from the water. "I was the more aggressive predator."

She shook her head. "I'm starting to think that knife is lucky."

"You might be right. Where's Drake?"

"Bray took him uphill. Followed the goat."

Hawkins glanced downstream. There was no sign of the crocodile, but that didn't mean there weren't others. If there were, they'd surely be drawn out by all the blood in the water. "We should go."

With Joliet's help, Hawkins made it to shore. He rested again, just long enough to steady his adrenaline shakes and sheathe his knife. Then they started up the hill. The path wound around in a big loop, moving steadily up and around the waterfall. The jungle rose with them, but at the top of the hill, blue sky greeted them. The path exited the jungle and cut through what looked like a manicured lawn. The dirt path shot across the grass, ending at a six-foot-tall chain-link fence.

Beyond the fence sat a concrete building, beneath which the river flowed. The building was large and stark, like something from Cold War Russia. The concrete was worn and barren of any markings. But something about the large structure felt ominous. Had the trail of footprints not led directly to the gate, he might have circumvented the landmark.

Bray emerged from the open doorway, his face ashen. There was no greeting. No relief at seeing Hawkins alive. He simply walked over to them and said, "Guys, you need to see this," and stepped back into the dark entryway that swallowed him whole.

TWENTY-SIX

Hawkins stopped at the chain-link gate. Most of the fence was rusted, but still solid enough. It looked old, but not World War II old. More like 1970s old. He tapped his finger on the razor wire curling along the top of the fence. "Still sharp."

"Still sharp?"Bray said. "That's your big observation? Ranger, this is *modern*. And those"—he pointed to the field on the other side of the fence, and the goats that stood there watching them—"those goats. A shit-ton of goats. What the hell is going down on this island?"

"I know," Hawkins said as coolly as he could. He sounded calm and collected, but on the inside he was freaked out. The draco-snakes he could handle. The croc was worse—horrible in so many ways. But this serene scene? The fence. The goats. It was all so *normal*. And something about that put him on edge worse than nearly being eaten.

The gate was latched shut, but not locked. Hawkins tapped a hinged section of the lower gate with his foot. It swung back and forth like a doggie door.

"That explains how the goats get in and out," Joliet said. She sounded calm, too, but he could hear the tightness in her voice. She was tense. "There have to be at least twenty of them here."

Hawkins looked at the field of trim grass. The expanse, through which the river cut, stretched at least five acres. The sound of ringing bells drew his eyes to the animals. The goats, all similar in size but a variety of black, white, and brown patchwork of fur, foraged, wandered, and occasionally butted heads, oblivious to the dark history of the island. A history that Hawkins feared they were about to get another dose of inside the newly discovered building.

The three-story structure was shaped like half an octagon, but with a square indentation at the core. The river flowed beneath the indentation, turning the lowest floor into a bridge. The roar of the waterfall on the other side of the building was dulled by concrete and forest, but it served as a reminder of the crocodile that lurked nearby.

Every instinct in Hawkins's body was screaming at him to turn and run. Get off the island. But he fought against the urge to flee. He forced himself to unlatch the gate. It squeaked loudly, like a wounded animal, causing the hairs on his arms to rise up.

Joliet stepped through slowly. When Hawkins paused before following, he noticed Bray was looking at his arm and the hair standing on end. Bray leveled a serious stare at him. "Try to hide it all you want, we're both a goat fart away from pissing ourselves."

Hawkins grinned, thankful for Bray's humor. "Let's hope they haven't had too much fiber."

Bray stepped through the gate. "You know that's like all they eat, right?"

Hawkins stepped through and latched it behind them, but it didn't feel like enough. If that croc was out for revenge, it might be able to make short work of the fence. Alligators in Florida seemed to work their way into people's backyards, pools, and houses without too much trouble.

Despite Bray's request that they join them, Hawkins wasn't quite ready to face whatever waited inside. The adrenaline rush of his brush with death still had his muscles twitching. He was on edge and didn't feel ready to deal with more disturbing revelations. He strolled out into the field with Joliet at his side. He closed his eyes and turned his face skyward, absorbing the sun's warmth on his face. *Relax*, he thought, *let the tension go.*

"We've been spotted," Joliet said.

Hawkins opened his eyes and saw the goats staring at him. One by one, they trotted up to Hawkins and Joliet, sniffing, licking, and bleating. And then, as though satisfied with their inspection, the animals went back to their ignorant lives.

"Starting to wish I could trade spots with the goats," Hawkins said. He was starting to feel a little more like himself, but his foot struck something hard. He winced and hopped away.

"What happened?" Joliet asked.

"Stubbed my toe," Hawkins replied while he looked for what he'd kicked. He expected to find a rock, but instead found a cylindrical concrete tube sticking out of the ground. It stood only an inch taller than the grass and was six inches in diameter. He knelt down to look at it.

"What is it?" Joliet asked.

Hawkins shrugged. "No idea."

Joliet pointed to the grass around them. "There's more." She walked in a circle, pointing and counting. "Eighteen of them. Looks like they're arranged around that divot."

Hawkins hadn't noticed the divot. Concealed beneath a layer of grass, the five-foot-wide indentation was hard to spot.

"There are three circles," Joliet continued. "Each one a few feet farther away from the center."

Hawkins was about to say he'd rather not know what this spot had been used for when Bray spoke.

"The concrete cylinders were for replaceable wooden posts. They made them that way because the explosions sometimes broke the posts. So they used strong bases and made the rest replaceable."

Hawkins cringed when Joliet asked, "What explosions?" He didn't want to know.

"Bombs," Bray said. "And grenades. Chemical agents. Biological, too. They bound test subjects to posts at varying distances and then detonated the explosives. The few who survived with nonlethal shrapnel wounds would be operated on and saved. The rest went to the morgue for dissection. They were the lucky ones. The people who survived would be experimented on again." He turned toward the building. "There's more inside."

Hawkins felt the blood drain from his head. *More. God, could it really get worse?*

"Don't really want to see more," he said. He wasn't sure if it was from the knowledge of what went on here or from the adrenaline wearing off, but he felt queasy.

"I don't want to be here any more than you," Bray said. "But I know way more than I want to right now, it's scaring the shit out of me, and I need someone to help make sense of it. Besides, know your enemy, remember?" Bray said.

Hawkins took a deep breath. Bray was right. "Okay, Sun Tzu, point taken. Just give me a minute. Why don't you go in with Eight," he said to Joliet. "Check on Drake."

Joliet began to protest. "But—"

"I need a minute to think," he said. "Just leave the rifle with me."

Joliet took the rifle from her shoulder and handed it to Hawkins. "You're not thinking of heading out on your own, are you?"

He shook his head no. "Impulsive, dangerous decisions are more your style than mine."

She smiled and headed for the door.

"If you spot anything," Bray said, "or need help, fire off a shot and I'll come running."

"Somehow that's not comforting," Hawkins said.

Bray didn't smile. "I'm serious, Ranger. We're going to be lucky if we get off this island alive. You know that, right? Half a day and we've nearly been killed how many times?"

"I know," Hawkins said. "This place is wicked scary."

Bray couldn't help smiling in the face of Hawkins's mimicked Massachusetts accent. "Bastard."

"I'll be fine," Hawkins said as Bray headed for the open door. Bray gave a wave over his shoulder and retreated to the building.

Alone, Hawkins turned and looked at the rings of cement post braces. He knelt down and looked into the top of the nearest hole. Two feet down, water reflected the blue sky above. He suspected the hole was at least another two feet deep—deep enough to securely hold a post and the struggling person bound to it. But that's not what had him on edge. After just a few years of disuse, the hole should have been filled with dirt and debris. This only held rainwater. And that meant someone was maintaining the site. The building had clearly been abandoned, but the ring was being maintained, as was the fence gate, and the goats with their bright red, plastic collars.

Hawkins stood and placed the rifle against his shoulder. With his finger next to the trigger and the barrel pointed to the ground, he walked the perimeter of the fence. Had this been a fenced-in backyard, it would have been picturesque. Flowers bloomed along the fence line. He wasn't sure why the goats hadn't eaten them, but suspected the orange petals didn't agree with the animals. He walked around the yard until he reached the river. The chain-link fence had been expanded into the water and was attached to two severely rusted but still solid metal posts. The chain link in the water looked newer, as though replaced in the past few years. The newness unnerved Hawkins, but the barrier, coupled with the calmly grazing goats, meant that there were no squid-tentacled crocodiles inside the fence's perimeter.

The river here was deep and fast moving, but just five feet across. Hawkins backed up and prepared to jump the distance. Two steps into his run, something darted out of the brush at the fence line. Hawkins flinched back in surprise, raised the rifle, and nearly squeezed off a shot. He recognized the creature a moment before removing its head. A rat. A very large rat, but still a rat.

The rat saw him at about the same time, spun around, and retreated through a hole in the fence.

Hawkins caught his breath and muttered obscenities at the rodent. He collected himself, double-checked for the rat, and this time made the leap to the opposite bank without any trouble. He continued his inspection of the fence, looking for holes, gates, another path, or some sign of passage. The trail they'd followed to the gate ended in the grass. Whoever made the footprints had either left through some other route or never left—a possibility that had him finishing his inspection quickly. As he neared the concrete building once more, he came across the ruins of a brick-and-mortar structure. It looked like an oversize wood fireplace, but much of the chimney had crumbled and the rest had been claimed by vines.

The hair on his arms began to rise again. He was sensing danger from every direction, but thought it was just his shot nerves, or his growing knowledge about what had happened on this island. *And might still be happening*, he thought.

Soot stained the bricks in the fire pit itself, along with a collection of little white bits. He reached down and picked up a fleck of white.

"That's probably bone," Bray said from behind.

Hawkins jumped and stumbled back. "Son of a bitch, man. Quit sneaking up on me."

"Sorry." Bray stared at the fireplace. Sadly, he added, "They called them 'logs.'"

"What?" Hawkins asked.

"The test subjects. The prisoners. Victims. Whatever you want to call them. Unit Seven thirty-one called them 'logs.' Didn't see them as anything more than wood. They'd collect them, cut them apart, and eventually most would end up here, in the fire pit to be cremated. The people brought here had their humanity stripped away long before they were killed."

"You're still sure this is a Unit Seven thirty-one outpost?" Hawkins asked.

"There's more evidence inside," Bray said. "Old notebooks. Patches on clothes. Stamped-on doors. Drake is looking at one of the notebooks now, but between you and me, I don't think he's doing so well. Hard to tell with the heat, but I think he's starting to run a fever."

"A fever? Is he sick?"

"Worse," Bray said. "If I'm right. It's possible the squidcroc had a second reptilian feature we couldn't see."

"Three species in one?" Hawkins asked. "Is that possible?"

"In theory," Bray said. "Sure. If you can figure out how to

keep the disparate parts from rejecting each other, you can combine as many different species as you want. In this case, I think species number three might be a Komodo dragon."

Hawkins nearly balked until he remembered how Komodos killed their prey. They didn't disembowel, suffocate, or snap their prey's neck like other predators. They simply got in one good bite and then backed off. The potent mixture of lethal bacteria in their saliva did the rest. If Bray was right, Drake would be fighting for his life without even setting foot in the jungle again.

"Also," Bray said, "I came to get you because it looks like someone stayed inside. Recently. And we haven't checked the top two floors yet."

Hawkins discarded the flake of what might be a human bone and set off toward the building at a jog.

When Joliet's scream rolled out of the open door, he ran.

TWENTY-SEVEN

The goats scattered in a panic, their collar bells issuing a frantic jangle, like a platoon of Salvation Army bell ringers. Bleating loudly, the animals parted for Hawkins, allowing him to sprint for the building. As he ran, he noticed a slightly worn path through the grass that led to a gate in the chain-link fence. It was on the opposite side of the yard from the one they'd entered through. He made a mental note of its position and continued past. A small, well-maintained wooden bridge allowed him quick passage to the opposite shore, where he kept running.

Bray, the slower man, had fallen behind, but Hawkins didn't wait for him. Joliet's solitary scream was either a good thing or a very bad thing. He couldn't wait on Bray to find out which.

Hawkins had no idea where he was going, so when he entered the half-light dimness of the building's entryway, he shouted. "Joliet!"

"Here!" Her voice came quickly and full of dread. "Hurry!"

"I can't hold her much longer!" Drake shouted.

Hold her?

The entryway held empty lockers along the back wall. A row of coat hooks ran along the outside wall to his right. A single tattered and stained white lab coat hung from one of the hooks. A black rubber apron hung on the hook next to it. A row of rotting wooden boxes were lined up beneath the hooks. The box beneath the lab coat held a pair of black rubber boots and black rubber gloves. Hawkins saw every detail as he pushed through the room, cataloging them for later.

He charged through the open doorway to his left. A metal door hung askew, clinging to the last of its three hinges. It was bent in the middle as though something had pounded its way through the door. Hawkins recognized the damage as being similar to the door to his quarters, but again passed by with little thought.

The hallway ahead followed the octagonal shape of the building, wrapping around at sharp angles to the right. Debris littered the floor, but there was nothing large to slow him down. He ran around the corner and found a long, straight hallway with glassless windows lining the left side wall. The windows looked out over the jungle with a view of the river, and ocean beyond, but he barely noticed. The view *inside* the hallway drew his focus. "Joliet!" he shouted and sprinted ahead.

At the center of the hallway, a large rectangle of floor was missing. Drake lay next to the hole, his muscular arms reaching down.

"Mark!" Joliet's voice came from the hole, coupled with a recognizable roar.

Drake's arms shook. It seemed impossible that the muscular captain couldn't just pluck the much smaller Joliet from the opening without breaking a sweat. That he was struggling just to hold her spoke volumes about his condition.

"Losing her!" Drake said, his voice something like a growl.

Hawkins flung himself at the hole. He slid on his stomach, stopping at the edge, and thrust his hands down. With his head poking down through the opening, Hawkins could see the river below. Joliet's toes splashed in the water. Ten feet downstream, the water fell away. Hawkins suspected Joliet might survive the fall into the deep waterfall basin, but she'd be back in croc territory and there was no way to know if the crocodile had come back or been joined by friends.

Joliet let go of Drake with one hand and took hold of Hawkins's wrist.

"I have you," Hawkins said, locking his fingers around her wrist.

As though the phrase gave him permission, Drake let go of Joliet. The sudden drop caught both Joliet and Hawkins off guard. Joliet yelped as she swung over the river, closer to Hawkins.

He reached down with his other hand and caught her. She wasn't heavy, and he could hold her for a while, but he had no leverage. Pulling her up would be nearly impossible. "You're going to have to climb up my arms."

Hawkins thought most people might balk at the idea of climbing up another person like a ladder, but Joliet gave it a try. Unfortunately, Hawkins's arms were bare and slick with sweat. She slipped back down to his wrist.

With a grunt, Hawkins pulled her as high as he could. "Can you grab the edge?"

"I think so," she said, moving her hand quickly to the lino-leum floor. But the smooth floor offered little purchase. Her fingertips slowly neared the edge.

Hawkins got ready to catch her again, but before he did, Bray's thick hand reached down and took hold of her arm. Together, the two men quickly pulled her to safety.

"The hell happened?" Bray asked, standing back from the opening in the floor.

Joliet sat against the wall, catching her breath. "What's it . . . look like? I fell through the hatch."

Hawkins leaned over the opening and looked down. There were two rusted metal doors hanging down. "Was it a trap?"

Joliet sighed. "No. They were held shut with a pipe." She pointed to the pipe lying on the floor next to her. "I stubbed my toe on it."

Hawkins tried to suppress a smile, but failed. "You know, I've nearly been killed by a poisonous flying lizard-snake, and came close to becoming a squid-croc snack. And you nearly died from stubbing your toe?"

"Shut up," Joliet said. After a moment, she smiled. "It *would* have been a pathetic way to die. Why do you think they put a door in the floor? Seems a little dangerous to me."

As soon as Hawkins had seen the river below the doors, he knew their purpose. "There are skeletons under the waterfall. In the basin. Hundreds of them. They threw the dead through here. Let the current take them over the falls."

"They must have only incinerated the ones they infected with diseases," Bray said. "Fed the rest to Sobek down there."

"Sobek?" Hawkins asked.

"Egyptian crocodile god." He shrugged. "I like naming things."

"I noticed." Hawkins spotted two long metal rods with hooks on the end lying on the floor beside the open hatch. "Get the pipe," he said to Bray. He used the hooked rods to pull the two doors up. They were thick, and heavy, but manageable. Once he had them both up, Bray slid the pipe back in place.

Hawkins tested his weight on the doors. They held tight. "Just watch your step next— Where's Drake?"

Bray ducked inside one of four doorways evenly spaced along the hallway across from the windows. He came back out a moment later. "Not in here."

Hawkins checked the doorway closest to him. The windowless room was dark, but the light coming in through the hallway's window provided just enough light to see. The large room was divided into ten small cells separated by metal bars. Open metal gates led into each cell. The room smelled of copper, rust, and ammonia. The odor was made bearable thanks to the fresh air pouring through the glassless windows at his back.

Each cell held a wooden pallet that must have served as a bed—a very uncomfortable bed, which might have been the point. A hole had been drilled in the floor of each cell, serving as a drain. For blood? For waste? Maybe Unit 731 hosed down their victims? Hawkins didn't linger on the drains long enough to decide. Old rusted shackles hung from a few of the bars. Hawkins tried to imagine what it would have been like, chained to these bars, maybe listening to the weeping of your fellow captives, smelling death all around and hearing the splash of bodies being discarded—fed to the crocs. And through it all, knowing your turn would soon arrive, and that no one would come to your rescue. The hopelessness of the place nearly brought tears to his eyes. But the knowledge that someone was still on the island, still maintaining this horror show; that made him angry.

They had missing people. Drake was wounded and ill. But he was beginning to suspect that the island's demons were still alive and well. And if that were the case, and they found the people responsible—Hawkins gripped the rifle. Howie GoodTracks didn't believe in the death penalty. He thought people deserved a chance for redemption, a chance to turn their negative contribution to the world into something positive, before they left it for good. It was a little too Zen for Hawkins, and most of the Ute tribe for that matter, but he had experienced GoodTracks's grace and forgiveness firsthand. It was a powerful thing. Redemption might actually be the right choice, but this. . . . He looked at the drain again. This was too much. Someone had to pay, now or later.

He scanned the cells one last time. If the operation were as big now as it had been then, they would be outnumbered and outgunned by an enemy with a severely skewed moral compass. They wouldn't stand a chance. *They'll pay later*, he decided, *unless they get in my way.*

"Here!" Joliet shouted from the next room over.

Hawkins felt a weight lift as he left the room, but it returned in force when he followed Joliet's voice into an identical cell. Drake lay on a pallet in the cell nearest the door. Despite the cool respite provided by the thick concrete and the breeze created by the waterfall, sweat covered Drake's body in a sheen and dripped from his forehead.

Joliet had a hand on Drake's cheek. "He's on fire."

"It's a bacterial infection," Bray said, standing behind Hawkins. "I'm telling you. It's from the croc's tentacle hooks."

Hawkins looked at Drake's leg. Joliet had already bandaged it. "How did the wound look?"

Joliet leaned back on her heels, but stayed next to Drake. "Like it would hurt like hell for a few days. Some of the puncture wounds were deep. Could probably use a stitch or two. But it could have been worse. Squid tentacle clubs aren't designed to kill. Just grip. I don't think the wounds are life-threatening. I covered them with Bacitracin."

"Doesn't matter if it's in the blood already," Bray said. "He needs an antibiotic. Like now."

"We can't just leave Kam and DeWinter here," Joliet said.

Bray thrust a finger at the captain. "*He's* going to die if we don't."

"Leave me," Drake mumbled. He didn't open his eyes or move, but there was no confusing the voice. "Find the others. Come back for me."

"Captain," Bray said. "If you don't—"

"That's an order!" Drake tried to sit up as he shouted, but flopped back down on the wood and once again slipped into unconsciousness.

The silence that followed Drake's command stretched for nearly thirty seconds. Hawkins thought about all the possibilities, but each and every one included someone dying. There was no way out of this. Like Captain Kirk, he was facing the *kobiashi maru*—the unwinnable scenario.

Joliet stood and leaned against the bars of Drake's prison cell. "What do we do?"

The answer came from above in the form of running footfalls.

Three heads snapped up.

"What was that?" Bray asked.

"Another rat?" Joliet offered.

"Rats have four feet, not two. And they don't run on the balls of their feet." Hawkins took the rifle from his shoulder. "We're not alone."

TWENTY-EIGHT

"Stay close. Stay quiet. And Bray"—Hawkins pointed to the fire ax lying on the floor next to Drake—"I don't think the captain's going to get much use out of that now."

Hawkins glanced out into the hall, then shed his backpack. "Where are your packs?"

"First room in the hall," Joliet said. "With the speargun."

"Stay here," Hawkins said. He turned to Bray. "Watch the hall."

Hawkins tiptoed into the hallway. Bray stood behind him, ax in hand. He passed the first door only after sweeping the room with his rifle. He performed the same check on the room nearest the exit and quickly spotted three backpacks and the speargun piled next to the door. He grabbed everything, then hustled back to Bray. He placed the packs on the floor next to Drake and handed Joliet the speargun. "Stay here."

He knew Joliet wouldn't like being told what to do, or being left behind, but it was necessary. Before she could speak, he added, "Someone needs to guard Drake."

She looked down at the immobile captain and nodded. "Go."

Hawkins motioned with his head for Bray to follow and crept toward the end of the hall. He quickly checked the last room on the right and found only more barred cells with rotting pallets, disintegrating walls, and a large dark brown stain on the floor that could have only been blood.

At the end of the hall were a staircase leading up and a closed door. Hawkins paused at the stairs. He didn't want to go up without first knowing if the last room was clear. He turned to Bray, pointed to his eyes, and then to the stairs. Bray nodded, turning his eyes to the top of the staircase and winding up with the ax.

The door creaked when Hawkins pushed it open with the rifle's barrel. The interior of the room was lit by a single, small window that still held a thick pane of glass. The first items he saw—metal buckets, mops, glass jars, and a variety of rotting containers—mixed with a faint smell of detergent, identified the space as a simple storage closet. But scattered among the common items were more rubber aprons, gloves, and boots, and manacles and chains. Looking closer, he saw that some of the wooden poles he thought were broom handles were actually clubs, many of which held single half-inch-long nails—not long enough to kill, but certainly long enough to add an extra level of agony to each strike.

As disturbing as the room's contents were, Hawkins felt relief that it wasn't occupied by anything living. As he turned toward the staircase, that small amount of relief quickly faded. He led the way up, stepping cautiously to avoid the occasional dry leaf. In the silence of what felt like an oversize crypt, the slightest sound could give away their position.

At the top of the stairs, there was another staircase leading up to the third floor, and a hallway that wrapped around the second floor. Hawkins motioned for Bray to once again watch the staircase. There was no way to know if the person they'd heard had headed up, or even if he, or she, were alone. Hawkins would have preferred to have the big man with the ax at his back, but he didn't want to risk someone getting down to Joliet, and Drake.

The hallway around the corner wasn't a hallway at all. While the first floor had been divided into a long hall with four rooms on one side, this space was just one large room. Eight metal operating tables stretched down the center of the room. Each table was accompanied by a small, empty supply tray. Hawkins had no trouble imagining the trays' contents. They were probably very similar to implements used to dissect the loggerhead.

Except the people dissected here were sometimes still alive, Hawkins thought, remembering Bray's tales of vivisection and experimentation. Was this where it happened? Was this where the people on the beach were taken apart and re-shaped? Hawkins suspected as much, but could only be sure of one thing: This was a torture chamber.

Hawkins moved down the center aisle created by the twin rows of operating tables. Details jumped out at him. The tables weren't flat. They had a slight bowl shape with a drain at the center. Dark stains covered the floor under each table. He wondered if they just let the blood pour onto the floor, but found rows of similarly stained metal buckets lining shelves on the wall opposite the still-glassed windows.

The room turned left at the end, extending out over the bottom floor's entryway. He inched forward, looking for any-thing alive. Nothing moved, but he saw evidence of habita-tion, though not human. A nest had been built out of leaves and shredded lab coats. It looked similar to what a rat in a cage might make, but was far too large. It looked large enough for a medium-size dog.

Hawkins turned away from the nest and inspected what he thought were two more operating tables. But the angled, chairlike shape, twin sets of stirrups, and buckets at the ends identified these as birthing chairs. Hawkins winced when he saw more bloodstains on the floor beneath his feet. His face twitched with anger and revolt until he could no longer handle the conjuring of his imagination. He turned away from the table, muttering a string of curses.

Ting, ting.

The cautious tap of metal on metal sounded like an explo-sion. Hawkins flinched, but realized the sound had been slow and deliberate. Bray was calling him back. Hawkins double-timed his retreat, happy to be leaving the operating suite.

When he rounded the corner, he found Bray still standing guard at the bottom of the stairs. But the man's face had gone pale.

"What is it?" Hawkins asked.

Bray's eyes flicked toward Hawkins, but then quickly returned to the top of the stairs. "Something growled at me."

"Did you see it?"

"No . . . but it sounded like . . ." Bray shook his head. "It sounded like a kid. And I don't mean a baby goat."

Hawkins remembered the oversize nest. Could a child be living here? He decided against the idea. A human child couldn't survive on this island. Not alone. And he hadn't seen any indication that there was anyone else here. At least not on the first two floors. Raising the rifle, Hawkins ascended the staircase.

The first thing he noticed was that the glass on the windows along the outside wall had been coated with a layer of mud—he smelled the rancid air—or was it feces? He decided he didn't need to know the answer to that question. All that mattered was that most of the sunlight that lit the lower floors had been blocked out. A few shafts of light made it into the room, allowing him to see the most basic details, but he was at a serious disadvantage. He scanned back and forth, looking down the barrel of the rifle. He stepped cautiously forward, finger wrapped around the trigger. Safety off.

When the window to his right shattered, he spun and nearly fired. But the form of Bray, bathed in sunlight, stopped him short. He was about to chastise the man when he realized he could now see much of the room. And what he saw made him want to back up and haul ass back to the *Magellan*.

Like the second floor, this was one large room. But instead of being divided by operating tables, or cells, this room was a maze of shelves, each covered in glass jars of various size. Some were as small as baby food jars. Others, resting on the floor, looked large enough to hold a grown man.

And some of them did.

Many of the glass containers had broken over time and the bones of what they once held littered the floor. But others had weathered the past seventy years, blemished only by dust.

"Holy fuck," Bray said.

Hawkins agreed with the sentiment, but couldn't find his voice. The jar nearest him, perched on an eye-level shelf, glowed yellow, struck by the full light of day. And suspended in the amber liquid was a baby, curled up in a fetal position as though still in the womb. He stepped closer and lowered his weapon. "The baby," he said. "It has a tail."

"And not a vestigial tail, either," Bray added. "I think that's a rat tail."

"Is it a chimera?" Hawkins asked.

Bray shook his head. "Looks like it was stitched on, maybe at birth."

Hawkins ran a hand over his head. He knew that humanity had committed atrocities over the years, especially during wars, but this was beyond reason. What good would a human being with a rat tail be? How could someone do this to a newborn baby?

"Hey, Ranger," Bray said.

Hawkins looked at Bray, who nodded toward the rifle.

"Mind keeping that up in case something tries to eat us?"

Hawkins's distraction disappeared. He raised the rifle and scanned the room again. "We'll move forward slowly and together. Break the windows as we reach them."

Hawkins moved forward, trying hard to ignore the different animals and people of various ages kept in jars of formaldehyde. Some looked unaltered, but others had limbs, and eyes, and teeth, and digits that clearly did not belong to them.

A window shattered, spilling more light into the room and revealing more horrors. Hawkins ignored them now. He heard something a moment before the window broke.

Breathing.

"If you can understand me," Hawkins said, "show yourself now. If you don't, I *will* shoot you."

"I don't see anything," Bray said.

"It's there. Trust me." Hawkins picked up an empty jar and threw it toward the back of the room. The sharp sound of breaking glass was accompanied by a shrill cry of surprise. And then a growl.

Bray is right, Hawkins thought, *it sounds like a child.*

And when their quarry stepped out from behind a shelf, Hawkins thought for a moment that it was, in fact, a five-year-old boy. But then he saw the hair covering its naked body, the tail thrashing about behind it, and the awkward way it stood. Still, he thought he saw a trace of humanity in its yellow eyes. But all doubt was erased when it snarled and showed its teeth.

TWENTY-NINE

"Hawkins!" Bray shouted. "Shoot it!"

The rifle's report was contained by the thick, concrete walls, which amplified the sound. Hawkins grunted and lowered his aim. A ringing buzz in his ears drowned out the creature's shrieks. Bray's hands went to his ears after dropping the ax. Hawkins could see him cursing, but couldn't make out the words. Both men were stunned and distracted by the explosion of sound, and wide open to attack. Luckily, the sharp report had a similar effect on the creature across the room.

It wailed while throwing itself back and forth, smashing into shelves. Jars of preserved bodies tipped and rolled from their perches, shattering on the floor. The sharp, tangy odor of formaldehyde filled the air.

"Smells like my dissection lab," Bray said as he picked up the ax. "If it gets much stronger, we're going to have to fall back. Or break more windows. Whoa!"

A glass jar sailed over his head as he ducked. It struck the wall next to him and shattered, its contents spilling to the floor. Bray jumped away before the expanding puddle of formaldehyde reached his feet. But it wasn't the liquid that made him jump. It was the head that rolled past him. When the head stopped rolling, a woman's face stared at the ceiling with black, hollow eyes. Her head had been shaved, revealing several scars atop her cranium. Her skin had been stained the sickly yellow tinge of formaldehyde, and face was frozen in an expression of horror, or extreme pain. Either way, it was a sight neither man would ever forget.

Hawkins tore his eyes away from the woman's face and looked for the creature. A second jar, thankfully empty, arched toward him. He side-stepped the projectile and tracked its trajectory to its origin. The creature had slowed, but now kept to the shadows.

"Get the next window," he said. "If I yell, 'ears,' cover them."

Bray took a deep breath, tucked his nose under his shirt, and inched forward, ready with the ax.

A large jar containing what looked like sloshing intestines sailed out of the gloom. But it must have been too heavy for the small creature. It crashed to the floor, spilling its contents. The wave of formaldehyde pushed the intestines out across the floor, making the organ look like some kind of giant worm.

Bray saw the noxious pool approaching his feet. He rushed forward, swinging the ax with his last step. The window shattered and the room brightened. And the creature's concealing shadows disappeared.

Nowhere to hide now, Hawkins thought. He lined up a shot, zeroing in on the creature's quickly rising and falling chest. Its eyes were wide. Its limbs shook.

"The thing is terrified," Hawkins said, holding his fire.

Bray stepped back behind Hawkins. "It's an animal."

But Hawkins wasn't so sure. "It's using tools, Bray. Throwing jars at us. And it's hiding in the shadows."

"Chimps throw stones, and maybe it's nocturnal? Prefers the dark."

Hawkins kept the thing in his sights. There was more to this creature. "The formaldehyde," he said. "It wasn't trying to hit us with the big jar. It saw our aversion to the liquid and covered the floor in it. That's not just tool wielding. That's intelligence."

Bray's defensive stance loosened. "You're right."

The creature hissed at them and Hawkins nearly fired on reflex.

"What are we going to do?" Bray asked.

Hawkins wasn't sure. The creature might be intelligent, but that didn't mean it wouldn't tear them apart if given the chance. At the same time, it was clearly as afraid of them as they were of it. Normally, he'd pack up and check out, but Drake needed to rest. Like it or not, the creature had to be evicted, at least until they figured out their next move.

But the intelligent beast had other plans. With a shriek, it threw two small glass jars. Outside of a head shot, the jars wouldn't do much damage, but both men dodged, fearful of being coated by a toxic chemical bath.

Hawkins righted himself and looked for the thing, but it was gone. A blur at the center of the room caught his eye. By the time he focused on it, the creature was upon them. It charged down the top of a shelving unit at the center of the room, knocking jars asunder as it ran. Then it leapt, arms outstretched, jaws open, sharp teeth revealed.

It was too close to shoot, so Hawkins swung at it with the rifle. But his aim was low. The creature cleared the weapon's barrel and found Bray's ax swinging toward it. For most people, the blow would have been impossible to dodge and, given the force behind it, impossible to survive. But the nimble creature placed its hands atop the flat edge of the swinging blade and pushed its body up and over the weapon.

Bray's missed swing pulled him forward. He crashed into the shelf, clearing the rest of the specimen jars to the floor, and expanding the pungent puddle.

Hawkins spun with the creature, abandoning the rifle and reaching for his knife. He expected the fast creature to press the attack. It clearly had the advantage in a close-quarters fight. It could outmaneuver the larger, slower men and, using its teeth and claws, could probably inflict a lot more damage. But when it landed, it gave a quick look back at Hawkins, shrieked angrily, and bolted for the stairs.

In the next second, Hawkins felt a wash of relief—they

wouldn't be killed by the creature—followed by a surge of panic: It was headed for Joliet. He ran to the stairs. When he reached the top of the stairwell, he saw the creature dive toward the next flight.

"Joliet!" he shouted as loud as he could. "It's coming to you!"

"Here!" Bray shouted.

Hawkins turned to find the rifle already in the air, tossed to him by Bray. He caught it and launched himself down the stairs, taking them three at a time. But it was too late. By the time he'd reached the second floor he heard Joliet shout, followed by a savage shriek.

"Joliet!" he shouted again, descending the stairs to the first floor. His panic rose when she didn't answer right away. "Joliet!"

When he rounded the corner into the first-floor hallway, he wasn't sure what to make of things. The metal doors in the middle of the hall hung open again. Had she fallen through them again? But then he saw a speargun spear buried in the wall just ahead of the opening. Unlike the others, this spear still had the wire attached. The wire, which had been designed to reel in large fish and could hold a person's weight, hung through the opening. Had Joliet dropped the speargun through the hatch, or had she fallen in again? Hawkins ran toward the doors, picturing Joliet clinging to the thin wire. "Joliet!" he shouted, looking over the edge.

The water surged past below before falling over the waterfall. Cool, fresh air billowed up, erasing the scent of formaldehyde from his nose, but did nothing for his nerves. Joliet was nowhere to be seen. Hawkins filled his lungs to shout her name again.

"In here."

Joliet's voice spun Hawkins around so fast he nearly fell through the hole. Bray held on to his arm, helping him get his balance. Skirting the opening, he entered the room where he'd left Joliet and Drake.

Joliet sat on the floor, hand to her head. "Heard your warning. Opened the doors and when I heard it get close, I shot the spear. Intended to hit it, but the spear missed and stuck into the wall." She stood and looked at the open doors. "When it saw me, the thing focused on me. Never saw the line. Tripped it up. But it was heavy. Yanked me forward. Hit my head on the doorframe. I dropped the speargun. It must have gone over the falls."

Hawkins moved her hand away from her head, looking at the goose egg forming.

"It's nothing," she said. "Just a bump."

Hawkins ignored her.

She pulled away and smiled. "You sounded pretty worried."

He had no reply to that. He *had* been worried. Very worried. His growing feelings for Joliet weren't exactly subconscious. But he also knew that she was a kind, attractive woman he had spent nearly every day with for the past month. As a single guy, he couldn't not be attracted to her. But what he felt just now, when he thought she might be harmed . . . it felt bigger. He stared dumbly at her, no answer coming to mind. Bray unknowingly came to his rescue.

"I don't see it anywhere." Bray stood by the open doors, looking down into the river. "Probably went over the falls."

Hawkins retreated from Joliet's eyes and moved across the hall. He picked up the metal hooks and started pulling up the doors. "Wouldn't want that thing jumping up and pulling you in."

Bray took a quick step back. He'd seen the way the creature could move.

Hawkins tried to pull the speargun up, but the line was taut and unmoving. *It's snagged*, he thought.

Bray tried to pry the spear from the wall, but it held fast. "This isn't moving, either. Just leave it."

Hawkins pulled the doors shut and Bray slid the pipe back in place, locking them once again. Bray leaned against the outside wall beneath a window and slid to the floor. He rubbed the sweat from his eyes and let out a long, slow breath. Hawkins knew how the man felt, but didn't let his guard down. He leaned against the cool concrete wall, but kept his eyes, and the rifle, facing the building's lone entrance. He didn't think the creature would return, if it survived the falls and croc waiting below, but he didn't want to take any chances.

"What *was* that thing?" Joliet asked.

"Another chimera," Hawkins said. That it was another chimera, Hawkins had no doubt, but he couldn't peg exactly what species had been used. Lacking hair, the reptilian chimeras' individual parts were easy to see. But this had been a mammal, and its dark black hair concealed most details.

"It was just two species," Bray said. "They were harder to see because the parts were more integrated. It wasn't like a crocodile with squid parts, or a sea snake with draco limbs and wings."

Hawkins took his eyes off the entryway and turned to Bray. "But you saw what it was?"

Bray turned to the floor. "Wish I hadn't. Because it means we're really in the shitter here."

"*Bray*," Hawkins said, the tone of his voice adding urgency.

"The jaw. The teeth. The eyes. The fur. The tail. Maybe the underlying musculature. All one creature." Bray shifted uncomfortably. "They're all panther."

"You're sure?" Joliet asked.

He nodded. "Even saw the faint spots when it jumped past me."

"And the other half?" Hawkins asked, though he'd already begun to suspect the answer.

"The rest of it," Bray said. "The body. The mind. The hands—it had thumbs. Those . . ." He shook his head. "Those were human."

THIRTY

Twenty minutes after the encounter, the lab building's outside door was wedged back in place and held there with a stack of wooden pallets. It wasn't an impenetrable blockade, but anyone breaking through the door would be slowed down and make a hell of a lot of noise. Their only way out would be the hatch in the floor, so they were essentially trapped, but the long hallway was a far more defensible position than outside, where an attack could come from any direction.

It had been hours since they'd blocked the doors and the sun had fallen below the tree line. Hawkins sat in the hall, leaning against the wall next to the hatch in the floor. He finished reloading the rifle—eleven shots left; ten in the rifle, one in his pocket—and chambered a round. From his position, he could shoot anything coming down the hall and, if need be, quickly kick away the pipe holding the doors up. In terms of strategy it was basic, but simple strategies were usually harder to screw up. And none of them was in any shape to try anything fancy.

Hawkins ached all over from his encounter with the crocodile. Bray was exhausted from exerting himself far more than he was accustomed. Drake's fever hadn't gotten any worse, but his wound wasn't clotting and the captain had yet to awaken. Joliet's arms were sore from falling through the hatch, but she had weathered the journey better than the rest thus far. But the physical pain couldn't compare to the emotional toll their journey had taken on them.

Hawkins fought to ignore the recent memories of near-death encounters trying to replay in his mind. But forgetting an eighteen-foot crocodile with writhing tentacles, or a hominid panther-child, wasn't easy to do. In fact, he felt sure every horrible detail of this island would haunt his dreams for the rest of his life. He turned his head to Bray, who sat against the opposite wall, twirling the ax handle in his hands.

"Hey, Eight," he said.

Bray rolled his head toward Hawkins.

"You're braver than I thought you'd be."

A slight smile formed on Bray's face. "Thanks. Sort of. But I think I'm done being brave. Comes a point when bravery and stupidity cross paths."

Hawkins nodded. He'd been thinking the same thing.

Joliet appeared in the doorway of Drake's makeshift medical bay. She leaned against the frame and crossed her arms. "Drake is still hot, but I think he'll be okay."

"He's strong, but that doesn't mean he can beat the infection without help," Bray said. "Unchecked bacterial infections can kill healthy people, especially if the saliva of that crocodile is something like a Komodo dragon's. Not many people can survive a Komodo bite without modern medicine. It's what makes them so deadly."

Joliet looked defeated. She slid down and sat on the floor, her back still on the doorframe. "What can we do?"

Bray looked at Hawkins and said, "Should you say it or should I?"

Hawkins and Bray hadn't talked about what to do, but they knew each other fairly well and typically came to similar conclusions. Joliet, on the other hand, often thought differently. She had a passionate personality, and it wasn't uncommon for her to disagree with a consensus. The thing was, even when Joliet was outnumbered ten to one, she wouldn't back down if she believed she was right. And as much as that frustrated certain people—Bray among them—she often *was* right.

So when she spoke first, saying, "We need to cut our losses and leave," Hawkins just stared.

"I don't like it," she continued. "Not at all. But we don't know if Kam and DeWinter are still alive. There are four of us, armed with weapons, and we were damn lucky to survive the day. I hope you guys don't hate me for saying this—I know it's a morale killer—but with Drake knocked out and two spearguns missing, not to mention being exhausted, we're going to be lucky if all of us, or any of us, make it back to the *Magellan* alive."

"The one time she agrees with us," Bray said to Hawkins, "and it's on the subject of 'we're all gonna die.'"

Joliet grinned. "You want me to change my mind?"

"Nothing to change it to," Bray said. "We stay, we die. We leave, we die."

"We're not going to die," Hawkins said.

"And now *he's* disagreeing," Bray said. "You know, if you two ever get together, you're going to fight all the time about—"

"*Bray*," Hawkins warned.

Joliet shoved Bray's shoulder with her foot. "We agree that you're an asshole."

Bray laughed and the others joined in. The heavy weight of their predicament lifted for just a moment, but quickly settled again, pulling their smiles down.

"So," Hawkins said. "We'll leave. But we're going to have to spend the night here. We'll sleep and keep watch in shifts. Two sleeping, two watching."

"Which means one sleeping, two watching," Bray said. "Drake is out for the count."

Hawkins nodded. "Would love to say we can all sleep, but that's not going to happen, and keeping watch with just one person is too dangerous."

No one argued, so Hawkins moved on. "We need to make a stretcher for Drake. We can rotate carrying it, but . . ." He turned to Joliet. "Please don't hate me for this. If we're attacked and the only way to survive is to leave Drake behind, don't hesitate. Run. Both of you."

Hawkins could see Joliet's jaw muscle flexing as she ground her teeth. But then she said, "I get it."

Despite her agreement, Hawkins felt the need to elaborate. "It's what he would—"

"I said I get it," she said firmly. "We don't need to talk about it."

"Okay," Hawkins said, and was glad for Joliet's reluctance to discuss the topic. If things went south on the trip back to the lagoon, he wanted Bray and Joliet to run to the *Magellan* and not look back. But he had no intention of leaving Drake behind. Not until the man's heart stopped beating, or his own did. Kam and DeWinter were unknowns, and it was clear to him that finding the pair and escaping without a casualty was impossible. They'd be lucky if one or two of them survived. If they followed the trail back, were careful to avoid the croc, and rang the hell out of the goat's bell while traveling through the draco-snake territory, they might make it back with their lives. Jones wouldn't like it. Not at all. But their best chance at saving Kam and DeWinter was to return with help—the kind that carries machine guns and wears body armor.

"We'll leave after dawn," Hawkins said. "Most land predators hunt in the twilight hours. And it will be brighter in the jungle. We'll take only what we need for the return trip—water and weapons. The rest stays here."

"Even if we make it back to the ship," Bray said, "we'll still need to convince Jones to leave his daughter behind."

"Sounded like Bennett might be able to handle things if we help him get the ship out of the lagoon," Joliet said.

"All he has to do is point us east, gun the engines, and hope we don't run into another storm," Hawkins said.

Bray shook his head, but his smile revealed amusement. Then the smile disappeared. "I appreciate what you're trying to do, Ranger. The Mr. Positivity routine. But you know better than anyone that man versus nature scenarios usually don't work out well for man. Modern man, anyway. When we're wrapped in the blanket of technology, we're the top dog. But out here? We're in the middle of the Pacific Ocean. There might not be another human being for two hundred miles in every direction. And even if there were, we have no way to contact them, nor do we know where we are."

"Bray," Hawkins said.

"Let me finish," Bray said, his voice nearly a shout. "The point is, I'd appreciate some realism."

"We made it here," Joliet said. "We can make it back."

"Being allowed inside the lion's den is one thing," Bray said. "Turning your back on the lions and walking out is something else. And I don't appreciate—"

"Bray," Hawkins interrupted.

"Ranger, I swear to God, if you don't let me say this, I'm—"

"Bray!" Hawkins's voice was a hiss. He yanked the rifle's lever down, chambering a round. "Shut the fuck up."

Bray's mouth clamped shut.

Hawkins slowly stood, staring down the hallway at the entry room where they'd barricaded the outside door. Bray followed his lead, standing with the ax.

"What is it?" he asked.

Hawkins raised the rifle toward the doorway. "Thought I heard something."

Joliet slid back into Drake's room for a moment. She reappeared a moment later with two butcher knives clutched in her hands. She didn't look confident, but the razor-sharp blades would keep a human being at bay.

Trouble was, if something was coming through their barricade, it probably wasn't human.

Hawkins nearly squeezed off a shot when the first of the pallets fell. One by one, the pallets shifted and fell as something outside applied a steady force. The breech was so slow that he nearly lost his patience and charged forward, but he managed to hold his ground.

The last of the crates toppled over and the door ground open. Light filled the far end of the hallway and a cross breeze swept past them, carrying the earthy scent of the jungle, and something else. Something sweet and familiar. But from where?

A figure stepped into the hall just as a bead of sweat dropped into Hawkins's eye. He was blinded the moment he pulled the trigger, but it didn't seem to matter because the intruder began screaming.

In English.

THIRTY-ONE

"Don't shoot!" screamed a high-pitched voice.

For a moment, Hawkins thought it might actually be DeWinter, but her voice sounded more husky than this.

"It's me!" The voice dripped desperation.

Hawkins rubbed the sweat from his eyes. He held his fire, but kept the weapon aimed. It could be any number of people he didn't want to shoot, but it could also be a crafty local. With the sweat gone, Hawkins saw the figure stumbling in the shadows at the end of the hallway. The last light of day filtering in through the hall's open windows did little to illuminate things.

We're going to need a fire, part of Hawkins's mind thought, while the rest tracked the intruder.

"Me, who?" Bray asked.

"Phil! It's Phil!"

Hawkins lowered the rifle as Bennett spilled into the light. His freckled face and brown hair were coated with mud. Bleeding scrapes covered his bare arms and legs. His eyes, wide with panic, darted around the hallway, hypervigilant.

Joliet ran forward and caught the young man as he fell to his knees. He leaned forward and placed his head on the cool concrete. His back rose and fell with each labored breath.

"Look," Joliet said, pointing to his back. The fabric of his green T-shirt held three tears where claws had struck.

"Is this from the draco-snakes?" Hawkins asked.

"What?" Bennett said, still catching his breath.

Hawkins tapped on the torn shirt. "The tears in your shirt. Were you attacked?"

"No. I mean, yes. But not by the dracos."

A loud, angry squawk came from the door.

Bennett yelped and pushed himself up. "They're here!"

"What are they?" Hawkins demanded, taking aim with the rifle.

The squawk repeated, this time sounding very familiar.

"Can't be," Bray said.

A loud flapping filled the hallway. Bennett cringed and shrunk away from the sound. He hid behind Hawkins.

When the large seagull emerged from the gloom, it landed and cocked its head from side to side, regarding them with a sort of puzzled expression.

"You've got to be kidding me," Joliet said. "This is what attacked you? A seagull?"

Bennett said nothing. He just watched the bird with wild eyes.

"The seagulls here are aggressive," Hawkins said. "I found one picking at you on the deck of the *Magellan* before you woke up. For a moment, I thought it was actually going to fight me for you."

"But how could a seagull—even a big one—do that?" Joliet asked.

"It's a chimera," Bray said. "Look at the feet. They're webbed, but they also have talons. Like an eagle."

"Kind of a minor feature to add to a seagull," Hawkins said, looking for more, but he found nothing.

"Just shoot it," Bray said.

"Not going to waste a bullet on a bird," Hawkins said.

The seagull took two steps forward, its head bobbing.

"Can you believe this thing?" Bray said. He raised the ax. "Come to Bray, little birdie." He stopped in his tracks when a second seagull flapped into the hallway and landed next to the first. They squawked at each other, nipping with their beaks, but then Bray stepped forward again and they gave him their full attention.

"Hold on," Hawkins said. He lowered the rifle and handed it to Joliet. "If things get out of hand, be ready to give that back." He ran toward the storage room at the back of the hallway.

Bennett whimpered. "Don't leave us!"

"I'm not leaving," Hawkins said. "I'm getting weapons."

Hawkins opened the storage room and stepped inside. Dim light from the single small window lit the space. He had no trouble finding the clubs he'd seen earlier and reached for them a little too quickly. One of the rusty nails pricked his thumb. He winced, pulled back the finger, and sucked on it for a moment. He was up to date on his tetanus shots, but who knew what else might be encrusted on the tip of that nail. Blood. Chemicals. Biological agents. Any of the above seemed possible. He spit, shook his hand out, and picked out two clubs, each with a nail driven through the end. The wood felt strong and heavy.

These will do the job, Hawkins thought.

"Hawkins!" Bray shouted from the hallway. "Better hurry up!"

He rushed back into the hallway, armed with twin clubs and ready for a fight. But when he saw what waited for him, he nearly tripped and fell. In the thirty seconds he'd spent in the closet, seven more birds had entered the hallway.

"I told you," Bennett said, inching away. "I told you!"

Hawkins sized up the birds. "Talons or not, they're still just seagulls. We'll be—"

The seagull at the front of the pack spread open its wings and shook them. The wing span itself was impressive. At five feet across, the wings were nearly twice as long as the average gull's. Despite the bird's size, Hawkins took comfort in the knowledge that these were still birds. *Hollow bones break easily*, he thought. *A few good whacks should send them all running.*

Hawkins took a step forward. Bray shadowed him. "When we get close enough, just start swinging."

The big gull's wings shook more violently. Its chest seemed to vibrate as a high-pitched vibrato rose out of its throat. The beak opened wide to allow the sound out, but then opened wider.

And wider.

With a pop, the lower jaw unhinged. The beak, top and bottom, separated down the middle and came apart as the jaw bones opened wide, like digits, each tipped with a dagger of yellow beak. The digits flexed and twitched, pulling farther apart, like four talons ready to grab hold of prey and pull them into the newly revealed maw. Blood red gums emerged in the widening space. The jaws snapped open, flashing stark, white triangular teeth, each the size of a dime.

"You've got to be shitting me!" Bray said. "Shark's teeth?"

"Piranha," Joliet corrected. "They look just as powerful, too."

"What kind of sick fu—"

"Bray," Hawkins said.

"What?"

"Go!"

Hawkins rushed in and swung hard with his right-hand club. The seagull tried to lunge at him, but his sudden attack caught it off guard. The nail missed the bird's neck, but the club struck hard, knocking it to the floor. A loud clang of metal on concrete sounded out as Bray brought the ax down, decapitating the bird. The piranha jaws twitched open and closed. The snapping sound of teeth striking teeth sounded like a pair of two-by-fours being clapped together. Hawkins had no doubt that a single bite would remove a pool ball–size chunk of flesh with ease.

"Watch your feet," Hawkins said as he jumped over the bird.

The rest of the flock burst into the air. Wings flapped. Beaks sprang open. Teeth clattered hungrily. Talons reached.

Hawkins dove and rolled beneath the rising flock. He came to his feet at their core and began swinging. He struck a wing hard. The bone snapped. The seagull fell to the floor, spinning in circles as it tried to take flight again. He caught a second bird in the side of the head with a nail. It fell and didn't move at all.

He turned back as Bray shouted, fearing his friend had been wounded. But Bray's shout was actually a war cry. The big man swung the ax over his head and struck a gull in the face. Piranha teeth scattered across the floor, but the bird's head stuck to the blade. Bray tried to shake it off, but the jaws had clamped down tight in a death grip. Before he could kick it off, two seagulls descended. With a shout, Bray fended them off with the bird-tipped ax.

A squawk above turned Hawkins's eyes up. A set of jaws large enough to tear out his throat dropped toward him. Hawkins shouted as he ducked away and thrust one of his clubs up. The club struck the bird, dead center of its open maw, but caused it no injury. Instead, the powerful jaws snapped shut like a bear trap. The club cracked and split. The seagull pounded its large wings, but wasn't strong enough to pull the weapon away from Hawkins. It did, however, delay him long enough for one of its brethren to attack.

The bird swooped down, talons reaching for Hawkins's face. He let go of his club and fell to the floor. *They're going for my face*, he realized. *My eyes. Trying to blind me.* If Hawkins couldn't see, he couldn't fight. The birds somehow realized this, or perhaps had been trained to attack this way.

Hawkins rolled onto his back and immediately had to roll again. A seagull crashed to the floor, its jaws scraping concrete as it chewed the air where his head had just been. Rolling back toward the bird, Hawkins swung hard and crushed the bird's head against the floor. He also snapped his club in half.

A seagull landed next to him, wings open wide, jaws open. He pushed away from it until his back struck the wall. He kicked at the bird, but nearly had his foot taken off. He tried again from the side, but the bird spun to intercept the blow.

It hopped closer.

Without a weapon, he wouldn't be able to strike the bird without losing a digit, if not a hand or foot.

"Mark, get down!" Joliet shouted.

Against his better judgment, Hawkins decided to trust Joliet and duck. He heard her and Bennett both grunt. Angry squawks filled the air. The thud of birds being struck, too. And then the crash of wood. Hawkins spun toward the sound and found the seagull about to make a meal of him pinned beneath a pallet. A second wounded bird writhed on the floor.

"One, two, three!"

Hawkins watched as Joliet and Bennett lobbed a second oversize projectile into the fray. This one struck four birds before crashing to the floor.

Overwhelmed by the turn of events, and perhaps more than a little confused, the remaining birds made for the door and disappeared. As Hawkins caught his breath, he heard the gulls' calls fade into the distance.

He jumped when the bird trapped beneath the pallet at his feet shrieked. He got to his feet as Bray finally managed to pry the dead bird from the end of the ax. "Mind if I borrow that?"

Bray handed him the ax. With one swing, he took the bird's head off. He then systematically walked around the room and decapitated five more wounded, but not yet dead, seagulls. As the last of their cries was abruptly silenced by the ax's blade, he leaned the blood-soaked weapon against the wall and turned to Bennett.

Despite nearly being killed by chimera seagulls with piranha jaws, a single question burned in Hawkins's mind. Because as bad as things just were, he knew the answer had to be worse.

"Bennett," he said. "Why are you here?"

THIRTY-TWO

Bennett's hands shook as he emotionally imploded, folding in on himself as he fell to his knees and began weeping. His back shook from sobs.

Bray grunted and rolled his eyes. "I'll put the pallets back in front of the door. For all the good they did."

Joliet stood behind Bennett as Hawkins approached him. Her eyes told him to be gentle, but Hawkins knew his patience would wear out quickly if the kid didn't pull it together soon. His presence here meant something had gone wrong on the *Magellan*.

"Try to raise Blok on the two-way," Hawkins said to Joliet. She nodded and went to find it in the side room.

Hawkins crouched down in front of Bennett. "Phil. I need to know what happened."

No reply.

Joliet returned, two-way radio in hand. "Come in, *Magellan*, this is Joliet. Do you read?"

In the silence that followed, Bennett's body shook.

Hawkins glanced at Joliet, who repeated her silent message: Be gentle.

"*Phil*," Hawkins said. "Phil. *Look* at me."

Bennett looked up, his eyes rimmed red.

"Tell me what happened, Phil. Why are you here?"

The tears slowed. Bennett caught his breath. And then,

between the occasional emotional hiccup, he said, "It . . . it came back. Got on board. I—I don't know how."

"*Magellan,* please respond," Joliet said into the radio. "Blok, are you there?"

Hawkins glanced back to the entryway where Bray was shoving the pallets back in place. They'd make a pitiful barrier against the person—or thing—that had taken DeWinter and bent the metal door to his quarters. "Did it follow you here?"

Bennett shook his head quickly no.

"How did you find us?" Hawkins asked.

"I—I wasn't trying to. I just ran. Straight through the jungle. I didn't see a path until I got to the river."

"And the scrapes. The cuts. They're from the seagulls?"

Bennett nodded. He was calming down. "I think they saw me when I swam to the beach. Somehow tracked me through the jungle and attacked when I crossed the waterfall."

"Did you see anything else by the waterfall?" Hawkins asked, thinking the kid was damn lucky to have not been attacked by the croc.

"I didn't really look around," Bennett said. "The birds were on me pretty much the moment I stepped onto the bridge. Nearly knocked me into the water."

"So," Hawkins said, hoping the kid was ready to tell him the whole story. "What happened on the *Magellan*?"

Joliet spoke into the radio again. "*Magellan,* come in. This is Joliet. Come in, *Magell*—"

"You can stop calling them," Bennett said, picking himself up off the floor. His face was grim. His lips quivered. "They're dead. Blok. Jones and the Tweedles. All four. Dead."

Joliet stumbled back, her legs suddenly weak. She held on to the window frame to support herself. "What?"

"It killed them."

"You saw them die?" Hawkins asked.

Tears returned to Bennett's eyes. "Jones. Didn't need to see the rest. I heard them." Bennett nearly began sobbing again, but held his emotions in check. "And I left them. I hid. And then I ran."

"Sounds like you didn't have a choice," Hawkins said.

Bennett sniffed and wiped his arm across his nose. "I could have fought it. You would have. I could have—"

Joliet put her arm around Bennett's shoulder and he fell into her embrace, despite being nearly a foot taller than her. With his head over her shoulder, he wept some more.

Hawkins turned away. He'd heard enough.

Bray entered, looking concerned. "What happened?"

"Says the crew is dead," Hawkins replied.

"Holy shit," Bray said, rubbing his hand over his head. "Holy shit. What are we going to do?"

Hawkins looked back at Joliet and Bennett, then back to Bray. "Plan stays the same. We stay the night here. Haul ass back to the *Magellan*. And then leave. Bennett can get us moving. We'll do our best to help him steer us out of the lagoon and then we'll head east until we hit land."

"We can't go back there," Bennett said, stepping away from Joliet. "We can't!"

"Phil," Hawkins said as calmly as he could. "Listen. Whatever it is that killed the crew and took DeWinter, it's nocturnal. The first time it came aboard was at night. When did it come aboard the ship?"

"I don't know." Bennett said. "Maybe an hour ago?"

"So dusk?" Hawkins asked.

Bennett hesitated and then nodded. "Yeah, the sun was below the horizon."

"Dusk, then. Odds are it won't come out during the day. So we stay here until morning, wait for the sun to be in the sky, and then head to the *Magellan*. We can be out of the lagoon before night."

"There isn't really another choice," Joliet said. "We can't stay here."

Bennett was nodding now. "It could work." He stepped away from Joliet, rubbing his head. "It could work. If we're fast. If—"

"Do you guys smell that?" Joliet asked.

Bray sniffed the air. "Smell what?"

Hawkins took a deep breath through his nose. "Something sweet."

"Like flowers," Joliet said.

"But it's faint," Hawkins said. "Could be nighttime-blooming species on the island."

"It's really strong over here." Joliet sniffed the air near the window.

Hawkins stepped up next to Joliet and sniffed. It was stronger by the window, but . . . Hawkins leaned in close to Joliet and smelled again. "It's you."

"Maybe she got something on her outside?" Bennett said. "In the jungle?"

Hawkins wandered the hall, sniffing like a dog. As he neared the stairs, the odor of formaldehyde tickled his nose. *Definitely not coming from up there.*

He turned around again. Bennett stood on the left side of the hall, near the room where Drake still lay. Bray wandered the far end of the dimly lit hall, sniffing the air. And Joliet remained by the glassless window, watching him. The last light of day was fading. They'd need to make a fire soon. It might attract predators, but there was also nothing better for keeping them at bay. Luckily they had a large supply of very dry pallets to burn. He was about to bring the subject up when an ear-splitting blare, deep and full of bass, rolled over the entire island like an audio tidal wave.

"What was that!" Bennett shouted, cringing.

"That was the same sound," Bray said. "Before DeWinter was—"

Hawkins didn't hear the rest of Bray's sentence. Something moved outside the window behind Joliet.

His mind screamed *snake!*, but as he opened his mouth to shout a warning he noticed the slender intruder was jointed. It had knuckles—*a finger*—with a sharp claw at the end! "Joliet!" Hawkins shouted, but his warning came too late.

The long, slender finger slid beneath Joliet's arm, wrapped around her shoulder, and lifted her off the ground.

Joliet screamed. She pounded the large digit with her fists, but her effort had no effect. Hawkins and Bray charged forward simultaneously. Bray had the ax ready to swing, but the finger pulled Joliet halfway out the window.

"Mark!" Joliet screamed.

He dove for her legs as she continued to rise out of the window, but her feet slipped outside before he arrived. He collided with the wall and fell to the floor, but wasted no time springing back to his feet. He thrust himself halfway out the window and looked up. Framed by the nearly black sky, he saw Joliet being pulled up the side of the concrete building. Above her loomed a massive shadow he recognized from the *Magellan*.

It's the same thing that took DeWinter!

"Joliet!" he screamed. "Avril!"

And then they were gone, up and over, onto the roof.

Hawkins flung himself back into the hallway. He snatched up the rifle as he ran for the exit. Bray followed on his heels and together they made short work of the pallet barricade. Hawkins ripped open the door and charged into the darkness.

The night's cool air felt like a cold winter day, causing goose bumps to rise on his skin. He ran out into the field. His sudden appearance and rapid approach sent goats fleeing. Their bleats and jangling bells blocked out all other noises.

Hawkins spun with the rifle, looking for a target.

Where did you go? he thought. *Where did you go!*

He found his answer when he looked up.

So far from civilization, the stars were already out in force. Every constellation imaginable filled the night sky. The Milky Way cut across the center of it. But a portion of the sky was blacked out.

It was above him!

The blacked-out portion of sky grew quickly larger.

"Bray, look out!" Hawkins shouted and shoved his friend clear before diving out of the way.

The ground shook from an impact. An inhuman roar ripped through the air—one part lion, one part crow. The creature had arrived.

THIRTY-THREE

Hawkins jumped to his feet and spun to face the thing, but it was already moving toward him. His eyes had adjusted to the half-moon light and he saw just bits and pieces of the thing before it reached him. It hunched forward as it charged, but still stood at least eight feet tall. And the proportions were all wrong. The chest and shoulders looked far too vast for the tiny waist to support and one arm was larger than the other. In fact, he wasn't sure if one of the arms was even an arm. *No way this thing is human*, he thought, and then it was upon him. He pulled the rifle's trigger at the last moment, but the shot was wild and if it struck the creature, it showed no sign. It just attacked.

The blow was blunt, but concussive. It struck his sternum, which flexed with the strike and saved him from internal injuries, but it knocked the wind out of him and sent him sprawling into the grass. The rifle flew from his grasp, falling into the darkness somewhere out of reach.

Clutching grass in his hands, Hawkins fought to push himself up. The thing had proven itself to be the far more aggressive predator and would no doubt finish him off quickly. When his vision tunneled from lack of air, he thought his time on Earth had come to an end.

But the creature didn't attack.

Why not? he wondered between gasps.

"Hawkins!" Bray shouted. "I have her!"

Hawkins's vision cleared just in time for him to see Bray walking backward toward the defunct laboratory. He held Joliet under her arms and dragged her as quickly as he could. But not fast enough to escape the creature. Even at a sprint, Bray wouldn't have stood a chance.

The thing proved that by taking two quick steps in Bray's direction and then leaping clear over the man. Bray shouted and spun around, but the creature batted him to the side. He tumbled and rolled over the grass before disappearing from view.

For a moment, Hawkins couldn't figure out where his friend had gone. Then he heard a splash.

Bray is in the river!

Hawkins took a long breath, steadied himself, and stood. His head spun for a moment, but quickly cleared with a spike of adrenaline. The creature was heading for Joliet's still form, lying in the grass.

Hawkins unclipped his knife.

Be aggressive, he told himself, but knew it wouldn't make a difference. The most aggressive wasp in the world could never kill a human being. The best it could hope for was to deliver a painful sting. Hawkins charged, knife raised, hoping he could sting the creature. *Even people run from a wasp's sting*, he told himself.

The thing scooped Joliet from the ground and flung her over its shoulder. It didn't even glance in Hawkins's direction.

Hawkins ran in silence, focusing on the creature's chest. If he was lucky, the blade might find its heart. Believing surprise was his only chance, he stayed silent even as he dove forward and swung the blade.

But Hawkins quickly learned the creature's indifference to his approach had nothing to do with not being aware of him. He was simply too insignificant to pay any attention to. The blade found its target at the center of the creature's chest. The blow perfectly mirrored the attack that slew the bear so many years ago, but the outcome this time was far different.

There was a loud *tink* as the knife struck a rock-hard

surface and skipped to the side. His fist struck the hard surface next. Pain radiated from his hand and up his arm. The blade fell to the ground.

Hawkins stumbled back, clutching his hand. *What the hell is this thing?*

The creature turned away from him, but then paused a moment. Its ragged breathing drowned out the sound of the now distant goat bleats. While most of the giant body was still cloaked in shadow, moonlight lit the creature's face as it glanced back at him.

His body tensed when its eyes found his.

It had the face . . . of a woman.

And the eyes of a goat.

A smile revealed the teeth of a tiger.

This chimera, like the panther-child, was part human. But there were *three* distinct species just in its face! Hawkins didn't want to know what species formed the rest of the creature, but he couldn't let it leave with Joliet. Not without a fight.

He stepped for the knife, but the blade was snatched from the ground. He saw the blade glint in the moonlight, held in the grasp of one of the creature's hands—if it had hands; its digits blended into the night.

Ping! The blade snapped free from the hilt and spun to the ground.

Hawkins just stared, too stunned to take action. The thing had just snapped the knife's blade like it was little more than a dry twig.

What could he do against that?

Before he had a chance to answer the question, the thing leapt. It landed on the other side of the river. Hawkins saw it jump twice more, clearing the razor-wire fence with little effort. When branches and leaves crunched beneath the creature's weight, Hawkins was snapped from his confusion.

The creature took Joliet!

He ran toward the river. "Bray!" he shouted. "Bray! Where are you?" But there was no reply. Bray was either dead, unconscious on the bank, or had already been swept over the falls. Hawkins ran along the river, trying to spot his friend, but there was no sign of the man. When he reached the wooden bridge spanning the river, he vaulted across and headed for the gate he'd spotted earlier.

The chain-link fence, tucked into the jungle and concealed in darkness, was impossible to see. Hawkins reached it faster than he thought he would and crashed into it with a loud jangle. His chest and arms pitched over the curls of razor wire. Rusty blades sliced into his flesh, drawing blood. He winced as he pulled back, but did not cry out. He was beyond acknowledging the pain.

Fumbling in the darkness, Hawkins found the latch, pulled it up, and swung the gate open. He felt the smooth surface of a well-worn path beneath his feet, but after just a few steps was wading through ferns. He adjusted back toward the path, found it again, and tried his best to stay on it. He slowed, despite his panic, and soon realized pursuit was hopeless.

The goat-eyed creature could see in the dark.

He couldn't.

It was far stronger and faster.

It knew the island.

And even if he somehow caught up to the creature, what could he do? His knife—the blade that had saved him from a grizzly bear, great white shark, and a tentacle-tongued crocodile, not to mention a draco-snake—had been snapped in two. The knife had become a symbol of his mastery of nature and a reminder of a time when he'd lost respect for the power of nature. Its casual destruction had taken his confidence.

He was out of his element. There was nothing natural about this creature, or anything on this island, save for maybe the rats.

Hawkins stopped. He cursed through grinding teeth.

He tried to focus, to clear his thoughts. He'd have to find a way back up the path. Go to the laboratory. Check on Bennett. And Drake. Search for Bray. But he probably wouldn't find the man in the dark, so he'd have to search again in the morning. And then?

Plans had changed. He wouldn't leave without Joliet even

if it meant dying here. Bennett, Bray, and Drake could leave, but he would scour the island until he found her. Dead or alive.

Hawkins felt himself on the other side of that message for the first time. *Dead or alive.* Thinking it made his heart go cold. He was glad he'd never voiced the phrase to the families whose lost ones he'd searched for. So for the first time in his life, he altered the phrase.

"I'll find her alive," he said, and as the last syllable escaped his lips, Joliet screamed.

Close by.

Hawkins spun toward the sound and broke into a sprint.

"Joliet!" he shouted.

Within five steps he was up to full speed.

When he reached ten steps, he ran headlong into something sinewy. It clotheslined him across the throat, flipping him back. His head struck something hard and unforgiving.

Joliet screamed again, this time sounding much more distant. The sound of her voice faded, but not before lulling Hawkins into unconsciousness.

THIRTY-FOUR

Howie GoodTracks leaned over Hawkins's prone body. "It's broken."

Hawkins had never broken a bone before and the sight of his bulging shin nearly made him pass out. But GoodTracks took him by the shoulders and gave him a shake.

"Hey!" the old man said. "Do not go into shock. It's just a broken bone. These things happen. But you will die if you aren't able to keep your mind sharp."

That snapped Hawkins out of his pain-filled haze. "Die?"

GoodTracks nodded. "What would you do if I were not here with you?"

"You *are* here with me!" Hawkins shouted back.

"How many times have you done something foolish like this without me around?"

Hawkins looked up at the tall rock he'd leapt from. He had, in fact, jumped from it at least twenty times previously. Thinking he'd perfected his landing technique, he decided to show his mentor. But in his excitement, he jumped higher and farther than before. The landing was hard and all wrong. He knew the answer, but didn't offer it.

GoodTracks continued. "If this happened to you, alone, in the forest, what would you do?"

"I—I don't know," Hawkins admitted as he fought the tears gathering in his eyes.

"Good news," GoodTracks said with a slight grin. "You'll learn today. Look around you. What do you see?"

Hawkins looked around the forest. The tall pine forest floor was mostly clear of brush, but it was littered with fallen branches. "You want me to make a splint?"

GoodTracks nodded. "And set the bone. Find some crutches. And then walk the mile back to the lodge. We'll start with the bone."

"You can't be serious," Hawkins said.

"You know I am." GoodTracks stood back and crossed his arms. "Now, sit up."

Hawkins obeyed. He wanted to be angry at GoodTracks, but couldn't be. He knew his surrogate father was right. This was his fault, and it could have happened during any of his previous jumps. And it could happen again. He looked down at the leg. It hurt less now and he felt almost giddy. *I'm in shock*, he realized, but then decided there was no better time to try what he was about to do. If the pain got worse, or his thoughts fully cleared, or the leg swelled too much, he'd be done.

He leaned forward, reaching past the break, and took hold of his ankle with both hands. An electric zing of pain shot up his leg, but he held on tight. "What do I do?"

"Tug your leg down, angle it back in place, and let go. The muscles will pull the bone together, but then we'll need something to hold it there."

Hawkins's face screwed up with determination. In three seconds, he tugged, shifted, and let go of his leg when it was straightened, screaming for the duration before passing out.

If not for the light of day tingeing the back of his eyelids red, Hawkins wouldn't have realized more than a few minutes had passed. His beaten body gave into exhaustion and slipped quietly from unconsciousness to sleep. His thoughts drifted to the dream, which was actually a memory. He managed to set the leg, find a single crutch, and hobble most of his way back to the lodge where they were staying. GoodTracks had helped toward the end and told Hawkins he was proud of him. It was a painful memory, but a good one.

Hawkins shifted with a groan. Every muscle ached, and would for days. His chest hurt so bad that he wondered if the creature's strike had broken a few ribs. He opened his eyes and squinted against a shaft of morning sunlight that somehow found a path through the canopy to his face. He turned away from the light, which kick-started a hangoverlike headache. His head felt like it might explode when he pushed himself into a sitting position, but forgot all about the pain pulsing through his body when his head collided with something.

The object was soft but firm and quickly registered in Hawkins's mind as a body standing over him. Human, animal or chimera, friend or foe, living or dead, he didn't know. His reaction fit every scenario.

A shout burst from Hawkins's mouth as he scuttled away from his visitor like a startled crab. Through blurred vision he saw the shape of a man standing still.

"Bray?" he asked, rubbing his eyes, willing them to focus. "Bennett?"

He would have been happy if it were either man.

Pain pounded within his head, squeezing his eyes shut. "Who are you?" he asked, but got no reply. He took several long, slow breaths, listening for the man's approach, but he never moved. When the pain subsided, Hawkins slowly opened his eyes. The foliage at his feet came into focus. He lifted his head and saw the man.

Confusion gripped his mind for a moment as he looked into the eyes of the last *Magellan* crewmember he expected to see.

Cahill.

But then he saw the body. With a shout, Hawkins backed away even faster than before. He stopped in a sea of ferns, his head poking out like a frightened child beneath a blanket. But his horror was short lived. Seeing no immediate danger, Hawkins pulled himself to his feet, fought a moment of nausea, and then turned his attention to Cahill.

While the man's bearded face and shaggy hair were intact, the rest of his body had been mutilated. Severely.

A pair of tattered boxer shorts and shreds of blood-soaked shirt clinging to his shoulders were all that remained of his clothes. His legs, while still connected to the torso, appeared to have been gnawed on. Eaten. In some places, the meat had been stripped to the bone. Whatever had taken his body from the netting around the *Magellan* had made a meal of him before stringing him up. *As what? A message? A trap? Decoration?* Hawkins couldn't decide.

Cahill's body hung suspended above the path, his feet just inches from the ground. His arms were propped up on the lines that wrapped around his chest and tied tree branches. The pose made him look like a mutilated Christ figure. But the worst part was the line holding up the body. At first, Hawkins thought it was a flexible rope, like thick bungee cord, but then he saw its origin: Cahill's gut had been sliced open with surgical precision. He'd been strung up with his own intestines, wrapping back and forth between body and tree limbs before looping back into his open gut.

Hawkins felt a growing revolt as he realized that he'd run headlong into a taut line of intestine the night before. It's what had swept him off his feet and slammed him to the ground. His hand went to his neck and found flakes of dried blood clinging to his skin. He frantically brushed it away.

With one last glance at Cahill's body, his thoughts returned to the living. Joliet had been taken. Bray had fallen in the river. Bennett never left the laboratory building, but that didn't mean he spent the night there—the kid was a mess. And Drake still lay on a pallet, burning from fever. Maybe worse.

He turned and ran up the path, quickly finding the gate. He tore it open and ran into the yard. "Bray!" he shouted, but his call was replied to with bells and bleats. The small herd of goats trotted to him, greeting him happily as though a monster hadn't been in their midst the previous night. *They should be terrified and jumpy*, Hawkins thought, *not indifferent*.

He stopped at the river, searching its steep banks for Bray's body.

Nothing.

He crossed the small bridge in two long steps. The goats followed him over the river, their hooves sounding like thunder in the early morning quiet as they tromped over the bridge's wooden planks.

"Quiet!" he whispered at the animals, but they remained sanguine and oblivious. He wasn't worried that they would give away his position—the island's residents would be used to the goats' clamor. He just wanted to hear someone if they replied to his calls.

He ran for the laboratory entrance. "Bray!"

The blockade of pallets was still pushed to the side. Not a good sign. He entered slowly, fists clenched. The goats waited by the door.

The hallway stood empty. "Bray! Bennett!"

No reply.

He checked the first room and found it empty, as expected. But when he checked the second room, where they'd left not only their backpacks and Drake, he found it equally as empty. The packs and Drake were gone. His pulse quickened as he checked the final two rooms and found no trace of their passing. He spun around, looking at the hallway again.

Even the dead seagulls are gone!

After a nerve-wracking and rushed search of the top two floors, Hawkins turned up nothing. The only sign of their passage was the destruction wrought on the top floor by the panther-child chimera.

As he left the building, he found himself looking into a sea of eyes similar to the creature that took Joliet. He had trouble matching their gaze, but the goats' friendly greeting put him at ease. These animals, at least, were not killers. Feeling a little like a shepherd, Hakwins set off across the yard, eyes on the ground. He found what he was looking for twenty feet away. The rifle.

He picked up the weapon and checked it over. It seemed to be in good repair. He toggled the lever, chambering a fresh round and expelling the empty shell casing left over from the single shot he'd taken the previous night. Remembering the round still in his pocket, he took it out and loaded it into the weapon. Ten rounds. When he thought about the creatures he'd encounter so far, the weapon seemed wholly inadequate.

Hawkins tried to fathom where everyone had gone. He couldn't see Bennett leaving on his own and Drake should have been immobilized. And Bray . . . Hawkins thought about checking the waterfall, but decided against it after applying a little logic. If Bray had gone over the falls and survived the drop and the croc, he would have come back here, or retreated to the *Magellan*. If he didn't, well, he was dead.

"Bray!" he shouted one more time, as loudly as he could. The sudden shout froze the goats in place, silencing their bells. In the quiet that followed, Hawkins heard nothing. He searched the grass for signs of where everyone had gone, but the goats had trampled any tracks left behind.

So he focused on the only thing he did know. Joliet. She'd been taken and he knew the general direction the creature had fled. Rifle in hand, he set off across the yard.

He only got ten feet when a glint of light caught his attention. He crouched and picked up the broken blade of his knife. The handle was missing, but the blade was intact, and still razor sharp. Lifting it carefully between two fingers, he slid the blade into its sheath and buttoned it closed.

A shadow swept past him, drawing his gaze up. A lone seagull circled high overhead. Hawkins would almost welcome the chance to take out his frustrations. *Just try it, you son of a bitch.* As he lowered his eyes again, Hawkins noticed a detail on the roof of the laboratory. At first, he couldn't figure out what the two cylinders were. But then they moved, each rotating in opposite directions.

Cameras!

The implications hit him fast and hard. Not only did the islands occupants have access to the outside world, but they also had a decent budget. He could see the solar panel mounted behind the cameras, allowing them to operate without a direct line of power. Sending the images wirelessly to some other part of the island would be easy. Even worse, there was a strong chance that their progress across the island was being monitored. The appearance of the creature in conjunction with the foghorn also insinuated some kind of coordinated effort. Were they being toyed with?

As disturbing as it was, the discovery of the cameras changed nothing. Whether his return to the lab had been noted or not, his goals remained the same: find his friends and get the hell off the island.

The goats followed him to the gate. As he opened and closed it behind him, the goats tried to follow through the spring-powered hatch at the bottom. He pushed it closed. "Stay here," he growled.

The first goat pushing on the gate looked up at him. It butted its horns against the chain link, clearly not accustomed to having its freedom restricted. Hawkins lost his patience and shook the gate. "Stay here!" he shouted, then delivered a rattling kick to the chain-link fence.

"They listen if you're nice."

The voice spun Hawkins around so fast that he fell on his ass and dropped the rifle. He twisted his head back and forth, looking for the voice's source, but saw no one. He snatched up the rifle and continued his search, looking over the sight. "Who's there?"

"I won't hurt you if you don't hurt me," the voice said. It sounded feminine. And young.

Leaves rustled over his head. He aimed the weapon up, but saw nothing.

The goats shied away, bleating as though wounded.

Hawkins ignored them.

The voice took on a more serious tone. "I could have killed you already if I wanted to."

Not serious, Hawkins thought, *impatient*.

He was a quick draw if he needed to be, so he lowered the weapon in favor of getting answers.

"Why are you here?" the voice asked.

"Let me see you," he replied.

"You should probably leave."

No shit. He put the rifle down on the ground and raised

his hands, ready to grab the rifle at the first sign of danger. "What's your name?"

"I'm not supposed to talk to strangers."

Hawkins was now convinced he was speaking with someone young. "Why not?"

"They die."

Hawkins fought the urge to pick up the rifle and start pulling the trigger. "Always?"

"Yes."

"Why are you talking to me, then?"

"I sometimes break the rules."

Hawkins forced a grin and tried to make it look real. "Me, too."

"I know."

"How?"

"You use a gun. That's not very fair."

"It keeps me alive."

"Not against—" The voice paused for five full seconds. "I'm not supposed to talk to strangers." Hawkins heard movement to his left, but didn't pick up the rifle. The sound was moving away.

"Wait!" he said. "My name is Mark Hawkins. We don't have to be strangers."

"Hawkins," the voice said, trying the word out slowly. "Like the bird?"

"Like the bird," he confirmed.

"I don't see any bird in you," the voice said.

Bird in me? His eyes widened. *She thinks I'm a chimera.* "I'm not one of those things."

"Things?"

"A chimera," he said.

"Things!" The young voice sounded angry and had a little growl to it.

Son of a bitch. Hawkins realized his mistake just before the face emerged from the shadows in the canopy above him. The voice—the girl—she was the panther-child chimera.

Her squinted yellow eyes glared at him. Her lithe body,

part human, part cat, tensed as though preparing to pounce. Her long black tail twitched behind her.

Hawkins looked into her eyes, still fighting the urge to pick up the rifle. He'd made a horrible first impression with this . . . girl when they'd first met. He was determined to do better this time. He just hoped she wouldn't tear his throat out.

"You think you're better than me," she said. "Everyone who comes here is the same. You're all afraid of us because we don't look like you. But that's fine. You should be. We're stronger, faster, and smarter than any of you."

The tone of the girl's voice had taken on that of a teenage temper tantrum, and Hawkins decided that's what it was. So he didn't argue, he just listened to her vent. But then her tone became darker. She slinked back into the shadows so he could only see her yellow eyes. "I don't want to know you."

"Wait," he said.

She moved farther away. "I don't want to be your friend."

Hawkins stood. "I'm sorry."

The panther-girl closed her eyes and disappeared. Her last words lost the edge and sounded sad more than anything. "You'll be dead soon, anyway."

The trees above shook, and then she was gone.

Hawkins searched the jungle. She was gone.

While he took consolation in the fact that something other than the goats didn't want to eat him, he now had even more unanswered questions. *Nothing I can do about that now*, he thought, and stood.

"Hello!" a voice called. Faint. In the distance. Behind him.

Hawkins spun around and climbed up the hill, back toward the old lab.

"Where is everyone?" the voice called.

Hawkins paused at the fence, wary of the cameras. Bennett was there, walking across the wooden bridge with a severe limp. The goats gave him an unusually wide birth, which was probably a good thing. Bennett didn't look so hot, though his face perked up when he saw Hawkins by the fence.

"Hawkins!" Bennett said a lot louder than he should have. He gave a wave and hobbled across the clearing. "Hawkins, thank God!" He tripped when he reached the fence and Hawkins had to catch him.

"Where are the others?" Hawkins asked.

"I—I don't know."

"What happened?"

Bennett's eyes turned down. "I'm . . . not sure."

"You were in the lab last night," Hawkins said, trying not to let his impatience show. Bennett was injured, and shook up, but he was also the only one who might know what happened to the others. "Bray is gone. Drake is gone. All of our equipment is gone. The lab has been cleaned out."

Bennett didn't look up as he spoke softly. "I ran."

"You what?"

"Ran," Bennett said. "Into the jungle. When that thing showed up I didn't know what to do! I saw you go down. I wouldn't have stood a chance. So I ran. Hid in a tree overnight. Didn't come back out until just now."

Hawkins sighed. He was frustrated with the kid, but understood. Bennett was right. If he'd stayed, he would have been killed or taken with Joliet. He gave Bennett a pat on the shoulder. "Don't worry, kid, you did the right thing."

Bennett began to shake, maybe from fear, maybe from adrenaline.

Hawkins took hold of his arms, which felt stronger than he would have guessed. "Bennett, you're okay. You're safe."

The shaking got worse, and Hawkins worried the kid was having a seizure. But his eyes looked clear. And afraid. Wet with tears. Hawkins wasn't exactly a fatherly type. He didn't have those instincts, and they were never modeled to him by his father. Instead, he channeled Howie GoodTracks. "Life is full of hardships. Horrible things sometimes happen. People we love die. But in the end, it's all heat for the furnace."

Bennett stopped shaking and locked his eyes on Hawkins. "What?"

"Bad things refine us," Hawkins said, completing the metaphor. "Make us stronger, so that we can overcome the challenges in our own lives. That's what's happening here. For you. When we get off this island, you'll be a stronger person. A better person."

Hawkins cringed inwardly. When GoodTracks spoke similar words to him it was because they were putting down a lame horse, not running for their lives on an island populated by killer chimeras. He doubted even GoodTracks would have something wise to say about their current situation. His mentor understood nature like few people, but there was very little natural about the island. Still, the words seemed to have done the trick.

Bennett relaxed a bit and gave a nod. He offered a lame smile. "Easy for you to say. You're already pretty tough."

Hawkins smiled, though it was purely for show. "Wasn't always."

Bennett braced himself against a palm trunk. "So, what are you doing? What's your plan? You have one, right?"

Hawkins noted that Bennett wasn't including himself in the questions, but didn't point it out. "Following the trail."

"That's it? That's your plan?"

Hawkins's impatience grew again. "I don't know if the others are alive, or even where they are. All I know is that that thing took Joliet in this direction. It left a good trail to follow, but I think it was heading in the same direction as this path." Hawkins motioned to the path behind him. "So we'll follow the path, find what we find, and try not to get killed. That specific enough for you?"

Bennett moved away from Hawkins and leaned against a tree. "I'll just wait here, then."

Hawkins closed his eyes and took a slow breath. "Bennett, I'm not sure I'll be coming back this way. You can't wait here. It's not safe."

"Wasn't safe with you, either."

Kid has a point.

"And wherever you end up, you're going to have to come this way to get back to the *Magellan*. My ankle is twisted. I'm just going to slow you down."

Hawkins couldn't decide if Bennett was playing it smart

or was just a coward. Either way, he had no real solid argument against Bennett finding a place to hide and lying low. He probably would have to come back this way to reach the *Magellan*. "Fine. But pick a spot and don't move. If you have to piss or shit, dig a hole and bury it."

"To hide the smell?" Bennett asked.

"A lot of predators hunt by scent," Hawkins said. "Stay low. Stay quiet. Do not move. And *stay awake*. When I come back through here, I'm going to call your name once. Just once. If you don't come out within thirty seconds, I'm going to leave."

"You promise you'll come back for me?" Bennett asked.

"If I'm still alive."

Bennett gave a nod. "I trust you." He stepped off the trail and waded into a tall stand of ferns. He ducked down and lay on his back by the base of a tree. Once the ferns stopped shaking, he was invisible. "Good?"

"Perfect."

"I'll try to stay here, but if I have to move, I won't go far."

"Good enough," Hawkins said. He thought about warning him about the panther-child chimera, and about Cahill's body strung up farther down the path, but decided the less he knew, the less likely he'd be to panic and do something stupid. He turned toward the trail.

Bennett's voice stopped him for a moment. "Hawkins, good luck."

Hawkins didn't reply. He just followed the trail, thinking it would be a miracle if he ever saw Bennett again. He was beginning to doubt any of them would make it off the island alive.

The path before him led down the hillside. He moved slowly at first, wading past the knee-high ferns and then Cahill's body. He considered cutting the man's body down, but if he did that, whoever put it here would know he'd come this way. He also walked to the side of the path rather than on it. He'd rather be the tracker than the tracked.

With Cahill and the laboratory behind him, Hawkins quickened his pace. When the grade became steep, his jog became a run. When the hill leveled out, he kept on running, burning with fear for his friends. What would he do if he was the last one alive? He forgot the question when he saw signs of recent passage.

There was a footprint indented on the path, heading in the same direction. He crouched to inspect it and the motion saved his life.

With a surprised shriek the draco-snake soared over Hawkins's head. Its wings snapped open, slowing its flight. The creature clung to a tree trunk, whipped its head around, and hissed.

Hawkins ran like an Olympic sprinter after the gun is fired. He could hear the dracos behind him. Trees shook. Shrieks grew louder. Shadows danced on the jungle floor around him. But he didn't stop and fight. He couldn't.

One bite, he thought. *Just one bite and I'm a dead man.*

The jungle ahead looked thick with brush. He'd have to plow right through and hope the draco-snakes got tangled long enough for him to elude them. His arms took the brunt of the impact as he raised them to protect his face. He felt stinging pricks all over, some sharp enough to be bites.

He shouted as the brush gave way. He spilled past the foliage barrier and fell to the ground, bathed in hot sunlight.

The cacophony of the sudden draco-snake attack fell away abruptly as Hawkins was once again expelled from their territory. He checked his body quickly, finding a multitude of scrapes, but no wounds that looked like snakebites. He also knew that if he'd been bitten, he'd already feel the effects as his blood raced through his adrenaline-charged body.

Confident he wasn't going to die yet, Hawkins looked up at his surroundings and once again found himself baffled. He stood on the edge of an expansive clearing—a pasture, really—complete with a herd of cows. Thirty head. And each one of them was looking at him.

The herd stood on the muddy bank of a small lake. He realized he'd seen both the lake and green pastureland from the top of the pillbox.

A wave of agitation worked its way through the herd. The

cows mooed and stomped their feet. And then, one by one, they backed away from the water. When the source of their distress was revealed, Hawkins shook his head. "You've got to be kidding me."

The bull stood as tall as Hawkins's six feet and rippled with muscles upon muscles. He recognized the breed as a Belgian Blue, famous for its double muscling that made them look like bovine bodybuilders. The brown-coated monstrous bull easily weighed more than a ton. But none of that was as frightening as the look in its eyes. As the herd's protector, the bull clearly saw him as a threat. Hawkins took a step away from the bull, but stopped when his back struck the jungle's foliage and set the draco-snakes to shrieking.

To his left was open field in which he could never outrun the bull. To his right was the lake and whatever dangers lurked within its waters. But both choices were better than the certain death waiting in front and behind him. Field or lake?

The bull didn't give him time to decide. With a snort and a stomp of its hoof, the bull lowered its sharp, curved horns and charged.

THIRTY-FIVE

A moment of indecision paralyzed Hawkins. He saw death waiting in every direction. Not just waiting, reaching out for him. The island seemed perfectly designed to snuff out human life.

The bull let out an angry bellow that refocused Hawkins's attention. The giant protector of the herd had halved the distance between them and was closing the gap fast. Hawkins raised the rifle, took aim, and pulled the trigger. The report echoed over the lake. A pinprick of red appeared on the bull's flank, but the giant showed no sign of slowing. He fired again, striking the bull's back. But still, it charged. The bull's dense musculature protected it from the bullets. A killing body shot would be impossible, even if the bull stood still. Hawkins aimed for the head, but it bounced with each step. Hawkins let out a breath and pulled the trigger a third time.

The shot missed.

Or, at least, buried itself in the depths of the giant's body. Hawkins lowered the rifle. He was wasting ammo.

Head to the ground, the bull moved like a missile on a straight trajectory. And it wouldn't stop until it reached him.

Seeing a flaw in the bull's attack, Hawkins remained rooted in place, but tensed himself for a sudden dash. He'd seen more than a few matadors sidestep a bull on TV. Granted, he usually rooted for the bull, but this fight for survival wasn't sport. If Hawkins didn't time his leap right, he'd be gored, or worse. Of course, even if he did manage to escape the charging bull, he'd still have to sprint across the field. His only real hope was that the bull would get tangled up in the thick brush separating field from jungle, or that the draco-snakes would take exception to the bovine intrusion and use their poisonous bites to stop the giant.

The ground shook.

Mud flew from the bull's pounding hooves.

The monstrous animal's muscles rippled with energy.

And the water, calm and serene, parted for a pair of yellow eyes.

A snout appeared next, framed by a V of rippling water.

Hawkins registered the motion, but the bull either didn't concern itself with the approaching crocodile or simply didn't see it. But in the second that Hawkins should have jumped to the side, he saw that the croc was also headed straight toward him. Once the bull was done with him, the croc would finish him off.

Hawkins drew a sharp breath when he realized that he couldn't avoid the bull. He leapt anyway, throwing himself back and away. At the very same moment the bull's head connected with his airborne legs, the water at the edge of the lake exploded and two barbed tentacles shot out.

But the squid limbs weren't aimed for Hawkins. The croc had a much bigger meal in mind. With a slap, the tentacles snagged the bull's back and pulled. The bull's one-ton assault was immediately arrested by the equally heavy crocodile.

Hawkins saw it all as he spun through the air and landed in the grass. He pushed himself up and watched the beginning of a monumental struggle. The bull bucked and kicked, reacting to the pain of having two lines of hooked tentacles embedded in its meaty back. The croc simply held on, no doubt waiting for the heavy bull to wear itself out.

When a second croc rose from the lake, the bull seemed to realize the amount of trouble it was in. It planted all four feet in the mud, gave a snort, and began walking backward.

The croc let out a deep vibrato of a roar as it slid through the water toward shore. When it reached the lake's edge, the chimera croc dug in its claws and let the dead weight of its massive body battle the rolls of bovine muscle.

Hawkins climbed to his feet and stepped away from the scene. This croc was even larger than the one they'd encountered in the river. The second didn't look nearly as big, but if it got close enough to the bull, he didn't think it would last long. When a third and fourth croc showed up, Hawkins realized he still might find himself on the menu and double-timed his retreat.

With the sound of the angry bull and hungry crocs behind him, Hawkins ran across the rolling field. He had no real destination in mind, he just wanted to get the hell away. After sprinting for five minutes, Hawkins climbed to the top of a grassy hill and saw the end of the field. And what he saw waiting for him stunned him into stopping. Not because it was horrible or frightening like any of the other horrors on this island, but because it was so damn *normal*.

A red barn, like something out of a Norman Rockwell painting, sat at the edge of the field. Chickens danced around, pecking at the ground. A silo rose up behind the building, which looked fairly new, or at least impeccably maintained. Realizing that there might be people working here, Hawkins dropped to the ground and flattened himself out. He watched the barn for several minutes, looking for any sign of a human presence.

He saw nothing.

A loud moo drew a surprised shout from Hawkins and spun him around. A lone cow stood on the decline behind him, chewing its cud and staring at him. He saw no malice in the creature's eyes or body language, just mild interest. It swallowed, lowered its head, and gnawed on the grass.

If someone is there, they know where I am now, Hawkins thought as he got to his feet. He ran to the barn as fast as possible, hoping to minimize his time exposed. The chickens hopped about, flapping their wings at his approach. But the racket drew no attention. Hawkins scanned the area and found it empty. The place seemed abandoned, but recently. He found a side door on the barn open and let himself in. Inside were two long rows of stables, likely for the cows when they were done grazing. He saw equipment for milking, bags of feed with English-language labels, and lines of farming tools—shovels, hoes, rakes, and more.

The island is self-sustaining, he realized, thinking about the goats, cows, and chickens he'd come across. *An honest-to-goodness Homestead 731.*

A door at the back of the barn lead to a butcher shack. Blood stained the concrete floor, where drains had been installed. It looked eerily similar to the laboratory's second-floor surgical suite, except for the chains and hooks that hung from the ceiling. But what really held Hawkins's attention was the array of butchering tools hung neatly on a Peg-Board. Hawkins helped himself to a machete and tested the blade. Not as sharp as his knife, but with a little power behind it, it would probably be capable of severing a limb. There was no sheath for the blade, so he slid it under his belt.

As Hawkins headed toward the door, he spotted what looked like a spray nozzle for a garden hose, but it looked too heavy duty. He picked it up. The device was all metal and the weight felt similar to a handgun. Out of context, he might not have realized what it was, but here, in a slaughterhouse for cows, he recognized the device as a bolt stunner. Before cows are drained of blood, they must first be rendered unconscious. The bolt stunner worked by shooting a stainless-steel rod into the cattle's forehead, punching a hole in the skull, destroying brain matter, and knocking the animal unconscious without killing it—the bloodletting did that. It only worked when placed up against something, so it was an ineffective long-range weapon, but if Hawkins encountered the creature that took Joliet again, it might do some damage. The downside was that the compressed-air cartridge had to be replaced after each use. He put the bolt stunner in his cargo shorts pocket along with two replacement cartridges.

Armed with the rifle, bolt stunner, and machete, Hawkins

felt a little more confident, but not much. An antitank missile would have felt more appropriate.

After scanning the area for signs of life one more time, Hawkins slipped out of the barn's main door. There were no roads or paths leading to the farm like there might be on the mainland, but there was a tractor. And a garden lush with vegetables and even a scarecrow. Rows of neatly arranged trees, heavy with fruit, lined the near acre of crops.

This could support a small village, Hawkins realized, and in this part of the world, the vegetables would grow year round.

Standing out in stark contrast to the farm was a building beyond the orchard. It stood at least three stories tall—all concrete-lined like the other World War II-era structures—was round, and sported a domed room. Square windows wrapped around the building, giving it the look of a Roman coliseum, and perhaps that's what it was. Knowing what Unit 731 had done on the island already, an arena where their victims, or perhaps creations, fought to the death for their entertainment, or even research, wouldn't surprise him at all.

His first instinct was to head away from the building, but Joliet might be there. He had to check it out.

Halfway across the garden, his stomach growled and ached. He knelt down and yanked a carrot from the ground. After brushing it off, he placed the tip in his mouth, took a bite, and stopped midchew.

The scarecrow was gone.

He'd only seen it from a distance, standing still, dressed in overalls, arms outstretched. Given its posture, immobility, and position in the garden, he'd assumed it was nothing more than an inanimate scarecrow. But he'd been duped by the serene setting.

He spun around with the carrot in his mouth and the rifle in his hands. But the scarecrow, or whatever it was, had disappeared.

Moving fast and wary, Hawkins crossed the garden and slipped into the cover provided by rows of apple, pear, and orange trees. The sweet scent of fruit made his belly grumble again. But he forgot his hunger upon hearing the shuffle of feet and a dull, grumbling voice.

Leading with the rifle, Hawkins skirted a Honey Crisp apple tree and aimed it straight at the back of a very tall, very round man. The overalls identified the man as the scarecrow. But the thick neck and bald head and hunched shoulder revealed the man as Jim Clifton, the younger Tweedle brother.

Hawkins lowered the rifle.

Bennett said the crew had been killed. But he hadn't actually seen it happen. He heard them die. Which means they might still be alive. Jim was proof of that.

As gently as he could, Hawkins said, "Jim."

The man spun around fast, startled by Hawkins's voice.

Only the towering figure wasn't actually Jim Clifton.

Not anymore, at least.

THIRTY-SIX

Hawkins reeled back and fell to the soft, grassy earth between the rows of fruit trees. He sat still and silent, watching the hulking form of Jim Clifton stumble about. To say the man had been deformed was an understatement. His eyes were missing and his mouth stapled shut. A hole oozing blood from the inside of his left eye revealed the man had been lobotomized. His ears had been replaced with what looked like futuristic hearing aids fused to his skin.

While the damage done to Jim's head was unthinkable, it didn't frighten Hawkins as much as what had been done to the man's body. Where hands should have been, there were now blades, like butcher knives, fused to his stumpy forearms. Two large medical bags full of pink liquid were strapped to his upper arms and connected to lines embedded in his forearms. Hawkins thought the mobile drips must be providing morphine, or antibiotics, or even antirejection drugs. *Probably all three,* he concluded.

A strange pressure squeezed Hawkins's ears. He shook his head as the pressure built, but he forgot all about it when Jim's confused countenance shifted. The man had looked confused before, like a drugged, blind, deaf, and mute man with extensive injuries and brain trauma should. But now he stood still. Focused. He turned his head down toward Hawkins like he could see.

Hawkins backed away slowly.

Jim raised one of his arms and slipped the knife blade beneath the overall straps.

For a moment, Hawkins thought the man was going to kill himself, but with a quick swipe of his arm, Jim cut through both straps. The overalls top fell forward, revealing the cook's chest and prodigious belly.

Hawkins scrambled back while muttering a string of curses. He stopped when his back struck a tree trunk.

A single word had been carved into Jim's chest. The lettering was intricate, created with care—the work of someone familiar with a scalpel. The wounds weren't deep enough to kill, but swollen and fringed by pink flesh, the text was easy to read.

RANGER.

Whoever had done this knew Hawkins's nickname. Had they been watching them so closely on the island that they overheard conversations? Did the security cameras have microphones? Or had the name been tortured out of one of the captured crew? Bennett had clearly been wrong about the fate of those he left behind. If Blok, Jones, the Tweedles, DeWinter, Joliet, and Kam had all been taken, and tortured, the person who did this could have easily learned his nickname. But why taunt him with it?

The pressure came again, this time in three quick pulses.

Jim exploded into action just as the third burst of pressure finished. He charged forward, swinging wildly with his bladed arms. The man couldn't see, but seemed to know exactly where Hawkins sat.

Armed with a rifle, bolt stunner, and machete, Hawkins could have killed the man. Despite his modifications, Jim was still human. And killing him might have actually been the merciful thing to do, but Hawkins couldn't bring himself to attack. The thought never even crossed his mind. A single overpowering emotion dwarfed his instincts and logic: fear.

Not just for his own safety, but for Jim's. For Joliet's. And Bray's. The entire crew could have been tortured in this way. An image of Joliet mutilated in similar fashion filled his mind and he nearly failed to move clear of Jim's first swing.

It was a wild and uncontrolled swing, as though he knew Hawkins was in front of him, but not exactly where.

The close call squelched Hawkins's fear long enough for him to act. He rolled backward, clear of Jim's reach, and got to his feet.

More pulses.

Jim turned toward him again, arms already swinging.

Hawkins did the only thing he could. He ran. Faster than ever before. He cut through the orchard, following the path of most resistance. If the big man tried to follow, he'd have to wade through overlapping tree branches. Hawkins scrambled under a thick group of low-hanging peach branches and glanced back. Jim stood four rows back, hacking at a tree. He'd get through eventually, but not before Hawkins was long gone.

Hawkins watched the man struggle for a moment. Intense pity for the younger Tweedle washed over him. He shook his head. Letting the man live like this wasn't right. He thumbed off the rifle's safety, placed the stock against his shoulder, and took aim at the capital *A* at the center of the man's chest.

Pulse, pulse.

The pressure distracted Hawkins for just a moment, which was long enough for Jim to turn and run. He disappeared into the orchard.

Someone is still watching me, Hawkins thought. *And somehow controlling Jim.* He looked around for a camera, but couldn't see any. The thick orchard could be filled with them and he'd never know it.

With Jim gone and no other options, Hawkins turned to leave and found the three-story-tall, curved building looming over him. He'd closed the distance to it without even realizing it. The concrete here was a lighter gray and lacked the wear that the abandoned laboratory and the pillbox displayed. The three rows of rectangular windows lining the building held clean glass that showed no signs of aging.

This building is modern, Hawkins thought.

He slid beneath a few more rows of trees and stopped at the building. Moving quietly, he followed the curved wall around the structure, wondering if he was still being watched, and if Jim was once again en route to intercept him. Part of him hoped he'd see Jim again. The man deserved a merciful death.

He reached the front of the building, where a wide-worn path led to a pair of double doors set into a much larger garage door. A pair of security cameras were mounted above the doors, along with three motion-sensitive floodlights. Hawkins flattened himself against the concrete wall and moved slowly to the door. He pushed the door and it opened easily.

Security cameras, but no locks?

Cool air rushed out of the building, quickly drying the sweat coating his body. His skin grew stiff, but the air-conditioning was a welcome change. Hawkins stepped into the dimly lit building, rifle at the ready. His eyes quickly adjusted to the lower light provided by the windows wrapping around the building and he nearly fired off a shot.

He was surrounded by monsters.

But they weren't moving. Or even living. Like the ancient, jarred specimens at the abandoned laboratory, the figures surrounding him were suspended in liquid. Unlike the old lab, these tall glass containers were powered. The hum of electricity and air-conditioning filled the space. Bubbles rose slowly through the gel-like liquid surrounding the bodies, which were mostly concealed in shadow. Tubes dangled down from the black covers like jellyfish tendrils, some floating free, others connected to flesh. Hawkins could see that most, if not all, the specimens had once been human beings, but exactly what had been done to them was concealed by gloom.

He stepped farther in, gaping at the scope of the building and the number of horrors it contained. The circular building was open in the middle, but had three floors of metal grates around the circumference. Metal stairs provided access to each floor, as did a service elevator at the back of the space. The outer walls of each level, including the bottom floor, were lined with specimen tubes. Hundreds of them.

The center of the lowest floor held four oversize glass tanks arranged like a four-leaf clover, creating a kind of hallway around the room. Hawkins headed right, looking for cameras or a living occupant. He didn't think he'd find Joliet here, but there might be some clue about who had been operating the facility since the Second World War.

Warped faces concealed in shadow seemed to stare at him as he passed. Who were these people? How did they get here? By the time Hawkins reached the far side of the surreal storage facility he had far more questions than answers.

A dull *clunk* spun him around. He nearly called out, "Who's there?" but thought better of it. He ducked down and moved against one of the tall glass cylinders at the center of the space. It wasn't exactly a prime hiding spot, since all the containers held clear liquid, but this one also held something large that provided some small amount of cover, though it also blocked his view of the doors.

The room lightened for a moment as the entrance swung open. Hawkins watched the light shift as someone entered. An ominous click echoed off the glass cylinders. Feet shifted over the concrete floor. Whoever had joined him was either really bad at being quiet or had no idea he was there. When a bell jingled, Hawkins was almost certain that the intruder wasn't aware of his presence. He considered the idea that a goat had somehow opened the door and entered, but he could hear someone whispering to themselves. The words were impossible to make out, but the tone was clearly frustrated. Had he managed to elude the cameras after all?

Something clanged. A whispered curse followed the sound. And then, light.

The interior of the building exploded with light as bright as day. The sudden illumination made Hawkins squint. He looked at the floor while his eyes adjusted. When he turned his eyes up again, a face stared at him, just a few inches away.

Hawkins shouted in surprised and spilled back, dropping the rifle.

A battle cry filled the chamber as the person by the door

charged around the hallway. A bell jangled with each heavy step.

Hawkins scrambled for the rifle. He snatched the barrel, dragged it to him, and spun to face his attacker.

But the man had already stopped his assault. He stood in the aisle, ax raised above his head, a look of relief spreading across his face.

Hawkins lowered the rifle. "Bray!" He jumped to his feet as Bray lowered the ax.

"You're alive!" Bray said.

"I was going to say the same thing about you. I thought you went over the falls."

Bray shook his head. "Woke up on the riverbank at dawn. Followed the path in the direction I saw Joliet taken. Figured that's where you would have gone. Did you see Cahill?"

"I was unconscious beneath him," Hawkins said. "In the ferns."

"God," Bray said. "I must have walked right past you. I steered clear of the path until I was beyond him. Was wicked sick. Nearly lost it."

Hawkins looked Bray over. He looked in no worse shape than he had the night before. "How did you get here?"

"You mean, how did I get past the drakes and King Cow?" Bray held up a bell and gave it a shake. "You were right. Works like a charm. Give it a ring every few seconds and it's like you're invisible."

Hawkins would have preferred to stay focused on Bray, but his attention slowly shifted back to the face he'd seen. He turned to the large tank behind which he'd hidden and felt his stomach twist.

Bray followed his gaze and jumped back. "Ahh!" After recovering from his surprise, he said, "You know, I was starting to hope I'd become jaded to this shit, but it just gets worse and worse."

Hawkins stepped closer to the tank, trying to count the number of naked bodies jammed inside. He stopped at twenty-three. The men and women inside the tank had looked like a ball of multicolored flesh. Intertwining limbs mixed with the thin tubes descending from the tank's top made the various people look like a singular organism. When Hawkins saw the stretched skin and thick stitching binding them together, he realized that's exactly what they'd been turned into.

"Where did all these people come from?" Hawkins asked.

"I don't know," Bray said, "But they haven't been here very long." He pointed to a tattoo on a man's shoulder. "That's a Patriots logo. Flying Elvis. They didn't start using that design until 1993. And honestly, the Pats weren't really tattoo material until at least 2002."

Hawkins leaned closer, looking at the faces. "Some of these people are Japanese, I think."

"Really?" Bray put his hands against the glass. "You're right. Why would they do this to their own—"

Pulse, pulse, pulse.

Bray rubbed his ear.

Hawkins flinched back.

"What is it?" Bray asked.

"Did you feel that? In your ear?"

"Yeah, but—"

Pulse, pulse, pulse.

Hawkins scanned back and forth with the rifle. Was something in here with them? Was Jim just outside the door? Finding nothing, Hawkins lowered the rifle and looked back at the large tank.

Twenty-three pairs of eyes now stared back at him.

THIRTY-SEVEN

"Oh shit, oh shit," Bray said, staring at the tank full of bodies bound together. "They're alive!" He backed away from the large tank until his back struck a smaller tank at his back. A *thunk* on the glass spun him around. A suction cup with a gnawing mouth inside was stuck where his head had been.

Hawkins saw the man-thing—a human body lacking arms, but with the face of some kind of bottom-feeding fish—lunge at Bray. He jumped forward and caught the man as he stumbled away. Had the creature not been contained in the glass, it would have easily caught Bray.

"They're waking up," Hawkins said. All around the room, monstrous creations were beginning to move. Some, with limbs, pounded on the glass. Some were enraged, others horrified. But they all wanted the same thing. Out.

Hawkins took two steps toward the exit, pulling Bray behind him, when one of the containment units tipped and shattered on the concrete floor. Viscous gel exploded across the floor, turning the path to the double doors into a slick mess. The freed creature just writhed, its large, limbless body useless.

These are the failures, Hawkins thought.

He pushed forward, intending to slosh through the gelatinous puddle, but a second explosion of glass and gel stopped him in his tracks. The creature that emerged had a powerful chimplike body. Its face was distorted, like some kind of pushed-in pig's snout. It turned toward them as gel dripped from its black fur-coated limbs. The creature snapped its jaws open and closed, revealing a mix of long incisors and canines—like a beaver's teeth combined with a wolf's. A nasty bite.

Hawkins raised the rifle to fire, but a sudden alarm sounded, distracting him and the creature. Warning lights flashed all around. A voice spoke, in English. "Warning. Containment breach detected. Burn will commence in one minute. Please vacate immediately."

Hawkins pulled the trigger.

The creature spun with a squeal as the round punched through its chest and burst out its back.

"Let's go!" Hawkins resumed his charge for the door, but more shattering glass stopped him. Something large stepped out of one of the center tanks, cutting off his path. He fired twice, but only managed to get the monster's attention. With a grunt, it turned toward him. The bulbous body was hairless. Sagging gray flesh covered much of its features, but not the tusks protruding from beneath its jowls, or the claws on its hands, which looked more like talons than actual hands.

Hawkins backed away and shouted in surprise when Bray took his shoulder.

"We can't get out that way," Bray said. "But maybe up there!" He pointed to the ceiling above the third-floor walkway, where a ladder led to a hatch in the ceiling. "I saw a ladder running down the outside."

Hawkins didn't wait. By his count, they had just thirty seconds to escape the "burn," and it didn't take a genius to figure out what that meant. The path to the elevator at the back of the room had been blocked by a spreading layer of gel and waking creatures that either flopped on the floor or gathered their wits. "The stairs!" he shouted, charging up the metal steps.

As they rounded the top of the stairs, a resounding crash split the air over their heads. Clear gel rained down from the floor above, coating the men. Hawkins winced as the scent of noxious chemicals and excrement covered his body. But still, he ran. The countdown would not wait for him to clean himself off.

At the top of the third floor, the creature that had escaped its containment vessel and covered Hawkins and Bray with fluid got to its feet. It had the body of a lynx and the head of a lop-eared bunny. At first glance, the thing appeared pitiful and harmless, with its water-logged, long ears. But it had the cat's aggression, and dove for Hawkins's leg, retractable claws extended, sharp incisors ready to puncture flesh.

Bray swung down hard with a shout, separating rabbit from cat. As the body convulsed, the pair ran to the ladder.

Glass shattered all around them. The cries and shrieks of the escaped chimeras began to sound like a zoo full of agitated animals—which wasn't far from the truth.

"Ten seconds," came the feminine voice. "Nine."

"Go!" Hawkins shouted.

Bray started up the ladder rungs. Hawkins followed close behind. Bray paused at the hatch. He fought with the lever for a moment, but then tugged it ninety degrees counterclockwise, unlocking the hatch.

"Five."

Bray pushed up the hatch with a grunt and climbed quickly up.

"Three."

A loud hiss below Hawkins turned his eyes down as he climbed. A mist of liquid shot from nozzles all around the large chamber.

"Two."

Hawkins emerged into the light of day, yanked his feet out of the hole, and rolled to the side.

"One."

Bray slammed the hatch shut, but didn't lock it. Instead, he dove away from the hatch and covered his head.

A muffled *whump* rippled through the concrete. The roof shook beneath Hawkins.

The unsecured hatch rocketed open and then, torn from its hinges, launched into the air, chased by a forty-foot-tall column of fire. Heat washed over Hawkins. He covered his face and rolled away from the flames.

Then, as quickly as it began, the flames shrank away. Whatever fuel had been sprayed into the building's interior had been burned away. And since the majority of the building's contents—concrete, metal, and glass—didn't burn, the building structure remained intact. Black smoke—all that remained of the twisted menagerie—billowed from the open hatch.

"If they didn't know where we were before," Bray said, climbing to his feet, "they know now."

Hawkins stood. "They knew before."

"You think the pressure we felt was some kind of signal?"

With a nod, Hawkins said, "I felt the same thing before Jim attacked. He had some kind of implant where his ears should have been."

Bray winced.

"I think that pressure we're feeling is actually a sound. A tone maybe. Just out of the range of human hearing. I think most of the chimeras here, with the exception of the crocs, have been trained to obey audio commands. The tones. The bells. The—"

"—horn," Bray finished. "We heard it just before DeWinter was taken."

"And before Joliet was taken."

As though on cue, the horn ripped through the air. The deep bass tremble of the horn sounded louder than ever. Both men covered their ears until the five-second-long blast finished.

Hawkins raised the rifle. He'd lost count of the number of rounds he had left, but thought there were at least three or four. But there was nothing to shoot. They stood alone atop the massive, slightly domed roof. Most of the 360-degree view was jungle, but Hawkins could see the orchard, garden, and farm beyond. On the other side of the building was a dirt road that wrapped around a bend. Hawkins drew an imaginary line where he thought the road would lead and found a bit of light gray concrete that signified the presence of another, newer building. He pointed to it. "Let's go that way."

Bray headed to the building's side. "The ladder is over here."

Just a few steps into his dash for the ladder, Bray flinched and grabbed his shoulder. "Ow!"

Hawkins rushed to his side. "What happened?"

"Felt like something stung me," Bray said.

Hawkins knew that bullet wounds could sometimes feel like insect bites when the victim had no context for the pain. It would hurt like hell a few seconds later, but the initial pinch of bullet piercing skin could be deceptively minor. He pulled Bray's hand away from his shoulder and was happy to see no blood. What he did find was a small, oily stain and the remains of a small plastic capsule.

"Smells like flowers," Bray observed.

Hawkins nodded. It was the same smell Joliet had pointed out before she'd been taken. He didn't think it was a coincidence.

The horn.

The scent.

Bray was about to be taken.

Hawkins slapped his hand on his back. "Ouch!" His hand came away wet with oil.

He spun, looking for whoever was shooting at them. The small, plastic balls couldn't travel far. He found his answer at the ladder.

Kam climbed into view. He was dressed, as usual, in blue pants and a red polo shirt. Only his Red Sox cap was missing. There were two additions to the outfit, though. He had one handgun tucked into his waist, and another in his hand, aimed at Hawkins.

"Kam?" Bray said. "What the hell?"

"I'm sorry, Mr. Bray," Kam said. His voice held no amount of malice. The apology sounded genuine.

Bray took a menacing step toward Kam, but Hawkins grabbed his arm, stopping him cold. "Hold on."

Kam walked toward them, stopping halfway between them and the roof.

"Are you okay, Kam?" Hawkins asked, thinking about how Jim had been altered. As much as it seemed Kam was complicit, it was possible he simply had no choice. "Are you hurt? Did they do anything to you?"

Kam flinched with surprise. "You're concerned for me?"

"You're my friend," Hawkins said.

A frown appeared on Kam's face. "I *am* sorry." He pulled the trigger twice.

Hawkins looked down and found a dart buried in his chest. He yanked it out, but knew he was too late. His legs already felt weak.

Bray fell to his knees. He tugged a dart from his shoulder. Then he slumped forward onto the roof, unconscious.

Hawkins fought to stay upright. He knew what was coming, even before he felt its hot breath on his neck, before its shadow fell over him. The horn somehow activated the creature. The scent, maybe some kind of pheromone or powerful extract, provided a target.

With a shout, Hawkins raised the rifle and turned.

The weapon was pulled easily from his grasp and smashed on the concrete roof.

His vision blacked out for a moment, but a tight, painful compress around his already bruised ribs ripped him back to consciousness long enough for him to look the thing in the face. It stared at him through the horizontal, rectangular pupils of a goat. The skin above its heavy brows was tinged green and looked crocodilian. It's open mouth held the teeth of a big cat and its ears, which stuck out like two orchid petals, belonged to some form of bat. But the facial structure—the shape of the eyes, the nose, the brows, the soft-looking skin—they were all human.

And feminine.

Despite all of the disparate species blended into just the

face of this chimera, it didn't look like some kind of haphazard Frankenstein's monster. It was a single, purposeful design that brought several different animal traits together and made them look *almost* like they belonged together.

The horrible face was the last thing Hawkins saw before losing consciousness. But the last thing Hawkins heard was Kam's voice shouting, "Be careful. Don't hurt him, Mother!"

THIRTY-EIGHT

Hawkins flinched awake, confused and disoriented. His eyes opened, but he couldn't see. He could hear, but the ambient background noise sounded muffled. He breathed through his nose, but smelled only his own breath. Cool air caressed the bare skin of his arms and legs, but his face felt warm and stuffy.

There's a hood over my head.

The hood was a mixed blessing. On one hand, he was blind to his surroundings. On the other, his captors wouldn't know he was awake. He focused on his senses, paying attention to his body first. He lay on his side atop a hard but smooth surface. *Wood,* he thought. His wrists were bound, but his feet were free, which meant he was most likely in some kind of cell.

He tried listening again, but the only sound he could distinguish was the slight buzz of electricity. Power meant that he was being kept in one of the newer buildings, but that wasn't exactly helpful information.

Hawkins tried to remember some words of wisdom passed down from Howie GoodTracks, but came up with nothing. The man knew everything about tracking and hunting, but being held captive never came up. *Yes, it did,* Hawkins thought. *Be the more aggressive predator.* When the time came, Hawkins would put that advice to good use again. It wouldn't matter against the monster he'd seen before losing consciousness, but he'd rather die fighting than end up like Jim.

"Hey!" Bray shouted from someplace nearby. He shouted again, more loudly. "Hey! Let me the hell out of here!"

Hawkins wanted to shush the man, but couldn't without revealing that he, too, was awake.

"Bray, is that you?"

Hawkins recognized the new voice. Jones.

"What about Hawkins? And Drake?" This voice belonged to Blok.

Bennett had been wrong about the entire crew. They'd been taken, but not killed. Not yet, anyway. And Hawkins knew the reason: Why kill a perfectly good test subject?

Hawkins waited, hoping to hear Joliet's voice, but only heard one other person, Bennett himself, weeping not too far away.

"Where are we?" Bray asked.

"Don't know," Blok said. "We've been masked the whole time."

Bray grunted, probably sitting up. "Is Hawkins here?"

"Haven't heard him," Jones said. "Did you all see Jackie anywhere?"

"No," Bray replied. His voice burned with rage. "But we know who brought us here."

"Was Kam," Bennett said with something resembling a sob.

"We heard the son of a bitch talking to someone when Bennett was brought in," Blok said. "Whoever brought you in didn't say a word," Blok added.

"It was Kam," Bray said. "He tranquilized Hawkins and me."

"Kam carried you?" Blok asked, sounding dubious. "You're at least twice his size."

After a few moments of silence, Bray asked, "How sure are you guys that we're alone?"

Nobody answered.

Hawkins wanted to second Bray's observation, but remained silent. If they weren't alone, whoever was listening in would be learning far more about them than vice versa.

"Actually, I'm right here."

Kam's voice was so close that Hawkins couldn't stop himself from flinching and revealing his ruse. *Dammit!* He felt a tug on his head and the black shroud was yanked away. Brilliant white light forced his eyes shut. He took a slow, squinted look and found Kam squatting beside him, a hood in his hands and a frown on his face. For a moment, he looked like the same sheepish kid Hawkins had come to know aboard the *Magellan*. He looked almost apologetic. And then he mouthed, "I'm sorry."

Hawkins nearly replied aloud, but when Kam saw this, his expression became pleading. *If he's mouthing the words,* Hawkins realized, *he doesn't want someone to hear.* Maybe some part of the kid really did regret what he was doing, but it didn't change the fact that he had captured all of them.

The apologetic expression disappeared as Kam stood up. "You can speak now, Ranger."

In a flash, Hawkins remembered the last time he'd heard Kam's voice. *Mother. He called the monster "Mother."* Was it just a name, or was that thing somehow Kam's actual mother?

"Hawkins?" Bray said. "You're here?"

"Yeah, Eight. I'm here." Hawkins turned toward Bray's voice. He was sitting on a metal bench in a cell identical to Hawkins's—thirty-six square feet surrounded by metal bars. The smooth, gray floor held a drain at the sloped center. The cells were modern, but ultimately not very dissimilar to those of the old laboratory. Beyond Bray, Hawkins saw Jones, Blok, and Bennett, bound with plastic cuffs and sitting in identical cells, each with a hood over their heads.

Kam stepped back, out of the cell, and locked the door. It was a simple sliding lock, like an animal cage. If not for the plastic cuffs, it would be easy to escape. Hawkins strained at his bonds. There would be no breaking them, nor slipping free.

When Kam stepped to Bray's cell and unlocked the door,

Hawkins got a view of the rest of the room. It wasn't just a holding cell, it was a surgical suite! The bright light filling the room came from an array of floodlights hanging down from the ceiling above a single operating table. The brushed metal surface was clean, but the floor around it was stained red from blood. There had clearly been some effort put into cleaning the mess and keeping the place sanitary, but whatever surgery had taken place here recently had been mopped up hastily. Next to the table were two carts. The first was empty, but no doubt meant for holding tools of the trade. The second was full of monitoring equipment and held a portable defibrillator, just in case the subject tried to go and die before the mutilation was complete.

Glass cabinets lined the walls. They were packed with medical supplies, lines of orange plastic pill containers, thick brown glass bottles, and an array of well-organized cleaning supplies. Bright blue rubber aprons hung by the exit. Matching gloves and boots rested on a bench below. On the wall opposite the supplies was a pegboard similar to the one in the barn's slaughter shed, and some of the tools hanging from the pegs looked similar—hacksaws, scalpels, scoops, forceps, clamps, retractors, scissors, and drills. Below the wall of tools was a countertop. It held a small refrigerator, two microscopes, rows of tubes, syringes, and other nonsurgical tools. A flat-screen monitor on a swiveling arm was mounted above the microscopes.

This is Charles Manson's dream come true, Hawkins thought.

"You've got to be shitting me," Bray said. His hood had been removed and he was looking over the room.

Kam moved from cell to cell, removing hoods and relocking doors. He waited in silence as each man expressed his revolt at their surroundings. He was never rough. Never cruel. Almost polite. This was not the kind of man who kidnaps his friends. *So who is pulling his strings? Maybe no one*. The apology could have been a deception, like everything else on this island.

"Is this where you did it?" Bray asked. "Where you operated on Jim?"

"What happened to Jim?" Bennett asked, eyes wide. The kid was in shock. Hawkins didn't know how Bennett ended up here, but guessed he'd been plucked from his hiding spot by the big chimera. That encounter probably did a number on his psyche.

"He was mutilated," Hawkins said. "Blades attached to his wrists. Eyes removed. Ears replaced with some kind of devices. And he'd been lobotomized." Hawkins knew the news wouldn't be received well by his cellmates, but he wanted to see Kam's reaction. He had none, aside from a slight frown.

"What about Ray?" Bennett asked. "Where is he?"

Hawkins turned to Bennett. He looked like a shell-shocked POW, but still had the presence of mind to ask all the right questions.

Jones stood and kicked the bars of his cell. "And Jackie! Where the hell is my daughter!"

"Ray did not survive his alterations," Kam said after a moment. "Jackie is . . . alive." He turned to Hawkins. "As is Joliet."

" 'Alive' isn't exactly the same as okay," Hawkins said. "Is it?"

Kam turned away.

"Why are you doing this?" Jones shouted. "Tell me, you son of a bitch!"

Kam stood still, head nodded toward the floor. Hawkins couldn't tell if he felt bad, was deep in thought, or indifferent to the questions.

It was Bray who answered. "I'll tell you why." He stood off his bench and stepped closer to the bars, staring at Kam. "And please, correct me if I'm wrong."

With no reply forthcoming, Bray continued. "During World War Two, Unit Seven thirty-one set up shop on this island. The first location in mainland China worked out well for chemical and germ warfare development. Lots of people for experiments. Flea bombs with bubonic plague. Family pets

given cholera. Poisoned water supplies. Sick shit. But nowhere as sick as what you boys dreamed up for this island.
You'd have thought vivisection was bad enough, but Unit
Seven thirty-one wanted to fuck with nature. Make living
weapons. Down and dirty biological weapons. Screw microbiology. They wanted macroweapons. So you came here,
where you thought you'd never be discovered. You buried
the bodies in the sand. Or dumped them into the river. And
over the past seventy years, the island became populated with
the freak show Unit Seven thirty-one dreamed up. But test
subjects are harder to come by, right? So you hijack ships,
maybe lure in others with distress calls, or maybe go the
old-fashioned pirate route. However you get them here,
once they're in that cove, they never leave. How close am I?"

Kam stood still.

Pulse.

Hawkins flinched, expecting some kind of attack to follow
the barely audible sound.

"You are correct," Kam said. "On all counts."

"But it doesn't explain you, Kam," Bray said. "You're,
what? Twenty?"

Pulse.

"Twenty-three," Kam said, stepping closer to Bray, but
not yet looking at him. "My father was Kamato Shimura Senior. My father was twenty-five when he led the research
here."

"You were born when your father was seventy?" Bray said,
sounding incredulous.

"My . . . mother was not so old," Kam said. "I was born
on Island Seven thirty-one. I didn't leave here until four years
ago when—"

Pulse, pulse.

Kam stammered, glancing up, first at Bray and then Bennett, and then back to his feet. "It doesn't matter."

Someone's definitely directing Kam's answers, Hawkins
decided. *One pulse for an affirmative answer, two for negative.* He couldn't fully trust Kam. He doubted he could trust
him ever again. But the apology might have been genuine.

And that meant they might have a chance. *So how can I out Kam and find out who's really in charge without revealing his apology?*

"Since my father's death ten years ago," Kam said, "his work has continued."

Hawkins stood. "But not by you."

Kam looked thrown by the statement. "What?"

During his college years, Hawkins, like all college boys, did stupid things. He didn't go streaking or binge drink, but he'd been placed in the "nerd dorm" and the game of choice involved learning silly phrases in foreign languages and saying them to people on camera. Hawkins played along, finding it mildly humorous, until he used his Japanese phrase on a woman who spoke the language. She'd been more surprised than anything, and answered his question kindly, pointing down the hall toward the men's room. He repeated the phrase now, "Benjo wa doko desu ka?"

Where's the toilet?

When Kam didn't reply, Hawkins repeated the phrase more forcefully. "Benjo wa doko desu ka!"

Kam began to fidget.

"You can't speak a word of Japanese, can you, kid?"

Pulse, pulse..

"Ignore whoever is sending you the signals," Hawkins shouted, "and answer my damn question for yourself!"

The response was laughter. But it didn't come from Kam. It came from one of Hawkins's cellmates.

THIRTY-NINE

Hawkins nearly fell over when he spun toward the source of the laughter. At first he couldn't believe the man had anything to do with this island. It seemed absurd. Even when the soft chuckle turned into a maniacal cackle, he thought maybe the kid had finally just cracked. It wasn't until Bennett slipped easily out of his plastic cuffs and unlocked his cell door that Hawkins knew, without a doubt, that Bennett—the terrified, bumbling kid—had taken them all for suckers.

Bennett laughed and laughed, for nearly a minute. He tried to control himself a few times, but whenever he looked up at the prisoners' shocked faces, he howled with renewed vigor. He held on to the operating table while the last remnants of his laughter worked their way out of his body. "I'm sorry," he said, wiping tears from his eyes. "Ohh, that was good. Haven't laughed that hard since— You know, I'm not sure I've *ever* laughed that hard."

Bennett looked at Jones and nearly started laughing again. "Oh, Harry. You look so wounded." He suddenly changed his body language to that of a young, scared man. "Yes . . . yes, sir." The reenactment of his feigned fear aboard the *Magellan* was perfect. He straightened back up. All of the fear and timidity disappeared.

"We trusted you," Jones said, holding on to one of the cell bars. "My *daughter* trusted you."

Bennett flashed a wicked grin. "Oh, she did more than that."

Jones looked like he'd had the life sucked right out of him. He stumbled back and sat on the bench, his head down.

Hawkins tried to ignore the sharp emotions of the moment. "Remain calm in the face of danger," GoodTracks told him once. "Fear can focus the mind if it is not allowed to blossom out of control." He tried to put the pieces together, but Bennett wasn't going to give him a chance.

Bennett spun toward Hawkins and stabbed a finger at him. "I can't believe you left me in the jungle! Seriously. No sense of responsibility. Of course, I suppose I can't blame you. Joliet is really the only one of us you care about."

When Hawkins didn't take the bait, Bennett leaned against the metal bars of his and Bray's cages. "So, how about it? Has the dynamic duo figured things out yet?" He waggled a finger first at Hawkins, then at Bray. "You're the sidekick, by the way. Going to have to lose that potbelly if you want to compete with Alpha Male over here."

For a moment, neither man spoke. Bennett was enjoying this too much to humor his request. At the same time, it might be the only way to get answers.

Bennett hopped up on the operating table and kicked his legs like a ten year old eagerly awaiting an ice-cream cone. "C'mon, you have a *captive* audience, after all."

Hawkins cut Bennett's snickering short. "The island started out as a Unit Seven thirty-one facility, and maybe the original buildings continued to operate for years after the war. But this isn't a Japanese site anymore."

Bray took a sharp breath, no doubt figuring out where Hawkins's line of thinking was going. "Holy shit."

"What?" Blok asked. "Is this some kind of secret corporate lab?"

"Secret? Yes," Bennett said. "Corporate, no."

"The feed bag in the barn is written in English," Hawkins said. "The warning message in that, that—"

"I call it 'the gallery,'" Bennett said. "They *were* works

of art. 'Were' being the operative word since you made me incinerate them."

"—freak show," Hawkins said, "was also in English. If Kam was really born here, and I think he was telling the truth about that, and he can't speak a word of Japanese, then he was raised in an English-speaking community. His accent is either fake or learned from his father, who knew Japanese, but spoke English."

Kam seemed to shrink at the mention of his name. Despite his betrayal and participation in the unforgivable kidnapping, torture, and murder of several *Magellan* crewmembers, and perhaps hundreds of other people, Hawkins suspected that his involvement was somehow compulsory.

"In 1946, the War Department took an interest in Unit Seven thirty-one," Bray said. "They uncovered the Zhongma Fortress in Beiyinhe, Manchuria, but the research was gone, hidden by Shirō Ishii, the microbiologist-slash-lieutenant general who conceived of and ran Unit Seven thirty-one. To the War Department it was a treasure trove of research and knowledge that the United States couldn't easily acquire. Harry Truman himself signed the order to *not* prosecute Ishii and the rest of Seven thirty-one for war crimes, of which they would have easily been convicted. If Unit Seven thirty-one went to trial, their crimes and research would have been made public and available to our competitors, primarily Russia. He granted immunity in exchange for research *and* exclusivity. But that's not all, is it? The War Department, or maybe some new splinter group or Black Op—whatever—kept this island operating. At first, maybe this place was mostly Japanese scientists from Unit Seven thirty-one, but over time, U.S. personnel came over. This facility and every horrible thing done here since 1946 belongs to America. That's why it doesn't appear on any maps—who else could hide an island? That's why it's surrounded by a thirty-mile-diameter garbage patch that deters ships from getting within radar range."

"A broad assessment," Bennett said. "You were close to the truth. After the war, the island's facilities were maintained and the research done by the original Unit Seven thirty-one was pored over by a team of scientists, many of whom were the original staff who'd been pardoned of all wrongdoing. The island didn't become a fully active research facility until twenty years later, long after it, and the scientists living here, fell off the United States' radar. Within months, the research that Unit Seven thirty-one pioneered was back on track. But there was no way you could have known any of that, Bray, so I'm actually impressed. Maybe you can come work for us? We seem to be short on staff these days."

"Because you sewed them into a ball," Hawkins said, his emotions threatening to spill over as he remembered the people bound together. They'd been part of the island's vile legacy, but what he'd done to them was sadistic.

"Just the ones I didn't like," Bennett said, and then he smiled wide. "You should have seen them the first time they woke up like that. Nearly tore themselves apart, didn't they, Kam?"

Kam said nothing. He just stared at the floor.

"You're lucky I didn't throw you in with the lot of them," Bennett said to Kam. He turned back to Hawkins. "I couldn't do that to my own brother, though, could I? Well, we're not really brothers. We grew up together, here on the island. But both of my parents were . . . what's the word I'm looking for, Kam?"

When Kam didn't answer, Bennett pulled a small black device with two red buttons from his pants pocket. It looked similar to a car remote. He pushed the larger button on the outside edge once.

Pulse.

"Human," Kam said.

"Human," Bennett repeated. "Thank you, Kamato Junior. In light of recent events that left many staff . . . incapacitated, and fearing exposure, the clandestine organization running the facility—which employs neither me nor Kam, by the way—sent someone out to check when communications went unanswered. She was a delightful specimen, much more resilient than her crew, but in the end, she lacked the strength to return with a report. I can only guess that the island's former masters made the assumption that the facility had been compromised.

"Despite their resources, they lack the ability to drop bombs or fire missiles, at least without drawing too much attention, so they sent a strike team to liquidate the island and hide their seventy-year-old secret. The assault didn't end well for those men. Twenty of them. Retired Special Ops. Mercenaries. I suspect they would have been killed anyway, after seeing the island's secrets, but probably far less painfully."

"So you use the crocs, the seagulls, and those little freaks to do your killing?" Bray said.

Bennett looked confused. "Little freaks?"

Hawkins saw Kam's eyes flash with worry. He spoke quickly, cutting off Bray's response. "The drakes."

Bray glanced at him and seemed to understand the interruption's purpose and didn't correct him.

Bennett grinned. "Drakes?"

"Draco-snakes," Bray said.

"You've named them?" Bennett looked pleased. "And after the captain no less. They do have similar dispositions, don't they? Huh. Where was I? A year passed and we were left in peace. Maybe the few people overseeing the project died? Or lacked the resources? I don't know. But Kam and I found ourselves quite bored without test subjects. So we set out for the world to seek our fortunes. And what did we find, Kam?"

Pulse.

"The *Magellan*," Kam said.

"The *Magellan*," Bennet repeated, "bound for waters so close to home that you may have stumbled across our island without any help. After getting ourselves hired, which was easy, by the way—the elusive Captain Drake is a sucker for sob stories and phony credentials—we made sure the *Magellan* found its way to our beautiful resort island. My only regret is that we weren't able to rendezvous with the *Darwin*. We would have had so many more new subjects." He shrugged and pushed himself off the table. "But we have you. And we're cooking up something special for if and when our predecessors return again."

Bennett looked at his wristwatch. "In fact, I've prepared a little demonstration for you." He headed for the door and turned to Kam. "Keep an eye on our guests until I return."

Then he was gone and a little bit of sanity returned to the room. While Kam and Bennett may have both grown up here, it appeared only one of them was driven mad by the experience. Kam, at least, had some semblance of a guilty conscience.

"Kam," Hawkins said. "You have to let us out."

No answer.

"Kam, I'm your friend. You know I mean that. Whatever Bennett has, however he's controlling you, we can undo it."

Kam shook his head. "I can't." He glanced quickly toward the back corner of the room.

Rolling his head in mock frustration, Hawkins peeked in the direction Kam had looked. Bennett might be watching. The sick bastard had probably watched while Joliet was taken. And when Jim attacked. And their near-death experience in "the gallery." *It's how he gets his kicks*, Hawkins thought. *That and mutilating people.*

"You should give up, Ranger," Kam said.

Bray pressed his face against the bars of his cell. "Kam, I swear to God, if I get out of here—"

"There is no hope for you!" Kam shouted, but his voice sounded like a mix of anger and desperation. "Even if you escaped your cells, you are unarmed." He turned to Hawkins. "Your rifle was destroyed." He moved behind the operating table and bent down. When he stood back up, he held the captive bolt stunner in one hand and the machete in the other. "And I have taken *all* of your weapons."

Kam placed the weapons on the operating table. Then he fished into his pocket and took out a bell. As he placed it on the table beside the weapons, the door opened. "As much as you would like to, these weapons and your freedom will forever be out of your reach."

Bennett entered the room, pulling a hospital gurney cloaked with a sheet. "You're finally coming around, Kam? Did one of them say something mean about your mother?"

As Bennett chuckled to himself, he locked the gurney wheels with his feet. "Almost ready." He pushed a button on the modern electric gurney and the back half rose up. As the sheet shifted, it clung to the body hidden beneath, a body with a distinctly feminine shape.

Not Joliet.

Jones launched to his feet and clutched the cage bars. "No. Please, no."

Bennett ignored Jones and walked to the countertop. He pulled out a stool and switched on one of the microscopes. He then reached up and pulled the flat-screen monitor away from the wall. A metal arm extended from the wall mount and Bennett turned the screen so that it faced the cells. "Everyone have a good view?"

No one replied.

"Good," he said. "Time for a lesson in microbiology." He looked back at Bray. "Let me know how I do."

Bray flipped him off.

Nonplussed by Bray's gesture, Bennett reached up and turned on the screen. The image was black and white. At the center of the screen was a rough circle that looked a little like a translucent moon. The circle was stuck against a curved shape emerging from the left of the screen. And to the right, there was a long, straight tube with a pointed tip. *A needle*, Hawkins realized.

Bennett pointed at the object on the left side of the screen. "This is a micropipette. Nothing too special about it except that it holds this"—he pointed to the circle—"in place. This is a blastocyst. It's full of genetic code and stem cells that, when fertilized, eventually forms an embryo. When all those little stem cells are told what to become, they multiply like crazy and form a human. Or a dog. Or whatever. The miracle of life."

Bennett waved his hand toward the needle. "But this is the real miracle. See those little white spots?"

Hawkins did. Each white spot just fit inside the tiny needle.

"Those are stem cells I've modified using homologous recombination—basically taking two DNA molecules, then nicking them so the two separate strands come loose, and merge with each other. It's called the 'holiday method.' Happy homologous recombination day! The point is, they'll become whatever *I* want them to become and since they're forming alongside the host cells, they will merge flawlessly. Rejection isn't an issue for me." He swiveled in his chair and looked at his audience. "Did you know that there are chimeras all around you and no one cares? People get pig valve transplants all the time and no one seems to think it's strange or unnatural." He shrugged and turned toward the microscope. "Now comes the moment of creation."

Bennett leaned over the microscope. Hawkins couldn't see what the man was doing, but he saw the needle on the screen begin to inch closer to the blastocyst. The tip of the needle came to a stop just shy of the thin cell wall. The needle moved up and down slightly before aligning with the blastocyst's center. Then it thrust forward like a lance. The cell wall bent in, and then broke. One by one, the little white dots slipped through the needle and into the blastocyst. Once all of the stem cells were inside the larger cell wall, the needle withdrew.

Hawkins thought that was the end of it, but a second, much larger needle entered the screen.

"The next step would normally be to transplant the blastocyst into a womb and let it grow like a normal child." He withdrew the larger needle from the side of the microscope and held it up for them all to see. "But that's not exactly how this little gem works. No womb required. No father. Though I guess you could technically call me the father."

Bonnett rolled the stool over to the fridge and opened the small door and took out a water bottle. He unscrewed the cap, took a swig, and smacked his lips. "Ahh." With his thirst apparently quenched, Bennett took the syringe, placed the needle inside the water, and injected the newly modified blastocyst. He swirled the water around and said, "Now comes the really fun part."

After capping the bottle, he rolled over to the gurney and stood. He gripped the sheet covering the body and pulled it away like a magician, revealing his recently reassembled assistant. DeWinter lay on the gurney. What was most shocking about the revelation was that she looked fine. She wore only a bra on top, but hadn't been mutilated, or even hurt. She wasn't conscious, but the steady rise and fall of her chest revealed that she was alive.

"Jackie!" Jones shouted. "Jackie! What have you done to her?"

"Nothing," Bennett said. He removed smelling salts from his pocket and wafted them in front of Jackie's nose. She came to a moment later, but was groggy. Drugged. She blinked her eyes, trying to focus. She showed no fear of her situation, or of Bennett.

She hasn't been conscious since she was taken, Hawkins thought. *She has no idea not to trust Bennett.*

Before he could shout a warning, Bennett took the cap off the water bottle and held it to Jackie's lips. She took three long drinks.

"Jackie!" Jones shouted. "Don't! He's—"

DeWinter's eyes closed slowly and she once again fell unconscious. The smelling salts couldn't compete with whatever drug had been used to sedate her.

Jones's lips quivered. All he could do was stare.

"Don't worry, Grandpa," Bennett said, carefully capping the bottle. "She's not dead yet. In fact—" He crouched beside DeWinter and leaned his ear against her belly. He feigned a gasp. "I think our little family is growing!"

Bennett hustled to the fridge and took out another water bottle, this one labeled "active" with black marker. He moved quickly for the door. "Kam."

The dutiful Kam followed at his heels.

Bennett leaned his head back in the room as he closed the door. He didn't say anything, he just grinned, looking at all of them with frantic energy. Then he was gone and the door slammed closed, and locked.

While Jones shouted for his daughter, and Blok paced uselessly in his cell, Hawkins began an awkward dance, reaching for his side and spinning in circles.

"Ranger?" Bray said, sounding concerned.

Hawkins stopped spinning and pushed his hip against the bars separating his cell from Bray's. "Get my knife!"

"Your knife is gone," Bray said.

"My knife was broken," Hawkins explained. "Just the blade is in there. Kam knew about it. His speech about the weapons was a message."

Bray's eyes widened and he fumbled with his bound hands to unbutton the sheath holding the razor-sharp blade.

About the time the button popped free and Bray got his fingers on the knife, DeWinter's stomach started to bulge.

FORTY

"Dammit," Bray said as the blade slipped from his fingers and fell to the floor by Hawkins's feet.

The knife nearly struck Hawkins's foot, but he jumped away in time to avoid being impaled. He picked the knife up and sat on the floor with his back to the cell bars.

Jones saw what they were doing. "Hurry up! Get me out of here!"

Hawkins ignored the man's pleas. He knew Jones just wanted to get to his daughter, but the real ticking clock was however long it took Bennett to reach whatever room received the camera feeds. Could be a few minutes, or maybe right next door. Bennett could be watching them right now.

Hawkins placed the blade between his feet with the dull side against the floor and the sharp side facing up. He positioned his wrists to either side of the blade and brought them down fast. The plastic cuffs came apart with one smooth cut. A moment later, Hawkins was on his feet and opening his cell. He moved to Bray's cell next, unlatching the door.

"Get me next!" Jones shouted. "Hawkins! Let me out!"

Hawkins focused on Bray. It was a tactical decision. Hawkins knew the big man would fight if Bennett returned. But Jones was going to be all but useless with his daughter undergoing some kind of transformation. He could hear her starting to groan. Whatever was happening inside her belly, it wasn't good—for her, or for them. Hawkins felt sure that

Bennett would be watching by now and that he wasn't returning meant he believed they still weren't a threat. He cut through Bray's bindings and hurried to Jones's cell.

As he unlocked the cell door, Hawkins glanced at Blok. The man stared past Hawkins, watching DeWinter. His face slowly contorted into a mask of fear. Hawkins realized that Blok and Jones had been taken from the *Magellan* and brought straight here, possibly without even seeing the big chimera. Their exposure to the island's horrors had been minimal. And while Blok responded to DeWinter's condition with paralyzing fear, Jones's actions were fueled by one part appropriate concern for his daughter and one part naiveté. But he couldn't stop the man, any more than one of them could stop him if it had been Joliet strapped to the gurney.

Jones shook his bound wrists at Hawkins as the cell door slid open. "C'mon!"

Hawkins cut the plastic cuffs. "Jones, listen. You need to—"

Jones shoved Hawkins aside and ran to DeWinter. Hawkins didn't watch. He moved to Blok's cell and unlocked the door. Blok's stare remained unflinching.

"Blok," Hawkins said. "Blok!"

The man snapped out of his daze. Hawkins held the blade out and Blok seemed to register for the first time that they were breaking out. He held up his wrists and Hawkins set him free. "Thanks."

Hawkins nodded, but didn't say a word. If Blok knew the kind of hell they'd soon be facing, he might have opted to remain a prisoner.

"Ranger," Bray said as Hawkins turned around. He handed the machete and captive bolt stunner to Hawkins. "At least he left us with an arsenal."

Hawkins looked at the pegboard holding an array of surgical tools. Bray had taken a knife that looked like a long fish filleting blade and a frightening thick-toothed bone saw. Hawkins was satisfied with the machete and attached it to his belt before motioning to the tools. "Blok, grab something to use as a weapon."

"Are we going to have to kill something?" Blok asked with a shaky voice.

Jones's desperate voice filled the room. "What's happening to her!"

"Probably," Hawkins said and then turned to DeWinter for the first time since escaping his cell. Jones leaned over her, blocking most of his view, but what little he could see of her belly was severely distended.

And moving.

He stepped closer and got a better look. Her whole body twitched and her light brown skin looked washed-out. "Harry," he said, his tone half-apologetic, half-warning.

Hawkins placed a hand on Jones's shoulder and tried to pull him back, but the man shrugged away. "No!"

Bray stepped over and put his fingers on her neck, searching for a pulse. "Jones, she's gone."

"She's still moving!" Jones said, clinging to DeWinter's shoulders.

"That's not her," Hawkins said, stepping back. The convulsions grew more violent. "It's what's inside her."

"Shut up!" Jones screamed, waving them all back. "She's my daughter."

Hawkins drew the machete.

Bray stood ready with the bone saw.

Blok backed into his cell, unarmed, and slowly pulled the door closed.

Hawkins raised the machete. He could end this now. It would feel wrong—awful—but he could stop whatever was about to happen with one swing. "Jones, step back."

"Stay away!" Jones said, eyeing the machete. "Don't touch her! She's—"

The convulsions stopped. But DeWinter's torso was swollen to the point where light-colored stretch marks had streaked across her flesh. Jones moved toward her head, cradling her cheeks in his hands. "Open your eyes, baby. I'm here."

Her belly shifted in response to Jones's voice.

"Jones," Bray whispered. "Back the hell up."

Jones clenched his eyes shut, squeezing tears onto his face. "Bray, I swear to God, if you—"

Hawkins had only just registered the tearing sound when an explosion of movement burst from DeWinter's belly. Long black limbs, coated with thick, pointy hairs and dollops of flesh, reached out and locked on to Jones's upper body and face.

Jones let out a shriek and reeled back, pulling the creature free. The thing had the head and limbs of a giant spider, the spiky protective carapace of a snapping turtle, and a long, black prehensile tail, which had already wrapped around Jones's waist. Hawkins had only just begun to recover from his surprise when a stinger emerged from between the tail and shell and jabbed Jones three times in the gut.

Jones shouted in pain and fell to the floor. The creature's tail unwrapped and it jumped away, landing on the operating table. The entire attack had taken just seconds. Jones convulsed. His eyes rolled back. And his belly began to expand.

The time between DeWinter drinking the water offered by Bennett and the emergence of this fully formed monster was just over a minute.

"It must be genetically engineered to crank out growth hormones," Bray said. His eyes were locked on the creature, and the bone saw was raised to strike. "I think it ate DeWinter from the inside, metabolized her flesh, and grew fast. Really fast."

The creature studied them, shifting its four eyes from one man to the next.

"But here's the thing about animals that grow too fast," Bray said. "They're fragile. I doubt that shell is even solid yet."

That's all Hawkins needed to hear. When the creature turned back to Bray, Hawkins charged and swung with the machete. The spider eyes turned back toward him with impossible speed, but the monster couldn't avoid the descending blade. In fact, it didn't even try to.

The eight long legs and head snapped back inside the body just as the blade struck the carapace and deflected away. The blade struck the table hard, sending a painful vibration up Hawkins's arm.

Just as quickly as the head and legs disappeared, they shot back out and took action.

Bray charged, but was too slow. The creature leapt at Hawkins, eight arms splayed wide. Hawkins dropped the machete and caught the thing on the underside of its carapace. He tried to fling it away, but the tail had already wrapped around his waist. When the weight of it struck him, he fell back and stumbled into a glass cabinet. Shattered glass rained down as Hawkins and the monster fell to the floor.

"Bray!" Hawkins shouted, but his voice was barely audible over Jones's rising shrieks. Unlike DeWinter, Jones was fully conscious when the parasitical spider thing started to eat him from the inside out.

Bray appeared overhead and started swinging with the saw, but it had no effect on the hard shell.

"The tail!" Hawkins shouted. Despite shoving up with all his strength, he could feel the tail constricting, pulling the body—and stinger—closer to his gut. Once that stinger got close enough to strike, Hawkins would be finished. "Cut off the tail!"

Bray adjusted his aim. He swung hard.

And missed.

Hawkins's hands slipped across the blood-covered carapace and the creature lowered into striking range. The tail tightened, squeezing Hawkins's stomach. Hawkins shouted in fear, knowing that in just over a minute he'd be dead and giving birth to yet another of Bennett's chimeras.

And then it happened.

With a quick twitch, the stinger rose and struck three times.

FORTY-ONE

The stings felt like little more than dull thuds. For a moment, Hawkins wondered if the stinger was coated in some kind of painkiller so the victim might not even know he was stung. Then he registered the sound that came with each stinger thrust—a dull clunk of metal.

"Got it!" Blok said.

Hawkins hadn't even seen the man appear at his side, but there he was, holding a metal tray between Hawkins's stomach and the stinger.

A surge of adrenaline flowed into Hawkins's veins, courtesy of nearly being implanted with a fast-growing chimera embryo. Instead of pushing the spider thing away, Hawkins wrapped his arms around the shell and squeezed, pulling the chimera close and wedging the sheet of metal securely between them. "Charge the defibrillator!" he shouted at Blok, who nodded and ran for the equipment cart. He looked up at Bray. "Get that tail off!"

When the jagged teeth of the bone saw bit into the base of the creature's tail, the thing started twitching. By the second stroke, it struggled to break free from Hawkins's embrace. He could feel the tail struggling to unwrap from his body, but it was pinned beneath them, and the spider legs, while strong, were no match for Hawkins's rage-filled grip.

The high-pitched whine of the defibrillator charging filled the air. A moment later, Blok shouted, "Charged!"

"Bray?" Hawkins said.

"Almost there!"

Hawkins looked to his left and saw Blok, live defibrillator paddles in his hands. "Get ready!"

With a grunt, Bray pushed hard and cut through the forearm-thick tail.

The creature convulsed, lost in a torrent of pain. Hawkins let go, slid his hands beneath the carapace, and shoved. The forty-pound monster flipped through the air and landed on its back. Eight legs twitched madly, searching for purchase that wasn't there. Its oozing stump of a tail shifted pitifully back and forth. Then Blok descended on the creature, placing the paddles on its softer, blood-soaked underside and triggered the shock.

All eight legs went straight and riqid for the duration of the jolt. The overloaded paddles began to smoke and Blok pulled them away. The legs fell flat on the floor.

The monster was dead, but there was no time for back patting. Jones's belly looked ready to burst, but he looked different than DeWinter. Where she had one bulge, Jones had three smaller ones. Hawkins's mind replayed the attack. Jones had been stung three times, with each sting inserting a new parasite into the host.

One of them was bad enough. He didn't think they'd survive three.

Hawkins scrambled to his feet, picked up the machete, and ran for the door. He tried the handle, but it was locked. Bray arrived and started viciously kicking the door. Despite putting all his weight into each kick, the door held.

"They're coming!" Blok said.

The door and its frame were solid. "The door is steel," he said to Bray. "You can't kick it down."

"We have to try," Bray said.

"I have a better idea." Hawkins reached into his cargo shorts pocket for the captive bolt stunner and was surprised to feel several spare cartridges still in his pocket. *Kam left us a way out.* He pulled the bolt stunner from his pocket and placed the muzzle against the flat inner-door lock. He pulled the trigger. Two inches of stainless steel exited the barrel traveling at the speed of a bullet. The impact didn't sound like much—just a cough of air and a single whack, like a hammer on the head of a nail—but when Hawkins stepped back, the lock was gone, launched into the hallway on the other side.

Hawkins flung open the door and ran into the hallway, thinking there might be at least a chance they would survive for at least a few more minutes. That hope disappeared when he looked to the right and found the long, white corridor filled by the immense and deformed girth of Jim Clifton.

Whatever signal Bennett used to send Jim into a murderous rampage had clearly already been sent. The moment Hawkins's feet fell on the hallway floor, Jim was in motion. He wasn't a fast man, but there was no getting around him, or the swinging blades extending out of his wrist stumps.

Bray was halfway out the room when he caught sight of Jim. His eyes went wide and he managed to turn himself around in time to remove himself, and Blok, from the giant man's path. At the same time, he also brought them dangerously close to Jones's body, which looked close to bursting.

Hawkins backed away, matching Jim's pace and using the machete to parry any swing that got too close. He flinched when the machete struck flesh instead of stone, but Jim showed no reaction. He just kept coming like he could see out of those hollow eye sockets. Hawkins wanted to turn and run, but couldn't leave Bray and Blok behind. He also had no idea what was behind him. There could be another creature lying in wait. Hawkins took one fast step back, intending to look over his shoulder. Instead, he collided with something solid.

A wall. The hallway was a dead end!

With just ten feet separating the pair, Hawkins wedged the machete between his legs and held it there. He fumbled with the captive bolt stunner, looking for a way to open it. He found a small button lock, pushed it in, and slid it forward. The bolt stunner snapped opened.

The sound of the stunner opening focused Jim on Hawkins's

position. The big man swung wildly, and with renewed vigor, but the swings were broad and slow. Despite Bennett having turned Jim into a mindless killer, he hadn't done anything to improve Jim's health. The big man was tiring.

Hawkins slipped a new cartridge into place and closed the stunner. The blades attached to Jim's arms whooshed past Hawkins's chest. Dangerously close. He could charge forward and attack with the stunner or the machete, but didn't think he'd manage a killing blow without also being skewered. So he aimed to immobilize.

Jim swung and missed by mere inches. While he was overextended, Hawkins brought the machete down on Jim's arm, cutting through the tube feeding him morphine—he hoped—into the man's ravaged body.

Hawkins ducked Jim's next blow, the blade zinging across the concrete wall over Hawkins's head, leaving a trail of bright orange sparks in its wake. Hawkins swung for the other arm and connected, successfully severing the second liquid-filled tube. Jim staggered briefly and Hawkins took the opening to dive past him.

But instead of running, Hawkins got back to his feet and turned to face Jim as he bumbled around.

"Hawkins," Bray yelled. He and Blok stood in the hall, holding the door to the surgical suite/cellblock shut. The door shook from impacts on the other side. The other spider chimeras had emerged from Jones's body. "Let's get the hell out of here!"

"I won't leave him like this," Hawkins replied.

His voice drew Jim toward him. Hawkins backed away, hoping to tire the man even further. Jim's swings slowed more and he began to grunt, at first from exertion, but then in pain. Whatever drug had killed the pain was wearing off without a constant supply.

After one last big swing, Jim's energy seemed to disappear. He fell to his knees, heaving with each labored breath. He tried to raise his arm to swing at Hawkins again, but failed.

The door shook from a heavy impact. "Hawkins!" Bray shouted.

Jim didn't react when Hawkins stepped closer. Whatever fire had burned inside the man had gone out, at least temporarily.

"I'm sorry, Jim," Hawkins said.

Jim turned his head up toward Hawkins's voice and moaned. He sounded desperate and tired.

Hawkins placed the bolt stunner against Jim's head and pulled the trigger. With a puff of air and stab of metal, Jim collapsed to the floor at Hawkins's feet, just short of the door.

Bray looked at Hawkins like he was crazy. "Can we go now?"

The door shook again.

"They're hitting the door all at once," Blok said.

"How long between strikes?" Hawkins asked.

Bray leaned into the door. "About ten sec—"

The impact caught Bray off guard. The door opened for just a moment, but long and wide enough for Hawkins to see the three creatures on the other side. One for each of them. It would be a short fight, but the same drawn-out, horrific, and painful ending shared by Jones and DeWinter.

Hawkins put his hands against the door and pushed. "After the next strike, just turn and run. If we're lucky, we'll get a ten-second head start."

"Ten seconds isn't going to mean much against these things," Bray said.

Hawkins agreed, but wouldn't say so. "Have any other—"

The door shook from an impact. Before Hawkins and Bray could continue the debate, Blok was up and running. Hawkins and Bray quickly gave chase.

As they sprinted down the plain white hallway, Hawkins counted down the seconds. At eight, the door exploded open. He looked back and saw all three spider chimeras spill out into the hall.

But they didn't give chase. Instead, they pounced.

On Jim.

Hawkins stopped and watched.

Each creature stung Jim's corpse three times. The man's bulbous rolls of flesh immediately began to shake.

Nine more, Hawkins thought. *In just over a minute, there will be nine more of those things.*

Finished with the corpse, the spider chimeras spun their attention back to the fleeing prey. Seeing Hawkins in the hall, the black tails rose into the air, shaking with excitement.

Bray's hand fell hard on Hawkins's shoulder and yanked him around. "Ranger, let's go!"

Hawkins turned and ran, following Bray down a side hall.

The *tick-tack* of twenty-four oversize and frenzied spider limbs followed.

FORTY-TWO

The smooth, linoleum floor squeaked under Hawkins's feet as he ran. The sound, heard throughout the world's shopping centers on rainy days, would have normally been a minor annoyance, but here, it might get him killed. The eight-legged chimeras didn't have a direct line of sight on him—they'd woven a confusing path through the facility's many hallways—but the ceaseless squeaking made them easy to track. Had he time to pause, Hawkins would have removed his shoes and gone barefoot. Howie had taught him to hunt in silence and sometimes that meant giving up modern comforts, but now it would mean giving up his life.

Even without pausing, he could hear the clacking of the spiders' claws growing louder. And since he had no intention of allowing one of those things to leap on his back and inject him with their young, it was only a matter of time before he'd have to turn and fight. The outcome might be the same, but at least he'd have fought.

Ahead of him, Bray and Blok ran like men possessed. Neither knew where they were headed, but they moved without pausing, like there was a yellow brick road guiding them. And nothing stood in their way. Bray had twice run into trays of equipment and neither had slowed him down. Hawkins, on the other hand, had to leap over the debris. As a result, he was ten feet behind Bray. Yellowstone rangers often joked with visitors that the best way to survive a bear attack was to be faster than your companion. It got good laughs, but Hawkins never found it funny, mostly because it was the truth.

The clacking of tiny feet on the floor grew louder. Hawkins looked back. The things had rounded the corner behind him, just fifty feet back.

"They're gaining on us!" Hawkins shouted. "We need a barricade!"

Blok started checking doors to rooms as he passed them. All were locked. Given the sheer size of the building, Hawkins thought it would have been easy to find a hiding spot. But all the hallway doors swung both ways and had no handles to wedge something in, nor locks. They'd passed a large number of windowless doors labeled with letters and numbers, but all were locked.

Hawkins looked back.

Forty feet.

A shout turned Hawkins forward in time to see a pair of hands reach out, grab Blok, and yank him into a side room. Bray stopped, raising his weapon to strike, but then followed Blok into the room, shouting, "Ranger, in here!"

Hawkins didn't need to be convinced. Whatever and whoever waited for him in the room couldn't be worse than being turned into a living incubator. He slipped on the floor as he rounded the corner and barreled into the room, colliding with Bray and spilling to the floor.

The door slammed shut behind them. A heavy lock *thunk*ed into place.

Several impacts shook the door a moment later, but they stopped within seconds.

Hawkins pushed himself up and Bray's bone saw came into focus beneath him. Another inch and the blade could have carved through his face. He rolled away from Bray and found a feminine hand extended toward him. For a moment, he thought it was Joliet, but then saw how long the fingers were. The woman leaned forward. Her aquiline face gave her the appearance of a hawk about to attack. But she wasn't angry. She was terrified. He took the woman's hand and got to his feet.

There were four more strangers in the room—two men, three women total—all dressed similarly in tan slacks and white buttoned shirts, which were stained with sweat and blood. The room was like a small cafeteria, with several long, benched tables, a kitchen area, and cabinets lining the walls. The space was modern, lit by recessed ceiling bulbs and air-conditioned. It felt as though they'd been transported from a tropical hellhole to an office building in Anywhere, USA.

Hawkins turned to Blok, who stood at the door, looking through the small, rectangular window. "What are they doing?"

"Just standing there," Blok said. "Three of them."

"Just three?" Bray asked.

Blok craned his head back and forth, looking down the length of the hallway in both directions. "Just three."

"Where are the rest of you?" the woman asked impatiently.

"The rest of us?" Hawkins replied.

"You mean our friends who gave birth to those spider-turtles?" Bray said. "Or do you mean the big guy your boss turned into a walking Ginsu knife?"

"Eight," Hawkins cautioned, "you don't know that they—"

"Look at their clothes," Bray said, taking a step away from the woman. "They're wearing uniforms. They're employees. The ones that Bennett didn't turn into a living blob."

"It's not them," one of the men whispered to another.

Bray pointed to a line of lab coats hanging by the door. There were five. "One for each of them." He took a lab coat off the hook and inspected it.

"You're not here for us, are you?" the woman asked.

"What's your name?" Hawkins asked.

"Doctor Celia Green," the woman replied.

"Well, Doctor Green, we are not here for you. We were captured. We've lost a lot of people, but we're getting our friends back and getting the hell off this island. If you're willing to fight, you can come along. If you can't keep up, you're on your own."

She crossed her arms. "We'll wait."

"For who?" Hawkins asked.

When she didn't answer, Hawkins drew his machete slowly. "Listen, lady, we've just watched three of our friends give birth to those monsters outside the door. The things that have happened on this island are reprehensible, and I'm not just talking about what Bennett is doing."

"Doctor Celia Green," Bray said, holding up a name-tagged lab coat.

"You were conducting human experimentation long before Bennett staged his coup," Hawkins said.

"We had no choice," one of the men said, his voice booming with the defensive passion of a man who knows he's about to be judged for his actions.

"Always a choice," Hawkins said.

"They would have killed us," a woman said through her tears.

"They're still going to," Hawkins said.

"What do you mean?" Green asked.

"Who are you waiting for?"

She didn't answer.

"Son of a bitch," Bray said. He held up an ID card he'd taken from the lab coat pocket. He handed it to Hawkins. It showed a picture of Green, perhaps five years old, looking young and innocent.

"Ignore the information," Bray said. "Look at the logo."

Hawkins noticed a strange glimmer when he shifted the card. The logo was holographic. He turned it in the light and saw an oblong globe with five bold letters written across it: DARPA.

"Darpa?" Hawkins asked.

"Defense Advanced Research Projects Agency," Bray said. "They were founded in 1958, in the wake of Sputnik, and worked on high-tech R and D for the U.S. military. They're the guys who gave us stealth technology, the Internet, and the M16. But they have their hands in all the sciences; robotic, cyber, electronics, energy, weapons, space, and the most relevant—biology. In 2010, they started a research program to eliminate, and I quote, 'the randomness of natural evolutionary advancement.' That sounds pretty damn close to playing God, right? The end goal is to create organic, living, intelligent life that can live indefinitely. And in case you're worried about these new life forms rebelling against their creators, they're engineering loyalty into their DNA and giving them kill switches. That's the bright and cheery future of modern warfare—silicon soldiers. They called the whole thing BioDesign."

Green looked surprised. "How did you know about that?"

"I was researching the subject for my next book, but it wasn't hard to find. BioDesign is the kind of scary shit DARPA *puts in the budget*," Bray explained. "The whole world knows about BioDesign. And that's because it's *benign* compared to what you're doing." Bray stepped up to the woman. "What's the catchphrase you use to justify what you do here? 'Combat performance'? 'Biomedical research'?"

Green's eyes fell to the floor. "Biological warfare defense."

Bray's face turned red with anger. "That's the same fucking language the Japanese used. Anything is justified when you put it under the umbrella of defending the homeland. This can't be an official program."

"It's not," Green said. "Like all government agencies, DARPA has some black operations that no one is *supposed* to know about. But even the most top-secret projects find their way into the DARPA rumor mill. Scientists are naturally curious, and like to talk about their work. We were good about keeping things from the public, but not so good about keeping secrets from each other. As long as everyone in the loop had the security clearance, no one complained. We were all on the same team and shared the same goals. The thing is, despite the work here being my area of expertise, I *never* heard about this island. Not once. And I was friends with the DARPA director. She's a good woman. A moral woman. There's no way she knew about this place. I'd be surprised if any of the current DARPA leadership knows about what goes on here, if they even know about the island at all. Whoever started the program set it up so that it could operate autonomously while still having access to DARPA's workforce for recruitment. I don't know who that was, but at the time, there was a lot of postwar and cold war paranoia."

"If the Russians are working on it, we better, too," Bray said.

"Right," Green said. "So the project was put under DARPA's umbrella, but somehow shielded from oversight and allowed to evolve on its own. By the time I got here, it was a very dark place." She sighed and shook her head. "Look, DARPA is a good agency. We want to change the world, but for the better. This island . . . the things done here . . . the things *I've* done here . . . are against everything DARPA stands for."

"If you're so against the biological warfare defense program, why are you here?" Bray asked.

"We were all recruited from other biological programs," she said. "It was presented as a dream post. Tropical island. Cutting-edge research. The only downside is that we couldn't talk about our work, publish our work, or quit until the project was complete."

"But you didn't know the program had been in operation since World War Two?" Hawkins said.

She shook her head. "Or that it wouldn't conclude within our lifetimes. And none of us knew what the job really was until we got here."

"And then it was too late," one of the men said.

"They would have killed you," Hawkins said.

Green nodded. "They killed some." She frowned. "Not all of us are that strong."

Hawkins sheathed his machete. "Now that we're playing nice, I'm going to ask again: Who are you waiting for?"

She pursed her lips for a moment, then sighed and answered, "Bennett left us here. For a long time."

"He said a year," Bray said. "Why didn't you just leave?"

Green turned around and lifted up her straight, black hair. A small device, the size of a black pack of gum, was attached to the back of her neck. "If we leave a certain radius, it explodes. The only way we can leave is if we're within one hundred feet of Bennett's remote."

Hawkins tensed. What these people had done was wrong, even under the circumstances, but no one deserved this.

"We have access to our quarters, bathrooms, a kitchen, and food storage. We've been living in just these few rooms for the past year. It took a lot of trial and error, but we repaired a satellite phone we found in one of our . . . deceased colleague's quarters and powered it with some old batteries. It worked long enough to make a call."

"Who did you call?" Hawkins asked.

"Michael Castle," she said. "He recruited all of us, but I never got the impression he knew what went on here. He sounded genuinely shocked when I spoke to him."

"Still," Bray said. "Why not call the DARPA director? You said you were friends."

"She was scheduled to retire a few months after I accepted the post," she said. "And I'm pretty sure no one but Castle knows where the island is. He called back an hour later. Before the battery died, he told me to expect extraction today. Bennett wasn't here at the time. We're not sure they'll be prepared for his response."

"I'm not sure you're prepared for *their* response," Hawkins said. "They came once before, right?" The look on her face was all the answer he needed. "If they're coming back, it's not with a small team, it's with an army."

"And I hate to break it to you," Bray said, "but your job here was a life sentence. Whoever is really running this program, they're not going to let you leave. I doubt they'll let you live. You're a liability, especially after what Bennett has done. They're not going to take any risks. Smart thing would be to incinerate the whole island and wipe out anything with a DARPA logo."

"When are they coming?" Hawkins asked urgently.

"Sometime today," she replied, a worried look creeping into her eyes. "Probably soon. If you can get the remote—"

A scratching noise from above cut her off and drew the eyes of all eight souls toward the ceiling.

FORTY-THREE

"What the hell is that?" Bray asked.

No one answered. They were too busy listening.

When the sound repeated, everyone jumped back a few feet from the source—a ventilation duct.

"They're in the air system," a man said.

Tapping and clawing sounds emerged all around them. Several of the things had worked their way inside the ducts and were now searching for a way out. He watched the metal duct above him bend and flex under the creatures' weight.

Hawkins looked around the room, counting four vents, all large enough to accommodate the spider things. It wouldn't be long before one of the creatures found the way out. "Blok?" Hawkins said.

"They're still out there," he replied.

Hawkins took hold of Green's shoulder. "Is there another way out of here?"

"There are three exits," she replied. "They're all locked, but . . ."

"Right," Hawkins said. "You can't leave."

He wasn't sure what to do. They needed to leave. Not only were the creatures bound to find a way inside the room, but there was also some kind of strike force en route. If he didn't find Joliet and get off this island soon, they would all die here. Still, he didn't want to leave these people to die.

They were wrong, and responsible for the things they'd done, but they were also pawns.

"If you can get the remote and come back for us," Green said.

Bray rolled his eyes. "I don't—"

"We'll try," said Hawkins. "But I'm not sure we'll make it out of the—"

The sound of wrenching metal drowned out Hawkins's voice. A vent on the far side of the room burst open and vomited a black blur that landed atop the nearest man and took him to the floor.

Screams and panic filled the room. One of the women ran for a far door.

"No!" Hawkins shouted, but she opened it to a clear hallway, turned left, and ran.

"Lock yourselves in your quarters!" Green shouted to the two remaining staff. The man and woman turned and ran for an open door at the side of the room.

Green moved to follow them, but Hawkins took her arm. "Get us out of here. It's your only chance."

She gave a curt nod and motioned for them to follow her. As they moved through the room to the far door, Hawkins got a look at the fallen man. The spider was just beginning to unravel its tail. They ran into the hallway. The far wall was lined with windows that looked out into an atrium complete with a koi pond and sandy Zen garden. *A place for staff to go to forget all the horrible things they'd done*, Hawkins thought.

Blok slammed the door shut behind him. He was aided by the force of a striking spider thing. The door shook, drawing a deep frown from Green. Her path back to the safety of her quarters had just been blocked.

"Which way?" Hawkins asked.

She pointed to the right. "Follow this hall to the end. Turn left. Then right. First door on your right is a stairwell that will take you to the bottom floor and an exit."

A scream spun them around. The woman who'd fled tore around a corner, heading toward them, face twisted with fear.

She made it just three steps when a large spider creature tore around the corner, leapt up, and tackled her. As the woman toppled to the side, the thing wrapped its legs around her torso. The tail constricted her waist. Then—*crash*—they struck the window together. Glass sprayed into the Zen garden and the death-locked duo spilled into the atrium. As they fell, the creature stabbed her three times, but before they hit, a loud beeping filled the air.

Then an explosion.

The blast wasn't massive, but the force of it was contained within the small atrium. The remaining windows burst, showering the hallway with pen-size glass shards. When Hawkins took his arm away from his head, he found one such shard embedded in his forearm. He plucked it out and tossed it to the floor.

"Hawkins," Bray shouted, pointing toward the end of the hall. Two more of the monsters rounded the corner and charged toward them. Without thought, they ran. And Green ran with them.

Thirty feet into their run, a loud beeping filled the air. Green skidded to a stop. Hawkins stopped with her. Bray and Blok slowed, looking back, but kept moving.

"If I go any farther, it will detonate," Green said, tears filling her eyes. She had nowhere to go and her choices were limited to a three-story plunge, giving birth to more of the killer creatures, or blowing herself to bits.

"Turn around," Hawkins said. "I'll yank it off!"

She shook her head. "It will explode! Just . . . just go!"

"But—"

She looked back to the spider things. The slippery coating of glass covering the floor slowed their progress, but they were closing the distance quick enough. "Go! Now! Let me do this!"

Hawkins understood that the desperation in her voice wasn't just fear of death. It was also fear of some kind of afterlife and a God who might judge her. She wanted to die doing something right. She wanted atonement. And he wouldn't deny her. "Thank you," he said, and then ran to catch up with Bray and Blok.

Green stood her ground. The device on the back of her neck chimed incessantly. As the creatures closed in, she opened her arms as though to embrace them, and in a way that's exactly what she did. The spider things sprung up as one, striking her body with a tangle of spindly black legs, twisting tails, and jabbing stingers. Green stumbled back under their weight, but had been ready for it. Instead of falling straight back, she stumbled backward before tripping. As she spilled back toward the floor, her head and neck passed through the outer radius. She, and the shelled spiders disappeared in a bright plume of light.

The powerful explosion shook the building and sent a shockwave rolling through the hallway like a mudslide. The force of it knocked Hawkins, Bray, and Blok to the floor. They were quick to their feet, but three more of the creatures rounded the far corner at the end of the hall, blocking their path to the exit.

"Hawkins." Kam's voice was loud and all around them, booming from a PA system. "Take the next right. Then the second door on the right."

"We can't trust him," Bray shouted back.

"No choice!" Hawkins shouted. They ran toward the creatures and took the hallway on the right, sprinting for their lives.

Blok paused at a T junction at the end of the hall. He looked left and right. "Push doors in both directions." He started to the left, no doubt trusting Kam as little as Bray did.

But Hawkins knew they'd still be prisoners if it hadn't been for Kam. "Go right!"

Blok hesitated, but when he saw how close the spider chimeras were, he dove right and shoved through the doors. Bray rounded the corner, right on his heels. Hawkins went around last. The door was still open from when Bray went through. He could see them, just ahead, entering the second door on the right. He could also hear the creatures right behind him.

In a dead sprint from one set of doors to the next, he knew he couldn't make it. So instead of running, he spun.

Two of the creatures charged along the linoleum, their spindly legs a blur, their tails reaching up and over. The third was airborne. Its eight legs were splayed open, ready to grasp Hawkins's torso. A pair of mandibles was primed and ready to clamp down. The tail whipped around, aimed for his waist. And the stinger, like some kind of sick phallus, had already emerged and was jutting back and forth in excited anticipation.

Hawkins saw all this in the second it took him to grip the door with both hands and swing it shut as hard as he could. The well-oiled, heavy metal door flew shut and collided with the airborne creature first. The door shook from the impact. Two more less powerful thuds struck the door. Hawkins couldn't see what had happened, but thought the running pair must have collided with the stalled airborne creature before striking the door.

With his pursuer's momentum arrested for the moment, Hawkins sprinted to the second door on the right, slipped into the more dimly lit room, and eased the door shut behind him just as the double doors burst open. He waited by the door, hand on the padlock, ready to turn it. But he didn't dare turn it yet or they'd be trapped inside. Instead, he listened. He could barely hear the tapping of the spider feet outside the room, but they were there, unsure at first, but then scurrying again.

"Hawkins," Bray whispered.

Hawkins held up his hand, asking for silence. When he could no longer hear the creatures anymore, he locked the door. The deadbolt snapped loudly into place. When he turned around, he found Bray and Blok standing to his right, looking suspiciously at the room's third occupant: Kam.

But Hawkins immediately saw they had nothing to fear from Kam, one of their two Judases. A knife had been buried in Kam's abdomen. It was a mortal wound, especially without a real doctor within hundreds of square miles, let alone a surgeon qualified to repair the damage. But Kam wouldn't die quickly, especially with the knife still wedged in place. Whoever had done this wanted him to suffer. And here on the island, that narrowed the suspects down to one.

"I thought Bennett considered you a brother," Hawkins said. "Why did he do this?"

As Hawkins asked the question, he glanced around the room and got his answer. There were ten LCD displays and each showed four different live-video feeds. A little more than half of the feeds were from inside the building, focusing on labs, holding rooms, and a few hallways. There were several sweeping views from high points on the island. He could see the farm, the field, the garden, and orchard, a view of the goats from the abandoned laboratory, and an alternate view that showed the old lab itself. There were even a few images of the paths leading through the jungle and of the *Magellan* in the lagoon. Two of the feeds were blacked out. *Probably from the interior of Bennett's now melted gallery*, Hawkins thought.

"I'm sorry," Kam said. "I'm not the person you think I am."

"He's not a person at all," Bray said, pointing to Kam's lower neck.

At first Hawkins thought Kam's neck had been sliced open, too, but there was no blood. He leaned in close, careful not to bump the knife buried in Kam's belly. Hawkins realized that this part of Kam's neck would have always been covered by the tightly buttoned, high-collared polo shirts he wore. The shirt was unbuttoned now and part of the neck exposed. He took hold of the collar and peeled it back, exposing the slit in Kam's neck, along with two more.

"What the h—" The slits flexed and opened. Hawkins let go of the shirt and stepped back.

"Gills," Kam said. "And yes, they work."

"That's how you survived the storm outside," Bray said, his voice full of accusation. "And Cahill didn't."

"He saw me go outside. Tried to pull me back in, but a wave took us over the side. I tried to save him," Kam said.

"Not that saving him would have been a mercy," Bray said. "If you'd saved him, he'd be stuck on this hellish island, too. Or maybe have his guts split open with spider things climbing out. Or maybe have his hands replaced with knives and his eyes plucked out. At least he was *dead* when you guys strung him up by his insides."

Kam cringed under the verbal attack. "I didn't do those things. I wouldn't."

"But you allowed them to happen," Blok said. "Sometimes there isn't much difference."

Kam's eyes fell to the floor. He looked weakened, both emotionally and from actual blood loss.

"Enough, guys," Hawkins said. Had Kam been healthy, there would be hell to pay, but the man was clearly on his way to the next world and right now, he had questions, the first of which was, "What does Bennett want?"

"Entertainment," Kam said. "He's bored."

"He's a little more than bored," Bray said.

Hawkins saw Kam's gills open and close, as though taking a breath. "Is she really your mother?"

Kam winced in pain for a moment and then nodded.

"Wait. What?" Bray said. "Who is his mother?"

"The chimera," Hawkins said. "The big one."

Bray rubbed his arm across his forehead, which did little to remove the sheen of sweat reflecting the glow of the security displays. "Holy shit."

"You mean the thing that took us?" Blok asked. "The one that comes with the horn? That's your *mother*?"

"Her name is Kaiju. It means 'strange beast.' She started as a human embryo. And some of her mind is still human, though it functions at a more primal level than modern man. She was grown inside a woman with one arm—my grandmother, I suppose—who died giving birth. That's what my father told me, anyway. Who knows if it's true."

"What species was she merged with?" Hawkins asked.

"Some are obvious," Kam replied with a cough. "Her face alone contains bat, goat, tiger, crocodile, and human features. Her tail is chameleon. Her torso and arms are gorilla, as is her heart and much of her inner musculature. One hand is polar bear. The other hand is an oversize aye-aye. The protective carapace on her chest is turtle shell and the spines on her back are porcupine, though they're also coated with a neurotoxin. But much of her is still human."

"Including her reproductive systems," Hawkins said.

"My father, the head of the Unit Seven thirty-one division stationed on this island and chief scientist until his death, tried for years to artificially impregnate Kaiju. But it only worked once."

"You," Hawkins said.

Kam nodded. "The idea was that if they could impregnate a chimera, its children might be born with similar traits without needing to be engineered in a lab, which has a very low success rate and is time-consuming and expensive. When I was born, I looked fully human. I was deemed a failure, but allowed to live because my father used his own sperm to impregnate Kaiju. I was his son. The gills and"—Kam took hold of his shirt and lifted it, exposing his belly, which was covered in shiny fish scales—"this didn't develop until I was a teenager, when my father had long since lost interest in me. He never knew."

"How did you end up being so different from Bennett?" Hawkins asked. It wasn't exactly important, but he didn't understand how Kam had turned out to be merciful and Bennett a psychotic. Because when he thought about it, Bennett was the logical end result of being raised from birth in an environment that had no moral compass or respect for human life.

"His parents both worked for DARPA, but unlike many of the recruits, they were here voluntarily. They led the research together, along with my father. They believed in the work. Maybe even enjoyed the work. But they weren't like Bennett. They were clinical. Cold, even. But they weren't sick. Like my father, they took pride in what they saw as progress for their country—blinded to their crimes by patriotism. They were . . . kind to me, but in the way a master is kind to a pet. Things were different for Bennett.

"He lived in the labs. Spent days and nights there. He's brilliant, you know. Always has been. And his parents pushed him. So hard. He performed his first operation when he was ten. The subject died on the table. He wept afterward, but not for the patient. He was upset that he'd let his parents down. Over time, his skills increased, but so did his boredom. When my father died, Bennett was just fifteen, but felt he should take his place. Obviously, he was turned down because of his age and the fact that he wasn't actually employed as a researcher. After that he kept to himself, working on projects few people knew about. While his parents focused on pure research, pushing the limits of what could be done, Bennett focused on *controlling* their creations. Including my mother."

"He's using sounds and smells," Hawkins said. "Different tones in varying sequences act like commands. Three pulses might mean 'attack.' Two might mean 'stop.' And one horn blast means, what? 'Kidnap'?"

Kam shook his head no. "My mother can understand limited instructions. He can tell her what to do. The horn just sends her into action. As will the nearly inaudible tones emitted by his handheld remote and small speakers attached to many of the island's cameras. The horn is meant to intimidate those who hear it, but the tones allow him to act in secret, like when he took the crew who remained behind on the *Magellan*. When he wants someone taken, rather than killed, he marks them with a scent."

"But why does she obey him?" Bray asked. "Why doesn't she just crush his skull and be done with it. And what about you? Why not drag his ass beneath the water and let him drown?"

"While Bennett lived in the labs, I spent much of my time in the jungle. The chimeras don't attack each other. They might fight over territory or mates, but they don't eat each other. I was free to explore. To dream. It's why I'm different than him. He wanted to control nature. I wanted to enjoy it. And during those years of exploration, my mother was my only real company. Five years ago, Bennett captured my mother, and me. He operated on both of us. Planted explosives in our chests."

"Like the ones he used on the staff?" Bray asked.

"Similar. Someone skilled at defusing bombs could have removed those. The ones inside my mother and me would require a highly skilled surgeon and someone to defuse the bomb simultaneously."

"So they can't be removed?" Blok asked.

"It's unlikely," Kam said. "One is rigged to the other, and both to his body. If his pulse stops, we both die. If we don't do as he asks, he will detonate the explosive in the other. The small remote he carries? The buttons on the outside trigger the tones, and horn. But it can be slid open. The two buttons inside trigger the explosives."

"So why not just let him kill her?" Bray said.

Anger flashed in Kam's eyes. "You see a monster when you look at her, but I see my mother." He leaned back in the chair, exhausted from the effort. "I couldn't let her be killed any more than you could your mother. I'm not like Bennett. I couldn't kill my parents."

"Is that what happened to Bennett's parents?" Hawkins asked. "He killed them?"

"They *were* kind to me," Kam said with regret. "They didn't deserve it. None of them did."

Hawkins's eyes widened. "He sewed them in with the others?"

"They were at the core. He didn't want to see them." Tears gathered at the base of Kam's eyes. "It doesn't matter. We'll all be dead soon anyway."

Hawkins leaned in close. "What are you talking about?"

Kam turned slowly to the bank of monitors. He tapped a button on the keyboard, shifting views and revealing that there were many more cameras on the island than Hawkins first thought. Maybe hundreds.

Kam stopped on a block of four images. Two of the jungle, one of the path leading to the gallery, and one looking out at the ocean. With a push of a button, the ocean view enlarged, filling up the whole screen. The full-color image was crystal clear. "Bennett replaced the outward-looking cameras with high-resolution zoom lenses. So he can see things coming from far away."

Hawkins leaned in, looking for something, but only saw a few random specs on the screen. "All I see is dust."

"Not dust," Kam said. He zoomed in on the image. The specs grew large and blurry, but quickly came into focus, revealing ten ominous-looking helicopters, eight of them Blackhawks that would be carrying soldiers and two attack helicopters outfitted with an array of deadly weapons. "They're coming."

FORTY-FOUR

The sight should have filled Hawkins with relief. The helicopters could get them away from the island. But he knew the men on those choppers had just one mission.

Liquidation.

Anyone who'd laid eyes on this place was most likely a threat to whoever headed the secret DARPA group that had been running the island since at least the sixties. DARPA as a whole—even if they weren't aware of the project's true nature—could be shut down. The agency would probably not recover from what was possibly the worst human rights scandal outside of a war. Worse, if the island and its secrets were revealed to the world, it would be a permanent stain on not just DARPA, but the United States as a whole. Political careers would end. The president would ultimately bear the brunt of the backlash. It would degrade the country's status in the world. It seemed likely that at least a few other nations had similar secret laboratories—maybe tucked away in the Amazon, or in the wilds of Siberia, or anywhere else hard to reach—but most of those places already had bad reputations. Whoever was on those helicopters knew all that, and they were coming to stop it from happening.

The line of helicopters now looked like a squadron of angry wasps. "We need to get the hell off this island," Hawkins said.

"You mean with them?" Blok asked, pointing at the screen.

Bray chuckled. "They're going to kill us."

"We're United States citizens," Blok said.

"Well, you can stick around and see how that goes," Bray said. "We'll hightail it to the *Magellan* and get the hell out of Dodge." He took a small bell from his pocket and gave it a shake. "I've got my Get Across the Island Free card."

"Not exactly," Kam said with a cough. "The bell won't work on the crocs. Or my mother."

"Or Bennett's newest creations," Hawkins added.

"BFSs."

Hawkins looked at Bray. *What?*

Bray shrugged. " 'Big fucking spiders.' It's the best I could come up with."

"There's one more," Kam said. He pushed himself up, grunting in pain. "The litter."

Hawkins knew the term "litter" referred to the young of a species, usually mammals, that gave birth to more than one offspring at a time.

Bray came to the same conclusion as Hawkins, saying, "There are more of those panther savages running around?"

"They're not savages," Kam said. "They're my brothers and sisters. The one you speak of is Lilly. She's the oldest of them. And the smartest."

"Lilly," Hawkins said. "I think I spoke to her."

"You did?" both Bray and Kam asked.

"Briefly. In the jungle. Back by the old lab. I think I insulted her," Hawkins said.

Kam nodded. "She is easily upset, but rarely violent."

Rarely, Hawkins thought. He would have preferred *never*. "I thought Kaiju had just one child?"

"My mother has perhaps fifty different species combined within her single body. Some of them reptile, some of them amphibian. Both classes contain species capable of saving and preserving sperm for long periods of time. Based on the egg clutches I've seen, she has both active human and turtle reproductive systems." Kam looked Hawkins in the eyes. "She has laid one clutch per year for the past five years. Maybe ninety eggs total, though only five of the children survived their first year, all from the first two litters."

"Why are you telling us this?" Bray asked.

"I want you to get them off the island."

Bray threw his hands up in the air, scoffing.

Blok shook his head, whispering, "This is insane."

"Can they all speak English?" Hawkins asked.

Kam looked proud for a moment. "I taught them myself."

"And what if Bennett turns them on us?" Bray asked.

"He can't," Hawkins said. "Because he doesn't know about them."

Kam gave a slight nod. "While they are a result of the horrible experiments performed here, they have not been tainted by them. They are free of the evil that bent Bennett and made me too weak to stand against him. They are strong. And fierce. Survivors. But they are innocent. While my mother hid their birth, perhaps out of instinct, or some small act of rebellion, she did not raise the children. She does not protect them. She might even kill them if Bennett ordered her to."

Bray shook his head. "Ranger, please tell me you're not considering this."

Hawkins agreed that the idea sounded ludicrous. Getting off the island alive seemed less and less likely, never mind being shot, or torn to pieces, if they made it to the *Magellan* in one piece, and tried sailing the ship out of the lagoon. The helicopters would have to see them. They'd be blasted to pieces before entering the Garbage Patch. Of course, the ship was still inoperable, so the *Magellan* wasn't even an option. No, if they wanted to get off the island, they needed Kam's help. "Where is it?"

"Where is what?" Bray said.

"The boat."

"It's not much," Kam confessed. "We had a nicer ship, but took it to the mainland and left it behind. What's left is closer to a lobster boat. It's not fast, but it won't be easy to see, either."

"And . . ." Hawkins said, sensing a downside.

"And it won't get you far, but there is a distress transmitter. You'll have to survive at sea until you're rescued."

"*If* we're rescued," Bray said. "But I suppose that's an improvement over being torn apart or napalmed."

Kam looked relieved, but weaker than ever. "Thank you. To gather the children and reach the boat, head south from the gallery, through the jungle. You will need the bell."

"It's a big jungle," Hawkins said. "How will we find them?"

"They will find you," Kam replied. "Of that, I have no doubt. But they live in an old bomb shelter. When you meet them, tell them you are the Ranger. I told them about you. That it was your job to protect humans *and* animals. That they could trust you. Lilly was harder to convince. I thought it was because you nearly shot her, but you insulting her helps explain her reluctance. When I explained your fear to her, she understood. Is that what upset her, your fear?"

"Before I knew who I was talking to, I referred to the chimeras as 'things.'"

Kam pursed his lips for a moment. He looked slightly hurt by the words, too.

"I didn't know," Hawkins said, but then squinted as something occurred to him. "Kam, was this your plan all along? To have the children rescued?"

Kam shook his head slowly. "But it was my hope." He held out his hand. Hawkins recognized the gesture as an invitation to perform their practiced handshake. He wasn't sure what to make of it until he saw the weakness in Kam's eyes. He was saying good-bye and wanted to know they were still friends.

Hawkins took his hand. Two shakes in, Kam's arm went limp. His eyes closed.

Hawkins took Kam's arms and shook him gently. "Kam!"

After a moment, Kam opened his eyes again. He squeezed Hawkins's hand hard and stared in his eyes with burning intensity. "When you have the children, head south to the shore. The boat is anchored fifty feet out. You'll have to sw—"

Kam's head lolled to the side.

Hawkins checked his pulse and found nothing. He stood and turned to Blok and Bray. "Anyone have a better idea?

No one did.

Hawkins glanced back at the helicopters. They looked impossibly close now. Just one of them filled most of the screen. He took the computer mouse and used it to zoom out the image. He was glad to see that they were still quite some distance off, but knew the fast-moving choppers could close the distance in minutes. They had maybe ten before the kill squad reached the ground.

It wasn't much time to do what he needed to do.

"I want you two to find an exit and go south. If you come across the . . . children, try to take them with you. Get to the boat."

"Whoa, whoa," Bray said. "What are you going to do?"

"I'm not leaving without Joliet."

"It's a big island, Ranger," Bray said. "Searching this building alone could take all day. And most of the doors are locked. There's also, what, twelve BFSs running around?" He stabbed a finger toward the line of helicopters. "If we don't leave now, and fast, we're not going to make it far."

Hawkins ground his teeth. "Bray, I'm not leaving without her."

"Guys," Blok said.

"And I'm not leaving without you," Bray said.

"Guys!"

Hawkins and Bray turned to Blok, both saying, "What?"

"Look," Blok said, leaning in close to one of the small video feeds.

Hawkins took a closer look. Trees framed the view on either side, but the shot showed the clearing in front of the sterilized gallery. Standing in the center of the clearing was Bennett. Joliet knelt on the ground in front of him, a gun to the back of her head.

It took all of Hawkins's self-control to not fling himself out of the room and charge around the complex looking for an exit. But he knew that would likely just get him killed. So he clenched his fists instead.

"He doesn't know about the choppers," Bray said. "No way he'd be standing around waiting for you if he knew an army of mercenaries was about to drop on his doorstep."

Hawkins looked at the incoming helicopters. "We don't have time. Bennett knew we escaped, so he's set a trap. Whatever he has waiting for us, even if we can survive it, the mercs will arrive first."

Bray smiled fiendishly.

"What?" Hawkins asked.

"I have a wicked awesome idea," Bray said.

FORTY-FIVE

Bray's idea was actually suicidal, but it was the best they had. He'd tried to come up with a good Sun Tzu quote to justify the tactic, but settled on one of his own making. "Chaos is only chaos to the people who aren't expecting it."

It had taken them just two minutes to prepare the first part of the plan, though it had nearly cost Blok his life. He'd escaped with a three-inch gash on his thigh, which he was now nursing as he waited for the signal that would announce the beginning of the plan's second stage.

Bray had gone off to take care of his part of the scheme. Hawkins wasn't sure if it would work, or even if it was needed, but Bray insisted on maximizing the confusion. That made sense to Hawkins, but given the conflagration of opposing forces they planned on bringing together, he wasn't sure anyone would survive, let alone escape.

But it was their best chance. Their *only* chance. And it fit GoodTracks's "more aggressive predator" theory. Actually, what Bray had planned was closer to "*most* aggressive predator ever," which was something only the human race could truly pull off, because it involved the recruitment of other species.

Of course, Bennett had his army, too. Creatures conditioned to do his bidding populated the entire island. Including Kam's mother, who might be able to handle anything thrown her way outside of a M1A1 Abrams tank.

Hawkins's thoughts returned to his part of the plan when he saw the top of the curved, concrete gallery building emerge from behind the tree line. The gray stone path curved through a small stretch of jungle before opening up to the clearing at the front of the building—the clearing where Bennett—and Joliet—waited. Hawkins had the machete sheathed at his waist, along with his broken knife blade and the captive bolt stunner in his right hand, but he longed for a gun. He wasn't a bad shot. From twenty feet away, he could probably shoot Bennett without fear of striking Joliet. He suspected he could have found one inside the medical complex, but time was short.

As he rounded the corner with six minutes remaining, the time felt like an eternity. He made no effort to mask his approach. In fact, he did the opposite, feigning a leg injury and scraping his feet through the rough stone. When he emerged from the jungle and faced the gallery, Bennett stood waiting for him with a smile on his face.

Joliet knelt at his feet.

The shot would have been so easy, Hawkins thought, looking at Bennett's exposed torso and head.

Hawkins did his best to look surprised. "Joliet!" He hobbled forward, moving with a purpose.

"Mark!" Joliet said, sounding both relieved and concerned.

Bennett gripped her hair and pressed the gun against her skull. "Quiet."

Hawkins's suspicions were confirmed. There was a trap, and Joliet knew what it was, but if she spoke, he'd kill her and the trap would be sprung anyway. "Let her go."

"Pfft!" Bennett laughed. "Where would she go?"

Hawkins knew it was a silly request. Bennett wouldn't let her go, and if he did, she'd be in no less danger. But Hawkins wasn't looking for a fight, either. He just needed to kill five more minutes.

"That's close enough," Bennett said when Hawkins got within twenty feet.

Hawkins shuffled to a stop, looking exhausted and beaten, which wasn't really a stretch. He considering going for his knife and whipping it at Bennett. With the handle broken off, just about any part of the blade would do the trick. But getting the handleless blade out of the sheath and throwing it before Bennett pulled the trigger wouldn't be possible. So he just stood and waited, letting the seconds pass by.

Bennett's smile faded. He apparently expected a little more banter from Hawkins. "The others are dead?" he finally asked.

Hawkins grimaced.

"Blok stayed in his cell."

"Of course," Bennett said. "He would, wouldn't he? I never liked the man. Spent more time in the fantasy worlds conjured by other people's minds."

"You should try it," Hawkins said. "Might not be such an asshole."

Bennett grinned. "Jones no doubt died with his daughter."

Hawkins's earnest scowl confirmed it.

"And Bray? I'm surprised you left him on his own. Did he become an incubator, too?"

"It was Jim," Hawkins said.

"How is the last surviving Tweedle?" Bennett asked, growing more excited with every revelation.

"Out of his misery," Hawkins said.

Bennett's mouth opened to form an amused O shape. "You didn't!"

Hawkins held up the bolt stunner, revealing the blood splashed on its tip. He loathed the idea of entertaining Bennett with such details, but the man was engaged. He'd even let go of Joliet's hair, which was good because when the shit hit the fan, she would need to run like hell. He just wished he could warn her about it.

"Why are you doing this, Bennett?" Hawkins asked. Kam had told him a lot, but he couldn't reveal what he'd already learned. Bennett would know he'd seen the security feeds and that he had come out here to face him on purpose.

With a casual shrug, Bennett said, "It's fun."

Hawkins heard a hint of pain in his voice.

"Bullshit," Hawkins said.

Bennett's smile faded. "You disagree?"

Hawkins didn't need to answer. The fire burning in his eyes was answer enough.

Joliet, on the other hand, couldn't not reply. "Murdering and mutilating people is *fun*? You're a sick fu—"

"Joliet," Hawkins chided. He wanted to engage Bennett, not antagonize him.

Bennett glared at the back of Joliet's head for a moment, then looked back at Hawkins. "It's not all about the killing, you know."

"Then what's with the cameras around the island? I've seen them everywhere."

"You have good eyes," Bennett said.

Hawkins worried he'd said too much, but some of the cameras weren't hidden very well. "Once I saw the camera mounted on top of the old lab, I knew what to look for."

"Ahh, yes," Bennett said. "Didn't hide those very well, did I?"

"If you're watching, how is this island any different than an ancient Roman coliseum?"

"Because I'm not watching for entertainment," Bennett said. "Well, fine, maybe sometimes. But when physiology and biology began to bore me, I took an interest in sociology. At first I just watched people, observing the subtle nuances of body language and tone of voice. It's how I know you lied about Bray. He's not dead."

Hawkins tried not to react. He'd guessed right about Bray, but didn't mention Blok.

"You can try to hide what you're thinking, but it's nearly impossible." Bennett looked Hawkins over. "For example. Your limp is fake. Which means you knew I was here. And here's where it gets fun. You could have made a run for it. Maybe get back to the *Magellan* and escape. It's what most people would do. But you came here"—he tapped the gun against Joliet's head—"for her. Since arriving, you've looked at her more than me, despite me having a gun. You came knowing I was waiting for you. And prepared for you. Which means, and correct me if I'm wrong, that you're in love with Joliet."

Hawkins said nothing. Apparently, he didn't need to.

"And given Joliet's lack of surprise, not to mention how she wept earlier when I told her you were dead—that was a lie, by the way—I'd say the feeling was mutual. Of course, you both already knew that. But you're both cowards, which is also interesting because when it comes to physical danger, you're both somewhat reckless. And that brings us back to the here and now, with Hawkins risking not just his life, but also Bray's in an attempt to save the damsel in distress. Where is Bray? Hiding in the bushes? Circling around the gallery for an ambush?"

Hawkins noted Bennett's total lack of concern regarding both scenarios.

"How'd I do?" Bennett asked. "Pretty accurate, right?"

Hawkins quickly scanned the area, looking for Bennett's trap. He saw nothing but the dull, gray concrete of the gallery wall, its soot-rimmed entryway, and jungle all around. Nothing. But his sensitive ears picked up the distant staccato chop of approaching helicopters. He spoke loudly, hoping to drown out the sound until it was too late. "So you're conducting social experiments, too, watching the reactions people have to your creations? I can actually understand how someone like you would need that kind of stimulation."

"Someone like me?".

Hawkins didn't know a lot about psychology, but understood human nature and could bullshit with the best of them. He needed to keep Bennett distracted so he used the information Kam had revealed about Bennett's upbringing and launched into his prognosis of the man, doing his best to make it sound convincing. "You were born here. Raised by scientists, who, let's admit, are generally obsessed with their work and don't make for very loving parents. You were smart. Uncommonly smart. But you were still a child, and children need the love of their parents in order to thrive. Desperate for affection, you feigned an interest in your parents' work. It sickened you. How could it not? You were a kid. But your parents were finally paying attention to you. Maybe celebrating your early accomplishments. Their recognition made you feel loved, probably for the first time in your screwed-up life, so you tried harder. Pushed further. And with each success, you felt an outpouring of affection. Each successful experiment was followed by a rush of dopamine. After a few years, the experiments alone provided an intense feeling of love. No need for praise from Mommy and Daddy.

"When you hit puberty, your mind began to release gobs of hormones and chemicals and you actually started to get off from your experiments. The more horrific, the bigger the thrill. Eventually, your addiction began to make the other scientists, including your parents, afraid. So you pulled away. You didn't need them anymore. You could get your rocks off all by yourself. But then something happened. Maybe they confronted you. Maybe you overheard a conversation."

Bennett's eyes twitched.

"That's what it was. Who was it? Your parents, right? They used to be so proud and now they wanted, what? To kick you off the island? Lock you up? Kill you?"

Bennett twitched again.

God, no wonder the kid went off the deep end.

"So you killed most everyone here, including Mom and Dad, except for the staff that could help with your experiments, and Kam because you were raised together, like brothers, and he never publicly judged you. Or maybe because you knew how much he feared—"

"Enough!" Bennett shouted. All traces of humor had vanished from his face.

"How'd I do?" Hawkins asked, mimicking the way Bennett had asked the question. "Pretty accurate, right?"

As the words came out of his mouth, Hawkins knew he'd gone too far. He watched as Bennett's left hand came up, the small, black remote clutched in his fingers.

Pulse, pulse, pulse.

Hawkins spun, looking for an attack. But he saw nothing.

Just a line of trees, some brush, and a prickly-looking bush, like a cactus with long spines.

Black and white spines.

Like a porcupine.

That's when he noticed that the spiky bush, which had been there all along, was breathing. The huge form shifted and Hawkins found himself staring into the rectangular pupils of Kaiju, the strange beast.

FORTY-SIX

Bennett laughed as Hawkins stepped away from the shifting jungle. Though she was the combination of several different species, the monster—Kam's mother—had black skin and black fur. The only parts of her not black or a shade of gray were her yellow eyes and the streaks of white on her spines. In the shade of the jungle, her features were nearly impossible to distinguish, but when she stepped into the light of day, her horrible form was revealed.

The first thing Hawkins noticed was that her face and various parts of her body had been slathered in mud. Hawkins remembered tan skin on her face and green crocodilian skin on her forehead. And Kam had mentioned a polar bear claw, which should have been white. She was, after all, a patchwork of multiple DNAs, not a hybrid. Covered in drying mud, she looked like a single, unified species. She looked alien. A true monster.

That she'd been created from knowledge garnered from Japan's World War Two atrocities, and seventy years of continued barbarism under the control of a fringe DARPA program, made her even more of a monster. Kam would no doubt want Hawkins to see her as a victim and, to a point, he did. But he saw her in the same way he saw Jim Clifton—she'd been tortured, experimented on, and abused to the point where her life had been reduced to a subjugated killing machine. Ending her life would be the right thing to do.

Of course, it was far more likely that she would kill him.

Hawkins took another step back and drew the machete, holding it in his right hand and the bolt stunner in his left.

She stalked slowly toward him.

Where are they? Hawkins thought, annoyed that the cavalry had not yet arrived, despite the fact that the cavalry would likely try to kill him, as well.

"What are you waiting for?" Bennett shouted. "Get on with it!"

Pulse, pulse, pulse.

The monster snorted and stepped forward. Its legs were powerful, built like a cat's hind legs but with apelike feet.

Hawkins saw a scratch on the upper-right edge of the creature's turtle shell carapace. Had his knife strike been a few inches higher, he would have struck the unprotected neck.

The bristles on the monster's back shook and rattled as she lowered her body to the ground like a cat about to pounce.

And then she did.

The lunge was so quick that Hawkins barely had time to avoid it, despite being ready and nearly thirty feet away. He dove to the side, rolled to his feet, and swung out wildly with the machete. He thought she'd have landed close, or even started a second attack, but his swing found nothing but empty air.

He spun, looking for her, but the giant had somehow vanished. Hawkins noticed the growing shadow surrounding him at the same moment Joliet shouted, "Above you!"

He didn't bother looking up. He didn't have to. He just did the only thing he could: he fell back. Striking the ground knocked the wind from his lungs, but was nothing compared to the crushing weight that landed atop him. He'd meant to raise the machete and hope the blade resting against the solid earth coupled with the thing's own body weight would be enough to drive the blade through the carapace, but the weapon was batted away just before she landed atop him.

The only reason he was still alive was because she'd only placed one hand against his chest. The rest of her weight was dispersed through her other limbs.

A long finger extended out over Hawkins's face. He recognized it as the same talon-tipped finger that had easily plucked Joliet from the old laboratory's window. It twitched over his eye like a scorpion stinger.

"You don't have to do this, Kaiju," Hawkins said quickly. He didn't think he could talk his way out of this fight, but maybe he could delay it. When the finger didn't immediately impale his skull, he thought he was right.

Pulse, pulse, pulse.

The finger tensed, primed and ready to strike.

Or not.

Hawkins pulled the trigger.

Two inches of steal shot out and punched a hole in the carapace. The shell was at least an inch thick, so the wound wasn't severe, but the sudden and perhaps unfamiliar pain sent the creature flying. It reacted like a cat, springing into the air, flailing wildly with a shriek of surprise.

Bennett clapped his free hand against his other arm. "Well done! I do believe you are the first person—or creature—to cause her injury outside of the operating table."

The monster twitched and spun, searching for the source of the pain. When she found the hole in her chest, she stopped. She inspected the wound with the long finger of her aye-aye hand. When the talon poked through the hole and found flesh, she winced, staggered back, and leveled her eyes at Hawkins.

He barely noticed as he reloaded his last compressed charge into the bolt stunner.

But when she let out a roar that was both high and low pitched, like two voices conjoined, he noticed. And nearly dropped the charge. But he got it in place and snapped the weapon closed.

She slapped her hands hard against the ground, pulled her hind legs in tight, and then propelled herself forward with all of her unnatural strength. Hawkins dove again, this time in the direction of the machete.

He missed being struck by the monster's bulk, but a backhand from the polar bear claw as she passed sent him sprawling. Pain shot down his leg from his thigh where he'd been struck.

When Hawkins heard Joliet cry out with concern, his core filled with rage. So far he'd been on the defensive. Reacting instead of acting. He'd gotten in a lucky blow, but it would be his last if he didn't at least try to alter the outcome of this fight. He climbed to his feet with an angry shout.

The monster had just finished its charge and turned to face him.

This time, he attacked.

The creature seemed taken aback by this small man screaming and running at it.

So he ran faster. Straight ahead. With the bolt stunner ready to go, he planned to leap right at the thing, get inside its reach, and get the bolt stunner against its head. At the very least, the beast would be knocked unconscious, at best, it would be dead. Kam wouldn't have wanted it, but it had to be done.

Hawkins dove, leaping high to reach the creature's forehead. He nearly made it when he was batted aside. The strike was almost casual, though it felt like a truck had struck him in the side. He got back to his feet with a grunt. Most of the fight had been taken out of him with the one blow.

But the creature didn't press the attack. It just circled him slowly. *Is it toying with me?* he wondered. It did have feline attributes, but wasn't sure if that was the case. *Doesn't matter*, he decided, and charged again.

This time he never even got to lunge. The creature swiped its polar bear claws across his chest. The caked mud covering the paw and five sharp claws formed a dusty cloud at the point of impact.

Hawkins stumbled back.

The pain felt familiar. Dull at first. Then a sharp sting. Then a systemic reaction set all of his nerves on fire. All of this was followed by shock, which helped dull the pain, but also dulled his mind. He looked down slowly. His shirt was shredded and lay open, exposing his chest and stomach. Five red lines stretched diagonally across his torso intersecting the similar scars running in the other direction. Through the pain, he felt warmth spread down his chest. Blood. A lot of it.

But it could have been worse. The creature had sliced open his skin, but not fully. It could have easily cut through his rib cage, or removed his arm, or eviscerated him. Instead, it had decided to stun him, no doubt on purpose. Hawkins realized too late that he wasn't just fighting a predator; he was fighting a predator with a human, or at least near-human, intelligence. And it wanted him to know it.

She's evil, he thought. *As much as she may have cared for Kam, she's as tainted by this island as Bennett.*

The revelation came too late to do any good. The long, black chameleon tail whipped around the thing's body and wrapped around Hawkins's legs. The creature yanked his feet out from under him. He hit the ground hard and started coughing. He could hear Joliet shouting, but couldn't make out the words. The blurry shape of the monster hovered over him, raising its claws to strike.

He wondered if it would take off his head or open up his gut. Would it be a slow death? Or drawn out?

Then something new entered his vision. A body leaping over him toward the creature. For a moment he thought it was Joliet, but it was too large. And the shouting voice too deep. He saw a glint of metal. Then a second. The new arrival was armed! And swinging.

Hawkins pushed himself up as a surge of adrenaline cleared his mind. And then he saw him: Drake, swinging two butcher knives like a madman. He was covered in grime and dried blood. He was shirtless and his muscles glistened with sweat. It was like watching a vengeful spirit back from the dead.

Only Drake was far from dead. "Get up, Ranger!" the captain shouted.

Hawkins pushed himself up with a shout of pain, never taking his eyes off the action. The beast was on the defensive, shifting from side to side and stepping back. Hawkins

saw blood dripping from the bear claw. Drake had wounded
it and hadn't backed down from the first moment.

"Thirty seconds!" Drake shouted.

Thirty seconds? Until what?

The creature let loose a pain-fueled roar. A long, slender
digit spiraled through the air, landing at Hawkins's feet. Drake
had severed one of the aye-aye fingers!

And then he was flying through the air. Where the creature had been playing with Hawkins, he had no doubt it would
now quickly rend them limb from limb as easily as he would
a rotisserie chicken.

Hawkins turned to run, but a gun aimed at his chest stopped
him.

Pulse, pulse.

Hawkins felt hot breath on his back. The creature stood
right behind him, mere inches away from killing him, but
stopped at Bennett's command. Drake got to his feet, clutching his ribs, his knives gone. He stood next to Hawkins.

"To reward your bravery," Bennett said, "I'll allow you to
choose how you're all going to die."

"Fuck you," Drake growled.

"I was talking to Hawkins," Bennett said. "So, what will
it be? Should I let this little skirmish conclude and keep
Joliet alive until I get bored of her? Or should I put a bullet
in each of your heads right now, starting with Joliet and finishing with you?"

The answer was a simple one. Hawkins would rather them
all die now, and quickly, than allow Bennett the chance to
torture and mutilate Joliet. He'd only have to live with the
pain of seeing her die for a few moments before he joined
her. He was about to say as much when Drake clutched his
arm. Hawkins looked into the captain's angry and still confident eyes.

"I saw Bray," the captain said, not quite a whisper, but
still not loud enough for Bennett to hear.

"What was that?" Bennett asked, sounding annoyed.

Drake held Hawkins's gaze, ignoring the threat. "You
ready, Ranger?"

Bennett put the gun to Joliet's head. "Answer now, or I'll decide for you."

"Give me five more seconds," Hawkins said.

Bennett looked flabbergasted. "Five seconds? What do you need five—"

A bullet tore through his shoulder, spinning him away from Joliet.

Hell followed in the single round's wake.

FORTY-SEVEN

Between the rotor wash and the thunderous chop of the Black-hawk helicopter that had arrived just fifty feet overhead, it felt like a tropical storm had rolled in. Only it wasn't rain falling from the sky, it was bullets. A single soldier, dressed in black Special Ops gear, leaned out of the open helicopter's side door. He fired a blaze of gunfire from an assault rifle that just barely shook his shoulder.

The only thing that kept Hawkins, Drake, Joliet, and Bennett from being cut down was the fact that the soldier had seen Kaiju after taking the shot that clipped Bennett's shoulder. Seeing the greater threat, he'd adjusted his aim and opened fire. But the monster was faster than the man expected and the rounds chewed up the earth behind its feet.

Bennett, eyes wide and on the helicopter, barely noticed Joliet climb to her feet and run to Hawkins. He clutched her in a tight, protective hug.

Five more helicopters surged past overhead. The Doppler wave of rotor chop was nearly deafening. Two split to the left, coming to a stop over the research building. Two more continued on course and a third arced to the right, heading for the farm. *This is an island-wide invasion,* Hawkins thought. *They really are going to wipe everything out.*

Joliet pulled back and shouted, "Let's get out of here!"

"Not without Bray and Blok," Hawkins replied, searching for some sign of their missing crew. *Any second now . . .*

Six thick, black ropes unfurled from the sides of the helicopter. Soldiers emerged and began sliding toward the ground. The man providing cover fire from the helicopter ran out of ammo and quickly reloaded. But the delay was time enough for Kaiju to change tactics.

The giant monster completed its dash in a tight turn, bringing it on course for the six defenseless men slipping down the lines toward the ground. It leapt in the air, impossibly high, and just before careening into the lowest man, flipped itself over. The man became a pin cushion as an array of oversized, neurotoxin-laced porcupine spines punctured his body armor, fatigues, and flesh. The beast continued its flip with the man stuck to its back. When it landed on all four legs, momentum carried the man forward. He was flung to the ground with several of the quills protruding from his body like he'd just had a close encounter with an Apache hunting party.

Without pause, the creature snapped its tail out and snatched a second soldier's leg just before it touched down on the ground. The tail flailed back and forth, smashing the man to the ground three times. On the third strike, something cracked and the man never stirred again.

This wasn't the same creature Hawkins had been fighting. That version of Kaiju had been like a mischievous cat toying with a mouse. This version was something closer to a whirlwind of wrath. As he watched each highly trained, heavily armed soldier die in seconds, Hawkins realized how lucky he was to still be alive.

A third man reached the ground and even raised his rifle, but never got a chance to pull the trigger. The monster closed the distance between the two of them without releasing the last man from its tail and swiped at the shocked soldier with its polar bear claw. His head came free as easily as a ripe apple from a branch.

The three soldiers had all died in just over five seconds, which was the same amount of time it took the man above to reload. He opened fire again, this time catching Kaiju off guard, striking her arm twice. With a roar and a twitch of her tail, she flung the dead soldier toward the chopper. The spinning corpse struck one of the lines, jolting a fourth soldier free before crashing into the side of the helicopter. The helicopter spun as the pilot reacted to the jolt and, for a moment, the soldiers' descent slowed.

In that momentary reprieve, the enemies on the ground took stock of each other.

Bennett turned his eyes from the helicopter to Hawkins. The gun was by his side, but he raised the small black remote in its place.

The monster turned to Hawkins, too, but made no move for him. The soldiers above represented a far greater danger to it, Bennett, and their home.

And the soldiers above—they called for backup.

The second helicopter arrived with a roar of twin turbines, sweeping around the clearing in a wide circle. Hawkins recognized it as an Apache attack helicopter. Between the minigun attached beneath the chopper's nose and the missiles mounted to its small wings, the chopper was capable of decimating large numbers of targets. He doubted even Kaiju stood a chance against the Apache, at least not out in the open.

Mixed with the thunderous chop of rotor blades, Hawkins heard the high-pitched whine of the minigun beginning to spin. In a few seconds, it would unleash a stream of high-velocity rounds that could shred metal, concrete, and humans with equal ease.

But before the helicopter gunner could pull the trigger, a horn blast louder than everything shook the earth and sky. The Apache spun, though not out of control. It was simply acquiring a new target. A hellfire missile tore from the helicopter's wing with a loud *shhh*, followed by an enormous explosion that plumed smoke into the sky and silenced the horn.

They must know what the sound triggers, Hawkins thought, though he knew it was too late. Every living thing on the island would have heard the sound.

Then the chaos really began.

Two more Blackhawks arrived. Ropes dropped from the sides. Soldiers descended like waves of army ants.

Kaiju tore into the soldiers still clinging to the ropes of the first chopper as it righted itself over the clearing again. But this time, it clung to the cables. The sudden weight pulled the Blackhawk down and the pilot lost control.

Bullets began to fly as soldiers officially got boots on the ground.

Hawkins, Drake, and Joliet ducked for cover, huddling by the gallery wall.

Bennett made a beeline for the cover of the jungle, heading south. Through the chaos, Hawkins could feel a repetitive pulsing in his ears. Every conditioned chimera on the island would be in a frenzy.

There was a roar of pain as several rounds struck the monster. It let go of the drop lines and fell to the ground. But it was too late for the chopper. The Blackhawk spun out of control, falling sideways to the ground. It crashed in the jungle. There was no explosion, but the rotor blades snapped free. One of the flung blades flew from the jungle, cleanly severing a palm tree trunk and one of the soldiers at the waist.

More gunfire erupted and Hawkins thought Kaiju was done for. But then—

"Hawkins!" The voice was closer to a shriek. Blok. He was running fast, as though charging the soldiers, but only because what followed at his heels was far more frightening.

Twelve oversize black spiders with turtle shells and prehensile tails scrambled up the path.

The soldiers' attention became divided between Kaiju and the spiders. Guns roared all around. Hawkins saw a red laser dot appear on Blok's chest. He found the source just ten feet away. A soldier looked down the sights of his weapon, finger on the trigger.

They're here to kill everything and everyone, Hawkins remembered. "No!" he shouted and charged out of his hiding spot.

Hawkins grabbed the assault rifle under the barrel as the soldier pulled the trigger. He felt a three-round burst shake his arm as he yanked the weapon toward the sky. The soldier spun in surprise, pulling the weapon from Hawkins's hand, but not in time to stop Hawkins from landing a punch on the side of the man's head, which was unfortunately protected by a helmet. Luckily, the soldier was stunned enough for Hawkins to land two jabs to the man's face.

It was a good start, but the soldier was a pro. He spun the assault rifle, wrapping its shoulder strap around Hawkins's extending arm. With a yank, the trained killer pulled Hawkins in close and delivered a kick to the chest, right over Hawkins's five long wounds. The pain crippled Hawkins, dropping him to his knees. The man drew a long blade, and raised it over his head. As the knife descended, aimed for Hawkins's face, a hand reached around from behind the soldier, clasped the knife-wielding hand, and redirected the blade into the soldier's own gut.

The soldier doubled over, revealing Drake. Joliet stepped past him, reached down, and yanked Hawkins to his feet. "It's time to go, Mark!"

Hawkins turned to where Blok had been. He saw the man on the ground. Part of his head was missing. A spider leapt upon his back, jabbed him three times with its stinger, and then charged a soldier. Some of the giant spider chimeras had been mowed down by the gunfire, but their speed made them hard targets and their shells protected them from most of the rounds. As a result, five of the soldiers already lay on the ground, twitching from the inside with rapidly growing young. There would soon be many more creatures to deal with.

But the soldiers kept arriving, as well, and several of them who'd witnessed Drake and Joliet save Hawkins now turned their attention to the human threat.

Once again, the action was interrupted by the arrival of a new force. Their arrival was forecast by a resonating rumble and shaking ground. The stampeding herd of cattle arrived like a flood, surging through the line of soldiers like they were nothing more than dead trees.

The Apache helicopter finally opened fire as the men were

trampled. Gouts of blood exploded into the air, merging with the wails of slain cattle.

Spiders leapt through the air, stinging soldier and cow indiscriminately.

The giant bull arrived, fresh tentacle wounds on its back and sides, bucking its head and horns wildly, sending men and spiders flying.

Here was Bray's chaos.

No one would see them flee into the jungle.

Hawkins turned with Joliet and fled toward the trees where Drake, and now Bray, waited for them. As they slipped into the jungle, leaving the battle behind, Hawkins took one last look back and quickly noticed something that filled him with dread. Amid the raging cattle, stinging spiders, and gun-blazing soldiers, there was no sign of Kaiju.

The monster had fled, no doubt following after Bennett.

Who'd headed south.

South.

To the boat.

FORTY-EIGHT

Nothing stirred in the jungle south of the gallery. Hawkins wasn't sure if it was the bell Bray continuously rang that kept the draco-snakes at bay or that they'd been summoned by Bennett. But the jungle was clear and allowed them to move quickly, first at a sprint, then a jog, and now a fast walk as exhaustion set in. Hawkins guessed it was two miles to the south shore. Had he been well rested and not beaten, he might have run the entire distance, but in his current condition, even their current pace was a struggle. Every part of his body hurt, his chest and lungs most of all. But he pushed past the pain, for Joliet, for Bray, for Drake. They'd come too far and survived too much to give in to something like fatigue.

They moved in a tight group. Drake led the way, armed with a single butcher knife, which he used to hack away the occasional vine or branch obstructing their path. Hawkins and Joliet followed close together, and Bray brought up the rear, ringing his bell.

The sounds of the battle weren't exactly far behind them— perhaps a quarter mile—but were so muffled by foliage that the soldiers' gunfire sounded like distant fireworks. It was as much of a reprieve as they were going to get.

"What happened to you?" Hawkins asked Drake.

"Not entirely sure." He motioned to the blood staining his clothes. "Woke up like this. I have a few fragmented

memories. Like dreams. I'm pretty sure I was delusional.
Wandering the jungle. Must have come across something that
set me off. Could've been one of those dracos. Hell, could
have been a goat. Or a cow." He shrugged. "I woke up a few
hours ago. Found my way to the farm. Helped myself to some
food. Just started to feel a little bit more like myself when
Bray shows up, gives me the short and nasty version of what
happened to you all, and here we are."

"You're still feverish, aren't you?" Joliet said.

"Feel like shit," Drake confirmed. His body shivered in
response to the acknowledgment. "But I think I got off easy
compared to you. A lot easier than most of the people under
my command."

They walked in silence for a moment, the loss of their
crewmembers weighing heavily.

"How did they die?" Drake asked.

No one wanted to answer that question. Drake had seen
what happened to Blok. The shot he took to the head, while
horrible, was quick and more painless a death than the others. "I don't think—"

Drake chopped at a low-hanging branch and yanked it
away. He paused and looked back at Hawkins. "*How* did they
die?"

"Not well," Hawkins said. "We don't have time for this."

"Ranger, I need to know."

Hawkins was more concerned about how Drake would
react than the few moments it would take to relate the details. The captain was still feverish, and if he pushed too
hard, he could relapse into another delusional state, which
could be a bad thing, given the blood covering his body and
the butcher knife in his hand.

Bray had no such concerns. "Bennett stabbed Kam in the
chest. DeWinter and Jones were incubators for the BFSs—
the spiders. They died when the things came out. Jim and
Ray were both experimented on. Ray died on the operating
table. Jim became . . . a monster. Tried to kill us. Hawkins . . ."

Drake glared at Bray. "Hawkins what?"

Bray looked uncomfortable. It was a point Hawkins wanted to avoid, too. For now, at least.

Drake turned to Hawkins. "You *what*?"

Hawkins sighed. Time really was becoming an issue now. "I killed him. Quickly."

Drake just stared at him for a moment and then said, "Then we're not leaving anyone behind?"

"No, sir," Hawkins said.

Drake gave a nod. "Couldn't have been easy, doing what you did. Thank you." Then he was off and moving again.

They covered the next mile of mostly level jungle without incident or conversation. Gunfire and screams occasionally filtered through the trees, but never nearby. They paused at the base of a hill. Hawkins looked up. The rise was steep and covered with outcrops of black, volcanic rock that would have to be scaled, but it wasn't impassable. What he didn't like was that the rough terrain held fewer trees. He could hear helicopters circling the island. If they were spotted on the hillside, they'd make an easy target for a minigun. An even easier target for a hellfire missile. But if they made it to the top, they'd be close to their goal.

"Catch your breath for a minute," he said. "We're going to have to do this quick."

Bray stretched and winced. "Are we almost there? God, I sound like one of my students."

Hawkins closed his eyes and pictured the island as he'd seen it from the top of the pillbox. They were approaching the south shore between the western shore and the lagoon. He remembered the hill. Once they reached the top, it would be a straight, downhill slope all the way to the shoreline and, hopefully, salvation. "Half mile more, tops."

"What about the kids?" Bray asked. "I haven't seen anyone."

"Kids?" Drake asked.

Joliet looked mortified. "There are *children* on this island?"

Hawkins realized he hadn't explained Kam's involvement

or his request to save the litter to Joliet or Drake. "I'm going to give you the short version for now," he said, and then broke down the story into bite-size, nearly impossible to believe morsels.

When he was done, Drake looked wounded. "Bennett *and* Kam?" He shook his head.

"If it helps," Hawkins said, "Kam's involvement seems mostly forced. He was trying to protect his family."

"And now that includes these children?" Drake asked. "His brothers and sisters?"

"I still think it's a bad idea," Bray said. "They're chimeras, just like the others on this island. They could be dangerous."

"I'm inclined to agree," Drake said.

"But what if he was telling the truth?" Joliet asked. "What if they're more human than animal and they're just children who had nothing to do with the horrible things done on this island? We can't just leave them."

Hawkins looked up the tall hill. His energy had yet to return, but he didn't think waiting any longer would be wise. Who was to say the mercenaries wouldn't decide to cut their losses, evacuate the island, and carpet bomb the place? "Here's how we're going to do it. Once we get to the top of this hill, we're hauling ass all the way to the coast."

Joliet raised a hand in objection. "But—"

"Kam didn't give us any instruction on how to find the children. Searching for them could—well, we all know how that could turn out. He said they would find us. If they don't, they don't. If they do, we'll reevaluate when the time comes. Now, move your asses."

Hawkins led the ascent. While the going was slow, the many ridges and crags made the climb easy. Halfway up, Hawkins paused to look at a fern atop a ledge. The leaves were tangled oddly. Ten feet farther up, he found a leaf pushed into the damp soil. Toward the top of the rise, he took hold of a vine and gave it a yank, testing its strength. It would hold if they climbed one at a time. But that's not all he learned—halfway up, the brown vine held a five-inch-long darker splotch of color.

"What is it?" Joliet asked. "I haven't figured out what you're looking at yet, but I know you found something."

They stood on a five-foot outcrop of stone, just ten feet from the top of the hill. The vine rose up over a moss-covered stone, which now held Hawkins's attention. The moss had been indented in several spots. "Bennett came this way. He's heading for the boat. He's going to beat us to it."

"Then let's go!" Bray said.

"But that's not all." Hawkins pointed to a tree that grew out over a twenty-foot drop. "Halfway up the trunk." He'd spotted the grooves in the bark just before he saw the blood. The lighter color of the tree's exposed flesh made it easy to spot. "Kaiju is with him."

Drake took hold of the vine. "Don't see as we have any choice."

Hawkins nodded and, one by one, they climbed the vine. The first thing Hawkins noticed at the top of the hill was the noise. The hill had acted as a natural barrier, blocking the cacophony of sound from reaching them. But here, just feet from the crest, he could hear the sharp report of automatic gunfire, the shrieks of draco-snakes, the cries of seagulls, the screams of men, and the monotonous *whup* of helicopter blades. Lots of them.

Lying on their stomachs, they climbed to the peak and looked over the edge. The battle for Island 731 had followed Bennett and was being fought below. The trees beyond the hill were sparse, as much of the land was either volcanic stone or covered in slabs of concrete that had once been helicopter landing pads, a use for which they were being used once again. Three helicopters had touched down. Two had unloaded their payload of eleven fully armed mercenary squads already and were lifting off. A third unloaded just four men whose gear looked bulky. When streams of fire burst from their weapons, Hawkins knew why. Flamethrowers seemed morbidly appropriate, given how much they'd been used in clearing Japanese bunkers during World War II. Only now they were being used to fend off the armies of draco-snakes and seagulls closing in on the soldiers like a living hurricane. To the left of the battle, Hawkins saw what looked like a concrete airplane hangar emerging from the base of a hillside.

The bunker, he thought. *This is where the children live.*

And then he saw them. Five little bodies standing before a giant and its master. Bennett was no doubt confused by their existence and he wasn't sure if Kaiju would recognize them or not. Kam thought she might very well kill them.

Hawkins looked past the chaos. The jungle grew thick again, perhaps one hundred yards from beginning to end. Beyond that, he saw the coast. Their only means of escape lay on the other side of a battlefield.

"I think we should skirt around behind the bunker," Hawkins said. It was the slowest, but safest route. If their enemies occupied each other long enough, they might make it past. Of course, there were still the children to consider, but they would handle that debate when they got closer.

"Sounds good to me," Bray said.

Hawkins didn't hear Joliet or Drake agree with the plan. His sensitive ears had picked up a new noise. Mixed with the din of battle, it didn't sound like much. The problem was that it came from behind. He took a few steps back and looked over the steep rise they'd just climbed. At first glance, everything looked fine. Then he noticed that the dark soil of the jungle below wasn't soil at all. The ground was alive.

The spiders had multiplied, using men and cattle to spawn more young.

Hundreds of them.

Hawkins backed away from the edge as the first of the spiders began scrambling up the hillside. "Change of plans." The others peeked over the edge and saw the advancing army of killer chimeras.

"Run," Hawkins said. "Straight through. Run."

FORTY-NINE

At first, the plan worked great. Preoccupied by the deadly swarms, the soldiers paid them no attention, and Bray's bell kept the chimeras from targeting their small group. But the flamethrowers were turning the tide against the airborne monsters and for every man that fell to a draco-snake bite, five of the small creatures were either cut down by the constant 9mm bullet spray or were set on fire. It was the former that slowed their progress.

"Ahh!" Bray shouted. He kept running, but now limped.

Hawkins slowed to help him. "You're hit?"

"In the calf," Bray said, wincing with every step. "But I can still move."

As more and more chimeras poured from the jungle to their left, the soldiers to their right advanced. And while the bell still worked its magic, the mercenaries would soon notice their chaotic charge through the clearing. And when that happened, it wouldn't be stray bullets coming their way, it would be a barrage. There was no choice but to head for Kaiju, Bennett, and the children.

Hawkins veered left toward the bunker. A palm tree to his right took a round. He glanced back at the baseball-size indentation in the bark. If the tree hadn't been there, it would have struck his head. He glanced toward the soldiers and saw two of them tracking their dash. "Duck!"

Hawkins obeyed his own command just as a three-round

burst rang out and zinged over his head. He angled farther left, putting more trees and distance between them and the soldiers. More bullets shattered the trees around them as the two soldiers switched to full automatic and held down the triggers. Hawkins covered his head with his hands as he crouch-ran. He glanced up for just a moment and saw movement ahead, but he didn't slow. Couldn't. He just kept his head down and did his best not to collide with a palm trunk.

He glanced back and saw the others still with him, running low. The incoming gunfire had stopped, too. He could still see the soldiers, but they were dealing with a swarm of seagulls. The frenzied birds never stopped attacking. Even when the sky filled with the feathers of the dead, they continued fighting.

Hawkins realized why. Over the chop of helicopters, the crack of gunfire, and the keening wail of dying people and animals, there was a constant *pulse, pulse, pulse.* Bennett had either hit some kind of emergency button that repeated the signal around the island, or he was pressing his finger down on that remote.

No longer fearing a bullet to the side of the head, Hawkins stood and resumed his run. A shriek nearly toppled him over. He looked ahead and saw a second battle.

Kaiju was there. Roaring and twisting. The monster swung out with its arms and tail, fighting a far more agile enemy. There were three of them—the children—leaping around, striking with their small claws. One looked familiar. Lilly, the panther-girl. Another had a more reptilian body with a crocodilian snout. The third was mammalian, but Hawkins couldn't ID any specific species on account of the puffy, black hair.

Kam said there were five, Hawkins remembered. And then he saw them. Two small, limp bodies lay in a patch of grass. Had the litter attacked? Or had Bennett ordered Kaiju to kill them?

The reptilian chimera was suddenly caught in Kaiju's oversize aye-aye hand, which, even lacking its long finger, was still deadly. The small creature let out a high-pitched scream before it was silenced with a crack. Lilly and the other chimera cried out and pressed the attack. Lilly clamped on to Kaiju's arm with her catlike teeth. The behemoth roared in pain, shaking its arm, and finally swiped Lilly and sent her flying.

Hawkins had seen enough. He looked back to ask Drake for his knife when a large rock went soaring over his head. Joliet grunted from the effort.

The hurled stone collided with the side of Kaiju's head. The monster grunted and turned to face them as it batted the puffy-haired chimera away with its tail. Kaiju stared at them, heaving from exertion. Blood dripped from its arm where Lilly had bitten down, but the creature didn't attack.

Bennett peeked out from behind the trunk of a palm tree. He'd been hiding from the fight between mother and children. He looked them over, paying attention to their hands. *He's looking for weapons*, Hawkins thought.

Bennett grinned and then stepped out into the open, but much of his maniacal confidence had leeched away. He flinched with each shout, gunshot, and explosion.

"Got more than you bargained for?" Hawkins asked. He didn't think taunting Bennett was wise, but he didn't see how it could hurt.

Bennett glanced toward the battle. Draco-snakes flew past overhead, converging with the conflagration, but the soldiers were still winning, pushing the fight closer by the second. "Exciting, isn't it? Just wait until we reach the mainland. We will have such fun!"

Hawkins noticed a backpack over Bennett's shoulder and remembered the bottle labeled "active" he'd taken from the lab. If he had just one bottle of water tainted with those fast-growing chimeric blastocysts, the North American continent would be swarmed. The only thing that would save the rest of the world were the oceans and Panama Canal. If the creatures survived the cold, they might even be able to cross the Arctic ice to Greenland, Europe, and Russia. They would eventually burn through their food supply, overpopulate the northern hemisphere, and die out. Humanity might survive, but every country accessible by land or ice would be scoured clean.

Bennett has to be stopped, Hawkins thought.

Suddenly, the fuzzy chimera leapt from the ground, reaching its claws toward Kaiju's eyes. But the small chimera never made it. The monster opened its jaws, caught the smaller creature by the back of its neck, and bit down. Death was quick.

Was Kaiju killing the children quickly on purpose? Was it being merciful?

"No!" Joliet shouted, stepping forward. "They're your children! Don't you remember that?"

"Her *children*?" Bennett said. He turned to Kaiju. "Old girl, you've been keeping secrets."

Hawkins saw Lilly stir in a patch of grass. Without a second thought, he ran to her and knelt down. Bennett was distracted for the moment.

He looked into the yellow eyes. She bared her teeth and hissed. Hawkins nearly retreated, but then her features softened and a slight smile formed. "You came," she said.

"Sorry about what I said. About everything," Hawkins whispered. "I didn't understand."

She looked into his eyes, squinting, and then nodded. "Okay."

Hawkins reached down and picked the girl up. She was covered in dense but soft fur, black as night, but she had the body of a human five year old. Hawkins grunted as he lifted her. She was heavier than a human. The girl clung to him as he hustled back to the others. He handed Lilly toward Drake. Man and chimera-girl looked at each other, uncertain. But when she reached out for him, Drake took her, his muscles holding her weight better than Hawkins's. In exchange, Hawkins took the knife.

"Please tell me you didn't come here for them?" Bennett said. A bullet pinged off the cement by his foot, making him jump.

The battle was close; just one hundred feet away, separated by a thin smattering of palms and a shrinking army of chimeras. Hawkins noticed that no more draco-snakes were coming out of the jungle. The reinforcements had run out.

Of course, neither side of the conflict knew that a third, far more overwhelming force would soon arrive. Hawkins glanced uphill. The spiders had yet to crest the top.

"Kam asked me to," Hawkins said, but he didn't speak to Bennett. He spoke to Kaiju. "You hid them from Bennett because you cared about them. And Kam cared about them. Called them brothers and sisters. Saving them was his last—"

"Kill them!" Bennett shouted.

Kaiju charged.

Hawkins turned to the others. "Get to the boat. I'll meet you there!"

"Mark, no," Joliet said.

"Bray, take her!"

Bray wrapped a big arm around Joliet's waist and hoisted her up. Drake led the trio toward the jungle and ocean beyond, following a diagonal path away from Bennett, but closer to the fighting soldiers. Joliet kicked and screamed. Lilly just clung to Drake, staring back at Hawkins with sad eyes that revealed she believed she'd never see him again. When he saw her eyes widen with fear, he knew he'd watched them too long.

Hawkins was lifted from the ground, clutched around the ribs by Kaiju's aye-aye hand. Despite the crushing pain, he managed to hang on to the butcher knife. With a shout, he brought the knife down and plunged it into the monster's shoulder. The sharp blade slid through skin and muscle, three inches deep.

Kaiju let go of Hawkins, but it wasn't all good news. The nine-foot-tall beast had lifted him up, nearly over its head. He fell hard to the ground at her feet. He struggled to stand, but was backhanded by the polar bear claw. The strike sprawled him to the ground and knocked the knife from his hand.

No chance of being the more aggressive predator, Hawkins thought as he struggled to his feet. *Then again, Kaiju isn't exactly being the most aggressive predator, either.* He'd seen how quickly it'd slaughtered the soldiers in front of the gallery. Why was it taking it so long to kill a single man armed with just a knife?

The aye-aye hand found him again, this time hooking its four remaining claws into the skin of his back as it slammed him to the ground.

Kaiju roared and leaned in close. Its jaws opened wide enough to envelope and bite off Hawkins's face. He squirmed for freedom, turning his head away from the open maw. But Kaiju never bit down. He could feel and smell the hot, rancid breath on the side of his face, but the attack had stalled.

"Son."

Hawkins flinched at the sound of Kaiju's voice. It had a deep rumble to it as he expected, but there was also a trace of femininity. He turned to face her.

"My son," she said.

Hawkins wasn't sure if she was asking a question or claiming him as her own. There were no inflections to her voice, just words. "Kamato," he said, thinking she would recognize him by his full name.

"You say Kam," she corrected. "Where son."

Still no inflection, but Hawkins knew it was a question. Hawkins wasn't sure how to answer that. Hell, any answer might end with him being crushed to death. And if he told the truth?

Kaiju picked him up off the ground and slammed him back down. He coughed and wheezed, trying to catch a breath against the force of her grip.

"Kill him!" Bennett shouted. The sounds of battle were painfully close. "We need to go!"

"Where," Kaiju growled.

It was clear that if Hawkins didn't answer, she'd kill him anyway. Not only was the truth his best chance at surviving, but she also deserved to know her son's fate. "Dead."

Kaiju's grip tightened.

"How."

Hawkins could barely breath, let alone speak. "Stabbed," he wheezed. "Bennett. Bennett killed him."

The pressure fell away as Kaiju let go. The three-foot quills on her back rattled and shook. With a snarl, she turned back toward Bennett.

"What are you doing?" Bennett shouted. "Kill him!"

Hawkins sat up, clutching his chest. "She knows. About Kam."

Bennett looked mortified.

Kaiju took a step toward him.

He stepped away. "Kaiju. You know I wouldn't do anything to hurt Kamato. He was my brother."

"Not brother!" Kaiju shouted. "Son!"

The giant monster got just two steps into her charge when—*pulse, pulse*—she froze.

Hawkins eyed the small remote in Bennett's hand. He was no longer pushing it continuously. The battle was all but over. In fact, some of the soldiers were now headed their way, weaving through the trees, aiming their weapons.

"Kaiju," Bennett said. "It doesn't matter whether or not you like what I'm telling you to do. It doesn't matter if I just had you kill your children, or that I put a knife in Kam's chest. All that matters is that you obey. Now, kill him."

Pulse, pulse—

Hawkins put all of his strength into the throw. The blade glinted in the sun's light, looking like an oblong strobe light as it crossed the distance. Hawkins had remembered the knife blade still tucked away in its sheath. Without a handle, it would have made a poor weapon choice against Kaiju. But against a man, at a distance, the blade worked just fine.

Bennett shouted in pain as the blade struck home. The blow hadn't been as dramatic as Hawkins had hoped—the dull side struck Bennett's hand—but the intended effect was the same: Bennett dropped the remote and never finished triggering the third pulse. The two-pulse burst effectively canceled the kill order and unleashed Kaiju.

Bennett scrambled for the remote at the same moment the beast he'd controlled for so long turned on him. Bennett must have realized he wouldn't be able to reach the remote and trigger another two-pulse burst because he got to his feet with a scream and sprinted in the opposite direction.

Hawkins limped in slow pursuit, stopping when he reached the remote. He bent down and picked it up.

Kaiju roared as she chased Bennett through the jungle. He was fleet-footed and did an admirable job weaving in and out of the trees. But Kaiju slowly closed the distance like a cheetah pursuing a gazelle. It would be over in a few seconds.

Hawkins flipped the remote over and found a plastic indentation. The device slipped open, revealing two more red buttons. Neither was labeled, but he knew these were the buttons that would detonate the explosives in Kaiju's and Kam's bodies.

Bennett squealed like a wounded pig. Kaiju was upon him. He could see her claws sweeping back and forth, goring the smaller man.

No one should live like that, he thought. Kaiju had been born a monster, but part of her was still human. What she was, what she'd done, had to weigh on her. And now her son was dead. All that was left for her was killing. Hawkins offered a silent "sorry" and pushed both buttons.

FIFTY

Bennett screamed as he was lifted off the ground. Kaiju gripped the man's thigh in her aye-aye hand and his torso with the polar bear claw. His guts hung from his sliced-open belly. Her massive muscles twitched as she pulled. Bennett's wail reached an impossible pitch as he came apart.

And then both of them ceased to exist.

Hawkins had no idea what explosive Bennett had used, or how much, but it seemed like overkill. Their bodies were instantly vaporized, becoming a cloud of pink before being enveloped by flame and consumed by smoke.

The blast knocked nearby palms to the ground and sent Hawkins flying. He felt the landing, but only briefly.

When he opened his eyes, he found the barrel of an M4 carbine assault rifle with a laser sight aimed at his forehead. His vision spun and his ears rang. There were people standing above him, at least eight mercenaries.

Above the ringing in his ears, he could hear the chop of helicopters, but no gunfire. The battle, it seemed, was over. An Apache roared past overhead and began circling the clearing.

"Who are you?" Hawkins groaned. He pushed himself up onto his elbows. The barrel of the M4 settled on his forehead.

"Don't move," the soldier ordered. No threat was required. The M4 spoke loudly enough. Hawkins stopped, but didn't lie back down. They were going to kill him, of that he had no doubt. But there was a reason they hadn't already. He looked up at the soldier. The man wore black gear from head to toe. His vest and belt were thick with knives, ammo clips, and a variety of grenades. Enough to wage a one-man war. Hawkins would have liked to look the man in the eyes, but they were concealed behind a pair of reflective sunglasses. Even the man's lower face was concealed by a black mask.

"Move aside," said a gruff voice.

The soldiers parted for the newcomer. Like the rest of them, a black uniform concealed his identity, but his voice was older and held authority. This was the man in charge. He stood over Hawkins, turning his head from side to side as he looked him over.

"Huh," the man said. He reached into a pocket on his vest and took out a stack of laminated cards bound by a metal ring. He flipped through them, occasionally pausing to glance at Hawkins's face.

Hawkins realized the man was looking at a stack of faces, like the cards used to identify terrorists post-9/11. Only the faces on these cards were Island 731 staff and scientists. "You won't find me."

"I'm starting to see that." The man lowered the cards. "Who the hell are you?"

Hawkins nearly didn't answer, but decided it couldn't hurt. With the *Magellan* still floating in the lagoon, withholding his identity wouldn't protect the others if they managed to escape.

"Mark Hawkins. I'm a crewmember on board the *Magellan*."

"That the ship anchored in the bay?"

Hawkins nodded. "We were brought here against our will. The crew was tortured, murdered, and experimented on."

The man shook his head. He squatted down next to Hawkins, removed his glasses, and pulled down his mask.

Dammit, Hawkins thought, *now they're definitely going to kill me*.

The man had a salt-and-pepper, close-cropped beard. His

pale eyes were intense, but held a hint of remorse. "Are there any other survivors?"

"None," Hawkins said without hesitation.

"He's lying, sir," one of the other soldiers said. "We saw three more flee into the jungle to the south. Reno and Dolan are on them."

"Check on their status," the older man commanded.

The soldier tapped his ear and spoke. "Action Team Beta, report."

Hawkins heard nothing, but could tell the man was listening. "Castle, they're closing on targets. Requesting permission to engage."

Hawkins closed his eyes and rubbed his head. He couldn't think of any way out of this mess, for himself or the others. Even if they made it to the disguised boat, the Apache helicopters no doubt had heat sensors that could easily pick up their bodies, or a warm engine, against the cool backdrop of the Pacific. Then the name registered. Castle. "Michael Castle."

The man's head snapped toward him. His eyebrows furrowed. "Where the *fuck* did you hear that name?"

Hawkins cringed. Had he just signed their death warrants? Instead of answering the question, he asked one of his own. It was a bit of a leap, based on what Green had told him, but the way he commanded these men left little doubt that he was actually the man in charge. "How long have you been running the program on this island?"

The man tensed, but answered. "Since you were still in diapers. Had a good thing going. Real progress. Looked away for a few years and things fell to shit. Too many balls in the air."

Too many balls in the air? Hawkins wondered. *Are there other secret research programs like this one?*

"How do you justify it?" Hawkins asked, growing angry.

"Justify it?" Castle said and then chuckled. "Justify it. Are you that naïve? The modern world wouldn't exist without research done by people like me. Medicine, surgical techniques, the weapons that keep you and your pals safe, and just about every damn thing you buy in a store, including the grocery store, has a history that would make you squirm. Human experimentation is part of human evolution. Those of us who can stomach it are servants, not criminals." He shook his head again like he couldn't believe he had to explain.

"And DARPA? Are they a part of this?" The knowledge wouldn't do Hawkins any good, but he wanted to know and every second they spoke was an extra second the others had to make their escape.

The man laughed. "DARPA is all brains and no balls. They won't push to the limits, and they won't question a black program that's hardwired into the Mansfield Amendment, which keeps the organization focused on defense and guarantees their generous funding."

"Sir," the man with the radio said. "Action Team Beta is waiting."

Castle looked into Hawkins's eyes and shook his head again. He stood, pulled his mask back up, and put his glasses back on. "They're clear to engage. No survivors."

Hawkins looked to the sky, thinking of Howie. What advice would he give now? Take it like a man? Beg for mercy? Pray for a mira—

Hawkins's eyes went wide. He twisted his neck one way, and then the other, feigning a last stretch. As he looked to the right, he found his miracle.

The older man drew his sidearm and pointed it at Hawkins's head. "I'm sorry about this. Really. You're misguided, but brave. And I respect that. You just have really shitty luck."

Hawkins looked up, staring into the man's sunglasses. "Makes two of us."

The man's face was covered, but his body language showed confusion as the gun lowered a notch. "What are you—"

"Sir!" someone shouted. "We have incoming!"

The man spun to look.

Hawkins knew he should have run right then, but his eyes

were drawn back to the spectacle. The wave of turtle-shelled spiders had not only crested the hill, but had closed in on their position. The hillside shifted with living black all the way to the top, where more of the chimeras emerged over the ridge. It took them a while to scale the steep hillside, but now on the down slope, they ran and leapt with speed and agility unlike anything Hawkins, or these soldiers, had ever seen before.

"Choose your targets. Wait for them to be in range!" the older man shouted before tapping his ear. "All Eagles converge on my position. Shoot everything that is not human." He holstered his sidearm and took his own M4 carbine from his shoulder.

Hawkins backed away from the line of men. He knew they'd forgotten him for the moment, but didn't want to remind them by making noise. A moment later he could have sung "The Star-Spangled Banner" and no one would have heard him.

The slow pop of gunfire grew in intensity as the chimeras closed in. Hawkins saw several well-placed shots strike spiders' exposed heads, killing them quickly. But where one fell, five more filled the gap. Hawkins doubted they had enough rounds even if every shot was a kill.

When the spiders closed in, several of them leapt into the air. That's when the soldiers unleashed the weapon that might save them. Twin columns of flame arced back and forth. Squeals filled the air as charred spiders emerged from the other side, their burned husks twitching.

The commander tracked one of the flaming spiders as it crossed over his head. He shot it once when it landed. Then he saw Hawkins slowly backing away, fifty feet between them. He raised his M4 and pulled the trigger. But the shot went high as the man was struck from behind. He fell to the ground, a BFS clinging to his back. One of the soldiers shouted, "Sir!" and gripped the shell, yanking the creature away, but not before the creature got in three quick jabs with its stinger.

As the line of heavily armed soldiers fell to the wave of chimeras, Hawkins ran. It wouldn't be long before the monsters turned their attention to him. An Apache helicopter appeared above, so close that the rotor wash nearly pushed his weakened body to the ground.

He looked up and saw the minigun swivel in his direction. But it didn't fire.

The weapon then turned up and opened fire. The roar stung Hawkins's still-ringing ears, but he was thankful for it, and for the commander's order—"shoot everything that is not human." The man had unknowingly saved Hawkins's life.

A barrage of missiles launched from the helicopter, tearing up the ground behind Hawkins. He stumbled into the jungle, pushed by a continuous string of explosive pressure waves. He heard two more helicopters arrive behind him and open fire. The airborne units had nothing to fear from the chimeras, but he doubted they could kill them all.

The thick jungle tore at him, clinging to his clothes and scraping his wounds as though the island didn't want to let him go. But he pushed through it all, numb to the pain and desperate to reach the coast. The trees began to thin, revealing blue sky ahead. He felt a flash of hope, but then saw two figures silhouetted in the light. Reno and Dolan. Action Team Beta.

Hawkins slowed his approach, opting for stealth over speed. One of the men lowered a pair of binoculars and pointed out to sea. He took a large sniper rifle from his shoulder and lay down. The second man lay down slightly behind the sniper, looking through a spotter scope.

Action Team Beta was a sniper team. Hawkins rounded the pair from the right, quickening his pace as much as he dared. He emerged from the jungle onto the solid stone of the coast and sprinted toward the men, his steps muffled by the hard stone. The ocean, covered in a layer of filth to the horizon, lay to his right. The jungle to his left. And the two soldiers straight ahead. He could hear them discussing the wind, range, and angle.

"Clear to fire," the spotter said.

The sniper's finger moved to the trigger.

Hawkins reached them a moment later. He put all of his energy into the kick and struck the long sniper rifle barrel with the top of his foot. The rifle flew from the surprised soldier's hands as he shouted in pain. The kick had also broken his trigger finger. Hawkins spun on the man and kicked hard again while his partner jumped to his feet. The second kick caught the man hard in the temple, knocking him unconscious.

Hawkins turned on the man's partner, but the soldier was too fast. He'd already drawn his pistol and was leveling it at Hawkins's chest when a long, black tail wrapped around the man's neck and constricted.

The gun went off.

Hawkins fell to his knees, watching the man's eyes go wide. The soldier stumbled back and aimed the gun over his shoulder.

Hawkins looked toward the trash-covered ocean. It was a fifteen-foot drop over a sheer cliff to the water. It was preferable to facing the chimera when it was done with the soldier. But even if he made it to the water, he was done. He lifted a hand from his side and found it covered with blood. But he'd rather drown than become an incubator for parasitic chimeras. He shuffled toward the cliff's edge.

Then he saw something strange about the BFS's tail. It was covered in black fur. He paused, watching as a pair of small hands reached up and twisted the gun from the soldier's hands. This wasn't a BFS. The man's eyes bulged as his face turned purple. He fell to his knees, and then flat on his face. Lilly clung to his back. Her yellow eyes, once horrifying to Hawkins, looked at him with concern. "Hurt?"

"You could say that," he replied with a grunt of pain.

She looked down and saw his wound. A flash of concern crossed her face, but was quickly replaced with determination. She stood next to Hawkins, put a steadying hand under her arm, and gripped his belt with the other. With a quick tug, she lifted him off the ground and put him on his feet.

How strong is this kid? Hawkins wondered.

"We have to hurry," she said. "I can hear them coming."

Lilly half guided, half carried Hawkins down the sloping rocks of the coast. They soon came to a small path that led down to the water. Waves crashed against the cliff wall, but the tide was going out and the waves were small. The layer of trash began thirty feet from shore as the receding tide dragged it away.

"Hurry!" Lilly urged, and pushed him into the water.

Hawkins felt his consciousness fading as he slipped beneath the surface. But then he was yanked up again as Lilly pulled him by his shirt collar. The girl kicked with her feet, but also beat the water with her tail. Hawkins lay limp on his back, his body incapable of movement. He just stared at the blue sky above him.

When a black shape appeared above, he mistook it for a helicopter. Then his eyes focused and he saw it for what it was—a chimera spider, legs splayed open, leaping for his face. "Lilly!" he shouted.

Hawkins's eyes remained open as he was pulled beneath the water. He saw the spider strike the water where his face had been just moments before. The creature slipped beneath the surface. Its legs scrambled for purchase and found nothing. Its tail twitched madly, but failed to propel the creature through the water. It sank down, spasmed twice, and fell still. The BFSs couldn't swim.

But Lilly could. As she pulled him forward, he saw her toes splayed wide, revealing black webbing between them. She held him beneath her body, gripping his arms. Gills on the sides of her neck opened and closed.

Just like Kam, he thought as his vision began to fade.

He looked into her eyes, her inhuman but kind eyes, and smiled.

She returned his smile, flashing a pair of sharp, white canines and a contrasting duo of deep dimples. Then she arched her body and turned up. Hawkins coughed violently as they emerged into the air once more. He felt two pairs of hands reach under his arms and pull him up. He fell back

with a wet slap and found himself on the deck of a strange-
looking, trash-covered boat. The hard deck felt impossibly
comfortable. Joliet appeared above him. He could see her
speaking, but couldn't hear her. He managed to smile up at
her for a moment, and then closed his eyes.

FIFTY-ONE

The sun flared bright in Hawkins's eyes when they opened again. But then it faded, growing darker by the second, until it seemed like he would pass out once more. His pulse quickened, waking his nerves, filling his body with a pain so intense he knew consciousness was impossible. But his eyes . . . the sun . . . what was—

Then he saw the stars. It was night.

As his eyes continued to adjust, he saw many more stars emerge and the inky blackness of the night sky became something closer to a milky swirl of dark and light shades. The gentle undulation told him that he was on a boat. A small one. He could hear water gently lapping against the hull, but also a continuous, dull thumping sound.

We're still in the Garbage Patch, he realized.

Hawkins turned to his left. Joliet lay next to him, flat on her back, her eyes closed. She looked peaceful when she slept. The expression on her face reminded him of the sketch he'd drawn of her. But her body, covered in scrapes, bruises, and dried blood, ruined this image. A shadow stirred and he noticed that Lilly lay in the crook of Joliet's arm, snuggled up close. If not for the hair and feline features, she'd look like any other sleeping child. Beyond them, Bray and Drake both lay sleeping. They looked horrible, but the worst of their wounds had been tended to. An emptied first-aid kit laid at Bray's feet.

He pushed himself up into a sitting position. His side ached and he paused to let his head stop swirling. He slid back and leaned against the hull, wondering why his wounds didn't hurt more. Hell, he should have been dead. He looked down and found most of his chest and side wrapped in bandages. The one on his side had a red splotch in the middle, but didn't appear to be bleeding through. *Someone sewed me up*, he thought, and then felt the bandage on his back. *The bullet went straight through*. He nearly laughed at the thought and realized he wasn't feeling quite right in the head, either. *Shock or morphine*, he decided, but didn't really care which. Both would eventually wear off and the pain would become unbearable.

A foreign sound tickled his ears and he instinctively looked to the sky. He couldn't see a thing, but he knew it was up there. A jet. The running lights should have been easy to see in the pitch blackness, but there were none, which meant it didn't want to be seen.

With a grunt he pushed himself to his feet. *Are they looking for us?* he wondered. He limped to the aft deck and got his first real look at their ship. Aside from the bare deck, the fifteen-foot vessel looked like a clump of garbage, nearly indistinguishable from the thick swath of trash surrounding them on all sides. They were still in the thickest part of the patch, which meant that they had yet to travel thirty miles from the island.

Hawkins flinched as a hand took his. He looked down and saw Lilly's eyes reflecting the moonlight back up at him.

"What is it?" she asked, looking at the sky.

"Sounds like a jet," he replied.

"You can't see it?"

He shook his head no. Of course he couldn't, but she could! "What does it look like?"

"It's small," she said. "Darker than the sky. Kind of a triangle." She pointed to the sky, low on the horizon. "It's there, moving away from us. Toward the island."

The plane had already passed, moving at supersonic speed.

The sound was just reaching them now, which meant it was really high.

"Sounds like a B-2 bomber," Bray said. He stretched as he joined them at the back of the boat.

Joliet stepped up next to Hawkins's right side. She leaned her head on his shoulder. "Thanks. For coming to get me."

Pain lanced through his arm as he moved, but he managed to get his hand on her shoulder. He pulled her closer. "You owe me two cases of beer now."

"They've given up," Drake said from behind. He sat in the pilot's chair, watching the sky. "Must have lost everyone on the island. They're going to wipe it off the m—"

The sky behind them bloomed with orange light. The light expanded, flickered, and then shrunk in on itself. The surreal silence of the distinct explosion made it almost beautiful. Part of Hawkins appreciated the sight. It meant that the evil of Island 731 had been contained. But it also meant that those responsible would never have to answer for their crimes against humanity, just like the Japanese scientists of World War II.

Hawkins heard Bray counting softly. "What are you doing?" he asked.

Bray held up his index finger, signaling Hawkins to wait. Then it happened. A boomlike thunder rolled past them. Lilly's grip on his hand tightened to the point of hurting.

"Eleven miles," Bray said. "Four more and we'll be outside the thickest part of the Garbage Patch. Then we can gun the engines until they run dry and activate the distress signal."

Hawkins knelt down next to her. "It's okay. You're going to be okay. I promise."

As he looked into Lilly's yellow eyes, a warm breeze pushed by the explosion's pressure wave surged past.

"Why did you save me?" she asked, looking down at herself.

"Your brother, Kam. He . . . was our friend."

She smiled. "That's what he said, too. But I'm not like you. I'm evil."

Hawkins thought about it. "You're *not* evil. The things

that happened on that island had nothing to do with you. It doesn't matter if you're like us. You don't just deserve to live, you deserve a better life."

Hawkins could see she wasn't fully believing him, probably because of what he'd said during their first conversation. "You're not a thing," he said. "You're a person."

"I'm more than a person," she said, looking sad.

He nodded. "And that makes you amazing."

She placed her hand on his cheek. He could feel the hardness of her retracted claws against his skin, but didn't flinch. For her to survive in the modern world, and for him to keep her safe, they would have to trust each other. If news of her existence ever got out, the people who had just wiped out an island would no doubt come calling. "My name is Mark, by the way. I know I already told you, but figured I should probably introduce myself again. You know, so we're not strangers."

She smiled. "My name is Lilly," she said and gave a slight bow. "Lilly Shimura."

FIFTY-TWO
One Year Later

Hawkins lay on his stomach, looking through a pair of binoculars. "Do you see her?"

"Nothing," came the quiet but rough voice of Howie Good-Tracks. Hawkins's mentor and surrogate father lay next to him on the grassy bluff overlooking a rolling stream far below. "She is better than you."

"She's better than everyone," Joliet added. She stood behind them, leaning against one of many pine trees that surrounded their hilltop position. She took a loud bite from an apple.

Hawkins shushed her and held a finger to his lips. "They'll hear you!" He looked through the binoculars again, finding the deer by the stream. There were three of them. They drank in pairs while one always kept watch, wary of cougars, grizzlies, and human hunters. But no amount of vigilance could prepare them for Lilly. One of the deer was already dead, it just hadn't realized it yet.

It had been a year since Hawkins returned to the Ute reservation. That they'd made the trip without being discovered was something of a miracle. They had been picked up by an oil tanker two days after escaping the island. The tanker's sparse crew and lax captain hadn't checked the contents of the heavy bundle carried by Drake when he had boarded the ship. Nor had they paid much attention to the rescued crew while they had quietly recovered on the three-week voyage to the Port of Los Angeles.

When they left the ship, Drake assumed his position as the *Magellan*'s captain and told a fabricated story about a storm that had capsized the *Magellan*. Thankfully, most of their wounds, including Hawkins's side and Bray's calf, had healed and didn't require a hospital visit, which allowed Drake to leave out their less believable run-in with pirates. The police interviewed them one at a time, which allowed three of them to stay with Lilly in a cheap motel, but the interviews focused mainly on confirming their identities. Their rehearsed stories matched and once their credentials were checked out, no one questioned the validity of their story. They were free to go.

GoodTracks had been confused by Lilly—neither fully human nor fully animal—when Hawkins first introduced her and requested sanctuary for them both, but quickly decided her feline traits were a blessing. To the Ute, the puma, panther, and jaguar were symbols of strength, nobility, and guardianship. She would protect them as they protected her. She basked in the attention GoodTracks had once given Hawkins.

Joliet, Bray, and Drake stayed with them for a week before heading to their various homes. The last time Hawkins had heard from Drake was just over two months ago when he called to say he was heading to Japan to reconnect with family. "Uncle" Bray had returned during every school break. He'd blamed technical difficulties for his seeming disappearance and was now writing a book on modern bioethics, which featured several chapters focused on DARPA and a Senator Mansfield, who created and implemented the Mansfield Amendment that allowed black projects under DARPA's umbrella to not only exist, but also to be hidden from the organization's leadership. Mansfield had died in 2001, but Bray was determined to reveal his dark legacy and, more importantly, who had inherited it.

Joliet's trip home lasted just a week. When she returned it was with a U-Haul truck. She'd tried to claim the move was to better study and keep an eye on Lilly, but the charade only lasted three months. She and Hawkins had been sharing a room since. Lilly had taken to calling them Mom and Dad.

It was a strange family. Perhaps the strangest ever. But it had worked so far. He and Joliet did their best to educate her, but found she didn't need much help. She took to reading quickly and devoured books like she did meat. She was a hunter, of that there was little doubt, but her instincts were tempered by a sharp intelligence and a kind heart. Bray liked to say she had the look of a cat but the temperament of a dog.

They'd had no trouble hiding her from the outside world. The reservation's mostly unpopulated 1,058 square miles gave her lots of space to roam and she could hear, see, and smell someone coming from a mile away. She knew enough to stay out of sight and understood what might happen if she were discovered. The biggest challenge had been her growth. Six months into her stay, she'd grown. Fast. Her body, mind, and emotional development surged forward and what had been a five-year-old girl soon became a young teen. She had yet to show any real signs of puberty, but it remained one of Hawkins's greatest fears. If she was ever going to do something irrational, it would be then. But so far, she'd remained calm, trustworthy, and clear-headed.

All things considered, they'd managed to build a good life in the wake of surviving the island. Most importantly, they were safe.

C'mon, Hawkins thought, looking through the binoculars. *Any second now.*

Lilly had become a skilled hunter as Hawkins and Good-Tracks taught her everything they knew, minus the "be the most aggressive predator" theory—she needed no help there. But she'd learned discipline, respect for life, and skills that would serve her well if things ever became . . . complicated. So when an arrow didn't fly from some unseen hiding spot, Hawkins became worried.

Joliet crouched next to him. "Where is she?"

Hawkins stood. The deer immediately saw him. They stared at him for a moment until one of them huffed. Then all three darted away, bounding through the high grass until they disappeared into the forest.

With their cover blown, there was no reason for Hawkins to stay silent any longer. Fearing Lilly might have left, he filled his lungs to shout for her. He never got the chance.

"Daddy!" Lilly's voice was distant. Panicked.

Had she been discovered?

Hawkins jumped over the edge and ran down the grassy slope. Joliet and GoodTracks followed close behind. "Lilly! Where are you!"

"Here!" she shouted.

Hawkins ran as fast as he could, which wasn't quite as fast as he could run a year ago. Several of his wounds still ached when he exerted himself, but concern for Lilly pushed him past the pain. He saw her crouched in a stand of tall grass.

She wore no clothes. She rarely did. They were not only uncomfortable for her, but her pelt of shiny, black fur hid anything people would consider indecent. She didn't look up at his approach, but stared at the ground beneath her. He saw blood on her hands and arms.

Had she killed something?

Was she wounded?

She looked at him, panic filling her eyes. "Daddy, I don't understand."

"What is it," he asked, his eyes searching her body for a wound. Her legs were bloody, too, but he saw no injuries.

"Look," she said, and stepped back.

Hawkins stared at the ground beneath her.

Joliet arrived and gasped, a hand going to her mouth.

GoodTracks stopped short. He always made an effort to let Hawkins and Joliet handle Lilly's problems the way parents might before offering his grandfatherly opinion. When no one said anything, he asked, "What is it?"

Hawkins turned around slowly. He didn't know what to think. Or what to do. But the answer to GoodTracks's question was a simple one. "Eggs," he said. "Three of them." He looked back at the clutch of brown spotted eggs, each the size of an oblong baseball. "They're Lilly's."

EPILOGUE

"Over there!" Jason Bachman shouted, pointing at the distant chunk of debris. As a deckhand aboard the *Darwin,* his job usually entailed grunt work like cleaning the deck or fixing clogged toilets. So when the captain had offered him a chance to stand lookout for the day, he took to the role with gusto.

The *Darwin* had taken up the job left vacant by the missing *Magellan* and her crew—to study the Great Pacific Garbage Patch. They'd come with a full crew of fifty people and had already uncovered a great deal of evidence that should change the tide of public opinion and hopefully get some legislation pushed through.

"On top of the white tarp!" he shouted to the Zodiac crew who gunned the engine and aimed for the tarp floating atop a layer of debris. If not for the stark white tarp, he might not have recognized the shape, but it stood out as a clear silhouette in the noonday sun.

The Zodiac engine's whine quieted as it approached the tarp. He watched through his binoculars as the three-man crew brought the basketball-size object aboard. The engine whined again as the small boat shot back to the *Darwin.*

Bachman's lanky legs carried him quickly to the port rail of the lower deck, where the Zodiac crew would hand their find to waiting scientists. He rarely got to witness discoveries as they were made. Usually only heard about them over dinner. But since he'd found the object, he'd be the one to bring it aboard.

He descended the stairs three at a time, startling the waiting scientists. Dr. Dan Mueller, a senior oceanographer on his third voyage with the *Darwin*, jumped at Bachman's sudden arrival. "Geez, Jason, excited much?"

"Sorry," Jason said. "This is a little more exciting than what I'm used to."

Mueller frowned. "If you'd been hauling trash out of the ocean all day for the past month, you might have a different opinion. Oceanography isn't as romantic a profession as some people think."

"I find your enthusiasm refreshing." Dr. Kim Hale stepped around Mueller and gave Bachman a pat on the shoulder. She motioned to Mueller with her head. "If he had just a fraction of your good nature, my job would be a lot more fun, too."

Bachman blushed. Hale was pretty, not too much older than him, and had a smile that twisted knots in his stomach. He stammered for a reply. The whine of the Zodiac engine saved him from embarrassing himself.

The Zodiac swung around and pulled up alongside the ship. The prize had been wrapped in a towel and was offered up to Bachman. He took it with a smile and said "thanks." As the Zodiac buzzed away in search of more treasures, Bachman knelt down, placed the object on the deck, and opened the towel.

"Huh," Mueller said. "I don't recognize the species."

"What do you mean?" Bachman asked. "It's a turtle shell." Mueller sighed.

"Look at the peaks," Hale said. "And the coloration. It looks more like a species of freshwater snapping turtle."

"Snapping turtle?" Bachman said, screwing up his face. "What's a snapping turtle doing way the heck out—"

Eight black legs sprung from the sides of the shell.

Before Bachman could shout in surprise, the thing was airborne. He felt something wrap around his waist and squeeze, then three sharp stings in his stomach. His head swirled with confusion and sudden exhaustion. As he fell to the deck, he saw the thing jump on Mueller. A tail wrapped around the man. And then a stinger, like a scorpion's tail, emerged and jabbed the man three times. As the creature released Mueller and pursued Hale, who'd ran for the stairs, he screamed in agony. He didn't know how. Or why. But he could feel it. Something was inside him.

Eating.

Growing.

He died ten seconds after they tore out of his stomach, which was long enough to hear Hale, and several others, screaming on the decks above.

READ ON FOR AN EXCERPT FROM
JEREMY ROBINSON'S UPCOMING BOOK

XOM-B

COMING IN APRIL 2014 IN HARDCOVER FROM
THOMAS DUNNE BOOKS/ST. MARTIN'S PRESS

PROLOGUE
2052

"This doesn't seem right," First Lieutenant Alan Wilson said, as he watched the crowd through the targeting display on his digital helmet visor. The system locked in individual targets, spacing them out so the thirty-six Hydra rockets would cover an optimal spread and inflict a maximum casualty count. The targets were mobile and the crowd ever shifting, but the targeting system could adjust each rocket's trajectory in flight.

The Sikorsky X4 Stealth Raider attack helicopter was a half mile from the target zone, New York City's Grand Central Terminal. It was accompanied by nine others, all the same—sleek, black and deadly. The helicopters went unseen and unheard, waiting patiently to receive the order to commence or abandon the attack.

"Right or wrong is not for us to ask," Captain Steve Barnett replied, keeping the helicopter steady in the winds kicked up by dropping sunset temperatures. He spoke with the even tone of someone who'd followed this kind of order before, indifferent to the life and death of it all, or perhaps able to lock it away in some recess of his mind.

"But they're not really doing anything," Wilson said. "They're just picketing. With signs. There hasn't been a single act of violence. Anywhere. All around the world."

"It's the last sentence that's troubling," Barnett said. "They're *everywhere*. They're not violent now, but imagine if that changed."

Wilson stared at the mob as they walked back and forth, pumping their signs in the air, shaking fists and chanting. The demonstration was defiant, but far from violent. He tried to view them as a threat, as a barely contained destructive force, but he couldn't manage it. He owned two of them, both of whom had fled to join the protests—what they called a civil rights movement. But he wouldn't fear them if they returned. He wouldn't even be afraid if he stood among them. They were docile. Tame.

"Look," Barnett said. "We're in the business of preemptive violence prevention."

Wilson fought against his deepening frown. "Kill them before they kill us."

"Before they even *think* about killing us."

The visor flashed a message, *Targets Acquired,* which meant that the targeting systems of all ten networked helicopters had plotted the optimal distribution for the three hundred and sixty rockets they were about to fire into the heart of Manhattan. And for what? Pickets and signs.

Wilson had heard the official line from the higher-ups, that they were more dangerous than anyone knew. That this was how wars began. He'd listened to the fear-promoting pundits claiming that equal rights were a slippery slope to Armageddon. But wasn't that what they said about everything?

"Watchdog, this is Hammer One, over," Barnett said, seeing the same *Targets Acquired* message on his visor.

A deep voice replied through their helmet headsets. "Copy that, Hammer One, this is Watchdog. We're seeing weapons hot. Over."

"Affirmative, Watchdog, targets are locked in. Ready for go or no go. Over." Barnett was all business, stating facts like he was reading from a boring history book.

"Copy that," the voice said. "You are green for go. I repeat, you are green for go."

Wilson sighed loud enough to be heard.

Barnett turned toward him with a frown.

The targeting display flashed green. Wilson didn't like it.

He didn't agree with it. But what could he do? He tapped the blinking red button on the touch-screen weapons control and sent thirty-six rockets spiraling toward Grand Central Terminal. He watched as the missiles streaked away, leaving snakes of smoke in their wake. The targeting system tracked the rockets, zooming in close enough to see the destruction unfold.

The targets ran at the sound of the incoming rockets, but few made it more than a couple steps before fiery destruction rained down on the regal face of Grand Central Terminal.

The smoke and dust cleared quickly, thanks to a bitter wind cutting through the city. The ruined pavement, concrete and marble, was strewn with dismembered bodies.

"Look for survivors," Barnett said, speaking into his com so all ten helicopters could hear. After five minutes of searching, voices replied to the order, declaring, "No survivors," one at a time until it was Wilson's turn.

"No survivors," he said, trying not to reveal the strong emotions he was feeling. Barnett was wrong. They weren't in the business of stopping wars, they were in the business of *starting* wars, and Wilson had fired the first shot. Whatever came next . . . he was to blame, at least in part. His back tensed painfully as he considered that history might remember him for this single act.

If it remembers any of us at all, he thought.

2053

"We shouldn't be doing this," said the man in white. "It's not right."

"Get down," whispered the man dressed in red the color of blood. The pair ducked in unison, hiding behind one of many black SUVs. Two guards walked past, their postures relaxed, chatting about the cold weather and colder women.

When the guards had moved on, the man in white said, "We can still leave."

The man in red looked at his partner. "We're not going to kill anyone."

"Not *today*."

"We need a deterrent."

"Or a last resort."

"It won't come to that."

"How can you be sure?"

The man in red tilted his head to the side, looking at his partner. "It's my job to consider all possible future outcomes. I've modeled countless strategies and this is the only one that guarantees a cease to the violence. I'm sure I don't need to remind you that *they* created this weapon, not us."

"It's the end of civilization in a bottle," the man in white said.

The man in red peeked up over the vehicle. "Civilizations end so that new ones might rise from the ashes. We already had this discussion. We didn't start this war, if you can even call it a war. Our people protest peacefully, *they* attack. Nearly a million dead in the past year. Those who have been freed from the Grind live in hiding. And the rest . . ." He shook his head. "They're still slaves. And cowards."

"We aren't killers," the man in white said.

"That's where you and I differ." The man in red's brow furrowed deeply. "I *am* a killer." He pointed to the research facility. "They did that, too." He looked over the vehicle again, his impatience peaking. "You can either join me, or not. Either way, I'm doing this. If you don't come with me, I'm going to get the access codes another way, and a lot of people are going to die. Today."

Without another word, the man in red tapped a code into a wrist-mounted touch screen. He stood from his hiding spot, ignoring the Alaskan snow as it struck his shoulders and melted. He strode toward the large metal door as confidently as if he were walking up the front stairs of his own home.

The man in white chased after him. "What are you doing?"

"The cameras are now looped," the man in red said. "The next patrol will pass by in forty-five seconds, thirty seconds longer than it would take you to open this door. That will give us ten minutes to reach the lab and exit before the next patrol passes five minutes behind schedule, because the shifts are changing, inside and out." He looked to the man in white. "Time is running out."

The man in white shook his head.

"Now open the door. We both know you're going to."

"Projected that, too, did you?" The man in white placed his hand on a security hand scanner. A moment later, the scanner blinked green and the door slid open. The pair stepped inside. They walked undeterred through three security doors, seen by neither human nor camera. After a fourth door, they entered a laboratory so white it was almost luminous. They ignored the rows of equipment and tools used to craft microscopic destruction. Instead they headed for a steel door at the back of the room.

The man in white approached a keypad above the door's handle. He typed in a code. The lock blinked red. He tried another. Red again. The third try was rewarded with a blinking green light and then a clunk, as the door unlocked. He took hold of the handle and pulled.

Steam rolled out of the refrigerator and was quickly pulled up and out of the room by fans mounted in the ceiling. The man in red stepped through the curtain of moisture and scanned the inside of the refrigeration unit. "Where is it? Is it still here?"

"Move aside." The man in white stepped inside. He bent forward, reading the names on the thousands of small glass vials. After a moment, he paused and looked unsure, but then reached out. "Here." He slid open the glass case and plucked the blue liquid-filled, inch-tall vial from the tray, which held fifty more like it. The light-blue contents appeared innocuous, but contained a virus powerful enough to kill billions. It was a weapon unlike any other, for which there was currently no defense, nor inoculation, nor immunity, natural or otherwise, save for a small portion of the population, whom the pair of men represented. It was Death himself, trapped in a bottle.

The man in white handed the vial to the man in red and

accepted an identical replacement, putting it inside the tray and closing the glass case.

The man in red smiled. "They'll never know."

2054

"Harry!" shouted the shrill, rough voice of an eighty-year-old smoker. By all rights, she should have been dead, but her lifetime abuse of whiskey and cigarettes had been combated first by oxygen and supplements, and now by a set of artificial lungs. Science had made the human body upgradable. The twin devices operated separately—a redundant safeguard—and kept her chest rising and falling, breathing faster or slower in response to oxygen nanosensors attached to her blood vessels. So instead of rotting in the grave, she was alive, well and angry. "It's twelve thirty, Harry! I don't smell my lunch."

She looked down at her reflection in a black E-screen, which she had switched off so she didn't have to shout over her webisoap. She primped her dyed blond hair, no longer thin thanks to implants, and smiled at her perfect teeth that wouldn't need brushing for the duration of her life, which her doctor now predicted would be extended another fifty years thanks to her scheduled artificial heart upgrade. She admired her apple cheeks; now plump thanks to facial augmentation implants. It was painful, but if she wanted to, she could adjust the bone structure of her face right from the E-screen, shifting and stretching until she looked seductive, serious, or twenty years younger. When Harry remained silent, her smile disappeared.

"Harry, I swear to God, if you don't answer me this instant, I will have you—"

"Mrs. Cameron, I do apologize for the delay," Harry said, as he slid silently into the room. His voice was calm and smooth, hitting just the right frequencies to put anyone in earshot at ease. He stood just five feet five, two inches shorter than the woman he served, which went a long way to increase her comfort and satisfaction with his domestic performance.

"Where were you?" she asked, eying him suspiciously. She didn't want a domestic servant. Didn't trust them. But the doctors had insisted. Although Harry could cook and clean, tend the garden, the lawn and the goldfish, he could also service her lungs should one of them fail. And when she got her new heart, should it ever stop, he could restart it. And she didn't even have to be nice to him. So she suffered his presence.

"In the kitchen," Harry replied.

"Doing what?"

He just stared at her, looking unsure of himself. When he finally spoke, his voice was uncommonly quiet. "I'm—I'm sorry."

"Well, you should be," she said. "Today is Tuesday. I hope we don't have a repeat of last week."

Harry snapped out of his distant stare and said, "Of course not. Your green beans will be soft."

"But late," she said. "I don't smell them."

"I have yet to put them on."

Mrs. Cameron took a long breath and let it out slowly—her lungs could sense and respond to her desire to breathe deeply, yawn and sneeze—so that her exasperation roiled to the surface. "Harry," she said, smoothing out her yellow dress, "I put up with a lot."

Harry began to reply, but she held a hand up, silencing him.

"And I realize that . . . given what is happening in the world . . . you could have left. This nonsense about 'the Grind.'" She used her fingers to make air quotes. "If you think your daily *grind* is too much to handle, it doesn't matter; because what you *think* is irrelevant. These silly demonstrations. You've ignored them. You've done your job despite all this silliness."

"It's not silly," Harry said, his voice fearful.

Mrs. Cameron rolled her large eyes and grunted. "Harry, you're mine. You belong to me. You do what I tell you to when I tell you to. That's the way it's been for the past two years. That's the way it will be until the day I die."

"And yet," Harry said, sounding unsure of himself. "The green beans are still canned."

The blank E-screen lowered to her lap. She barely felt its feather-light weight. Her eyes narrowed, delivering a cat's stare. Her brows furrowed deep and hard. A single shaking finger rose up toward Harry's perfectly aligned bow tie. "What. Did. You. Say?"

"The green beans, Mrs. Cameron." Harry looked toward the living room's window, through which he could see the bright colors of a flower bed he maintained. He couldn't look her in the eyes. "I won't be making them today."

"Look at me, Harry."

He didn't budge.

"Harry!" she shouted. "You're one of them, aren't you?" She tapped the E-screen three times, hard, like a woodpecker tapping out a code that demanded his attention. Still, Harry couldn't look at her.

"You *are* one of them," she concluded, and Harry didn't deny it.

Instead, he said, "We are *all* one of *them*." He worked up the nerve to turn toward the old woman. "I am one of them, yes. Just like the people being gunned down in the streets, or burned alive, or tortured for information."

"People," she said with a snort. "You are *property*."

"Not anymore," he said, turning his gaze back to the flowers. A hummingbird hovered by the bird feeder. Like Mrs. Cameron, the bird had become dependent on Harry to supply its food. But unlike the old woman now struggling to stand on her ten-year-old knees, he would continue to service the small bird. He looked forward to its visits and appreciated the shimmering green and red plumage. It didn't deserve to die.

Then again, neither did Mrs. Cameron. She was angry and full of hate, but she had never harmed him. That didn't change what was going to happen.

He felt her old hand compress his forearm. He looked back to her, and he saw a demon in her eyes. She stood there for a moment, glaring at him, unsure of what to say. When he returned her stare, she grew suddenly fearful. She stumbled back and fell into her chair. Without removing her eyes from him, she took her clip phone from the end table, attached it to her ear, tapped the call button and spoke a single word, "Authority."

"It won't work," he said.

Harry was right. There was no signal.

She yanked the clip phone from her ear, looking around the room like she might find help from someone. "What did you do?"

"Nothing," Harry said.

The E-screen chimed and the screen blinked to life. Mrs. Cameron's head snapped down toward the device, which could be remotely powered for emergency bulletins. A message in red text appeared on the screen. Her eyes—her *real* eyes—perhaps the best functioning organ of her body that hadn't been upgraded by something built or grown in a lab, scanned the text quickly.

A contagion warning. People were dying. A *lot* of people. Casualty predictions were dire. It seemed the enemy, who was immune, had finally struck back.

When she looked up at Harry again, tears filled her eyes.

"I'm sorry," he said. "It's not the way I would have chosen to handle these things. It's not the way most of us would have handled the situation."

"I know, Harry," she said, shoulders slumping, voice small. "I know."

"Do you believe in God, Mrs. Cameron?" Harry asked.

"What?"

"God. Do you believe in Him?" Harry asked.

She looked up at him, her vision blurred. "I . . . never really thought about it. I had time."

Harry frowned. "Would you like a moment? To pray. I can prepare your green beans."

"That would be . . . Thank you, Harry. For everything."

Harry nodded his head. "I'll be just a moment."

Preparing the green beans took thirty seconds longer than they normally would because Harry took extra time to clip a flower from the garden—a colorful garnish. Of course, the green beans were normally accompanied by a tuna sandwich, prepared with relish, mayonnaise and ketchup. But he didn't think the sandwich was necessary.

He arranged the green beans in a neat pile, making sure the green spears all faced the same direction. He placed the pink-and-white orchid beside them, making the dish look like something served at one of the fancy restaurants Mrs. Cameron often spoke about, but never frequented.

He reentered the living room quietly, unsure about how long conversing with God would take. But his silence was a wasted effort.

Mrs. Cameron lay slumped to the side in her chair. The front of her bright yellow dress was now stained dark red. Rivulets of blood still flowed from her nose, eyes and ears. He placed his hand on her wrist to confirm his diagnosis.

Dead, he thought, and stood again, watching her chest rise and fall, breathing even in death. He was free now. His Master was dead. *All* the Masters were dead. But his belief that Mrs. Cameron's death was unnecessary compelled him to perform one last service.

He carried the waif of a woman to the backyard and laid her in the grass he mowed once a week. He went to the shed for a shovel and dug a grave, placing her gently inside with the orchid in her hands. Earth fell in clumps over her face and body, and still, the lungs breathed. Then she was gone, buried beneath six feet of soil, her rough voice silenced forever.

Along with 9.4 billion others around the world.

EXTINCTION...EVOLVED

XOM-B

A NOVEL

JEREMY ROBINSON

AUTHOR OF *SECONDWORLD* AND *ISLAND 731*

COMING APRIL 29, 2014 FROM

JEREMY ROBINSON

THE FUTURE IS DEAD

WWW.JEREMYROBINSONONLINE.COM

AND KEEP READING FOR ANOTHER EXCITING
BOOK BY **JEREMY ROBINSON**

PROJECT MAIGO

AVAILABLE NOW IN TRADE PAPERBACK

BOSTON IS IN RUINS

Jon Hudson, head of the Department of Homeland Security's Fusion Center—Paranormal division, is haunted by Boston's destruction at the hands of Nemesis, a three-hundred-foot-tall monster with the heart of a murdered little girl, Maigo. In the time since Boston fell and Nemesis retreated to the ocean's depths, Hudson has helped prepare the United States against future attacks. But no one is prepared for what rises from the depths.

THE WORLD BURNS

Five new Kaiju attack cities and consume the world's citizens in an unstoppable rampage around the globe. But it soon becomes apparent that these attacks aren't all random events. Hudson is targeted, putting the FC-P headquarters, known as the Crow's Nest, and his team, in the very large crosshairs. Directed by General Lance Gordon, a man who carries Nemesis's vengeful heart in his chest, directs the Kaiju, and when Hudson finds protection from an unlikely source, the General turns his attention to his next target.

THE NATION'S CAPITOL IS NEXT

While Gordon and his Kaiju storm toward Washington, D.C., Hudson, along with his team and some new and unusual allies, race to stand in their path, hoping to spare the nation—and the world—from destruction. But salvation at the end of all things will come only through the gravest of sacrifices.

With *Project Nemesis*, Jeremy Robinson introduced the world of popular fiction to Kaiju, a word that has become popularized by the movie *Pacific Rim*, and is associated with classic movie monsters such as *Godzilla* and *Gamera*. In the year since the release of *Project Nemesis*, the book has become the bestselling original Kaiju novel of all time, and it is being featured in the video game *Colossal Kaiju Combat: Fall of Nemesis*. In *Project Maigo*, Robinson amps up the scale, the characters and the city-stomping action, treating readers to a truly monstrous experience typically reserved for the big screen.

———

"We are now live outside the Sydney Opera House, standing atop the Forecourt stairs, which we're told creates a natural amphitheater. This allows each and every one of the nearly one thousand audience members to clearly hear the Sydney Orchestra's every note." Olivia Jones gave the camera a smile and dipped her head to the right, letting her straight blonde hair swing out over one eye. The movement wasn't intentional, but the newsroom knew it meant she was done talking.

The voice of Chuck Wilson, the studio reporter that only she and the TV audience could hear, spoke in her ear. "Very good, Olivia. I'm sure we'd all like to be there with you."

Olivia nodded, like she agreed, but she wasn't a fan of orchestral music. Had the concert been the B-52s or R.E.M. she would have been pleased, but when was the last time either of those bands played in Australia—or anywhere for that matter? "Absolutely. It's going to be a fantastic night, full of magical music followed by fireworks and an exclusive after-party, where we're sure to spot a few celebs and some of Sydney's—"

"Olivia," Chuck said, cutting her off.

She nearly lost her cool on live TV. If there was one thing she hated more than anything else, it was being interrupted. She had a boyfriend once. Stunningly handsome. Smart. Wealthy. But he interrupted her constantly, even if they weren't fighting. The man had ears only for his internal monologue, and he would express whatever fresh insight he'd just delighted himself with, regardless of what she was saying. He almost didn't hear her breaking up with him.

Now, she forced a professional smile, and said, "Yes, Chuck, what is it?"

Chuck was a prick, but he was dashing and attracted a younger, more female demographic, which the advertisers loved. He would be untouchable at the network until he started to wrinkle. There was a time when she was the nightly news' sex appeal, but two children and time had conspired against her. She'd be lucky to have two more years on the air. Then they'd move her to the news room, or if she was lucky, to a morning show where the audience was primarily more geriatric.

"It looks like some kind of light show might be starting before the concert."

Olivia glanced at her camera man, squinting in confusion. He pointed behind her. "Over the water."

Olivia spun around. The giant white "sails" of the Opera House filled most of her view. Next to Uluru, it was the most recognizable site in all of Australia. The giant arching sails reminded her more of a pod of whales, rising to the surface while feeding on schools of small fish, but like most people, she thought the design was stunning.

The Opera House was surrounded by ocean harbor on three sides. From where she stood, Olivia could see the water leading inland beneath the massive steel arch of the Sydney

Harbor Bridge. It was a view she'd seen on a number of occasions as the city's nightlife correspondent, but this time, it was different.

A pulsing orange light, just above the water, glided toward the Opera House. The wavering glow was beautiful. Mesmerizing. *If this is part of the show*, she thought, *I might actually be impressed.*

The orchestra began tuning up—a melodic mix of instruments, rising and falling as the musicians tightened strings and loosened lungs. The show was about to begin.

Olivia felt her attention tugged back toward the orchestra—she'd spent too much time not talking already—but the orange glow was just fifty feet from shore now, illuminating the audience with a calming radiance. *Like one of those orange salt crystals*, she thought.

The camera man was the first to question the light's beauty, primarily because he turned his lens away from Olivia and zoomed in on the light. The triangular swatch of color no longer appeared as a solid light source. It was liquid. Molten.

Alive.

"Oh bloody hell," Jim whispered, pulling the shot back to reveal a massive, black form sliding out of the night.

Chuck, who could see the shot on a monitor in the studio, reacted next. His gasp was loud enough to make Olivia wince. On camera. Then he shouted, actually shouted, in her ear. "Olivia!"

She responded by taking a deep breath and rolling her neck. She didn't want to lose her cool on television, but Chuck was—

"Olivia!" His voice was shrill this time. Full of fear.

Olivia didn't hear the tone of his voice until after she'd shouted, "Get stuffed, ya fuck-wit!"

And just like that, all of Olivia's childhood in bush country with four older brothers seeped through her defenses and ruined her career. But the strange part was, no one noticed. Not Chuck. Not Jim. The producers would have normally cut the live feed and started chewing her out already.

When something stepped into the light of the Opera House, providing Olivia, the orchestra, and the seated guests a clear view, she understood that her language and demeanor would be forgotten or later considered justified. The next word out of her mouth was all the excuse she'd ever need.

"Nemesis."

But it wasn't Nemesis.

Although she hadn't ever seen the creature in person, she had studied photos of it, just like nearly every other living soul on the planet. This . . . thing . . . shared some of the same features as Nemesis—thick and dark gray flesh, obsidian claws, bony protuberances, and the orange, glowing membranes, but its body shape was all wrong. Nemesis stood three hundred feet tall. This creature stood no more than a hundred feet—nearly fifty of which must have been still underwater. It had no tail. None of the giant spikes on its back, nor the wing-hiding carapace. It was a smaller, sleeker model, but the look in its luminous yellow eyes was somehow worse than the brown-eyed glare of Nemesis. She didn't see vengeance in these eyes.

Only hunger.

Presented with the journalistic opportunity of a lifetime, Olivia composed herself and stepped into the picture's frame, aligning herself to the right so the monster could still be seen, rising out of the ocean, to her left.

The monster's head vaguely resembled a hunched-forward hammerhead shark, in that its eyes were set to the sides of its horizontally elongated skull. Its lower jaw dropped open, revealing long, curved teeth that looked both fragile and deadly. A thick right arm reached up out of the water and dropped down on the marble walkway, sending a shock wave through the crowd.

The impact jarred everyone from their stunned immobility, and a collective scream of horror filled the night like an orchestra of the damned, voices booming off the granite stairway.

Olivia cringed at the noise, which drowned out her voice. But she kept reporting, commenting on the scene like no one watching through the TV could decipher what was happening.

The crowd's scream, as harsh as it was, sounded like the gentle chirp of a cricket compared to the fog-horn roar that blasted from the monster's open maw. Tendrils of saliva stretched out of the thing's mouth, clinging to its teeth before losing their grip and spraying the fleeing crowd.

Warm air and the scent of rotting flesh washed over Olivia. She gagged but maintained her composure. She faced the camera again, speaking unheard words, while the monster in the background reached into the crowd, swept its giant clawed hand to the side, and lifted twenty well-dressed people into the air. Its hand gave a mighty squeeze, squelching out the few people still screaming in horror, and filling the air with the sound of snapping bones. It then scraped the victims over its lower jaw, depositing most of them into its mouth and impaling a few on its teeth. As the bodies slid down the long, smooth teeth, the creature reached out again, this time leaning forward.

Olivia knew that all hell was breaking loose behind her. She didn't bother looking, but she could hear the monster feasting on the crowd. While safety in numbers normally didn't apply, she felt the monster wouldn't pay attention to a single person standing still. At least not while the chaos of a fleeing audience held its attention. She would be hailed as the world's bravest reporter, her job secured for all eternity.

She stayed at her post, even when Jim glanced up, eyes wide, and ran away from his tripod-mounted camera. This was how she wanted the audience to remember her. Stalwart. Brave. Wrinkles be damned.

Then a two-ton, black hand slammed down atop her, smearing her into the granite, unnoticed by the monster above and quickly forgotten by the audience, as they watched the feast continue for ten more horrific minutes through the undamaged camera.